UNBREAKABLE

Titles by Alison Kent

UNDENIABLE

UNBREAKABLE

UNBREAKABLE

ALISON KENT

HEAT | NEW YORK

THE BERKLEY PUBLISHING GROUP
Published by the Penguin Group
Penguin Group (USA) Inc.
375 Hudson Street, New York, New York 10014, USA
Penguin Group (Canada), 90 Eglinton Avenue East, Suite 700, Toronto, Ontario M4P 2Y3, Canada (a division of Pearson Penguin Canada Inc.) • Penguin Books Ltd., 80 Strand, London WC2R 0RL, England • Penguin Group Ireland, 25 St. Stephen's Green, Dublin 2, Ireland (a division of Penguin Books Ltd.) • Penguin Group (Australia), 250 Camberwell Road, Camberwell, Victoria 3124, Australia (a division of Pearson Australia Group Pty. Ltd.) • Penguin Books India Pvt. Ltd., 11 Community Centre, Panchsheel Park, New Delhi—110 017, India • Penguin Group (NZ), 67 Apollo Drive, Rosedale, Auckland 0632, New Zealand (a division of Pearson New Zealand Ltd.) • Penguin Books (South Africa) (Pty.) Ltd., 24 Sturdee Avenue, Rosebank, Johannesburg 2196, South Africa

Penguin Books Ltd., Registered Offices: 80 Strand, London WC2R 0RL, England

This book is an original publication of The Berkley Publishing Group.

Cover photograph by Claudio Marinesco.
Cover design by Sarah Oberrender.

PUBLISHING HISTORY
Heat trade paperback edition / February 2013

Library of Congress Cataloging-in-Publication Data

Kent, Alison.
Unbreakable / Alison Kent.
p. cm.
ISBN 978-0-425-25343-4
1. Man-woman relationships—Fiction. 2. Texas—Fiction. I. Title.
PS3561.E5155U527 2013
813'.54—dc23
2012018224

PRINTED IN THE UNITED STATES OF AMERICA

10 9 8 7 6 5 4 3 2 1

To Loreth Anne White, for #RWA12.
For the laughter and the tears and the Starbucks runs.
For all the fun as we talked lives and families and careers and story and dogs. I'll make you a viewpoint purist yet!

ACKNOWLEDGMENTS

To HelenKay for the legal help with Faith. To Margaret for the story help with Faith, and for loving Casper, then hating Casper, then loving Casper again. This cowboy's for you.

To the Berkley art department for the AMAZING Dalton Gang covers. Yee-haw!

To the couple at Millie Bush Bark Park with the Bernese mountain dog named Kevin. Bits and pieces of my own three mutts can be found in the Kevin I created for Clay. And thank you, Clay, for walking out that door when you did. This story wouldn't have been the same without you.

But really.

Kevin?

ONE

HIS BACK AGAINST the side of his truck, Casper Jayne braced for the bad news his gut said was coming. The same gut that had kept him in his bedroom when his old man had stumbled wasted through the door. That had sent him to the ground from his third-story window when his old lady had waved guns and threats. That had told him nearly two decades ago to get the hell out of that house if he wanted to live.

The very house he was now standing in front of.

The one-page handwritten letter folded to fit in his back pocket felt bulky and heavy. It made it hard to get comfortable as he watched the inspector circle the house he'd lived in before leaving Crow Hill at eighteen. The house was now his—as useless as tits on a boar hog—and would be hell to dump *or* to keep.

It had been a pit as far back as he remembered. His old lady hadn't done a damn thing to make it livable the years they'd called the rambling monstrosity home, or even later, when his life was rodeo, his old man in the wind, and she'd been the only one keeping the fires burning.

Gutting the interior and starting from scratch might be his only option, but first he needed to know if the structure itself was sound. *Check that.* He needed to know what it was going to cost him to make it so. Especially since he was cash poor and getting his hands on the money he did have meant barreling his way through the woman who held his purse strings.

A woman tighter than a ten-day drunk.

He suspected he'd have an easier time getting her to give up what she hid beneath the suits she wore than the funds he needed. And he wasn't sure he wouldn't rather have the first than the second. But since both options hung off the edge of possibility's realm, what he wanted didn't matter a lick.

He took off his hat, ran a hand across the bristled buzz of his hair, resettled the beat-to-hell straw Resistol and pulled the brim low. But he didn't push away from his truck. He stayed where he was, crossing his arms as the man with the electronic gadget in his hand and acorns popping beneath his feet kicked at the sidewalk, the cement buckled by the roots of the yard's hundred-year-old live oaks.

The inspector pecked out another note on the screen before walking through the thigh-high gate, which was missing two pickets and also hinged at a cockeyed angle. He stopped, swung it back and forth, then screwed his mouth to the side before looking at Casper from behind sunglasses that hid his eyes but not his expression. They both knew there was more wrong with this house than was right, but Casper didn't care what the other man was thinking.

He needed an official report to back up his request for the cash to do what was needed. Even shouldering the bulk of the labor himself, the supplies would set him back the cost of a herd of good horses. He doubted the house had been worth that much when he'd spent his nights staring at the holes in the ceiling and hoping the balls of newspaper he'd used to plug them would keep out the biggest of the spiders at least.

"Sure you don't want me to take a look inside?" This was the third time the inspector had pushed to get through the doors. "Let you know what you're looking at with your heating and cooling systems? Your plumbing fixtures? Your outlets?"

Casper shook his head. He wasn't ready for that. Besides, there was no cooling system. Never had been, unless he counted opening the windows and praying for a breeze. The space heaters he and his mother had used had been no match for the lack of insulation or the gaps in the siding—and the two of them hadn't done more than try to control the temperature in the four rooms they used of the two dozen in the house.

Summers and winters. Both had been hell. "Just give me the external damage. What am I looking at?"

The other man glanced at the house again—the wraparound front porch and badly canted columns, the Victorian gables over windows made of cardboard instead of glass, the oaks spreading from either side to meet in the middle, branches laced as if praying for the house to be put out of its misery—before turning to Casper with a shrug. "You could raze the whole thing and come out ahead."

Easiest solution, but it wasn't going to happen. "I know it needs a new roof—"

"A new roof's the least of it." Frustrated, the inspector made an encompassing gesture that took in the house and the trees and the entire half acre that resembled a landfill more than a yard. "Your fascia board's rotted through most of the way around. Eaves and gables both. Same with the soffit. Kid hits a baseball against the house, the vents are gonna fall plumb out. Your gutters are hanging on by a thread, and you don't have a single attached downspout. Both of the chimney masonry caps, the support beams on all the porches, the grade of your lot . . ."

"Yeah, yeah. It's a piece of shit. I got it."

With a shrug, the inspector said, "This house is not where I'd be pouring my investment money. Like I said. Razing's your best bet."

And, again, that wasn't going to happen. As long as Casper got his hands on the money, the risk of making over the house was his. What he did with it after that . . . He nodded toward the tablet the inspector held. "Can you print out a report on that thing? Give me a list or whatever?"

"I've got a printer in the truck, sure," the man said, making his way to where he'd parked his mobile office behind Casper's big black dualie.

"What about a fax machine?"

"Yep. I can send it wherever you want it to go." He opened the passenger door and glanced over as Casper approached. "I can send the bill, too. All I need is a name and a number."

For the first time since the letter from his old lady had hit his mailbox, Casper felt the hard tug of a smile. What he wouldn't give to be a fly on the wall of the office when this particular paperwork arrived.

"Send it over to the First National Bank."

"Attention of?"

His smiled tugged harder and grew just a little bit mean. "Faith Mitchell."

ONE MORE THING. That was all Faith Mitchell needed to go wrong today. One more thing and she wouldn't have any trouble telling the higher-ups to take this job and shove it. She got that the bank was not a charity and good business didn't allow for extending a loan indefinitely, or offering additional credit to account holders already unable to pay what they owed.

But after the chewing out she'd just received for daring—*daring*—to suggest the bank give the Harts another month before foreclosing on property that had been in the family for more than a hundred years, she was beginning to think it took a special kind of heartlessness to turn one's back on the honest-to-God need created by the nation's depressed economy and the state's ongoing drought.

The Harts were good people, struggling to make their living off the land the same way Henry Lasko, Nina Summerlin, and so many others were doing. The same way Tess and Dave Dalton had done for years, before passing on and leaving their ranch to Crow Hill's notorious Dalton Gang.

As teens instructed to give the elderly couple a hand, the three had earned the Daltons' love and trust while raising hell with the rest of the town. As grown men who'd returned to work the spread they'd inherited from Tess and Dave, the three were now fighting to get ahead like all of the area's ranchers.

Since Faith's brother Boone was one of the trio, she got to see his side of the picture as well as where the money men were coming from. That probably had a lot to do with the sympathy she felt for the Harts. Yes, they'd put up their land as collateral, but no one could've seen the drought coming—and staying—or anticipated the depth of the economy's downward spiral.

Turning one's back on the sort of ridiculous request outlined in the fax she'd received earlier was a different thing entirely. Casper Jayne knew exactly how tight the ranch's finances were. His own were no better, and he wanted to pour tens of thousands into a house that would be better served by going up in smoke? Please.

Her position as loan officer aside, the risks involved in his request were innumerable. The wiring in the house would have to be brought up to code before he could even think about powering the tools to do the job. Unless he *wanted* to start a fire as a way to get out from under this newest burden.

Hmm. The camel, the straw. Did he even have a homeowners policy? If he did, and if she approved just enough—

"Faith?"

"Not now, Meg," Faith said, dismissing the tempting thought of arson and waving one hand toward her assistant while reaching for the phone with the other. Might as well give the Harts the bad news.

But Meg insisted. "You've got a visitor."

"Okay. I'll be done here in—"

"How 'bout you're done now," said Casper Jayne, pushing past Meg before she could stop him.

Not that anyone had ever been able to stop him.

Abandoning the phone, Faith sat back and laced her hands in her lap to keep from jumping up and choking him. One more thing. Hadn't the thought just gone through her mind? And he qualified in ways nothing else did, all long and tight and wiry, with thighs he'd used for years to grip the backs of bulls. Thick thighs. Purposeful thighs. Thighs she wanted to ride and had her close to moaning.

Her reaction was just stupid. She'd known him since he was sixteen and she was fourteen and he'd become best friends with her brother, Boone, and Dax Campbell, the group's hell-raising third member. Playing his big brother role to the hilt, Boone had made sure she and Casper seldom crossed paths, and Casper hadn't pressed the point.

So what if she'd been broken-hearted? She'd been a girl, and that had been forever ago. She should be immune to him now.

For some reason, she wasn't. For some reason, as soon as he'd returned to Crow Hill her teenage crush had become a very adult fascination. And the way he wore his jeans didn't help.

But he was crazy reckless, a lesson in insane abandon, wild and out of control. She didn't need that in her life now anymore than she had in the past. If nothing else, that much was a given.

He was standing, staring, waiting. Taking up too much room in her office, breathing too much of her air. And God help her if she wasn't undressing him, peeling away those jeans, wrapping her legs around those thighs, grinding against him.

Could this day possibly go any further downhill? "What are you doing here?"

He walked closer, taking slow steps, lazy steps, his hips at her eye level and causing her so very much grief. *Please, please go away.*

But he and his thighs and his championship belt buckle stopped in front of her desk to tease her. "I came to see you."

"If it's about the fax, you're wasting your time and mine."

"I wanted to explain things in person before you had a chance to say no."

"No."

"C'mon, Faith—"

"No," she said again, watching his nostrils flare, his bright hazel eyes flash. Watching the tic pop in his strong square jaw. A bead of sweat crawled over his Adam's apple to the hollow of his throat.

She swallowed hard, but held his gaze. She knew him, and she would not be tempted. She would not. *She would not.*

"You enjoy this, don't you?" he asked, planting his hands on her desk blotter, leaning forward, bringing with him the scent of horses and hay. "Making it hard on a man."

She took a deep breath and a long pause, then said, "No. I

don't. But you know as well as I do that you don't have the money for the extreme makeover that house will need before you can even think about putting it on the market."

He frowned, hovered a couple more seconds, then straightened, crossing his arms and raising one slashed brow. "Who said I'm going to put it on the market?"

"You're going to live there? And still work the ranch?" She gave him a *whatever* shrug, because he needed to know he didn't bother her at all. "What else would you do with it?"

"Dax lives in town with Arwen, and he still works the ranch."

"Dax lives in Arwen's house. He didn't rob Peter to pay Paul for a place to stay."

"It's my money. I'll be using it for me. No Peter. No Paul."

"It's the ranch's money first, and only a third of that is yours. And not even that, really, because of the debt y'all are dealing with."

"I added my rodeo winnings to the coffers, remember?"

She did, but he'd obviously forgotten the rest. "And you signed paperwork turning it over to the partnership. It's not yours anymore."

"Not any of it?"

She thought of old dowries and entailed estates. "Not enough for what you need."

He paced the width of her office, his thighs, his jeans, his stride, and the roll of his hips bringing the word *yes* to the tip of her tongue. Bringing a sheen of sweat to her chest and her nape. Bringing one hand to her blouse's collar where she pulled the two sides close. This ridiculous feeling—*God, what was it? Lust? Longing?*—had to stop.

Across the room, he curled his fingers over the windowsill and parked his backside against it, his eyes downcast as if a solution lay woven into the carpet's pattern. "What about the oil money?"

She tried to contain her sigh. "You want a loan against your mineral rights when you don't even know what's down there?"

"The well's due to spud in a couple of months. Sooner if the rig can get there. Everyone's saying the prospect looks good."

"Until the well's producing, good doesn't mean anything."

"Well, fuck me."

She didn't get it. Why in the world would he want to put money into a second losing proposition? Why didn't he sell the lot and the house *as is* and be done with it? She didn't get it, but she wasn't going to ask because asking meant personal involvement, and even though her brother was a partner in the ranch, she had to separate her business from her personal life.

That's what he needed to understand. She wasn't singling him out or punishing him. As much as this was about his request, it wasn't. "Casper. If I approved this expenditure, I'd lose my job."

He brought up both hands, scrubbed them down his face, looking as exhausted as he was resigned. "Guess I'll have to get one that pays then."

Or he could start acting like he had some sense and let this go. "A job? Doing what? You already work dawn to dusk."

"That leaves me about ten hours," he said, walking back to her desk. He stopped between the two visitor chairs, gripped the back of both with strong, capable hands . . . hands with short, clean nails, golden hair trailing along the edges from his wrists. "That should be enough."

"To do what?" she asked, imagining the thick slide of his fingers and squirming in her seat. "And when are you going to sleep?"

"I don't sleep much as it is." He rocked back and forth against the chairs. "I hear Royce Summerlin's looking for someone to break a few horses."

"You. Breaking horses." She gave a scoffing laugh because he was too close, the seams of his jeans worn and nearly white and messing with her head.

"Why not?" he asked, his hat brim casting a shadow across his eyes.

She sat forward and picked up a pen, looking at the Harts' paperwork on her desk instead of giving Casper any more of her time. She had work to do, and he was bothering her. Making her itch. Making her damp. Making her heart race and her blood run hot.

Making her foolhardy. "Because you're a bull rider."

"I've ridden a lot more than bulls." He pushed up to stand straight. "And I've broken more than a few of my rides."

She brushed him off without looking up. "Don't be sex talking me. It's not going to get you anywhere. The answer's still no."

He came closer, until his thighs in her peripheral vision were the only thing she could see. "Sex talk? Really?"

Heat bloomed beneath her white blouse and blue blazer. What in the world was wrong with her? It was his fault. All of it. She wasn't herself when he was around. She wasn't anyone she recognized. She was imprudent, allowing in thoughts she had no business thinking, saying things that came with trouble attached.

"Sorry," she said, returning her pen to her desk and meeting his gaze. "It's just . . . I know you. Everything out of your mouth is a double entendre, and that's only when you're not being outright provocative or crass."

"Crass? Are you kidding me?" He narrowed his eyes. The corner of his mouth lifted dangerously.

Her laugh was more nervous than she liked. She knew she didn't have him wrong. "More like you're kidding yourself."

"You, Faith Mitchell, have wounded me."

"And you, Casper Jayne, are a scoundrel and you know it."

He took a minute to respond, as if first running his life through the filter of her words. He looked confused and suddenly not quite sure of where they stood, or where to go next. "Is that why you wouldn't have anything to do with me in high school?"

Now who was kidding whom? "*You* didn't want anything to do with *me*. I got that message loud and clear."

"Oh no, sugar." His voice was deep, hungry, his gaze sharp and to the point. "The message you got was your brother's."

"Whatever," she said because this conversation was one step away from precarious, and she could *so* easily fall.

"And anyway. You know the gang's got a hands-off policy about sisters."

That sounded as much like a coward's way out as a challenge. She couldn't stop herself. "You'll climb on the back of a two-thousand-pound bull, but you won't stand up to Boone?"

A vein throbbed in his temple. Heat rolled off his body to wrap her up, tangling her in his scent and the strength of his thighs. "You want me to stand up to Boone? Is that what you're saying here, Faith? Because all I need is a sign and I'll make it happen."

She'd been giving him signs for years. He needed to figure this out for himself. And she needed to figure out if this was really what she wanted—and why his company had her flirting with a trip off the path of straight and narrow and onto the road less traveled where so many things could go wrong.

Why it always had. "Look. Can we talk about this later? I've actually got work to do here."

She wasn't any keener on calling the Harts now than she'd been before Casper barged in. In fact, having to turn down his money request made her feel even worse about giving the family their bad news.

But she was too close to making a mistake here. She knew that. She couldn't think when he was around. She knew that, too. And so she waited for him to go.

A wait made in vain.

He hadn't moved, hadn't turned so much as his gaze away. It was as if he were looking for, waiting for that sign. "Later when?"

His voice, when it came, was gruff and demanding, and it was all she could do to breathe. *Be careful what you ask for, Faith Mitchell.* "I'm coming out to the ranch tonight to go over our parents' anniversary party plans with Boone. Will that work for your very busy schedule?"

"I'll be there," he said, and then strode out of her office. It took her a very long time to get back to work and stop thinking about his thighs.

TWO

BEFORE HEADING FROM the bank back to the ranch, Casper swung once more by the house. He wasn't sure why he bothered. Nothing in the last hour had changed. The place was still the nightmare it had been for years. Paint peeling. Shingles ripped away by high winds and branches. Weeds and rotting wood and broken windows and heinous neglect.

It was a home fit for rats and rattlesnakes, spiders and cockroaches—all apt descriptions of the woman who'd had zero interest in bringing him up.

He shook his head free of childhood memories no adult should have stuck there, thinking it strange the neighbors on either side hadn't gone to the city to have something done. Or maybe they had. Before returning to Crow Hill for good this summer, he'd only stopped by twice in sixteen years. Neither time had been to catch up.

The house had seemed an obvious place to recover after

getting hung up to a couple of rank bulls. He'd stayed out of sight and mostly drunk. He hadn't wanted anyone to see him busted all to hell. He sure hadn't wanted any curious sorts offering to nurse him back to health, coming into the house where he'd lived, sniffing around, getting all nosy, and breaking out their holier-than-thou.

Snorting under his breath, he climbed down from his truck and hopped onto the roller coaster of a sidewalk, tripping once before getting his feet solid under him. Most likely, the city had finally found his old lady plying her wares in Vegas, instead of on the interstate at Bokeem's, and told her to do something with the property before they did. As always, her solution had been to pass the buck, this time leaving him the one in a bind.

And because of that bind, if Faith was willing to talk tonight about the money he needed, because he couldn't imagine her wanting to talk about fucking him, it might be a good idea to decide where to start spending it rather than jumping into a time-suck of a renovation with no plan. Though, really, talking about the money was easy. Coughing it up was going to be the hard part. The woman was tight with a capital T.

So tight, in fact, he doubted she'd spare a thought to squeezing out the sign he'd told her to give him—even if everything he'd seen in her eyes told him the idea of doing so heated her up. Faith was a prize. More of a prize than he deserved, for certain. That didn't mean he'd turn her down if she offered, the Dalton Gang's no-sisters rule be damned.

Still, he couldn't see the two of them together. He was a broken-down son of a bitch who owned a ranch on the edge of belly up and a house turned over and waiting to be scratched. What he didn't have was anything to offer a woman like Faith.

Anything, he mused, but his damn fine cock, nearly losing his footing as he stepped over a tree root and into an ankle-deep hole. Served him right for going there, he supposed, and hell if the inspector hadn't been telling the truth about the grade of the lot.

'Course since rain wasn't an issue, neither was standing water, but cleaning the trash from the yard—newspaper, dead leaves and acorns, aluminum cans, cigarette butts, foam cups, and downed limbs—and getting a tractor over here along with a truckload of soil would go a ways toward making the place more picture perfect and less of an eyesore.

Set up a couple of spotlights, and he could get it done in three or four days, an hour or two a night as long as the neighbors didn't complain about the disturbance to their peace and quiet. Though where he'd come up with a generator and fuel to run it since the electricity to the place had been turned off ages ago . . .

Why the hell did everything have to depend on money?

He'd made a good bit on the PBR circuit, blown what he didn't spend on his gear on good times. But when he'd come back to Crow Hill, he'd poured what was left into the ranch's near-empty bank account. That investment could've given him more than a third of the ownership, but when Boone and Dax had pressed the point, he'd told them to make a fist and use it.

The Dalton Gang had always been an all-for-one, one-for-all proposition. As teens, they'd worked the ranch as a group. As adults, they'd inherited the business together. Things should've been just peachy. He was doing what he loved best with the guys he loved best.

But a lack of funds was still making a big, fat mess of his life—just as it had every day he'd spent here as a kid. Even after the piece of shit who'd been his old man had split, nothing had changed, he realized, glancing up as he rounded the northeast corner of the house where he'd taken most of his beatings from that man.

And that's when he saw the dog. Some kind of shaggy mutt, looking about as broken as he was feeling. It hadn't been here earlier, though with the gate unhinged it would've been easy enough for anyone to come through. The question was why? There wasn't any garbage for it to dig through, and there sure as hell weren't any enticing smells of home cooking to lure it close.

The animal had a round head, floppy ears, and fur that should've been white but was the color of coffee and mud. It lay on the back porch, between the swing hanging from one chain and what was left of the railing, chin resting on its front paws. Its black eyes were the only part of the mutt that moved, following Casper's every step as he zigzagged closer.

A dog meant dog shit and one more thing he didn't want to have to clean up. He picked up a stick, aiming to shoo the thing on its way, but had only taken two steps when the back door opened, and there stood a kid, maybe thirteen, fourteen, as unkempt as the mongrel and asking, "Who the hell are you?"

Huh. He was pretty sure that was his line.

"If you're vandalizing, I'm the guy who's going to call the cops," he said, knowing he wouldn't but watching the kid for a response. He got nothing, no fear, no attitude . . . just nothing. Had the kid and the dog been inside earlier? Watching while the inspector checked the outside of the house? "If you're squatting, I'm your landlord, come to collect the rent."

The boy let go of the screen door. It banged shut behind him as he disappeared into what had been designed as a pantry and mudroom but hadn't been used for anything but storing trash during Casper's day. Grumbling, he headed for the steps, stopped by a growl and a baring of teeth. He didn't retreat. He'd lost a couple rounds today already, and sharp canines or not, he was not backing down from this fight.

"Hey. Kid. Call off the dog or I'll shoot him dead." He

wouldn't do that either. He wasn't even carrying his piece, but the kid didn't have to know it.

"Kevin," came the boy's voice from inside the house. The dog quieted, returned to watching Casper with those big dark eyes.

Kevin? Seriously? Casper climbed the steps slowly, his eyes sticking to the dog as he pulled open the door. Blowing out an audible breath, he passed through the garbage dump into the kitchen. The dog followed him, catching the screen with his snout before it banged closed.

Even without shades hanging over the windows, it was dark inside, the film of dirt on the glass shutting out what light the trees didn't block, both keeping the room cooler than he would've expected to find. The floor tiles, never as white as originally billed, were now as brown as the yard.

Dishes were scattered from the kitchen island to the stovetop to the acreage of counters. Cereal bowls. A pan his old lady had used to heat Chef Boyardee and Campbell's Chicken Noodle. Beer cans. Aluminum TV dinner trays. Empty bottles of Jose Cuervo and Jack.

A box of Frosted Flakes had been knocked from the top of the fridge and torn open by varmints. Claw and teeth marks showed on the shredded cardboard and Tony the Tiger's head. And it was quiet. Quiet like a crypt, consuming memories and breathable air and dirty little secrets. A time capsule best left unopened.

Or as he liked to call it, home sweet home.

The smells kept him from getting totally maudlin. Mold and rot and urine and things once living that had to be dead. He shook it off—he'd deal when the time came—and followed Kevin, who seemed to know where he was going, from the kitchen down the long first-floor hallway to what would've been the front parlor had the Jaynes had use for such a thing.

There he found the kid sprawled on a sleeping bag, a paperback thriller in one hand, a backpack for a pillow. Some of the odor was coming from in here. The boy could use a bath. Tough to manage with the water off, but otherwise . . .

Casper looked around. The kid had certainly made himself at home. Matches, a candle, a flashlight. Crumpled foil and soda bottles and takeout containers that looked an awful lot like they'd come from a restaurant Dumpster.

He'd been here a while. And with no water. Which brought to mind the question of what he was doing about a toilet, and that was an answer Casper wasn't exactly excited to hear.

He pushed up on the brim of his hat, his hands moving to his hips. "Let's try this again. What are you doing here?"

"Trying to read," the boy said, his face hidden behind the book. "Do you mind?"

"And you're doing it in my house why?"

All he got in response was silence, so he moved closer, kicked at the worn sole of the kid's tennis shoe. "You answer me or you answer Sheriff Orleans."

The boy slammed the book shut. "That's uncool, dude, calling the man."

"I'm the man you need to worry about," Casper said, shaking off the idea of being the very authority figure he'd had his own skirmishes with back in the day.

"I found the house," he said, rolling up to sit, legs crossed, shoulders hunched. "It was empty. I needed a place to crash, okay?"

A fourteen-year-old should not need a place to crash. Casper might not know much, but he knew that. "You got a home? Family?"

"Would I be here if I did?"

Yeah. That's what he'd thought. "You got a name at least?"

The boy hesitated before offering, “Clay. Whitman.”

Whitman. Casper blinked, frowned. “Do I know you?”

“You just asked me my name, dude.”

Fucking smart-ass. “Okay, then. One more time. What are you doing here?”

The boy held Casper’s gaze as he gained his feet. He was all gangly limbs, awkward, but a solid five foot eight. Still growing. Still figuring things out, finding his place. On his way to being a man.

“I came looking for you,” he said, tossing off the bullshit for a man’s honesty.

This couldn’t be good. Casper was thirty-three. If the boy was fourteen . . . “What do you mean, you came looking for me? I just asked if I knew you.”

“But you didn’t ask if I knew you.”

“Do you?”

“Yeah. Or I did. About six years ago.”

Six years ago . . . God, how many places had he been? He recalled a good dozen. And then he remembered Albuquerque. That was where he’d met one of the bulls to nearly do him in.

He’d also met a couple of buckle bunnies who enjoyed tag-teaming their cowboys. One of their names, he was pretty sure, had been Whitman, though he’d been drunk a lot of that time.

“Are you from Albuquerque?”

Clay nodded, his face drawn and sober.

“You’re Angie’s kid?”

Another nod.

“She’s not here, is she?”

“She’s dead.”

Fuck me. Fuck . . . me. “I’m sorry, man.”

Clay shoved his hands deep in the pockets of his filthy jeans and shrugged. “Okay.”

"What happened?"

"She died."

Casper bit his tongue. Angering the boy wasn't going to get him any answers. "How did you get here?"

"Walked. Hitchhiked."

"How did you know I was here?"

"I didn't really. I knew this was where you were from. My mom used to caw like a crow when she talked about you. I couldn't think of any other place to go."

That didn't make a lick of sense. Casper barely remembered the eight-year-old Clay. It wasn't like he'd been the boy's father figure . . . And Angie making like a crow? What the hell? "What about social services? They didn't find you a family to stay with?"

Clay turned away, nudged his foot against his backpack. "I don't want to talk about it."

"You talk, or I talk." And then for some reason he added, "To the sheriff."

"I don't know why I thought you'd be cool about this," Clay said, the sentence ending on a break Casper did his best to ignore.

"Cool? About a kid I barely knew for a couple of months hunting me down?"

"Yeah. Like I said."

And way to be a dick. He yanked off his hat, worried the brim around and around as he weighed Clay's bravado with a narrowed gaze. "Are you hungry?"

It took a minute for Clay to answer, hunger warring with pride and with being pissed off and more than likely with his being a little bit scared. No doubt a pretty hefty level of sadness was mixed up in there, too. "I could eat."

Casper nodded. "C'mon, then. I'll buy you a burger."

Clay gave a snort. "And then drop me at the sheriff's office? No thanks."

Jesus. It was a wonder people kept having kids. "I won't drop you at the sheriff's office."

"You'll bring me back here?"

Casper considered his options. "No, but I'll take you to the ranch."

"What ranch?"

"Where I live. Where I work."

"This isn't your house?"

Casper made a scoffing noise. Did the kid really think he lived here? And why in the hell had he ever mentioned this place to Angie? Had he been showing off? Drunk bragging about growing up in a Crow Hill mansion? "It is, but it's not fit for man or . . . Kevin."

"He can come, too?" Clay asked, the question cracking as if he was only *just* holding himself together, and the smallest act of kindest would be the end of that.

"Sure. He can bunk with Bing and Bob." At Clay's frown, Casper explained, "The ranch's border collies."

"Then what?"

"Then what, what?"

"After you take me to the ranch. What're you going to do?"

That he did not know. There was a lot of legal stuff going on here and he was getting in over his head. He needed time and he needed advice. "I'll figure something out."

But Casper's non-answer had Clay backing up. "I'd rather stay here."

Jesus H. "You can't stay here. This place is a dump."

"I've seen worse." He dropped to his sleeping bag, digging in. "I can clean it up. You could pay me."

He could, if he had money, if the boy was of legal age, or even an emancipated minor. And if the house wasn't the size of the Crow Hill Country Club, requiring a crew of Clays to clean it. Casper shook off those thoughts for the one that mattered.

Where had Clay seen worse that made bunking in this hell-hole an option? "You can't stay here, Clay."

"Then me and Kevin'll split," he said, shoving the book he'd been reading into his backpack, rolling up the sleeping bag and tying it to the frame. His face was blank as he regained his feet. Then he shouldered his way forcefully by Casper, calling for the dog as he headed for the back door.

Hands at his hips, Casper hung his head, shook it, called out, "Wait."

He listened for the echo of the screen door's hinges, but heard only the reverberation of Kevin's claws clicking to a stop on the floor. He waited, but that was it, the cavernous house sounding of still air and old wood emptiness and hate and despair. He pulled in a deep breath and all the patience he had and returned to the other room.

Clay stood looking out, Kevin sitting at his side. Sunlight turned them into silhouettes, a boy and his dog, alone, the world theirs for the taking. And yet they'd chosen this piece of shit house to stay in. And they'd chosen him to come to.

The weight of that responsibility made the ranch and the house feel like feathers. Casper wasn't sure he liked being the voice of reason. What did he even know about reason? He'd measured a good chunk of his life in eight-second segments from the back of a ton of raw meat.

Jesus H. Christ. Okay. Basics. The beginning. He'd go from there and see what happened. Because, shit, what else could he do? "Let me go get us both something to eat."

"Sure."

"Will you be here when I get back? Or do I need to hog-tie you before I go?"

"I'll be here."

"I *will* come after you," he said, pouring that supreme truth into his words. "And I won't do it alone. So sit, read. I'll bring back the food and we'll figure this out."

Clay swung his backpack onto the kitchen's island, stirring up a cloud of dirt and stink. He dug for his book, curled his fingers in Kevin's ruff, and gave a shrug on his way back to the parlor.

Casper took a long minute to wonder what the hell he was getting himself into, then walked out the back door, hoping that sometime between now and later, he'd come up with more of a plan than the absolute nothing he had now.

THREE

FAITH HAD STARTED to think the lunch hour would never get here—and today, of all days, when she needed to unload on her girls. Sharing a meal with Arwen Poole and Everly Grant had become essential to her sanity, even though their getting together had nothing to do with the food.

In a community where a large percentage of the population was made up of ranching families, it was nice to sit down and unwind without the conversation turning to cattle prices and the lack of rain. Or cattle prices anyway—even if beef as an end product was a major part of Arwen's living.

The lack of rain, on the other hand, was killing everyone and everything. Even the apartment courtyard in Faith's hacienda-style complex was dry and crackly. These days, the grass shared by Arwen's cottage and the Hellcat Saloon was the greenest spot for miles, and her business was thriving because of it.

Hardly a surprise, Faith mused, dropping into her chair. With most of the area turned to some shade of brown, everyone was looking to relax in Crow Hill's only oasis. "I need Coke, ketchup, and french fries, stat."

Already in place at their out-of-the-way spot, Arwen returned her tumbler of iced tea to the table. "You look like you've been to hell and back. That's quite a trip to make before noon."

"No kidding." And unfortunately it would take hours, and more than junk food, to cleanse the morning from her mind.

"Is it work?" Everly leaned against the table's edge, her menu open in front of her. "More than usual, I mean."

"Work, yes, but . . . other stuff, too." Faith and the girls shared everything. And she'd confessed to them her renewed crush on Casper. But just in case it was completely pathetic, she didn't want to blurt out the things she'd been thinking about his thighs. "I told y'all about the surprise party Boone and I are throwing for our folks' anniversary, right?"

"Yep, their thirty-fifth." Everly closed her menu. "And my offer to help you design the invitations still stands."

"You're a doll." Faith turned to hook her purse on her chair. "And I *will* take you up on that. But I still need to make a list of everything else that needs doing."

Arwen narrowed her gaze. "You haven't done that yet? You talked about doing it last week."

Waving off the scolding, Faith said, "And then life got in the way, and here I am."

"So let's make your list now." Everly reached for her bag on the floor, and the pen and spiral notebook inside, tucking back her fall of honey-blonde waves as she straightened. "Number one. Invitations."

Faith nodded toward Everly's writing tools. "I thought news people these days were into digital recorders or iPads."

"Usually," Everly said. "But sometimes nothing beats writing by hand."

"Speaking of writing by hand . . ." Looking beyond Faith's shoulder, Arwen motioned for Luck Summerlin to take their order. But before any of the women could speak, the waitress pointed with her pencil to each at the table in turn.

"Faith wants an extra large Coke and a double order of french fries. Everly will have a club sandwich, and Arwen a grilled chicken salad."

Everly groaned. "God, are we that boring?"

"Not boring," Faith said, refusing the label. "Organized. Efficient. We know what we like, and it saves us from having to reinvent the wheel every time we order."

"Nice try, Faith, but I'm going to have to side with Everly on this one," Arwen said as she glanced at Luck. "I guess that boring order will be it."

Grinning, Luck nodded. "I'll get this put in and be right back with Faith's drink."

Her gaze following Luck across the saloon, Everly said, "You know, one of these days we're going to have to mix things up and throw Luck for a loop. I'll order meatloaf or something."

Arwen gave the other woman a knowing look. "And then a to-go box? Since you won't finish a plate of meatloaf the same way you never finish your club sandwich?"

"Hey!" Everly swatted Arwen's arm with her closed menu before dropping it into their table's fourth chair. "I get lunch *and* supper and only have to order once."

"Order once, pay once. I'd go out of business if everyone ate like you." Arwen turned from Everly to Faith. "Thankfully this one and her metabolism take up the slack."

Faith frowned at the thought of switching up her weekly junk food noshing. "I like my french fries. I like my Coke. I like coming here for the comfort of friends and food."

Arwen laughed. "Wouldn't that be for friends and comfort

food? We make a damn good plate of nachos, you know. If you ever wanted to go crazy."

"But I like my french fries," she whined, rubbing at her throbbing temples.

"And I like my club sandwich," Everly said. "But I don't want to grow stale. Next week, meatloaf for me, nachos for you. We're going to throw caution to the wind."

Throw caution to the wind. Words that made her think of Casper. She looked from Everly to Arwen and back, then took a deep breath. "How do you know if a risk is worth taking?"

"I don't think a few calories here or there is going to make a difference." Everly sat back, pinched lint from the knee of her skinny black pants. "Not with the way you burn fuel, damn you."

Faith only just managed to keep from rolling her eyes. "Not a food risk. A real risk."

"Oh. Well." Everly shrugged. "Depends on what it is. Are you talking personal or professional?"

"This one is definitely personal," Faith said, stabbing a straw into the glass of fizzing soda Luck set on the table before carrying the rest of the drinks on her tray to the next.

"That means it's a man," Everly said, leaning close to Arwen.

"And if it's risky," Arwen responded, leaning closer, "it's Casper Jayne."

Faith, who might as well have been sporting a bull's eye on her forehead, propped her elbows on the table and braced her chin in her hands. "Am I that obvious?"

"It's not about being obvious, sweetie." Arwen reached to squeeze Faith's arm. "Casper's been your weakest link for years."

A shiver slid the length of Faith's spine as she thought back to this morning. "He was in my office earlier, and dear God, those thighs. I could barely look at anything else."

"What was he doing at the bank?" Everly asked as Luck arrived with their food.

Faith waited until the plates had been served before answering. "He's got a burr up his butt about renovating the house on Mulberry Street."

"Good lord, why?" Arwen shook her napkin over her lap. "I'm surprised he didn't put it up for sale the minute he got his hands on the deed."

Faith reached for the ketchup. "He hasn't said a thing about selling. Only about wanting money to fix it up."

"Are you giving him the money?" Everly asked, tucking a strip of bacon back into her sandwich.

"I said the risk I was considering was personal. I'm not about to lose my job over his obsession with that house. Thing is"—she ate two fries before going on—"after he left, I dug into the county records. Property taxes and such. Did you know that house was built by Zebulon Crow? At least the initial structure. It's part of Crow Hill history."

"Zebulon Crow?" Everly asked, her reporter's antennae obviously twitching. "That makes it part of *Texas* history."

"I know. But I'm not sure Casper does."

"I'll bet the Texas Historical Commission would think it worth saving," Arwen said, forking up a strip of grilled chicken. "But if the house was built by a Crow, how did the Jaynes end up with it?"

The same thoughts and questions had crossed Faith's mind. "The inspection report was dismal, but I went ahead and called the inspector. He told Casper he'd be better off razing the place, but admits it looks like most of the damage could be repaired. It wouldn't be cheap, and he hasn't seen the inside, but he didn't write it off as a complete loss."

"Why hasn't he seen the inside?"

"I don't know," Faith said in answer to Arwen. "Casper only wanted the bad news on the exterior."

Her gaze holding Faith's before falling to her salad, Arwen was slow to respond. "I remember hearing talk at school about how bad things were in that house for Casper."

Faith's chest tightened. She'd heard the same things. "I asked Boone about it, but he wasn't spilling any beans. Even as teens, those three boys were tight."

"If the house holds a lot of bad memories, it's kinda strange he'd be wanting to pour a ton of money into it," Everly said.

"I don't disagree," Faith replied, swirling a fry through the ketchup on her plate.

"Enough about Casper's house." Arwen held up a hand. "I want to hear about this big risk you're considering and how he's involved. It's his thighs, isn't it? You want to wrap yours around 'em and let him buck you like a bull."

This time Faith did roll her eyes. "I absolutely cannot afford to get caught up in his drama, but I came *so* close to dragging him across my desk this morning."

"Aww, sweetie. You're a smart girl," Arwen said. "As long as you know what you're doing, why not take him for a ride?"

Biting into her sandwich, Everly nodded, then mumbled, "What she said. Just do it."

"Y'all make it sound so easy."

"If we're talking about the same Casper Jayne, then yes. It's that easy," Arwen said. "Unless you don't think you can keep things to sex."

That wasn't as much of a worry as what trouble she might get into with him during a fling. The man was a loose cannon. "Did sleeping with Dax get him out of your system?"

"No," the other woman said, wiggling in her seat. "But I kinda like the way that turned out."

"Which is all well and good for you. But I'm not looking for a relationship, and even if I were, Casper is hardly relationship material."

"I didn't think Dax was either. And I certainly wasn't looking for anything more than a good time. Things just . . . happened."

"Then you're the perfect poster child for why I shouldn't do this. I don't have time for things to just happen. Not with a man as reckless as Casper."

"Faith, it's an affair. It's fun, and Casper is gorgeous. You work hard. You deserve to play hard. And I can't imagine playing with Casper would be anything but."

The thought of Casper hard . . . Her nipples tingling, Faith reached for her Coke, sucked down a long cooling swallow. "He told me to give him a sign."

"What? When?"

"This morning. In my office."

"You talked about sex in your office?"

"I thought he was flirting with me. I accused him of not having the balls to stand up to Boone and the gang's no-sisters rule."

"Ouch," Arwen said with a grimace. "How'd that go over?"

"Not the way I'd intended." *To say the least.* "He said if I wanted him to stand up to Boone, to give him a sign."

"And did you?"

"Not then, no. And I haven't decided if I'm going to." Faith glanced at Everly who'd downed half her sandwich while listening to the conversation. "I know how Arwen feels. What about you? What would you do if you were me?"

Everly held up both hands. "I'm the last person to give sexual advice. It's been so long, I probably qualify for a re-virgin card."

"But if you were ready and there was someone. What would you do?"

"If he wanted me the way Casper wants you, I'd jump his

bones. But just his bones. Not his heart, mind, or soul, and I'd take mine out of the equation as well."

"See?" Arwen gave Faith a look that had her questioning every reason she'd listed for why getting naked with Casper Jayne was a bad idea. "You think he's too reckless, but asking for a sign instead of dragging you across your desk doesn't sound that reckless to me."

Faith thought about her keyboard, her paperwork, her desk blotter. Thought about Casper sweeping it all to the floor, reaching for her, pulling her to him, her skirt up, her panties down.

There wasn't anything about that scenario that didn't scream reckless. And she could not, for one minute, let any of what she was imagining happen.

Setting her napkin next to her half-empty plate, she reached for her purse and her wallet. "I've got to go. I've got tons of work before I can leave the office. I'm meeting Boone at the ranch for dinner so we can nail down what we can of the party details."

"Did you decide where you're going to have it?"

She turned to answer Arwen and laid her money for the bill on the table. "No. We can't even settle on that. I want the country club. Boone wants to do it at their house."

"That's because you have a good job and he's a struggling rancher."

And then there was the money she had that he didn't, that no one outside her family knew about. But Arwen was right.

Things would be a lot easier if Boone would let her pay for everything; instead, they'd agreed to split all the costs. "What he doesn't get is that having the party at their house means more work for the two of us. I don't want to have to play hostess and caterer. I want to write a check and enjoy myself."

"Why don't you have it here?" Arwen asked. "We'll close for private functions, as long as we've got plenty of notice. And we've got the room you need, not to mention the food. The two birds, one stone thing. You wouldn't need a separate caterer. Unless you've already talked to someone."

"I haven't, no." Faith had planned to ask for a recommendation in Luling, the closest town of any size to Crow Hill, but it hadn't occurred to her to ask Arwen. Which was really, really dumb. "And I didn't even think about the saloon. I'm so under the gun at work my head is ready to explode."

"Then think about it."

"I will. I'll let you know. And," Faith said, turning to Everly, "we'll talk about the invitations soon."

"This thing with Casper's house on Mulberry Street," Everly said, putting away her notebook and signaling to Luck for a to-go box. "He's not living there, is he?"

Faith shook her head. "No, he still lives at the ranch with Boone."

"And you're going out there tonight?"

"To see Boone, yes." And then the significance of Everly's question sunk in. "If you think I'm going to sleep with Casper with Boone under the same roof, you are out of your mind."

"Yeah, I can imagine the two of you would get pretty noisy."

"Oh my God, Arwen. Why would you even say that?"

"That's easy," Arwen said, her cheeks going rosy, her eyes dewy, her smile dreamy and warm. "I want every woman I know, but especially my dearest friends, to have what I have. To know what I know. Both of you deserve this . . . this . . ." She fluttered her hands. "I don't even know what to call it, but it's perfect and it's beautiful, and I don't know how I ever got through a day without having Dax in my life."

Faith got to her feet, twisting her mouth against a grin. "I'm going to get all weepy now."

"Oh, shut up and go back to work," Arwen said, stretching

to meet her halfway for a hug. "And let's talk more about the party."

"Definitely," she said. Then Everly whispered in her ear, "Just do it," leaving Faith to walk out of the Hellcat Saloon with thoughts of Casper Jayne's thighs heavy on her mind.

FOUR

WITH A BOOT on the counter's aluminum footrest, Casper pulled a Blackbird Diner menu from between the napkin holder and the salt and pepper shakers, and leaned his crossed arms on the speckled Formica surface. He pretended to study the items offered. Pretended, because he knew what he wanted. All he needed was to have his order taken—and to avoid eye contact with anyone still holding a grudge.

He hadn't exactly been a saint the last time he'd called Crow Hill home, and those people were still out there. Less of them were gunning for him lately since the Dalton Gang had toned down their hell-raising ways, but they were still there. No doubt watching, waiting, expecting some big fuck up.

Little did they know the fuck ups were being kept in-house these days. Most had to do with the crapfest of a ranch he and the boys were trying to make into something worth all the hours of sleep lost to work and worry. Others he blamed on too much beer. He hadn't been completely redeemed. And he was still giving Boone plenty of grief over Faith.

Just seemed the thing to do, a last vestige of the past when Boone and Dax had decided sisters were off limits, and Casper had made no secret of his lust for both the Campbell and Mitchell girls.

Funny about that, how teasing Dax about Darcy had really been more about throwing Boone off the scent of the truth. Casper had always had a thing for Faith. He just hadn't known what to do with it.

"What can I get you?" asked a voice into his musings.

"Let me have three, no, four cheeseburgers all the way," he said, stabbing a finger at the laminated menu. Clay could strip off any veggies he didn't like. "And two extra large orders of fries."

"Four cheeseburgers and two extra large fries. Anything to drink?"

He'd grab a six-pack of soda from Nathan's. A bag of dog food, too. A jug of water. A bowl to pour it in . . . Jesus. "No, but go ahead and toss in a couple slices of apple pie. Wait. Might as well give me one extra large chocolate shake."

"Got it. And Casper, no one here's going to bite."

He looked up, catching the wink Teri Gregor threw him before she turned for the order wheel hanging above the kitchen's pass-through window. He thought back over his history, weighed it, came away pretty sure he'd never crossed any lines with her, though he doubted Dax could say the same.

Who knew getting out and about was going to have him questioning all the wrong turns he'd taken when knowing better didn't mean shit? Whatever. He couldn't be bothered with any of that now. He had too much on his plate already, and the dog and the squatter weren't helping.

At some point today, he was going to have to stop by the city and have the water to the house turned back on. No doubt that would require a hefty deposit. Might as well count on one for the electricity, too. And the gas. Had to have both to run the water heater, a vacuum, the refrigerator and a fan, plus the stove, because in the end it would be cheaper than buying and fueling a generator.

And Clay had to take a bath. The boy was already ripe, and working up a sweat while cleaning would only add another layer of stink. Depending on what all Clay had in his backpack, Casper was also going to need to haul his clothes to the ranch, or at least to the Laundromat for washing.

Okay. Hold up. What was he doing? Making it easy for Clay to stay in the house instead of turning him over to the authorities or sending him on his way? Buying dog food and a water bowl for Kevin? A chocolate shake *and* apple pie?

He was asking for trouble. For himself, for the boy. Letting Sheriff Orleans know a runaway had taken up residence on Mulberry Street was the right thing to do for all of them.

But Casper couldn't find it in him to be right about this.

Movement to his left had him looking that way as attorney Greg Barrett boosted onto the neighboring stool. "Casper."

"Greg."

"How're things at the ranch?"

"Good. The firm?" Not that he gave a crap. Casper's loyalties were with his boys, not the half-brother Dax had only learned this summer he had.

Greg bobbed his head. "Busy now that Darcy's set up her own practice."

Again. Hard to care. Darcy as a Dalton Gang sister got the same loyalty as Dax. "Word has it she's keeping busy, too."

"Not surprising. She had her own clients. Others," Greg said, stopping as if to weigh what his position allowed him to say.

"Some of mine preferred to take their family law issues to a different attorney once the truth came out."

Because even though Greg's last name was Barrett, he was still a Campbell. And since Wallace Campbell's heart attack, the bastard son had been at the helm. Interesting that Greg didn't seem to be bothered by the gossip. And that he still had plenty of work.

Strange, though, for Crow Hill to have two law offices instead of one, both practices belonging to Wallace Campbell's get.

Casper wondered how many clients had come to Greg because he'd proved he could keep a secret. Yeah, yeah, attorney-client privilege and all, but Greg had kept his own. Kept Wallace Campbell's, too, until the old man had gone down with a coronary. And even then he'd only told Dax.

"My lunch appointment's here," Greg said, sliding from the stool. Holding Casper's gaze for a long beat, he said, "Give my best to Dax," before turning away.

The door to the diner opened, and Philip Hart walked in to shake Greg's hand. Casper watched the two of them settle into the diner's back booth, a waitress arriving with water glasses as soon as they'd taken their seats. Huh. He'd heard rumors about the difficulties the Hart family was facing. Hell, he and the boys were up against ones that could very well drop them in the same shit bucket.

They'd used an attorney in Dallas to handle the legalities of their shared inheritance. He doubted that would change. Dax hadn't wanted the family attorneys knowing his business.

And so far in his life, knock on wood, Casper had managed to avoid needing more than a public defender to get him out of the occasional drunk and disorderly. Though this thing with Clay . . .

He swiveled his stool, facing the pass-through window and

the bustle in the kitchen. Something about seeing that mess of a boy in that mess of a house took him back a lot of years to a lot of wrongs.

No kid ever needed to deal with what Clay was going through. With what Casper had gone through, and probably wouldn't have survived if not for his boys.

Clay didn't have a gang, he had a dog, and until Casper figured out a way to do things that wouldn't have him hating himself, he'd do what he could his way. Since his way usually consisted of winging it, he'd have to hope he didn't fuck up things worse than they already were, and that he could keep off the local law's radar.

Hmm. Maybe he should've asked Greg for his card—

"Casper Jayne?"

Wresting off thoughts knotting his gut like a catch rope, he turned and looked into the eyes of Royce Summerlin.

The older man nudged his hat up a notch, his face ruddy from more than the sun and his ancestry, his gaze sharp as barbed wire, his mind thoroughly whetted to getting his way. "Heard you were back but haven't had a chance to say hello."

Casper was pretty sure there wouldn't have been any reason for him to, but he took hold of the man's outstretched hand and gave it a firm shake. Royce was in his sixties, looked older, but had the grip of a man a decade to the other side. Dave Dalton had looked similar, aged by the weather and the worry of a life lived at the mercy of the land, a life made easier for Royce by the Summerlin fortune.

"Royce. How're things?"

"Good enough, but could always be better."

Casper nodded. It was a sentiment widely held. But he didn't have time to spend talking about beef prices and the drought. "I hear you're looking for someone to break some horses."

"I am," Royce said, standing tall beneath a hat that added to his imposing height. "Had a man doing it for me, but I've sent him over to help Nina."

"Banning?"

"That's him," Royce said with a nod. "I know you made your name and your money riding bulls, but if you've got any interest—"

"I do." He pushed up from where he'd been leaning, reaching for his wallet as Teri brought a big brown grocery bag to the counter.

"Hey, Royce."

"Afternoon, Teri," the older man said, sweeping his hat from his head. "What do you hear from Shane?"

Teri reached for the three tens Casper handed her, rang up his order, and made change. "He's doing well. Hoping to get home for a week when Shannon starts school. It's hard on her, going back without her mom or dad when the rest of the kids have a parent with them."

"Shane's a good brother, a good man. Can't be easy coming home to take on a little sister he didn't even know." Royce waited for Casper to pocket his wallet before continuing where they'd left off. "Walk out with me, Jayne. Teri, say hello to your folks."

"I will. Thanks, Royce. And see you around, Casper."

Casper gave her a wave without looking back, his mind on Summerlin's offer. He set the bag of his and Clay's lunch on the hood of his truck, then turned. "About the horses."

"Why don't you come out to the ranch and see them for yourself? Might help you decide—"

"I don't need to see them. I'll do the job."

Summerlin settled his hat back on his head, narrowed his eyes. "I can't pay you a lot."

That was a lie. “I’ll take what you can give me.” And that was the truth.

Royce glanced toward the diner as if taking the time to run a tally of a possible profit and loss. “It’s not my business how you manage your time, but I know the ranch is keeping you busy. I don’t want to take you away from that, cause you any problems with Coach Mitchell’s kid and the Campbell boy.”

Doubtful Dax and Boone would appreciate being referred to as a kid and a boy, but at least he and Summerlin were on the same page. “I can spare a couple of hours a day, if that works for you.”

“I’d rather have someone who can spare more, but since it seems we’re both in a bind, that’ll do. At least until I can find someone to hire full time.” He quoted Casper a figure. “It’s not much, but it’s something.”

Casper and all of Crow Hill knew Royce could pony up more, but he wasn’t in a position to ask for it. He needed anything he could get, and it wouldn’t hurt to prove he’d moved beyond his hell-raising ways. “It’s fine. I’ve got a couple stops to make before heading back to the ranch. I could swing by once I’m done and you can show me what I’m looking at. We can see what sort of schedule works best.”

“That’ll do. I’ll look forward to seein’ ya,” Royce said, slamming his palm against the hood of Casper’s truck before making his bowlegged way to his own.

Snagging an arm around the grocery bag, Casper watched him go, his stomach growling, his head torn between getting back to Clay and getting started with Summerlin, some part of what he supposed was his conscience pressing him to get back to the ranch and the chores waiting there.

But most insistent was his lower body, reminding him of his date later tonight with Faith. A date to talk. Not exactly his first choice of activities but he could be patient. Though the idea of getting his hands on Faith would most likely test the truth of that.

"You're going to be on your own until morning," Casper said, gathering the trash from the lunch he and Clay had inhaled. Kevin lay on the parlor floor nearby, having chowed on his kibbles and now begging with his big black eyes for their scraps. He could just keep begging. There weren't any. "I've a million chores waiting at the ranch, two partners breathing down my neck, and I need to see a man about a horse."

His buying dog food along with cleaning supplies at Nathan's Food and Drug had raised eyebrows in the aisles and at checkout. Folks knew Casper, knew the ranch ordered for Bing and Bob in bulk from Lasko Ranch Supply. He supposed word of his purchases would reach Boone and Dax before he did—meaning he might as well come up with an explanation now instead of stumbling over one later.

The cleaning supplies would be easy enough. They knew about the house. And he could pass off the six-pack of soda as his, though most of his six-packs were made up of longnecks instead of aluminum cans. The dog food, not so much. He couldn't see them buying a story that he'd developed a soft heart for a stray.

Ah, truth. You ironic bitch.

Clay shrugged, sucked down the rest of his milkshake, then belched. "You act like I've got a problem being on my own."

The kid was fourteen. He should have a problem with it. Casper sure as hell did, but he knew this wasn't the time to start digging into what had driven the boy to Crow Hill when he'd had a world of places to choose from.

That, more than anything, was getting Casper's goat. What the hell impression had he given the boy in Albuquerque?

And how was he going to reverse it without making things worse? "What I mean is that you're going to have to get started cleaning up without me here."

"Here to help?" Clay asked, tossing his head to get his lank and overlong hair out of his eyes. "Or to look over my shoulder?"

"Both, but since I won't be here, then neither. I'm going to stop and put in orders to have the water and power and gas turned on, but you can start with the obvious trash in the meantime. I bought an industrial-sized box of garbage bags."

"Garbage detail. Got it."

"And stay out of sight."

"Got that one, too."

"Good, because we could both be in deep shit if you're discovered before I can figure out what to do with you."

That had Clay backing up a couple of steps. "I don't need you to do anything with me. You don't want me here, say the word and I'm gone."

Jesus. Casper closed his eyes, rubbed the grit away instead of snatching up the kid and shaking him. "Just stay out of sight. If anyone comes around, find a closet or something."

"No one has to come in to check the utilities are working?"

"Shouldn't. Well, maybe the gas, but they can wait till I'm here if that's the case. Water'll get turned on at the meter, and the electric box is on the rear of the house. Just keep Kevin off the porch."

"And you'll be back when?"

He thought of all the things at the ranch he'd already put off too long. Thought of letting down Boone and Dax, not holding up his third of the partnership. He thought about Faith. Then he thought about growing up and having no one watching his back.

He grabbed one last plastic fork from the floor along with a wedge-shaped container that had held a slice of pie, and headed for the kitchen, calling back, "As soon as I can in the morning. I'll work out a schedule for the things that need doing."

"I can pretty much figure out what needs doing," Clay said, following.

"Yeah, smart-ass, I know. But some things take priority."

"How much are you going to pay me?"

"Over your room and board?"

"This isn't much of a room, and Vienna sausages with cheese crackers and Coke doesn't count as much in the way of board."

"Vienna sausages with cheese crackers don't require cooking or digging through restaurant trash. And it's only for the rest of the day. I'll get you a microwave and figure out what to do about a fridge once I see if that one," he said, nodding toward the ancient appliance, "has any life left in it."

Clay screwed up his mouth. "You saying I can't use the stove? I do know how to cook."

"Without setting the house on fire?"

"I used to cook for my mom. Really cook, not just heating up cans of soup and nuking pizza bites."

Huh. Interesting. "We'll cross that bridge. Best to keep things simple for now."

"Whatever."

Jesus H. A teenager complaining about eating junk for a few days? "I'll pick up kolaches or breakfast tacos in the morning, okay?"

"Thanks," Clay said with a nod, his gaze finding Kevin as if he needed a friend. "I like eggs."

"I'll pick up a fan, too. There's a window unit in what's supposed to be the master bedroom, but I imagine it's nothing but a big nest for mice these days. Depending on how my finances shake out"—and what a joke that was—"I'll eventually look into central air."

After a long moment spent blinking and staring, Clay asked, "You saying you don't have any money?"

"No. I'm saying I have to be careful with what I have." Another joke. He was becoming a regular comedian.

That seemed to satisfy the boy. "What happens once the house is cleaned up? Are you going to move back in?"

Casper hadn't thought that far ahead. "I don't know. Another bridge I'll worry about when the time comes."

"You had to have been thinking something. Before you found me here. You stopped, and all."

What he'd been thinking was best not put into words. "I'd just got the letter telling me the place was mine. Thought it best I see what I'd inherited."

"Your folks die or something?"

"Nah. My old lady just didn't want it anymore."

"Guess she hasn't lived here in a while."

"She's been in Vegas for years, but I don't know when exactly she moved. I've been gone since I was eighteen. Just came back this summer."

"You're like, what, forty or something?"

Jesus. "I'm thirty-three."

"That's a long time not to see your mom."

"Clay . . ." Casper hesitated. He was the least equipped person he knew to advise on familial relationships. "My mother wasn't much of one. Not all mothers are."

"Mine was," the boy said, his tone hurt, his posture defensive. "She was the best."

"I'm sure she was. I didn't know her well, but I do know she loved you." He didn't know anything of the sort. He just figured it was something the kid deserved to hear. "She talked about you a lot."

"Didn't figure y'all were into talking."

Because they were too busy screwing. Clay didn't have to say the words for Casper to hear them. "Spending time with women is a lot more fun when you both talk about things that matter, and me and Angie did that. About rodeo and about Albuquerque. And about you."

"Whatever."

Jesus H. Teenagers. Casper reached into the past, grasping for something. "She talked about you and your books. She was damn proud of that, you reading instead of spending all your time in front of a computer or Playstation."

Clay shrugged. "I like stories. The best games have stories. But I left my laptop at home so I've been grabbing books where I can."

Something about that had Casper's antennae twitching. "Whaddaya mean, grabbing books?"

"Used stores toss out old ones. New stores throw away ones that don't have any covers. It's trash. It's not like I'm stealing."

Eh, they might have to disagree on that. "What else have you been digging out of the trash?"

"Food for Kevin sometimes. And other stuff."

"Food for you?"

"You figure out the best places to look, the best times." He flipped his hair out of his face again. "I mean, I'm not going to eat spoiled meat or rotten eggs, but someone tosses out half a Big Mac? Yeah. I'll bite. Better than Vienna sausages and cheese crackers."

Jesus H. Christ. "Your mom talk to you about looking a gift horse in the mouth?"

Clay dropped his gaze to his too-big feet, shuffled them. "Thanks for the food."

That was better. "It's just for a night."

Another shuffle, his soles squeaking against the floor. "You say so."

"I do," Casper said, realizing such backtalk would've earned him a fist to the face from his old man. "I stopped by to take a look at the place. I wasn't expecting visitors. I'm a little blindsided, but I'm working to catch up."

"Yeah," was all Clay said.

Okay. Change of subject. "When did you get here?"

"About a week ago, I guess."

"And you've been here in the house all that time?"

"Except when I've gone out for food."

"Did you ever think about going out for a shower?"

Color stained the boy's cheekbones. "I washed up along the way. Gas stations. Rest stops. It's mostly my clothes that smell. I didn't have the money to wash them."

"Doesn't cost but a few bucks, soap included."

"I didn't have a few bucks."

"Did you . . . Do you have anything?"

"Money, you mean?" He shook his head, his hair falling back into his face. "Not anymore. I had a trucker in Midland give me a fifty. It lasted a while."

Casper didn't like the sound of that. "He gave it to you. You didn't—"

"Suck his dick? No, man. None of that shit went on. I wouldn't have taken rides if it had."

"Good," Casper said, though who was he to judge what a kid had to do to survive? He dug his wallet from his pocket, rifled through the bills stuffed inside, and pulled out twenty bucks. That left him with the nine bucks of change from the lunch he shouldn't have splurged on. He crossed his fingers he wouldn't have a blowout on the way home. "Take this. Not that you'll need it, but being without's not a good thing."

Clay shrugged, his hands in his pockets. "I'll make do. I always have. Mom taught me how."

Maybe so, but it still didn't sit well, and he waited until Clay gave in and took the money. "Guess you were on the road a while."

"I left when school was out."

"In June? You've been on the road two months?"

He nodded. "Sometimes we'd just hole up a few days. If the weather was bad. Or we'd walk early and late, and hang out inside somewhere to get out of the heat. Sometimes we were just tired and took a break. It wasn't like we were in a big hurry or anything. I didn't even know if you still lived here."

And if the Dalton inheritance hadn't fallen into his lap, he could easily have still been on the road. The thought had a bale of dread choking him. "You're lucky. I only moved back a couple of months ago."

"That would've sucked. To get here and you not be here."

He started to ask the boy what he'd have done if that had been the case, but decided there was no use borrowing trouble when they were both neck deep. "Okay, then. I'm going to see about the water and power and gas, and I'll be back as soon as I can tomorrow. Stay out of sight. You and Kevin both. A stray dog in ranching country doesn't raise the same curiosity as one roaming the streets of Crow Hill."

"I'll keep him in, but we've been careful, sticking to the east side of the porch when he needs to go. Not as much happening at the house on that side."

Casper thought a minute. Last he'd known, the Banyons lived on the west, the Taylors on the east, and most likely a bit of morning gardening and coffee with the old-timers at the Blackbird Diner was the only time Sheldon Taylor ventured out.

"You can go," Clay said, drawing Casper's attention away from his musings.

"I'm going," he replied, getting back to counting all the things he had to do before seeing Faith tonight. He dug for his keys, settled his hat square on his head, reached for his sunglasses where they hung by the earpiece from the neck of his T-shirt.

"We're fine, dude," came Clay's voice from behind him when he still hadn't moved. "We've been at this a while."

And that particularly disturbing fact was what Casper carried with him the rest of the day.

FIVE

"WHAT WOULD YOU think about having the party at the Hellcat Saloon?" Faith asked, wiping down the plastic tablecloth in the ranch house kitchen, then leaning to pick up stray potato peelings from the floor that always seemed in need of a good mopping.

"Mom? In the Hellcat Saloon? Are you kidding me?" Snorting more than laughing, Boone turned back to the stove, flipping the hamburger steaks he was frying up in a cast-iron skillet.

Such a simple supper, and yet Faith's stomach was rumbling from the smells. Considering her lunch had been nothing but french fries, and she hadn't stopped work for so much as a snack the rest of the day, being hungry shouldn't have come as a surprise.

That's what happened when she thought more about Casper Jayne than her own basic needs. Another reason not to risk an affair.

A stupid reason, but she wasn't above grasping for any and all straws at this point. He'd be here soon, and she needed her ammunition ready, because her thinking about seeing him after the way they'd left things this morning had her skin itching, her lust crazy hot.

"If the saloon is closed for a private party, why not?" she asked as she tossed the peelings into the trash. "There won't be any drunks there, except for her friends, and there won't be any bar-top kitten dances, unless she wants to climb up with Dad and two-step."

"Who put this idea in your head? Wait. It had to be Arwen." He pulled open the oven door, used a hot mitt to slide out a baking sheet of potatoes and onions broiling to a crisp, shaking them around before sending them back to cook a bit more. "Y'all had lunch and she sold you on using her place."

"She didn't sell me on anything. Not if you mean she's doing it for the money. She's not. She offered the food and the drinks at cost." A detail that appealed to the banker in Faith. "We wouldn't have to deal with renting a hall and hiring a caterer and hoping we can get the date and time and menu we want. And it would be a whole lot cheaper than the country club."

Boone grabbed two plates from the cabinet. "I dunno, Faith. The folks've got room at the house. I don't know why we don't just do it there."

"One, because it's kinda hard to throw a surprise party in the place where they live. And two, I don't want to have to play hostess *and* make sure none of Momma's Precious Moments figurines get busted by kids running from the one den door, across the patio, and back through the other." The way she and Boone had done for years, her chasing him to get her diary back, him chasing her for teasing him about dousing himself in Stetson cologne before a date.

"Grab a couple of beers from the fridge, will you?"

First she grabbed a couple of knives and forks from the drawer, then went for the drinks, her eyes lighting up when she did. "Ooh. You've got strawberries and whipped cream."

"And an angel food cake up on top of the fridge."

"Dessert. Mmm. What prompted that? Y'all are usually much more caveman with your groceries."

Another laugh, this one with less snorting. "Caveman?"

She found herself grinning, picturing Boone with a club and dressed like Fred Flintstone. "You know. Kill it and gut it and skin it and drag it home to eat."

"If you think that's what we do out here, you need to come around more often."

"Speaking of which, do you mind if I sleep over?"

"No, but why?"

Because Casper's not home yet, and he's been on my mind all day, and we have to settle this thing we started this morning before I explode.

"Because I'm tired and it's late and I don't want to drive home. And the Cowans next door are having their three-year-old's birthday party tonight, and I'm just not up for all that toddler noise." When Boone grunted what she took for acceptance, she went on. "I thought I could use the room Darcy fixed up when she was helping y'all go through the Daltons' things."

"Sure. She left it in pretty good shape. It's probably cleaner than the room Dax left when he moved into town."

"Eww. No one has cleaned it? He's been gone a month."

Boone shrugged, sliding the hamburger steaks onto the plates. "It's not like anyone goes in there, or that we've got all sorts of spare time."

"Note to self. Hire a maid for the Dalton Gang."

"Now that's funny."

"Why?" she asked, scooping potatoes and onions onto the top of her steak. Then scooping more before letting Boone go at it.

He settled into the chair at the table's end, piling his plate full, then heading to the pantry for the ketchup. "You think any woman's going to want to come out here and clean for us? With our reputations?"

"You earned those reputations in high school. It's hardly like you're running around town drinking and whoring the way you did then."

"You calling your only brother a whore?"

"A reformed whore, then," she said, taking a bite and savoring the crispiness of the potatoes, the savory juice of the meat.

"No, not reformed. Just temporarily grounded. Whoring takes a lot of money. I'm broke as a joke and it ain't funny." He sat again, the legs of his chair scratching over the floor as he scooted closer to his plate. "Which is why I wouldn't be able to afford a maid if you found anyone to take the job."

"I'll find you a janitor, then. And I'll pay for it. I don't like coming out here being exposed to who knows what communicable diseases." When he gave her a look, she added, "And I don't like thinking about you living in filth either."

"I'm not going to have another man cleaning up after me."

"Oh, good lord. What does it matter who does it as long as it gets done?"

"I don't want you paying to have my house cleaned. I don't care who's cleaning it."

"Too bad. You want me out here more often? The place is going to be clean." That thought brought her back to the reason for this visit. "That's another thing to consider for the party. Having it at home means we'd have to get Momma and Daddy out of the house for the day *and* get a crew in to clean. And they'll have to come back the next day because I'm not going to mop and vacuum and haul away all that trash."

Boone sliced into his meat with the edge of his fork, scraped up a huge bite, but before shoveling it into his mouth, said, "Almost sounds like you're trying to talk yourself out of this whole party thing."

"No. I'm trying to talk *you* into having it at Arwen's place. Yes, she calls it a saloon, but it's more like a Chili's, or an Applebee's even, than it is a drinking hole with swinging doors and barmaids draped over pianos." She reached for the ketchup, squirted ribbons over her crispy potatoes. "And it's sure not anything like the old Buck Off Bar."

That brought a grin to Boone's mouth, but still he shook his head. "Maybe not, but I have a feeling a lot of the folks' friends from church aren't going to want to step foot inside that den of iniquity."

"Are these the same friends who showed up last month for the barbecue cook-off Arwen hosted? Because I don't have time to factor hypocrisy into all the other things on my to-do list."

"You won't have to if you have the party at the house," he said, screwing off the top from his longneck.

She took a deep breath instead of growling at him. "If we go that route, and I'm not saying we're going to, then what money we save by not renting a hall we'll have to put toward security on top of everything else. I'm not going to play hall monitor."

"You're not going to cook or clean or round up heathens. Check."

"Boone, it'll be *so* much easier to hire pros."

"I get that, Faith. But I want Mom and Dad to be comfortable, and I can't see that happening at the saloon. I mean, hell.

We could throw the party here, if it comes to it. I know it's a drive, and that might be an issue, but at least put the ranch on your list of locations to scout."

The party wasn't for six weeks or so. Not every decision had to be made immediately. And it wasn't like the guest list would be peppered with Crow Hill society who might turn up their noses at stepping out of their hilltop mansions.

But she would put her foot down about some things, and her brother would just have to deal. "I will, but don't count on it, okay? It'll be late when the party's over, and even if they leave early, some of the church folk are older than Momma and Daddy. You forget how dark it is out here at night."

"Look, just do what you think's best," he said, digging into his food again. "Bring me a list of what you're spending. I'll write you a check."

"I want you to have fun, too."

"As long as Mom and Dad have a good time, I'll have fun."

"No you won't. You hate coming to town and showing your face."

"If I hate coming to town, it's because I've got too much to do to enjoy being away. Plus, the fridge on the back porch is full of beer," he added with a grin.

Instead of grinning in return, she glared. "I don't like thinking about you out here drinking alone."

"I don't drink alone. I drink with Casper. That's assuming we don't both pass out in our supper plates first."

"That's it," she said, finishing up her food and pushing her plate away. "You're taking the rest of the night off. And not to spend in the barn doing more work. I'll clean up in here. You read or sleep or take a hot shower. Relax."

"I don't have time to relax."

"Uh-uh. No arguing. Move a chair outside and prop your feet up and have a couple of those beers."

"It's hot outside."

"There's a ceiling fan on the back porch."

"Yeah, circulating hot air."

She was going to strangle him. "Then sit in the living room. Watch a baseball game."

He cocked an arm over the back of his chair and took her in. "Are you trying to get rid of me?"

Yes! But of course she didn't say that. "I'm trying to take care of you. You're my brother. I love you."

"More like you're trying to get your way about the Hellcat Saloon."

"And here I thought I was so convincing," she said, getting to her feet and stacking their empty plates, leaning over to kiss his cheek. "Ugh. You smell like cow shit. Leave your clothes in the mudroom and I'll do a load of wash."

"I can do my own damn wash."

"I know you can, but tonight it's on me. And not because I'm trying to get my way, but because you stink."

At that, he laughed, pushing his chair away from the table and stripping out of his clothes as he left the room. Faith rolled her eyes and turned away to keep from seeing anything she shouldn't. But he was right.

Hiring a maid for this uncouth bunch would be a very bad idea.

SIX

GOOD THING SHE hadn't wasted her time deciding what sort of sign to give Casper, Faith mused, standing in the ranch house kitchen and staring into the fridge. It was almost midnight. She couldn't sleep, so what was she doing? Looking for relief from her insomnia in food. Sad, when the refrigerator shelves were next to empty, much like the ones in the pantry were close to bare.

She hated seeing the boys struggle to feed themselves, much less make ends meet. She hated being responsible for their purse strings and being forced to keep said strings drawn tight. Hated most of all that Boone wouldn't take any of the money she'd really never wanted, or any of the interest accrued in the ten years since she'd signed papers buying her silence.

He didn't want to cash in on her stupidity any more than she did. He hadn't used those words, but he hadn't needed to. They were close. And they both knew the truth.

Too bad that closeness didn't translate well to agreeing on their parents' party plans. After she'd cleaned the kitchen and he'd cleaned himself, they'd talked for hours, yet had settled very little beyond serving barbecue and a variety of beer. Their father loved discovering new microbreweries, and barbecue was a Mitchell family mainstay.

Boone had grunted when accepting her suggestions, like the menu items, and grumbled when he hadn't, like booking the Hellcat Saloon. The grunting and grumbling had only gotten louder until he'd headed upstairs at eleven. She hadn't meant to keep him so late—she knew he had to be up with the sun—but she'd wanted to make what headway they could.

And she'd been waiting for Casper.

She reached for the basket of leftover strawberries and the bowl of cream she'd whipped for dessert. And why not? Junk food was how she dealt with all her unresolved issues, and her lust for Casper Jayne was as unresolved as it got. She wanted him. He wanted her. They couldn't be worse for each other if they tried.

It had taken but a single, stupid incident in college to convince her she wasn't cut out for a life of reckless, inappropriate behavior. Casper, on the other hand, thrived on risks like the parched Crow Hill earth absorbed water, as if his very existence depended on access to a never-ending source.

Was that what was driving his crazy attachment to the house he'd grown up in? His need to pour money into a losing proposition? Did he expect to come out on top the way he did when he mounted a ton of bucking beef?

And what was the point of that? The adulation? The big, fat middle finger to his naysayers? To his mother? Did he ever consider what might happen if things didn't go his way? If a bull took his head off, or broke his back and left him bound to a wheelchair? If the house fell down around him and buried him in rubble so deep he literally—or metaphorically—couldn't claw his way out?

How could he live with disaster lurking right around the corner? And how could she knowingly step into that life, even if only for the physical pleasure he promised?

They made for a horrible fit, and yet when the heavy strike of bootheels sounded on the back porch she didn't move a muscle. She closed her eyes, frozen, the wait, and not the cold of the refrigerator, raising gooseflesh along her arms.

She swallowed at the whine of the screen door's hinges, at the squeak as the doorknob turned. She was stuck between wanting to be invisible and wanting him to find her in the camisole and boy shorts she'd worn to bed in lieu of nothing.

She wanted him to see her naked legs, her barely clothed body, her hair a mess from tossing on her pillow as she'd tried to sleep, thinking of having him beside her. Of having him *inside* her, deep and full and demanding.

The door creaked closed, latched. The footsteps slowed, then stopped. The air in the room grew heavy and close before a low, throaty laugh reached her ears. "Something tells me I'm looking at a sign."

God, what he did to her with just those few words. She was weak. He made her weak. Around him, she didn't have it in her to be strong.

Still facing the fridge, she opened her eyes, lifted her chin, and turned, taking him in from hat to belt buckle to boots. Then wishing they weren't going into this with this morning still fresh because she didn't want her control of his money to come between them.

But bringing her gaze back to his wasn't any better. He had some very naughty things on his mind. Things she couldn't help but wonder about. Things making the back of her knees sweat, her inner thighs grow damp.

"You're looking at someone who decided to spend the night and didn't want to sleep in her work clothes." She frowned, frustrated with herself, with him, with wanting him. "Where have you been?"

"I didn't know I had a curfew," he said, a look of surprise crossing his face.

She pointed at him with the strawberry she held. "I waited for you."

He pushed his hat back on his head, gave her a thorough once-over. "Wearing that? Because I would've made sure to be here if I'd known."

She doubted that. She was beginning to think he hadn't thought of her all day. "No. I came over after work to talk to Boone. You were supposed to be here, too, remember?"

He crossed his arms, that same flitter of surprise appearing briefly, as if he wasn't sure what to make of her, as if he didn't want to make a wrong move, say the wrong thing. As if she was unexpected. "I had a couple of errands to run. Got tied up."

"With what?" she asked, popping the strawberry into her mouth.

He tossed his hat to the table. "I went by the house."

"Why?"

He stiffened, his eyes going dark. "It's not going to go away just because you want it to."

"It would if you sold it. Or signed it over to the city. Or something that wouldn't cost you any money, and might even make you some."

"Money I can then turn over to you."

This morning's phone call to the Harts was still heavy on her heart, and she was being a bitch because of it. No, she didn't want to deal with Casper wanting money for something so totally out of the question. And she had no time to spend conjuring a solution because there was none. He had no money.

But she did. "It is what it is, Casper. I don't make the rules."

"It's okay, Faith. We're in debt up to our eyeballs. I got it." He came close to her, stopped in front of her, reached into the basket behind her for a strawberry, dragged it through the bowl of whipped cream she held in her hand.

But he didn't eat it. Instead, his gaze locked on hers, and he dotted the cold cream into the hollow of her throat. Then he leaned forward and licked it away.

His tongue was hot and deft, and her nipples tightened. Her camisole was thin, her arousal obvious, Casper too sharp not to see. But he held her gaze as he ate the fruit, saying nothing, waiting with her while the tension in the room grew thick and constricting, binding them.

She couldn't move, and her skin burned, and she felt as if she could reach out and catch the dust motes floating in the moonlight where it streamed through the curtains covering the window over the sink.

"What are you doing?" she asked, her voice a painful whisper when she forced it out of her mouth.

"Having a snack," was what he said, and she didn't know if he was talking about the berries, or about her. She didn't know if she cared, because he was here, and everything she'd wanted for ages was so close she could pull it around them like a cocoon.

He scooped two fingers through the cream then, his eyes on his hand as he brought it to her mouth. She licked her lips, swallowed, parted them and let him inside.

She swirled away the cream with her tongue, worked her way around his fingertips, in and out, sucking them, flicking them, watching his Adam's apple bob, his nostrils flare. His pupils dilate. Then she dropped her gaze and saw the truth of his cock straining to be free of his jeans.

Is this what it felt like to be reckless? Sex and Casper? After all these years? And with her brother sleeping upstairs—a fact that put the verifying stamp on her insanity, though the runaway beat of her heart in her chest told her that on its own.

Was his pulse pounding, too? Was he aching?

She used the tip of her tongue to push him away, her nipples begging for his mouth, her pussy for his hand. He knew what she was thinking. The look in his eyes said so, but instead of giving her what she wanted, he ate another piece of fruit, teasing her, making her wait.

She didn't want to wait, and she couldn't let him think he was running the show. They had to do this as equals, or they couldn't do it. She couldn't do it. And so she looked away, intending to return the fruit and whipped cream to the fridge, then return herself to her bed.

But he blocked her before she'd taken a second step. She lingered one long beat, devouring his heat and his meaning before meeting his gaze. His sizzled, caught on hers, his chest laboring as it rose and fell, his heart and his lungs struggling.

And then he shook his head, laughed, and gave in to whatever fight he'd been waging. He came closer, came lower, taking his time now that he'd made his decision, his nose against hers, his mouth hovering, *hovering*, and years beyond when she'd been ready, finally claiming hers.

He tasted like fresh fruit, cold and sweet, and then he was hot, his strawberry tongue tangling with the cream still on hers. He kissed like the devil he was, holding nothing back, burning her up. Making her want everything and more and all of it now, without a single thought for the consequences.

She didn't move. She couldn't move. She let him do all the

moving, taking the bowl from her hands and stepping into her, his belt buckle, his hips, his thighs. Oh, *God*, his thighs. Bold and full, and so, *so* powerful as he took charge of hers.

He was hard and strong and solid, like a tree, a brick wall, and he was heavy against her, making her feel small and precious and in more danger than she knew what to do with. Her chest shuddered with an unbearable ache, and her breasts tingled, as did her thighs, her belly, the core of her sex. His rose between them, full and thick and unapologetic, and moisture gathered at her entrance and wept from her folds.

He lifted her to sit on the counter, slid his hands down to her thighs, then draped her legs over his forearms as he leaned his weight into his palms on the tiled surface. He bent, his lips brushing the strip of skin above the elastic of her panties, the strip of skin bared by the hem of her cami that had risen up her rib cage to her breasts.

She let her head fall back on her shoulders. It hit the door of the cabinets behind her and she left it there, closed her eyes, covered Casper's hands with her own and gripped him tight with trembling fingers. This was the stuff of her dreams, and she wasn't even a dreamer, but oh, *God*, this couldn't be real because real had never been anything like this.

This was magic, his mouth, his breath heating her, his lips kissing and nipping, his teeth biting just hard enough to make her wince and yelp. And then he bit lower, nudging beneath the fabric of her panties to her clit and the swollen lips of her sex.

"Mmm, yummy," he said before he slid his tongue to separate her folds, licking and stroking until he reached her pussy's entrance, pushing into her, then pulling out and letting her panties snap back into place.

Then he kissed her. He stood straight, leaned in, and covered her mouth with his, showing her what she tasted like—the saltiness, the strange hint of grapefruit and musky olives, the scent of marine air. But all of that disappeared then, because this was Casper and he was kissing her, his tongue sliding against hers, his lips pressing to hers, his teeth glancing off hers with an audible click.

She wanted to taste him, to know him and learn him, but she couldn't think or focus. She tried so hard, but she found no purchase and could do nothing but let go and give in when he picked her up, when he turned her, when he walked them to the table where she'd shared dinner with Boone.

She couldn't think about that now. Wouldn't think about that now. Not when she was sitting where Boone's plate had been, leaning back on her elbows, her heels tucked to her hips. Not with Casper's hands moving to his belt buckle and zipper. Not with his jeans coming down, his briefs following, his cock jutting proudly, the tip ripe and red and wet.

"Lift up," he said, and she did, and he tugged off her panties before he stepped between her legs.

"What?" she asked when he stopped, a frown marring the hunger in his eyes.

"I don't have a condom, but I test clean. If we need to put this off—"

She shook her head. "I'm clean. I won't get pregnant. And if we put this off, we may never be here again."

He grunted, planting one hand at her hip, wrapping the other around his shaft and guiding himself into place. "Why's that?"

"Because once we're done, I swear I'm going to find my lost mind."

His laugh cut through her, a scythe of wicked humor and grit. "Who says we're ever going to be done?"

Then he pushed into her, and she closed her eyes, gasped because it had been so long, and it had never *ever* been like this.

He stretched her and hit bottom, and still he wasn't done filling her with the part of him she'd wanted for so long to know. She eased into having him, relaxing, adjusting, a smile tugging at her lips.

"What's the smile for?" he asked, his voice cracking just enough and in a way that let her know he was more worried than he was teasing.

She never thought of doing anything but setting him at ease, and let her smile reach her eyes as she opened them. "I like you."

"Good to know." He pulled out, pushed in. They both gasped, and Casper said, "You know we need to get this one over with."

Nodding, she bit down on her lower lip. The sooner they were out of the kitchen, the better, though she was well aware that wasn't what he meant. They'd danced around this first time too long for it to be anything but a prelude.

"You ready?"

She nodded again. "Could you try not to break the table?"

"Oh, baby. The table's not what I'm worried about breaking."

"Hurry. Just hurry. I can't wait anymore."

"Music to my ears," he said, leaning over her as she wrapped her legs around him and hooked her heels in the small of his back.

Then they fucked. There was no other word for the act between them. They did not make love, even though Faith's heart swelled and ached from the emotional surge. They rutted like animals, coming together in the most primitive of matings Faith had ever known.

And she loved it. She *loved* it. Every pounding slide of Casper's cock threatened to take her apart. She felt him in her pussy and she felt him in her head. Her toes tingled and her breasts beneath her camisole ached to feel his teeth and his hands.

But it wasn't enough. None of it. She wanted, needed more.

To see all of him naked. To know more than just his fingers and tongue and cock. To look down and see where their bodies joined, her pink flesh stretched to fit his that was similarly colored, and soft in as many ways as it was rigid.

And his abs. His ass. His thighs. She wanted to touch all of him, explore his muscles and his skin and the spots where he found the most pleasure. She wanted him to learn her. She wanted things that wouldn't fit on an old kitchen table in a ranch house where her brother was sleeping upstairs.

He was right. They had to get this one over with. And so she balanced precariously on one elbow, and hooked her other around his neck, bringing his head down to hers, his lips to hers, his tongue. He groaned into her mouth as he pushed deeper into her body, his weight pinning her, his movements rocking the table on old wooden legs Faith could only pray were built to last.

With each stroke of his cock over her clit, her nipples hardened, and her blood rushed hot beneath the surface of her skin. The hair on her arms stood on end. The hair at her nape snapped, electricity popping in the air around them.

Gasping, Casper pulled away, needing to breathe as he stared into her eyes, his gaze fiery and focused and full of lust and insanity. She'd thought nothing could be as crazy as her need for him. What she must look like, half naked and full of Casper Jayne without so much as a locked door to save her.

And she didn't even care. If that wasn't the height of madness she didn't know what was. She was soaring, so close to coming undone, and the things she read in Casper's eyes pushed her to the brink. He knew it. He saw it. And he shoved hard against her, grinding and taking her over the edge.

She cried out, squeezing her eyes shut and gripping his cock, milking him, coming all over him, holding onto the table's edges until she thought her fingers might break. Her release coursed through her and she shook and shivered and knew nothing but the thrill of surrender.

Above her, Casper grunted, rutting and grinding, shoving himself so hard against her, the table jumped. Her eyes popped open, and she watched his face, the deep grooves digging in around his closed eyes, the veins in his neck popped in relief. His mouth tight and grim as he strained, reached. His pulse ticking in his temple, a pounding drumbeat synced to his thrusts.

He slammed into her once more, then stopped, his upper body rising like a cobra from the place where his body was rooted to hers, and he came, juddering, quaking, his hands moving to her shoulders to hold her and anchor himself deep as he spilled his seed.

He finished quickly but with a force that alarmed her as she watched his orgasm play out in waves on his face, intense and vivid, muscles working around his eyes and his mouth, his nostrils flaring. Her heart pattered, her spine tingled, her sex ached and burned wanting him gone, wanting him always.

Finally, he looked at her, his eyes slowly opening, a smile sliding across his mouth and twinkling in his gaze. "Look at you. Faith Mitchell. All messed up."

"Get off me," she said, her words clawing the scant space between them.

But Casper had other ideas, settling his palms at her sides. "You are one tasty woman."

"Tasty? What does that even mean?" She moved her heels to his hipbones and pushed. "Get off."

"I could do that. Or I could just pick you up like this and carry you up the stairs."

"Are you out of your mind?" Then, since he wasn't moving, she did, scuttling like a crab across the table, missing the feel of his cock inside her the moment he was gone. She rolled from the tabletop to her feet, found her panties across the room, felt Casper's semen tickling the tops of her thighs. Reaching for a paper towel, she glanced at him and said, "Don't just stand there."

Because his standing there was bothering her. His jeans and briefs were bunched around his knees, her juices and his glistening on his cock that was still half hard. It hung between his thighs, thick and tempting as it bobbed above his balls. His hands were at his hips, his white T-shirt bunched up to reveal well-defined abs bisected by a trail of dark hair.

He nodded toward the towel she held in her hand. "Bring me one of those. Wet. Warm water, not cold."

What was she now, his concubine? But she did as he asked because it gave her a reason to look away and time to find some semblance of sanity. And she thought she had. Her breathing had calmed. Her heart had stopped trying to beat its way out of her chest.

When she reached him, however, she realized she wasn't herself at all. He didn't move more than an eyebrow, then told her, "Clean me up."

She waited—one heartbeat, a second, a third—weighing her pleasure against his, her acquiescence against his demand, then wrapped the damp towel around the tip of his cock to swipe away his cum. He shifted in her hand, lifting, hardening, going stiff and full as she held him, as she cleaned him, stroked him, her own hold tighter, feeling him throb.

He grinned, a slow, lazy move that grooved his dimples deep into his cheeks and brought a twinkle to his eyes. That had her heart pounding again, her blood rushing to pool low in her center the way his had done. She stilled her hand. He was clean enough for leaving. And that's what they both had to do. Now.

Or so she'd decided. Casper had other plans, hitching up his pants with one hand while he cupped the other at the base of her skull and brought her head to his, their cheeks together, his mouth lingering at the edge of hers. "Thank you."

"For what?" she whispered, the wash of her breath damp between them.

"The towel. The table. The countertop."

She pulled back far enough to meet his gaze. "You're thanking me for the kitchen?"

"I'm thanking you for making sure I'll smile every time I walk into this room from now on."

SEVEN

"SHH," FAITH SHUSHED from where she lay naked beneath him.

Casper's only response was to smile against her skin because he wasn't the one making the noise. He swirled his tongue in and around her navel, his hands against her inner thighs spreading her open. She wiggled and squirmed and her hands at her sides clenched his sheets in need of changing.

She groaned as he nipped at the cute pooch of her tummy, making his way lower and breathing deeply of her scent that was salty and warm. Whatever door she'd opened in the kitchen, he didn't want her to change her mind and lock it down tight. He'd waited half his life to get her here. He did not want her up and running.

"We can't do this," she was saying. "Not here. Risking it downstairs was bad enough, but now Boone's right down the hall."

He bit the soft flesh of her knee. "His door's shut. My door's shut. And locked. He sleeps like a dead man. So as long as you don't start praising the Lord when I slide my tongue inside you—"

"Shh," she shushed again, moaning as he slid his tongue inside her. "Don't say things like that."

He stopped the fun he was having and looked up at her from between her legs. "Faith Mitchell. Are you embarrassed?"

"No, I'm not embarrassed," she said, though he swore he heard that very thing in her voice, saw it in the denying slant of her brows.

He came at the problem from a different angle. "You're not much for sex talk then?"

She pushed onto her elbows and gave him a deserved glare. "Have I not been shushing you? I don't want Boone to wake up and find us."

Casper closed his eyes, dropped his head. They were going to have to deal with this now or their affair would be over before he ever had the chance to properly start it.

And boy did he want to start it. In all sorts of improper ways. To show her exactly what they could do together, be together—and to do so before she decided they'd made an epic mistake hooking up.

And that would happen sooner than Casper would like. Faith was too uppity, too straight and narrow for it not to. But since he knew to be forewarned and forearmed and all that . . .

He crawled up her body, braced his elbows on her pillow, and brushed her hair from her eyes. "And what if he does wake up and find us? What do you think he's going to do?"

"Besides beat the living shit out of you?" she asked, wiggling beneath him to settle his hips to hers.

His cock jumped when she moved, and he grinned when she sucked back a sharp breath. "Really? Is that what you think? That I can't handle myself with Boone?"

"I didn't say that—"

"Then you must be afraid that you can't handle yourself—"

"I can handle myself just fine, thank you."

Yeah. She could. "Then what's the big deal. You're, what? Thirty? Thirty-one?"

She nodded, but didn't pick door number one or two.

Though he was pretty sure he knew, he'd get the exact number later just because it bugged her so. "Okay. That makes you all grown up."

"I know that."

"Then why are you letting Boone kill the mood?"

"He's my brother. I don't want . . ."

And here it comes. Casper rolled away to his back, less pissed off than he was surprised it had taken them this long to get into class warfare. "You don't want to disappoint him by sleeping around beneath you."

Faith was still for a long moment, then she barked out a laugh loud enough for the dogs in the barn to hear. Raising up on one elbow, she stared down at him with the fire of a brand headed for his ass. "Sleeping around beneath me? Is that what I'm doing here? Sleeping around?"

He shrugged one shoulder. "I didn't mean it like that."

"Well, what exactly *did* you mean, Mr. Jayne, because I want to be sure before I say anything else."

Feisty little filly, wasn't she? He propped his head on one forearm, tweaked her nipple with his other hand. "You're sleeping with me. Having sex with me."

She batted him away. "I know that."

"I'm not done," he said, and tweaked again.

This time she let him, pressing her lips tight and waiting him out.

He let her go because it seemed the thing to do with this conversation looming, and tucked his other arm beneath his head. "You're a Mitchell. I'm a Jayne. There's something about never the twain meeting here."

"Why's that?" she asked, the tone of the question curious rather than patronizing, as if she hadn't heard all the stories told about the Jaynes through the years. "Just because I had a more comfortable life growing up than you did?"

"A more comfortable life?" That made him want to laugh. Or hit something with a chair. "Is that what you call it?"

"Sure. Why not? My parents both had"—she stopped, corrected herself—"both *have* good jobs working for the school district. Boone and I were well provided for. We didn't have to go without."

"Like I did."

"It wasn't a big secret, Casper," she said, her voice softer, her coffee-dark hair falling forward over her shoulder as she shook her head. "Everyone knew your father wasn't around for long after y'all moved here. And that your moth—"

"That my mother was a whore who put food on our table by selling sex at Bokeem's Truck Stop."

And fuck his big, fat mouth.

He sure as hell hadn't meant to say that, but without giving him a chance to haul them back, the words had fallen into a silence so complete he could hear his hair growing. But he had to give it to Faith. She held his gaze, no sympathy in hers, no *poor baby* tears or even words designed to soothe away the pain of his past.

Instead, she stayed true and no-nonsense. "I didn't know that, about your mother."

Really? She'd been that sheltered? That naive? "Everybody knew that about my mother, Faith."

"I didn't." She shifted beside him, reaching for the sheet and pulling it to her chest. "I knew she worked as a waitress at the truck stop, but that's all."

"Well, now you know the rest."

Thing was, he didn't really care that she knew. He was who he was. He'd gone through a lot to get here. What he didn't want was sorrow, or pity, or an emotional attachment that required he explain more than he wanted to, or share parts of himself he didn't let go of for anyone.

She wasn't like the women he'd had in the past, women like Angie Whitman who'd been a good time but no more a part of his life than he'd been of hers.

Faith, on the other hand, had been with him since his family had moved to Crow Hill. She hadn't been struck starry-eyed by any of his eight-second rides. She'd known him as a hell-raiser, as her brother's friend. As the extra kid at the supper table.

"Can I ask you something?"

"Sure," he said, turning to look at her.

She buried her nose in the sheet she held, grimaced. "How long have these sheets been on your bed?"

He snorted, and then said instead, "I'm a big boy, Faith. I'm not afraid of Boone."

"I'm not afraid of him either."

"Then what's the problem here?"

"I don't know. His being in the house . . . things changing between the two of you should he find out I'm here. I don't want the ranch partnership to go rocky."

"It won't."

"You say that like you're sure."

"We've been through a lot. And we're all still here."

"I suppose."

Her shrug had him wondering if she'd thought things through. "But if change worries you, you gotta know things would be different between you two as well."

"I know. We've had issues before."

Huh. "Anything I need to worry about?"

She shook her head, ran the tip of one finger down the center of his chest. "Just that I'm not a big fan of taking risks."

And risks had been Casper's whole life. "Sounds like I need to show you there's nothing to it."

He brought his mouth hard to hers, forcing his tongue inside to dance with hers, to slide along hers, stroking hers before coaxing hers into his mouth. The intimacy had his cock thickening along her bare thigh. And then he pulled away, moving his mouth to her jaw, her ear, breathing deeply of her scent that brought to mind the sort of soft summer he'd rarely seen.

He knew harsh conditions. His life had been nothing but. That made being here with Faith seem like something that should belong to someone else—even as he told himself he deserved every bit of what the woman beside him was ready to give up. Faith Mitchell. His for the night. No matter what she thought of him.

Tonight was about the slope of her neck to her shoulder, and the way her whole body shuddered when he kissed his way from her ear to her collarbone, then made his way lower to the rise of her tits that were lifting and falling with her efforts to breathe.

He tugged one nipple into his mouth. She gasped, and he bit down. She gasped again, and he leaned to the side, sliding the heel of his palm to the bone above her clit and pushing against it. This time her gasp became a groan, and her fight became less about breathing than about what he sensed was going on in her head.

"What do you want, Faith? From me. What do you want?"

"What you're doing. More of it. All of it. Everything."

He liked having a door thrown wide, but needed her to be aware of what she was saying. "Are you sure? Because I've had a lot of years to think about what I want to do to you. I don't know if you're ready to go everywhere I am."

She opened her eyes, met his gaze, wet her lips. "You think I'm sheltered, don't you? Because of the way I grew up. Because I haven't gone through the things you have. You think I have no experience at . . . this."

"This? You mean fucking?" Because if she couldn't even say it . . .

"Yes. Fucking. Is that better?"

"I tell you what would be better." He scooted up her body, hooked a leg around hers, and rolled to his back, taking her with him, ending up with her straddling his hips as planned. "This is better."

"Why?" was her only response. She just sat there, balancing, as if afraid to move more than the muscles it took to do that.

"Why?" he echoed, lifting his knees, a chair at her back, and moving his hands to her thighs where they created a vee on either side of his thick, jutting cock. "Well, from here I can see all the best parts of you at the same time."

Her shoulders had been hunched forward as if to hide her bare breasts, but the motion only served to plump them together, and when she hid her chest behind crossed arms, he tucked his beneath his head and sighed.

"This isn't going to be any good if you go into hiding."

She stared at him a long, hot moment, then flung her arms to the side before reaching for her hair and twisting it up against the back of her head. "Is this better? Is this what you want?"

"I want you to have fun. I don't want you to be nervous." He was surprised after the kitchen she would be.

"I'm not nervous. Not about the sex."

"About what then?"

"Everything that goes with it."

Did she mean all the emotional baggage he'd managed to keep out of his sexual encounters? "Like?"

"What happens tomorrow?"

"More sex?"

She hesitated, chewed at the corner of her lip, then, "And nothing else?"

Fuck. "Do you want there to be something else?"

"No, but I don't want things to get awkward."

He was beginning to regret the question. "Awkward how?"

She took a deep breath and closed her eyes, opening them once she'd found what looked like courage. "I don't want you thinking I'll plead your case at the bank because of this."

The thought hadn't crossed his mind. The fact it had crossed hers had him feeling mean. "Then this was a big, fat waste of time, wasn't it?"

Her eyes went wide like a newborn calf's. "Are you kidding me?"

Jesus H. Christ. "Give me some credit here, Faith. I haven't thought about money once since you climbed up there and started struttin' your stuff. But now that you mention it . . ."

She slapped at his hand as he reached for her tit. "Stop it."

"Stop touching you?"

"No. Stop making light of something that's serious."

"I'm always serious about sex."

"I'm not talking about sex." She gathered her thoughts,

blowing out a breath once she had. "I just don't want things to get weird."

"Weird how?" he asked as she covered his hands with hers.

"I want to be able to sit down to supper with you and Boone, and Dax and Arwen, even Darcy and Josh, and not have you look at me or say something that gives us away."

He thought about that. Decided he could live with it. "So you want to keep us a secret?"

She nodded, the ends of her layered hair brushing her chin and shoulders.

"And you're not going to blab to your girlfriends?"

Her face colored at that.

"Uh-huh. See. The secret's already out."

"I told Arwen and Everly that I wanted to sleep with you, yes," she said, her gaze falling from his eyes to his chest, his abs, the trail of hair that led to his treasure currently winking at her. "But they won't know that we have."

He laughed because she couldn't be serious. "Until they get a good look at you all drunk on Casper Jayne, you mean."

"Really?" she asked, cocking her head. "That's what we're doing now? You're that full of yourself?"

"Being full of me feels pretty good, wouldn't you say?"

She didn't say anything after that, just rose to her knees, aligned their bodies, and lowered herself onto his cock. Then she moved her hands to his thighs and leaned into them as she began to ride. She closed her eyes, lifted her chin. Her hair fell down her back, brushing his hands at her waist, teasing, tickling, the ends of the strands like bristles passing over his skin.

He shuddered at the contact, bucked up into her, shuddered again when she laughed, a sound he would never have thought to hear from Faith Mitchell. It was guttural and wicked, and said all sorts of things about the very naughty girl who wore tight suits and no-nonsense heels and kept a hand wrapped around his purse strings as if strangling his balls.

He was strangling now, watching her tits bounce, her nipples puckered and peached. Watching her teeth holding her lower lip one second, the tip of her tongue the next. Watching her pussy stretch around his cock, her clit bold and aroused where she ground it to the base of his shaft. He couldn't look away. She was the hottest thing he'd ever had his cock in. And he was in so much trouble because of it.

His balls and his bank account were one thing, but he'd broken the no-sisters rule. And he'd lied to Faith when he'd told her he wasn't worried about how things would shake out with Boone. But he couldn't think about that now. Right now was all about his cock and her cunt and the look on her face that had him tightening his abs and thrusting.

She took him and squeezed him, pulling him with her as she lifted her hips, then letting him go until she held nothing inside her but his very full tip. He was ripe to bursting, and every move she made worsened the urge he was fighting not to let go. He wanted to flip her to her back and slam into her, pounding her until neither one of them could breathe.

He wanted rough and he wanted wild and he wanted to knock a hole in the wall with the headboard. He wanted to tie her to it, climb up her body, and shove his cock in her mouth. But this was Faith and he had to think of her. If he ever wanted to have her again, and goddamn but he wanted her often, he had to make this worth coming back for, because Faith did not sleep around.

He moved one hand to her hip, his other to her pussy, his thumb pressing down on her clit, rolling over it side to side. She gasped, her fingers tightening on his thighs, and he did it again, then flicked the nub of nerves softly, a butterfly touch that had her muscles flexing, her breath hitching, her skin growing slick with the sweat of her lust.

"Casper," she whispered, her voice coarse and caught in her throat.

Hearing her force out his name, he nearly lost it. "C'mon, baby. Come for me."

"Shh. Quiet. You've got to be quiet." Her eyes were still closed, her chest rising and falling.

He grinned to himself because she was the one doing all the talking again. "As a mouse, baby. Just come. All over me. I wanna feel you milk me dry."

"I can't wait," she said, riding harder, faster. "I can't wait. I can't wait. *I can't wait.*"

She came before he could tell her to be quiet, that her brother might be a heavy sleeper, but she was nearing the waking-the-dead decibel level and even Boone might not sleep through that. And then he quit thinking about anyone but Faith because *Jesus H. Christ,* she was tight, and she was tugging him, and she fell forward, her hands on his shoulders holding her weight.

She rode him like a wild mustang, back and forth with her hips, up and down, grinding the base of his cock and dragging her tits across his chest. He wanted them in his mouth, but settled for his hands, pinching her nipples until she yelped, then braced her forearm on his collarbone to return the favor.

And she didn't stop with tweaking him, but breathed against his ear and nipped his earlobe, licking him, sucking his skin, bruising him, marking him. That was what set him off, the thought of wearing Faith's brand. He hooked a leg over hers and rolled the both of them to the other side of the bed, reaching for her knees and sliding his arms beneath them.

He held her gaze as he slammed his body into hers, his cock sliding deep and hitting bottom, her cunt slick and inviting, her eyes huge and damp. He wanted to ask why she looked so terribly sad, but he was too far gone, and it was all he could do to keep his mouth shut while his balls bucked up and exploded, his cum pulsing in jackhammer spurts he swore were going to tear him apart.

He thought he'd never finish, his muscles bunching until they were spent, and he collapsed on top of her, crushing her, knowing he needed to move, knowing he didn't have the strength. Faith didn't complain. She kept her ankles crossed in the small of his back, her arms around his neck, her fingers massaging circles at the base of his skull.

Later, when his blood returned to his brain, he was going to have to figure this out, what was going on here, what they'd just done. Why he didn't want to jump from the bed and find his boots and light the hell outta here. Why Faith smelling so sweet in his pigsty of a room had him wishing he'd given her something better than this. Hell, a bed of clean straw in the barn would've been better than this.

Finally, she lowered her legs and pushed him off. He fell to the mattress, his cock slipping from her pussy, then wrapped himself around her. He wanted to go again, but he wasn't going anywhere until he recovered. If his exhausted body let him . . .

He was just drifting off, Faith's weight at his side comforting and right, when she shifted, rolling away to sit up. Figuring she needed to pee, he drowsily asked, "You okay?"

"I'm fine."

"You weren't crying, were you? Earlier?"

"No, Casper. I wasn't crying."

"Good. Then come back here."

She shook her head, her hair brushing across her back. "I've got to go."

He wasn't so drowsy now. "No. You're spending the night."

"I can't. If Boone heard any . . . of this, I can't be here in the morning. He can't know I was the woman you had in your room. If he asks, I'll just tell him I couldn't sleep for the noise." She was on her feet, her ear at the door.

"What're you doing?"

She turned to him, brought her finger to her lips, then started pulling on her panties and top. "I need to get back to my room and get my clothes before he gets up for the bathroom or a drink or something."

He didn't want her to go. He could stand up to Boone. They could get this particular truth out in the open, let the chips fall. Life might get messy, but it would go on. That was about him, however, and he had to think of Faith. First, above all else, he had to think of Faith.

"Okay," he said, searching for his shorts. "You get to your room. I'll head to the john. If he hears anything, he'll hear me."

She gave a nod, pulling her hair from the strap of her top, then looked down to where his cock was jutting again. "Are you going to go like that?"

He waved his shorts. "I'll dress when I'm done."

"Men are disgusting."

"It's just a cock, darlin'. Nothing your brother hasn't seen before."

"Disgusting. Like I said." Then she hopped up on her toes to brush her lips over his before scooting down the hallway.

He headed in the other direction, glad for her sake to hear the epic snoring coming from Boone's room. He made enough noise himself in the bathroom to mask the sound of her taking the stairs to the kitchen, and he left the water running, the old pipes clanking as if ready to fall from the walls, until the small frosted window showed her headlights coming on once she'd made it from the ranch yard to the road.

Then he decided since he was already naked and the steam was heating up the place, he might as well shower to save the time in the morning. And he did, lathering away the stink of the day and all traces of Faith's smell, stripping the sheets from the bed once back in his room.

Not up to hunting down clean ones—did they even have clean ones?—he tossed the comforter on top of the seen-better-days mattress, collapsed on one half and covered up with the rest. But it was a long time before he fell asleep, and he did so missing Faith and feeling empty in ways he hadn't known he could feel.

And hurting in places he couldn't remember any two-thousand-pound bull ever making him ache.

EIGHT

THE SUN FALLING fast into the horizon behind him, Casper held his breath for a lot of the ninety-mile-per-hour drive from Luling back to Crow Hill. The plan had been to make a quick trip to town at first light, check in with Clay, and see where things stood with the water, the electric and gas, and the appliances.

Once he knew the state of things, he'd make a list of chores for the boy, before heading back for his own long day digging postholes for the new holding pen. That had to be done before he and the boys started a couple of days from now preconditioning steers.

Then, after knocking off this evening, it would be back to town to feed the kid and pick up whatever else Clay needed for cleaning. That done, he'd make a run out to the Summerlin ranch and put in an hour or two with the horses.

But today's schedule had been blown all to hell when he'd

arrived home last night, found Faith near to naked, and lost most of his mind.

God*damn*, what a night.

He hadn't been laid like that in months. Hell, he didn't think he'd been laid like that in his lifetime. For one thing, he'd been sober. But the biggest difference was that he'd been in bed with Faith. Faith with the gorgeous high tits and the willing mouth and that way she had of sounding like he couldn't do anything wrong. That every which way he moved was exactly what she wanted.

He'd moved a lot because of that, sweated a lot because of *that,* and passed out after like a damn dog. He'd slept straight through sunrise, only waking when Boone slammed a fist against his door and told him to put on his pants. He'd barely had time for coffee, much less breakfast, before the three of them had made for the holding pen.

He hadn't thought about Clay until lunchtime, when he'd been sitting on a stack of fence posts downing a ham sandwich, and Bing and Bob had raced by, making him wonder how Kevin would fit in. Yeah. He was the guy Clay had come looking for because he didn't have anyone else.

After that, he'd slammed through the rest of the day, taking off even though it had been his night to cook supper. Boone wouldn't be happy, but Boone was a big boy and could fend for himself. It was Clay Casper needed to get to.

Instead of raising more eyebrows shopping in town, he'd made a quick run to Luling for a microwave and more groceries, crossing his fingers the power company had come through. He'd thought about a mini-fridge in case the one in the house was dead, but decided not to be stupid. He'd wait until he knew before spending that money. It would make more sense to pony up for a full-size secondhand one anyway.

All that aside, he was still on the hook for abandoning the

kid. For all he knew, the boy had split, deciding his word wasn't worth shit. Hard to argue that one.

As he pulled to a stop in front of the house, he glanced toward the front windows, glad to see Clay was sticking to his end of their bargain and staying out of sight. It was a bargain Casper knew would get both of them in trouble, but it was the only way he could think of to keep the boy in Crow Hill.

Why he felt the need to do so was yet another question he couldn't answer, filed just beneath the ones about Faith coming to his bed. All he knew was that Clay had crossed two states to get to him. That was a responsibility he wasn't going to shirk more than he already had.

He left his purchases in the truck bed and walked to the back of the house, looking for footprints that would tell him if anyone had been inside the gate. Stupid, when he couldn't see his own, the damn yard being so dry. But there was a big pile of dog shit—oh fucking joy—a fresh one, telling him his squatters were still here, and at least one of them squatting.

He tested the faucet next to the back porch, glad to see the water running. Now to check the electricity, the gas, and the appliances. He took the steps two at a time, frowning at the vibration riding up his arm when he pulled open the door. Crap. If the pipes were bad . . .

He stepped into the kitchen just in time to raise his hands and deflect the full garbage bag Clay pitched at his head.

"Thought you were coming back this morning."

That had been the plan. And then he'd forgotten Clay even existed. "Yeah, sorry. I got hung up."

"Whatever," the boy said, turning to leave the room.

Casper tossed the bag into the mudroom, realizing the trash dump was gone and replaced by dozens of similar bags stuffed to bursting.

Then he realized the rattle he'd thought was the water pipes banging in the wall was the washing machine running instead. He walked back into the utility room, checked the hoses for dry rot and leaks, but found none. Then he looked up to catch Clay staring.

"Just checking things," he said, as if owing the boy an explanation, which he didn't.

"I checked things," the boy said, as if anyone who didn't know to do so was dumb.

Crabby little thing, wasn't he? "Where'd you get soap to wash your clothes?"

Clay gave a nod toward the garbage bags. "Found some detergent boxes in the trash. Scraped enough dried soap from the bottoms to do a load."

Clever kid. And clean kid. His hair was about ten shades lighter without all the grease weighing it down. "Looks like you had a shower, too. Scraped together some soap slivers, did you?"

"There was a bar in the bathroom upstairs. And I took a cold shower. I didn't want to light the hot water heater and blow shit up."

Smart kid, too, though since he'd known to check the washer's hookups for leaks, Casper shouldn't have been surprised. "Thanks. I'll put detergent on my list. I did buy a microwave."

"Cool. The fridge finally came on, but I didn't mess with the stove." He shrugged, stuffed his fists in his baggy cargo pants. "That blowing-shit-up thing."

"Guess you were the man of the house at home, huh?"

"Because I know how to work appliances?

"No one ever taught me."

"No one ever taught me either."

And yet they'd both had reasons to learn. Casper didn't want to think Clay's home life had been similar to his; Angie had seemed like a real good mom. But the more he was finding out about the boy, the more his curiosity was getting the better of him—and the more he was beginning to doubt that he'd ever had a clear picture of who she was.

Hardly surprising. He didn't think he'd ever been with her sober.

He pushed aside the past, rubbed at his jaw. "I'm still thinking it would be better for you to be at the ranch."

"I thought you didn't want anyone knowing I was here."

"I don't, but it doesn't seem right, you being here by yourself."

"Yeah. I get it." He kicked his sole at the floor, marking it. "Right is putting me in a foster home where I have to share a ten-square-foot bedroom and one chest of drawers with three other guys."

Anger itched its way up Casper's spine. "Thought things in those places were monitored. That there were rules. Regulations. To keep stuff like that from going down."

Clay only shrugged. "The girls' bedroom was a converted den. They used the built-in bookshelves for their clothes. But it was pretty big. They had space to fold up all the laundry. Towels and sheets and rags. Go through papers and magazines for coupons. Clean up old junk for garage sales."

Casper felt his blood pressure rising. "This was a group home? Or a sweatshop?"

"It was a foster family."

"With seven kids."

"It was clean. They fed us. Corn Flakes and ramen and hot dogs. I figure most of the state's money went to the fifty-inch flat screen, stuff like that."

And now he wanted to get his gun. "But they didn't hurt you."

"If you mean physically, no," Clay said, and left it at that.

Casper thought about the size of this house. He'd lived a lot of places before coming to Crow Hill. Apartments. Trailers. For a while in a car. But when he'd been Clay's age, this was the house he'd called home.

Thousands of square feet left empty while he'd holed up in a bedroom smaller than the one Clay had shared with three other boys.

He'd just shared his with spiders. "I'm going to talk to my partners, see if they mind me moving you out to the ranch."

"I'll be fine here, if it's going to be a problem."

"It won't be. And I'd feel a lot better having you out there. We're working on a new pen tomorrow, so I'll feel them out then. In the meantime . . ." He looked around the kitchen, walked across the big room to the door leading into the hallway, and flipped the switch there on the wall.

The bulbs in the fixtures along the corridor's ceiling burst to life. Three stayed lit, two fizzled and popped. The light was enough for now. "Grab a couple of trash bags. I'll get you started on the first floor. Should keep you busy till I can get back here tomorrow."

And then he took a deep breath, preparing to face six years he'd thought he'd put away forever. The closets where his old man had locked him, the marks cut into doorframes when he'd jumped out of the way of belts and fists.

The one deep gouge in the plaster left by a knife that had nicked him before cutting into the wall. He raised his hand and rubbed at his shoulder, wondering if the dried blood in that room was still visible, or if bugs had eaten it away.

If the papers he'd scribbled full of hate and silent screams were still hidden between the studs at the head of the bed where he'd slept.

"You okay?" Clay asked from behind him, the trash bags

rustling in his hands, Kevin shaking his head and flapping his ears in impatience.

Casper was still standing in the doorway, staring the hallway's length, wondering how many nests of wolf spiders lurked in the woodwork.

"Yeah. Let's go," he said, and swallowed as he tugged his hat brim to his eyes.

NINE

FOR TWO DAYS now, Faith had not been able to stop thinking about the things Casper had told her in bed. Not about loving her body, and getting off to having her, and what the sight of her naked on top of him did to his cock and his balls. She'd had to push that part of the night to the back of her mind so she could try to make sense of the rest.

The frightening, sobering rest.

His mother had sold sex at Bokeem's Truck Stop. She hadn't supported him with her waitressing income and tips after his father had left. And he'd known this the whole time he'd been at Crow Hill High, while she hadn't had a single clue.

How many others had known? Boone and Dax? The faculty? God, had his teachers known? His coaches? Her parents? Had Tess and Dave Dalton been aware of the life Casper had lived on Mulberry Street? For all intents and purposes, he'd raised himself, a thought that had her chest growing tight around the sadness it contained.

She couldn't imagine growing up without her family in her business. Sure, she'd bitched about curfews, and weeknight suppers eaten together at a properly set table, and Sunday mornings at the First Baptist Church. And she'd acted out. Not as far out as Boone had, but still. She'd never felt alone or adrift. She'd had a foundation, a place to feel safe.

How had Casper lived otherwise, knowing what his mother did, having no father or other family on his side? No Christmas dinner or help with homework or cheering section on the sidelines of the football field. Had that excuse for a home life been at the root of his hell-raising ways?

She couldn't blame him, even while finding it impossible to believe she'd never heard any gossip floating through the hallways at school, or in the parking lot of the Dairy Barn after. Especially the way everyone in Crow Hill loved knowing the business of everyone else.

His revelation about his mother had Faith wondering the same thing Arwen had the other day at lunch—why *hadn't* he arranged to unload that house? There couldn't be anything there for him anymore—if there had ever been anything there for him at all. So why the obsession? Why not let it go? And why was she letting the things he'd told her get to her this way?

That one, out of all the questions swirling in her head, was easy to answer. Thinking about Casper's high school years kept her from dwelling on what they'd done. His body, her body, their hands and mouths and tangled limbs.

She'd had sex, not a lot, and not often for a while, but enough to know what she liked, and she had no problem reaching that place on her own. But sex with Casper . . .

He'd caught her off guard, unprepared. She had no idea sex could be like that in the real world, without actors playing the parts, or authors creating the words, without fantasies.

She hadn't thought herself naive. She and Arwen and Everly didn't pull punches when talking about sex, or getting what they wanted from a clueless man. But what Casper had shown her . . . what he'd done with her, to her . . .

How was she supposed to process something so far removed from her experience? She was out of her league in *such* a huge way. Even in college, with Jeremy, and Jon—

No. She wasn't going to go there. She cut off the thought, reaching for the distraction of the dust cloud coming toward her, and recognizing Casper's big black dualie as the one causing the stir.

Her thoughts of the past keeping her heart in her throat, she slowed, pulled from the center of the road to the side to let him pass. But he didn't pass, obviously recognizing her car, too, and braking a lot faster than she did. His wheels locked up and his truck slid dangerously close to her front door before he straightened to come alongside her.

They both waited for the air to clear before rolling down their windows. Casper was the first to speak. "If I'd known you were going to come back for more, I would've made sure to be here."

She stuck out her tongue. "I was dropping off some price lists for Boone. For the party."

"Boone doesn't have any more money than I do. Just buy the cheapest booze and be done with it."

"You are such a man."

"And you like me that way."

She did, but he didn't have to know it. Or to know how conflicted she was about this thing they'd started. It couldn't go anywhere. They were completely wrong for each other. She knew that. Surely he knew that, too. "If you say so."

He stared at her for a minute, his mouth finally quirking before he glanced down the road, his profile beneath the brim of his hat all hard lines and stern focus. Or maybe avoidance. Or maybe he was trying to think of a way to talk to her now that there was more than money between them, now that the tension had become knowing and tightened because of it.

"Why don't you come back to the house?" he finally asked, still looking straight ahead.

No. Not to the house. "I've just been there. I don't have a reason to go back."

"Right." He rubbed a hand over his jaw. "Don't want to make the brother all suspicious and shit."

She closed her eyes, opened them. "Casper—"

"It's okay. I got it. Top secret. Lips sealed."

Wait. Was he pouting? Had she hurt his feelings? "We could compromise."

At that, he looked over. "How so?"

"Rather than me going back to the ranch, or you coming all the way back to town, we could both go to Fever Tree for supper. The Rainsong Cafe has an amazing—"

"—chicken fried steak. Yeah. I know."

"Is that a yes?"

"Is that all we're going to do? Eat?"

"We're going to a restaurant. So, yes. We're going to eat."

He gave a nod as if thinking, then said, "Last I was through Fever Tree, I saw a sign for a bed-and-breakfast. We could get a room."

Lots of Fever Tree residents banked in Crow Hill. She couldn't take that chance. "Let's start with supper," she said, clenching her thighs as she thought about that bed-and-breakfast, about clean sheets on a big soft mattress. About the hair on Casper's bare thighs. "We'll see about dessert later."

He was shaking his head, muttering beneath his breath, before saying, "You go on. I'll get turned around here and be right behind you."

Nodding, she pulled onto the road, watching in her rearview as he maneuvered his truck in a tricky three-point turn to follow. He bore down on her a lot faster than she'd expected, until the only thing she could see when she glanced into any of her mirrors was his truck, the big headlights, the row of amber fog lamps on top, the grill that seemed to be grinning like a devil. Or a fool.

She shivered, her blood racing beneath the surface of her skin, raising the tiny hairs at her nape and bringing her nipples to points. She pictured his mouth, the smirk there before he lowered his head to catch her between his teeth, to use his tongue to tease her, torture her. Arouse her unbearably.

Longing pulled at her with a sharp visceral tug, coiling in her belly and sending tendrils deeper to stir her lust until she was damp and ready. She told herself she wasn't being stupid. Her eyes were wide open. But her nipples were hard, and her pussy was tingling, and all she could think of was his cock full and jutting and pushing into her mouth.

Still shivering, she parked, got out of her car, watched as he pulled in beside her, as he walked to the front of both vehicles and waited for her. They made their way to the door side by side, no hand holding, no arms around waists, no accidentally brushing against each other, no touching at all. Inside, Faith took the lead, requesting a quiet table for two from the hostess.

With Casper behind her, she followed the young woman who escorted them to a corner with a window looking onto the patio, where a tiered fountain bubbled and flowed. The sounds of bamboo and brass wind chimes filtered softly through the glass, and as they sat, Casper rolled his eyes.

He filled his chair and his side of the table, and she felt trapped by his size and his presence. The width of his chest and shoulders aside, there was something about the way he ignored the rest of the room, the way he waved off the menus and told the server what they wanted, the way he looked at her while doing it.

As if he saw through her. As if he saw everything.

"Well, you've got me here. Now what're you going to do with me?"

"Eat dinner," she said after clearing her hunger for him from her throat. "Talk."

"Like a date, or something?"

"Or like friends. Eating dinner. Talking."

"Is that what we are? Friends? Because my cock would beg to disagree," he said, just as their server set her iced tea and Casper's beer on the table.

Faith waited until the other woman had moved on before leaning toward him, her eyes narrowed. "Thank you. That was amazingly thoughtful."

He laughed. "I thought you brought me here because no one we know would see us."

"There's less of a likelihood, yes. That doesn't mean you have to be crass."

"Right. I keep forgetting that's what you think of me."

"Good lord, Casper. It's not like I pulled my opinion out of thin air. Listen to yourself." She lowered her voice. "Most non-crass people don't talk about their cocks in public, much less at the dinner table."

"In your house, maybe."

That put a stop to her reprimand. Not that he didn't deserve it; he was a grown man and knew better. But the last thing she wanted to be was a nag. "You've got to know your experience growing up was not the norm."

"Because my father beat me bloody with whatever he had on hand?" he asked, holding his knife's blade against the table. "Or because my mother was a whore?"

She swallowed, remembered the scar on his shoulder, wondered now if it wasn't from a bull like she'd thought. "I didn't know that about your father."

He cocked his head, considered her. "First my mother. Now my father. And I'd thought you knew everything, the way you were always staring at me."

She'd known enough to wonder what it would be like to be so reckless. To walk out of school in the middle of the day while teachers looked on. To drive like a bat out of hell. To pack a longneck for lunch.

She'd known enough to realize he was like no one else in her circle, and that if Boone hadn't friended him . . . "I didn't stare."

"Oh, you stared. And I imagine when your hands slipped into your panties at night, you were thinking about me."

Heat rose. "Again with the crass."

He sat back. "Sorry. I didn't get a lot of schooling. I barely got fed."

He hadn't meant to say it. She could tell by the way he closed up, his gaze going to his plate as their food was served, his mouth a grim line, his pulse a tic in the vein at his temple.

"Is that why the house is so important to you?" she asked

once they were alone. "A reminder of how far you've come? That you made it out?"

He snorted, scraped his fork through his mashed potatoes. "Did I?"

"You're here. That's something."

"Yeah, well. It's just a house."

"One you're willing to dig yourself even deeper into debt over. Unless you're hoping to flip it for a profit. Which might not be as impossible as you think," she said, holding back the surprise of what she'd learned. No need to let him know she'd researched the structure's history.

He sawed through a bite of his steak, scooped it through the gravy, shoved it into his mouth. "I don't know what I want to do with it."

"Except pour it full of money you don't have," she said, reaching for her iced tea.

"It doesn't matter, does it? I don't have the money, so the house will stand there until it doesn't."

"Have you thought about asking your mother why she dumped it on you?"

"Have I thought about my mother at all?" he asked, looking down at his food.

"Surely you have. Since the letter came about the house . . ."

He glanced up at that, one eyebrow arched. "Boone told you about the letter?"

"Do you know?" she asked, refusing to be distracted. "Why she dumped it on you?"

"Because she's a stupid whore," he said, and went back to eating.

She toyed with her squash casserole, then with her potatoes, finally taking a bite when she sensed him staring, though her appetite was long gone. "Seems strange to come out of nowhere like that. Giving it away instead of selling it for whatever she could get."

"You're talking about my mother, Faith. She doesn't deal with anything that inconveniences her."

"Like you?"

"Yep. Mama's Big Inconvenience. I should've had a T-shirt made."

Then, because she wanted to know, and because she'd never heard from anyone what happened, she asked, "Do you know where your father is?"

He shook his head. "I don't even know if he's alive. Hell, I don't even know if the man who was around when I was a kid *is* my father."

"When did he leave?"

"Not long after we got here. Two of 'em had a big row one night after he came home shit-faced. He threw a wad of papers at her and said, 'Here's the house, you bitch. Now get the fuck outta my head.' Never saw him again."

"So it was your father, or . . . whoever he was . . . who owned the house?"

"I don't know. Maybe. I guess so."

"Hmm."

"Faith?"

She looked up.

"Why are you so interested in my house?"

"Just wondering what you might know about it," she said with a shrug, taking a bite of steak.

"Seems to me you'd know more, being born here and all." He finished off his potatoes. "Who lived in it before we moved to Crow Hill?"

"I don't remember anyone ever living there, though I suppose someone could have."

Casper shrugged. "It was empty when we got here. It needed some work, but it was livable."

"But the work never got done."

"Nope. And pretty soon it wasn't worth living in."

"But you stayed."

A grin pulled up one corner of his mouth. "I stayed because Boone and Dax threatened to hunt me down, tie me up, and take an emasculator to my nuts if I left without a diploma."

Gross. "And here all this time I thought you were the troublemaker. Out of the three of y'all, I mean."

"I've been known to cause a bit."

"A bit? Is that what you call it?"

"Boone did chase me down with an ax a few weeks back."

She gasped. "What? Why in the world?"

His forearms against the edge of the table, he leaned toward her. "Because I said something about having a thing for your ass."

"Oh, my God," she croaked out, her eyes going wide. "You did not."

"I don't remember the particulars," he said, still grinning. "But close enough."

"Did he hurt you?" It was a ridiculous question. Boone wouldn't hurt a fly.

He held his arms out to the side. "Did you find any recent injuries?"

Heat spread from her chest to her neck, and it took every bit of her self-control to keep from lifting a hand to hide her reaction. Especially since her fingers had run across a lot of scars she'd wanted to ask him about. "It was dark—"

"It wasn't *that* dark. And the fridge light lit up the kitchen like the sun. And your busy little hands would've found anything there was to find."

"Busy little hands?"

He gave her a wink, then said, "I like 'em," which had her rolling her eyes. "What?" he asked, feigning insult. "I'm being serious here. I like your hands. And I do have a thing for your ass."

"Casper—"

"Hey," he said. "This was before the kitchen mambo. I'm not breathing a word. I'm afraid I'll never get in your panties again if he knows I was there in the first place."

Honestly. She was about to give up, but first . . . "Here's the thing. It was hard, really hard, on my folks when Boone left after high school."

"What about on you?" he asked, as if only her hurt mattered.

"Me, too. I missed him. A lot."

"You saw him, though. He came home. He told me about the family holidays. That they weren't to be missed."

"Seeing him two or three times a year is nothing to having him here all the time."

"Even if you rarely see him now?"

"I've seen him twice this week already." She knew what he was getting at. "But, yes, it's fine not seeing him. Having him here is what counts."

He sat back, head shaking, a bit of a sneer drawing at his mouth. "I don't get that. I'll never get that. But if it works for you . . ."

"It does," she said with a nod, placing her napkin beside her plate, saddened by the truth of what Casper thought family was. "You hung with him in high school. You know what it was like around our house."

"It was loud. That much I remember. All that yelling going on."

"Yelling? Are you kidding me?"

"What would you call it? Using your outside voice inside?"

She laughed. "Well, yes. But I get what you're saying. We put on a good front, but no Mitchell I know would ever claim to be reserved."

"Is that why you wear those tight-assed suits? Proving you're reserved and respectable?" he asked. Then he managed to drop his voice to add, "Because it's not much of a disguise."

"Oh, my God. You cannot have a conversation without it turning to sex, can you?"

"Sex is good. I like sex. I know sex."

But he didn't know families. Normal relationships. Ones built on trust and loyalty and emotions that weren't dependent on physical intimacy to work. She gave it to him straight. "If you and I being together hurts Boone in anyway, you and I can't be together. At all. Ever."

"That's kinda harsh."

"That's the reality. I don't think Boone's that uptight, but I need to put that out there. I can't have what I'm doing with you cause trouble at the ranch so that he would think of leaving again. I can't do that to my parents. That's the bottom line."

He weighed her terms, his mouth a grim line, his eyes stony beneath his furrowed brow. "Then we don't say a word to anyone. Either of us. No Arwen. No Everly. No Dax. Deal?"

"Deal," she said, disbelieving it would ever be that easy.

"Okay. Let's go," he said, getting to his feet and tossing a handful of bills on the table.

"There's a register up front," she said, nodding that way.

"They'll figure it out," he told her, taking her by the arm and guiding her to the door.

The sun was just hovering over the horizon, the heat still

stifling, but the sky a gorgeous mix of Kool-Aid orange and red. She'd kept on her suit jacket while eating—the restaurant had their a/c set to arctic—but shrugged out of it now as they crossed the hot asphalt, the sharp, pitchy scent reminding her of family trips to Six Flags and the suffocating steam that rose from the ground.

Before she could find her sunglasses in her purse, Casper pulled her between their vehicles, but instead of reaching for her door, he backed her into it, spread her legs with his knee, and reached between them, leaning to nuzzle his face to her neck. He smelled like beer and like dinner and like dried sweat from a day spent outdoors. And he was intent on having his way.

"What are you doing?" And why wasn't she making any effort to stop him?

"If I have to explain it, then I'm obviously not doing it right," he said, his upper body pinning hers to her car door as his hands gathered the fabric of her skirt to her hips. "And what the fuck with the pantyhose?"

"I haven't been home from work yet."

"Yeah, well, you need a new wardrobe," he said, making his way behind the waistband to slide his hand into her panties, working two fingers into her pussy, using his thumb against her clit.

And then he brought his mouth to hers, his tongue finding hers, and kissed her passionately while fucking her with his hand. All she could do was hold on.

She rode his fingers, shifted her hips to grind against his palm, gripped his shoulders as if doing so was the only way she could keep from falling. She rose on her tiptoes and he rose with her, penetrating, impaling, rubbing the fly of his jeans against her hip and groaning when she rubbed back.

"This isn't fair," she tried to say, wondering how *fair* came out instead of *smart* or *safe* or *a good idea*.

"Don't worry about fair," he told her, the rhythm of his fingers increasing, the slide of his tongue along hers as intimate as it was suggestively bold. But before he pulled free, he added, "Don't worry about anything but getting off."

He made it sound so easy. As if sex was the only thing worth her time. And the way he took charge left her unable to think otherwise. Left her unable to do anything but feel.

He stroked her, fingered her, played her, hurt her. She gasped and clawed at his shirt and buried her face in his chest. He brought his mouth to her temple and urged her on, his words dirty and hot and entirely inappropriate for the parking lot of a restaurant known for its chicken fried steak.

Everything they were doing here was wrong, and she wanted to care, to find the Faith who was proper and appropriate and didn't come in public places, but her body and desire had misplaced her mind, and she cried her release into the fabric of Casper's shirt.

He brought her back slowly, easing his hand from her body but not from her clothes. It wasn't till she heard the material rending and felt the crotch of her panties being pulled between her legs that she realized what he was doing. It took another few seconds for her to realize why.

"Now we can talk about being fair," he said, popping his buckle and button fly and lifting his cock from his shorts, as bold as he pleased, before bunching the strips of torn cotton in his fist like a rag.

"You're not—" was all she got out before he started to stroke.

"I am," he said, his voice low and gravelly, his gaze piercing and hot. "Unless you want to."

She did. God help her, she did. She held his gaze and reached for him, so thick and ready, so proud and so fierce. She cupped her palm over the plum-ripe head, stroking in a circle, tugging down, over and over as his nostrils flared, as his chest labored.

As in the distance, the restaurant door opened and customers exited, their laughter spilling into the waning light.

"People are coming."

"Worry about me coming."

She swallowed, nodded, fearing discovery, loving the feel of the veins bulging on the underside of his cock. She licked her lips, and he jumped in her hand, giving her a look that dared her to drop to her knees. She wanted to oh so much. To wrap her lips around him. To tongue the slit that was seeping moisture into her palm even now.

She shook her head, stroked him faster.

"Chicken," he said, and laughed. But then he slammed his hands onto the roof of her car on either side of her and dropped his head back, his eyes screwed closed, his throat working, his pulse hammering as he tensed. Finally he grunted, grabbing her hand and holding her where he wanted her while he spilled semen into her palm.

"God*damn*," he said, collapsing forward and resting his forehead on his forearm still on the top of her car. Then he looked over, winked, and grinned before covering her mouth with his and kissing her senseless. She kissed him back, her arms caught between their bodies while he tucked himself back inside his jeans.

It was just about then that applause erupted. Faith froze, her eyes popping open before she pulled her mouth from his. He was still grinning, the jerk, and then he reached for his hat, removed it, and took a bow.

But he never looked at their audience. He had eyes only for her.

She, on the other hand, held her cum-filled panties. And the wild look in his eyes told her he loved that she had them, and that they were the only two to know.

TEN

"IF Y'ALL DON'T mind, I'm going do a little work for Royce Summerlin." Casper lifted his arms and slammed the posthole digger into the ground, his whole body vibrating with the contact. Boone and Dax looked on as he wiggled it, settled it, put a boot on top of it, and shoved it deep. Then, since neither had said a word, he added, "On my own time."

"Own time," Dax repeated. "You have that?"

"Sure. Same as you." Though the truth was that none of them had any at all. Hell, they'd started working on this very holding pen weeks ago, after Massey Construction had demolished the ranch's old bunkhouse, cutting the boys a deal for their services based on how much of the wood they were able to save.

Casper wasn't sure if his and the boys' delay in getting finished was due to their jam-packed schedules, needing to free up the money to buy the fence posts and boards, or guilt at having destroyed a piece of the ranch that had been so much a part of the summers and holidays they'd spent here as teens. Hard to think that was it, except when it came to Tess and Dave, all three of them carried a soft spot.

As Casper worked the dirt from the hole, Dax rolled the next post ready to be sunk away from the pile. "And when would my own time be? Because I must've mixed it up with the hours I spend here or something."

"I guess he means the time you spend with Arwen," Boone said, using the edge of a sharpshooter to scrape the dirt from beneath Casper's feet.

Dax snorted. "The only time I spend with Arwen is sleeping."

Boone grunted. "If that's all you're doing with that woman, then I am sorry for you."

Dax snorted again. "That's not all I'm doing. But it would be nice to have time to do more of the other stuff."

"Whatever you're doing," Casper said, getting his head back in the game and off the *stuff* he'd been doing with Faith, "that's your free time. Just like Boone uses his for—"

"Boone doesn't have free time," Boone said. "Boone eats and sleeps and works. And sometimes Boone eats while he's working and skips sleeping altogether. Boone is not a happy man."

Were any of them? Saddled with a ranch it was getting harder and harder to love? Pinching pennies? Skimping on sleep? Facing a to-do list that grew longer by the day? Casper grunted. "Boone needs a woman."

"Boone is not going to argue with that," the big man said. "But right now he's more interested in hearing about you cheating on your partners and your ranch with Summerlin and his spread."

"I'm not cheating," Casper said, ramming the tool another few inches into the hard-packed earth. "I just want to make some extra money."

"Don't we all?" Dax asked.

"Yeah, well, I've got a chance to." Casper handed the other man the tool when he offered to take a turn. "I ran into Royce a couple of days ago, he said he's shorthanded, and I told him I'd come out and see what he had in mind."

Boone shook his head. "So you already agreed to it?"

"Yeah, well, I didn't want him running into someone else with a ready answer while I waited to check in with y'all."

"What sort of work you talking about?"

This was where it got tricky. He looked over at Boone. "Breaking horses."

"You shittin' me?"

"Doesn't he have a man doing that already?" Dax asked, coming out of the ground with more dirt for Boone to get rid of. "What was his name? Banning or something?"

"Royce sent him over to work for Nina, so the spot's open." Casper took a moment to fill a tin cup with water from the Igloo lashed to the back of the flatbed. "We talked about me filling in for a while."

"What do you know about breaking horses?"

"More than you, I reckon."

Dax stacked his hands on the digger's handle, took a stand. "I dunno. I put my butt on the back of a few wild ones while in Montana."

"And if I recall correctly," Boone said to Casper, "your butt couldn't stick eight seconds half the time."

"How do you know what my butt was or was not doing? You were off working in New Mexico or wherever."

"And you think that means I couldn't keep up with you and the PBR? Seems you didn't do too badly one year in Albuquerque."

The year he'd met Angie and Clay. "Were you there?"

"Not at the rodeo, no. Had planned to come, but we had a nasty brucellosis outbreak and it was all hands on deck."

"Huh. Wonder how many times the three of us crossed paths over the years."

Boone cocked his head Dax's direction. "You and Dax did the nomad thing. I stuck to New Mexico, so any time you came through, we would've been in spittin' distance."

"Wish I'd known," Casper said, meaning it. He'd hid it, even from himself, but he'd really missed his boys. "I would've looked you up." He turned to Dax. "I hit Montana on the way to Calgary, but that was years ago. Doubt you'd settled in Bozeman yet."

"I never really settled in Bozeman." Dax reached for the cup. Casper passed it over. "It was just the last stop before getting the news about Tess and Dave." He stared into the water, frowning as he swirled it. "I'd already been thinking about heading south of the border. I hated the cold."

"And here I thought you were a Scotsman to the bone."

"Speaking of bones," Dax said, giving Casper the eye. "You got a woman who needs courting? Is that what the extra money's for?"

Casper's first response was to dig at Boone about his sister, the way he'd done dozens of times. But since having her in his bed, he couldn't go there. Mostly out of respect for Faith, but he also didn't think he could pull it off. "I need it for the house."

"I dunno," Boone said. "I heard his headboard bouncing off the wall the other night. Not sure I'd call what was going on in there courting."

"You didn't hear shit. You were snoring loud enough to wake Bing." Who snored loud enough to wake Bob. Who snored loud enough to wake all of Crow Hill.

"By the time you snuck her out, maybe. I couldn't get to sleep until the two of you stopped shaking the house."

"Fess up, partner," Dax said, tossing him the empty cup. "Who was it?"

"My dick, my business," he said, catching it and returning it to the Igloo. "About the house. There's something else."

"That where you're keeping her?"

"Godammit. I'm not keeping anyone anywhere." He stopped then and laughed because he was doing just that. "Except I am."

Neither of the other men said anything, with Dax lifting a brow, Boone kicking at the sharpshooter's blade.

Casper mopped his forehead with his sleeve before settling his hat back in place. This was his cross to bear, but he had to come clean. He couldn't do anything to hurt the partnership. That was the bottom line in all things.

And that included Faith. "There's this kid there helping me clean up. And he needs a place to stay that's not a pit. I was thinking of bringing him out here. His dog, too."

"That's going to need a lot more explanation, dude," Dax said.

Then Boone said, "Yeah. A kid and a dog who need a place to stay doesn't sound exactly kosher."

Casper looked from one man to the other. He needed them to know this wasn't a joke. "His mom died. He doesn't have any other family. He came looking for me."

"Shit." Dax forced the digger back into the hole. "He yours?"

"I can say with one hundred percent certainty he is not. I met his mother in Albuquerque six years ago."

"Met his mother? Or fucked his mother?" Boone asked, while Dax came at him with, "The same Albuquerque we were just talking about?"

"Both," he said to Boone, and gave Dax a nod.

In return, Dax gave him a whistle. "Let me get this straight. You were doing this kid's mother when you were in town for a rodeo. His old lady dies, and he comes looking for you? Must've made one hell of an impression."

"It's a mystery to me. If I wasn't at the arena or in her bed, I was drunk. I barely remember him. Hell, I barely remember her," he said, the admission carrying both shame and regret.

Dax nodded. "You ask him about it? Why you won the daddy figure lottery?"

"Not really. All he said was that he didn't have anyplace else to go."

"No family?"

"I guess not."

"And foster care?"

"He gave it a try."

"I'm pretty sure if he's under eighteen, he doesn't have a say. He goes. He stays. End of discussion."

"Well, he went. And he didn't stay. And now it seems I'm the one who's stuck setting things right."

"You going to see a lawyer?" Boone asked, finally weighing in.

Yeah. Since he had so much disposable income . . . "I figure a lawyer's better than going to the law. For now. Until I know exactly what's what."

Boone glanced toward Dax. "Darcy, maybe?"

"No," Dax said. "Leave Darcy out of it. Get Greg to look into it. He won't feel the need to get personally involved."

And because Darcy was a friend of the Dalton Gang, she would, even if it went against whatever code was meant to keep her impartial. Casper nodded. "What about him staying out here? The boy. Clay."

Dax looked from Casper to Boone and shrugged. Boone looked back to Casper. "Faith was just saying we needed a maid. He could take on the job, help as he could with other chores. But it's on your head. Anything happens. This can't blow back on the ranch."

"It won't," he said, taking the tool from Dax and slamming it into the ground, praying as he did that he could keep that promise. And that he wasn't about to make the biggest mistake of his life.

ELEVEN

While Faith sat at the bar in the Hellcat Saloon, looking at the menu and nursing a vanilla beer, the lunchtime conversation from earlier in the week came back to haunt her, steering her away from a double order of fries and toward something more adventurous. Though what she was hoping to prove, and who she thought she'd be proving it to, wasn't exactly clear.

Yes, she believed in being organized and efficient. And hadn't she proved in the ranch house kitchen and Casper's bed—not to mention the Rainsong Cafe parking lot, *for chrissake*—that the last thing she was was boring?

She just needed to take baby steps from the safe end of the pool to the dangerous one instead of launching her entire body into the deep end. The way she'd done in the past.

The way she was doing now.

"Good plan," she muttered to herself. "But bad planning."

Baby steps meant seeing someone safe. Like Dr. Mercer Pope. Or Greg Barrett, Esquire. Even Mal Breckenridge. Or Cameron Neal, DVM. Not sleeping with the Dalton Gang member most likely to ruin her reputation for good.

But that was exactly what she'd done since she'd been old enough to date, wasn't it? Choose the worst possible men. Never learning her lesson. Thinking a bad boy could give her whatever it was that seemed to be missing in her life.

All that after growing up with the best example of a good man a girl could hope for, a coach, a husband, a father who talked and played and disciplined, who took his kids' joys and sorrows to heart.

And then there'd been Boone. Boone and his hell-raising ways had gotten the most of their parents' attention. But really? Had she been that ridiculously self-centered? That envious of Boone?

Had she looked for love in all the wrong places because the enormous amount showered down on her at home hadn't been as much as that poured onto her brother? Lord, if she'd been that shallow, she deserved the hell she'd gone through in college. But she alone. Not her family.

Still, that disaster was done with, leaving her with no explanation for what she was doing with Casper now . . .

"Mind if I join you?"

Faith glanced over to see Kendall Sheppard holding the back of the neighboring stool, her straight blonde hair swept away from her face with a band. "Kendall, sure. Please, sit. It's good to see you."

"You, too." Kendall moved fluidly into the seat, her long dancer's body—kept in shape these days by climbing the rolling ladders attached to her bookstore's shelves—making it look effortless. "I didn't want to cut in if you're waiting for a date."

"I'm waiting for dinner. Or I will be as soon as I make up my mind what to order." Faith tapped the menu in front of her. "And I'm taking it with me. Which means my only hot plans for the night are with my food." She gave the other woman a grin. "And maybe Timothy Olyphant."

"Ooh, good choice," Kendall said, reaching for a menu from those tucked between bottles of Tabasco and Louisiana hot sauce. "Mine are with my food, and another three or four hours of work. I'm afraid if I streamed Timothy in the background, I'd never get anything done."

"He is a distracting man, isn't he? Just enough bad boy mixed in with the good."

"And those long, *long* legs. Watching him walk . . ." Kendall let the rest of the sentence trail, sighing at the same time as Faith.

Then Faith cleared her throat and got back to being thirty-one years old. "Sorry about the late hours."

"Thanks. There are lots of perks to being an entrepreneur, but sometimes I'd take a cozy nine-to-five over betting my future on ordering the right number of the right titles, and having them in stock when customers actually have the disposable income to spend."

Faith heard what Kendall was saying, but her mind was stuck on the word *cozy*. Is that what her job was? As safe as the finance degree that had never offered a moment of challenge? As predictable as her weekly double orders of fries?

Thing was, she'd gone to college not knowing what she wanted to do with her life. She wasn't even sure she knew now. It wasn't as if she'd been born to coach like her father, or like her mother, had a need to counsel struggling teens. A calling was too ethereal, impractical. Faith prided herself on being neither, and banking fit.

Still, the word *cozy* kinda stung. "Nine-to-five's not all it's cracked up to be. In my case, the perks come strangled in suits and pantyhose."

Kendall laughed. "Can I tell you a secret? I don't remember ever owning a pair of pantyhose. Unless tights count."

"I think I hate you now."

"And when I'm elbow deep tonight processing returns, I'll be hating you, your comfy bed, *and* your night with Timothy Olyphant."

"I guess that makes us even," Faith said, laughing, then looking up as Ned Orleans came to a stop between them. "Hey, Sheriff. Are you picking up dinner, too?"

Out of uniform for the evening, he patted a beefy hand against his big belly and laughed. "I'm here with the missus. We just topped off two plates of fried catfish with a big bowl of banana pudding. I didn't want to interrupt, but I saw Kendall here and figured it a good time to ask her if she'd had anymore trouble from her thief."

Faith glanced over, frowned. "You have a thief?"

"I know, right?" She shook her head. "Someone's been snatching books off my shelves."

"Well, that sucks."

Kendall's gaze traveled from Faith to the sheriff before she looked back to her menu. "I get that it's tough on everyone with the library's funding being pulled, and the school having nothing for the kids to check out except old Louis L'Amours, but this is my livelihood. I can't afford to keep taking these hits."

"I think those L'Amours were there when I was in school," Faith said.

"I'm pretty sure they were there when I was, too," Ned added.

"I wouldn't doubt it. And I'm happy to give away any of the trade-ins too worn to put on the shelf. But the Nesbø title was a special order, and now I have to order it again." She turned to the sheriff. "To answer your question, no, I haven't noticed anything else missing, but you might ask Arwen. She mentioned her trash being disturbed by something other than dogs or coyotes."

"How would she know it wasn't animals?" Faith asked, looking up as the third woman joined them.

"Because dogs and coyotes don't twist tops off soda bottles," Arwen said, swiping a rag across the bar. "And last time I looked, they didn't leave size twelve sneaker prints in ketchup."

"Sounds to me like someone's hungry." Faith lifted her beer, realizing again how even their small town hadn't escaped the economy's hit.

"That's why I haven't said anything about it to Ned." Arwen nodded at the sheriff. "Until now."

Ned frowned, bobbed his head. "I'll make sure the night patrol knows to keep an eye on your place."

"As long as whoever it is keeps his foraging to the Dumpster, it's not a big deal. Once he, or she, breaks into the kitchen, I will press charges. But right now, I'm more concerned about someone in Crow Hill being that much in need and stealing instead of asking for help."

Faith thought back to her conversation with the Harts. "These days, there could be more than a few people on that list."

"I know," Arwen said. "I hate it. Especially since Dax and the boys aren't that far from having their names added."

"At least they've got family here," Kendall offered.

"All but Casper," Arwen said, her gaze meeting Faith's and a look passing between them that had heat rising beneath Faith's skin.

"I'll leave you ladies to your supper then." Ned gave a pat to the bar. "Call if you have more troubles. Any of you."

Faith waited until the sheriff was out of earshot before giving Arwen her order. Kendall did the same, and once Arwen had torn the tickets from the pad, she asked Faith, "How're the party plans coming?"

"We're making progress, but if we can't agree on where to hold it, none of our progress is going to make a lick of difference. Boone is so hard-headed." Even though in this case he was probably right. "You know I really wanted to have it here."

"Don't even worry about it. I totally understand the thing with the parents."

"Thanks. You were so generous to offer, and I'm so bummed we can't work it out."

"You know," Arwen said, tapping her pencil to her chin. "It's too bad Casper doesn't have the money to fix up that house of his. Can you imagine having the party there? Empty rooms decked out with white linen cloths on the tables, tiny little Christmas bulbs strung around, candles in clear hurricane holders?" She tucked her pencil behind her ear and sighed. "God, I can just see it. The hardwood floor gleaming. The windows reflecting the lights and the flames. The moon shining down. It would be gorgeous."

Arwen's words conjured up a scene from an old Kevin Costner movie, one with a beautiful Pat Metheny ballad played at an outdoor wedding. The dancing, the lights, the trees and soft decorative greenery . . . Faith could *so* picture the same sort of atmosphere for the party. With one problem—the state of Casper's house.

A problem she could solve if she were willing to take the risk.

Days into thinking about doing so, and she still hadn't decided. But, yes. She could see it. And gorgeous wasn't a big enough word. "Do you realize the money it would take to get that house in shape for anything?"

"I do. But it would be a showplace. Absolutely stunning." Arwen shrugged. "Instead, it will remain the pit it's fallen into, and the Texas Historical Commission will mourn the loss."

"I doubt they're even aware of the house's existence," Faith said, closing her menu. "Only Crow Hill old-timers know its history."

"Which makes it doubly sad that Casper can't make it right," Kendall said, glancing over Faith's shoulder. "And speaking of the devil . . ."

Refusing her pounding heart's urging to turn, Faith swallowed, scraped a nail over the label on her longneck, pretended Casper's scent and heat didn't have her body tightening, longing, waiting . . .

He stopped just behind her, his shoulder brushing hers as if by accident, his voice deep and gravelly. "A man can't even stop for a beer without finding he's being talked about."

"Just be glad your name wasn't spoken in vain," Arwen said with a wink before saying to both Faith and Kendall, "I'll get these orders turned in. It'll be just a few."

"I ordered more than fries," Faith called at her. "I hope you noticed."

All Arwen did was lift the slip of paper over her head before disappearing between the swinging doors into the kitchen. And then Kendall slid from her seat, waving at someone in the dining room behind her. "I'm going to go say hi to Teri Gregor."

Faith glanced beyond Kendall's shoulder to where Teri sat laughing with eight-year-old Shannon, her Navy SEAL husband's half-sister who was technically her sister-in-law but who Teri had taken on to help raise. "Say hello for me, too."

"Sure thing. And we'll catch up again soon."

Once Kendall was out of earshot, Faith swiveled to give Casper a side-eyed glance, ignoring the gleam in his eyes when she said, "Thanks. Running off my friends that way."

"Did I?" he asked, boosting a hip onto the edge of the stool where Kendall'd been sitting, one leg straight, one bent, his jeans tight around his thighs. "Huh. That usually doesn't happen with me and women. What is it that I can't make right?"

"Your house," Faith said, refusing to think about what usually *did* happen with him and women. Refusing, too, to look at his thighs. "What're you doing here?"

"It's suppertime. I'm hungry," he said, his eyes more gray than usual and reflecting the color from the bar's neon signs.

"Thought you and Boone took turns cooking."

"We do. But I was on my way to the house to check on some things and saw you pull in. Thought you might want company."

She was not going to fall so easily for his charms. Not this time. Not after the last. "I had company, thank you very much, and I'm getting dinner to go."

"Want to bring it out to the ranch?"

"Why would I want to do that?"

"I changed my sheets."

She thought of riding him, the feel of his cock stretching her, the look in his eyes as he watched her come. She dropped her gaze to the bar top, searching for her voice. "I'm pretty sure this isn't the time or the place for this discussion."

"Right. The secret. Don't want it getting out."

It wasn't about the secret getting out as much as needing room to breathe. Space to find her footing. Distance to deal with what they'd done outside the Rainsong Cafe. She still hadn't been brave enough to analyze that encounter, to figure out how she'd let lust get the better of her in such an inappropriate way.

The fact that she hadn't made it easier to say, "It's probably best if we put things on hold for now."

"For how long?" he asked without missing a beat.

Until I can trust myself around you, she thought, but said, "I don't know."

"Uh-uh. You can't just climb all over my cock and then change your mind."

"Shh." Good lord. Did the man have no filters at all? She braced an elbow on the bar, rubbed at her forehead. "I think that's why they call it a one-night stand."

He spun his stool to face the bar, tapped his index finger against the surface as if counting. "Hmm. I'm coming up with two times, maybe three, depending if you include last night in the parking lot. And that's just this week."

"If you don't shut up," she said, reaching over to dig her fingers into his wrist, "those three *times* will have to hold you until your next buckle bunny comes along."

He frowned, looked from her hand to where a silver platter the size of a saucer lay flat against his abdomen. "I didn't think you'd even noticed my buckle."

"I noticed." She let him go. "I've got a bruise from it gouging me."

"What about you?"

"What about me?" she asked as she lifted her beer.

"Is thinking about me going to get you through until your next ride comes along?"

"My next ride?"

"Yeah, though I suppose you've got a drawer full of boyfriends. Why bother with the real thing?"

She did not need this. She did not need him. She had boring and cozy and a cautious lack of adventure on her side keeping her safe. “I’m going to go to the restroom,” she said, sliding from her seat. “Why don’t you use the same time to leave?”

“And here I thought you wanted me.”

“I want you gone.”

“Afraid I’ll follow you to the parking lot?”

“I’m not afraid of anything,” she lied.

“I parked beside you again,” he said. Leaning closer, his breath tickling her ear, he added, “Just in case.”

“That,” she said with emphasis, because he was too sure of himself and she was not his toy and she deserved better than his disrespect, “will never be repeated.”

“I thought you liked it.”

“Me liking it is not the point.” She blinked, her throat closing around the frustration that threatened to burst into tears. “God, Casper. Can we not have this conversation here? Or can we just not have it at all?”

“Fine with me,” he said, sitting straight as he tugged down his hat brim. “I’d rather fuck than talk anyway.”

“Then go. Find someone to fuck. And leave me the hell alone.”

HE WAS GOING to make her insane. Honestly. What was she doing with him? Business was one thing; she’d been the Daltons’ loan officer and had continued to handle the ranch’s finances after the couple’s passing. But she and Casper had stepped over the line into a very personal relationship, one that could never be anything but physical.

So why was she wasting her time searching for something he didn’t have in him to give her? For something more than the Dalton Gang hell-raiser he was? Why was she trying to change him? Why did she think she could? He was vulgar and base, and he didn't seem to care. Why should she?

She wasn't looking for a long-term partner. She wasn't ready for that. Not until she'd found a man to help her discover whatever was missing in her life. Casper Jayne was not that man. He wanted her body. He was not interested in the rest.

Her palms on the dark granite vanity between the two sinks, she stared at her reflection. She was still dressed in her corporate armor of pantyhose and sensible—though sexy—black pumps, and a sleeveless white blouse beneath a black designer suit. From the neck down, she still looked like the banking professional she was. But from the neck up . . .

After ten minutes spent with Casper Jayne, she looked like a woman in need of a good fucking. Her eyes were glassy, her pupils huge. She was breathless, and all she could think about was Casper's gorgeous cock, having him inside of her, coming around him, watching the way his abs contracted just before he let go.

How did he do this to her? Why did she let him? Where was her self-control? Had she learned nothing in her life about the consequences of inappropriate behavior? Was she going to be fighting this flaw forever?

At the sound of the door opening, she cleared her throat and straightened, tugged down the hem of her suit jacket, then looked up to meet Casper's reflected gaze. Her heart flipped, tumbling to crush her chest and choke her.

Before she could turn around, he moved in behind her and pressed his body to hers, from shoulders to hips to thighs. God, but he felt good. "What are you doing?"

"I'm about to do you," he said, holding her gaze in the mirror and reaching between them for his buckle and his fly.

Her sex throbbed and dampened. She took a step forward. "Are you insane?"

"No more than I've ever been," he told her, drawing flush with her again and this time trapping her, his body behind, the vanity in front.

This. This reckless behavior. She couldn't throw caution to the wind the way he did. She cared about her reputation. She could lose her job, being so indiscriminately . . . debauched.

And then he moved just enough for her to catch sight of his cock, jutting thick and proud as if he had every right in the world to be naked with her, to show himself to her. To make her want to look, and to ache for him.

He wrapped his arm around her, beneath her belly, drawing her ass back into his groin and grinding against her. "If it makes you feel any better, I locked the door."

"We're not going to do this. Not here. Not now."

"Yeah," he said. "We are."

"Casper—"

"Shh," he said, reaching between them for the button of her skirt, freeing it and pushing the garment to the floor.

"You couldn't just pull it up?" she asked, mindlessly moving while he tore away her panties and hose, stripped her out of her jacket.

"Shh," he said again, then told her, "bend forward." He grabbed her hip with one hand, his cock with his other, and aligned their bodies, dipping to work his way between her legs.

This was wrong. So, *so* wrong, and yet as she watched emotions play over his face, she couldn't stop herself from spreading her legs, from adjusting the angle of her body. From being stupid yet again and breathless as her heart beat the air from her chest.

He slipped into her, and she caught her tongue between her teeth, biting down on the groan filling her mouth. He was full and thick and long, and his balls heavy where they hung hot against her skin.

What was she doing, letting him into her body, here, behind a door so easily unlocked? She was out of her mind. She had to be. Standing here like this, unmoving, impaled on his imposing length.

She lifted her gaze from where he filled her, searching out his eyes beneath the brim of his hat, the flare of his nostrils, the hard line of his jaw as he ground it. He was shaking, his legs behind hers, his arm around her waist, and his breath hitched before he caught himself and buried that vulnerability in a wicked lift of his lips.

But she'd seen it, and she'd felt it, and his hiding it didn't erase the truth. And because of that slip, that tiny bit of the barest sort of honesty, she couldn't turn him away. But she could turn the tables . . .

He gave a nod to the front of her body. "Unbutton your blouse."

"No."

"I want to see your tits."

Tits. So crass, yet so much his word. "What about what I want?"

"That one's easy," he said, breathing the words against her ear. "You want me to fuck you."

Yes, she wanted that. Over and over, she wanted that. But she wanted it in her bed, in private, where she could let go. Not in a public place where at any minute someone could knock on the door.

"Look," he said, parting her pussy's lips to squeeze her clit from both sides. His cock stretched her, and his veins were blue and engorged, a relief map of his desire, his balls beneath driving him to lust.

"Watch," he said, dipping his hips and setting a slow, shallow rhythm that had just the tip of his cock sliding in and out of her, teasing her, the seam splitting the underside creating a furrow for her clit to slide, his flesh wet with her cream.

She didn't know what to do with her hands, so she moved them to the buttons on her blouse, opening them slowly, watching his eyes heat as she bared her skin, as she used two fingers to pull just her nipples from the cups of her white bra.

She toyed with them, and he grunted. She pinched and twisted them, and he shoved himself deeper inside of her, grinding his hips, gouging the flesh of hers where he gripped her. She cupped herself completely and lifted herself free, and he moved his hands from her lower body to hold her.

He covered her, hid her, hefted her slight weight in his very large palms, thumbed her nipples until she squirmed, until she lowered her hands and used her fingers to ring his cock.

"Look," she said, sliding the circle she'd made with her thumb and middle finger from beneath his head's cap to the base of his shaft.

"Watch," she said, this time drawing only one finger upward, finding the nerves bundled at the base of the underside seam and stroking him there.

"You're an evil woman, Faith Mitchell."

And you're the worst choice I could ever make, Casper Jayne.

She didn't say it, of course. Another woman would have. Another woman wouldn't have cared about hurting his feelings, or cutting him down when he was exposed and defenseless. Another woman would have fucked him and walked away.

Faith wanted to be that woman, but knew herself too well. She would fuck him, yes. And she would walk out of this room without a single backward glance. But she would care about his feelings because she didn't have it in her to hurt him. Not like this. Not ever. Not knowing who he was, where he'd come from, what he'd been through.

She moved one hand to the vanity, one to her clit, and leaned forward while he fucked her, while he held her hips and drove into her, while he ground down against dirty words and desire and thrust like a jackhammer, nearly taking her off her feet.

She watched him, the strain in his neck, the rise in his blood pressure reddening his face, the flaring of his nostrils as he caught her gaze before he screwed his eyes shut to finish.

His look of desperation took her over. She fluttered and shook, coming quickly, surprised she'd made the climb with her nerves so ragged, but what she'd seen in his face had displaced her anxiety just long enough for her to let go. Now, however, as sanity returned, so did her urgent need to escape and she pushed back to get him to move.

Grunting, he pulled free, dripping cum down her thigh and onto the floor. Then he stepped from between her legs, giving her the space she'd come in here to find in the first place. She tossed her pantyhose into the trash, found her torn panties, swiped them over the mess Casper had left on the floor, and tossed them away, too.

Her skirt lay in a puddle beneath the vanity. She used her foot to slide it out, then stepped into it, shimmying her hips as she zipped it up and fastened the catch at the waist. Her bra was next, though it took her three tries to line up the hooks, and two tries to match the buttons of her blouse with their holes.

A quick look in the mirror had her smoothing her hair, though since Casper hadn't even bothered to kiss her, her makeup had survived the assault intact.

It was when she reached for her jacket that she finally looked at him, shrugging into the garment as she did. His fly was buttoned, his belt buckled, his black T-shirt tucked in. The fabric stretched tight across his chest, and she thought of the hair there, how silky it was. Thought of his nipples, the muscles around them, how sensitive he was to her tongue, to her teeth.

He had his arms crossed, his shoulder propped against the tiled barrier separating the main part of the restroom from the door. His hat was pulled low, hiding his brow and all but the glittering heat in his eyes. But there was more there. An element she wasn't sure of. It ticked along his stubbled jaw, beat beneath the skin of his neck.

He was brown from his time in the sun. Strong from his time on horseback. He was rangy, leanly muscled but bigger than most bull riders. She wasn't sure that had served him well or worked against him when he'd climbed on the backs of the beasts.

He was also a survivor. The years of his childhood. The years in the arena. He was beat up and battered. Broken. And yet here he was, having come through it all and still standing. Hanging on. Working a ranch on the verge of collapse, owning a house worth more than he could afford. Giving her brother a reason to stay.

Pursuing her and making her feel rich.

"I have a proposition for you," she said before she could think better of the offer she was about to make. It wasn't like her thoughts hadn't been headed in this direction for days. Much like a train wreck, she thought with no small amount of trepidation.

"Does it involve more of this?" he asked, nodding from his crotch to hers, which was now safely beneath her skirt and away from his too hungry gaze.

"No. This was a one-time thing."

"So we're back to you and your one-time things? Because the parking lot in Fever Tree didn't count? The kitchen in the ranch house didn't count? My bedroom didn't—"

Her head was pounding again. "Stop it."

"Hey, it's your dime, but if it's not about sex, I can't imagine what kind of deal we might make." He looked down at his feet, one muddy boot crossed over the other, then at hers and her black pumps that gave her hips just enough lift to meet his. "Mitchells and Jaynes just don't have that much in common, remember?"

That cut her a lot more painfully than she would've imagined. "We don't need to have anything in common for me to loan you the money for the improvements to your house."

He waited for a long moment, not moving, barely breathing, doing nothing but staring at her, his eyes holding hers. He didn't flinch. He didn't blink. He gave nothing away. "What's the catch?"

"No catch. I've got the money saved."

"Really? Is that why I can't get the money from the bank? They're paying you enough to save that kind of fortune?"

She ignored his comment. "We'll draft an agreement. You'll pay me back with interest."

"What's the catch?" he repeated.

"Why do you think there's a catch?"

"Isn't there always?"

"Fine," she said, smoothing down her skirt while she gathered her wits. "First of all, before you sell it or move back in, I get to hold my parents' anniversary party there."

"Ah," he said, the pull of his lips more sneer than smile. "So you're doing this for you, not for me."

"And what if I am?" she asked, though the party had truly been an afterthought.

"You could've offered me the money the day I came to the bank."

"It didn't occur to me then."

"It didn't occur to you until you needed something from me."

Argue. Backtalk. Complain. Was that all he could do? "I'm giving you what you want. Are you going to turn it down because there's something I want attached?"

"How do you have that kind of money?"

"I told you—"

A knock on the door interrupted her. "Hey in there."

"Sorry," Faith called, still staring at Casper. "Be right out."

"No," he said.

"No? You don't want the money?"

He tipped his hat with a harsh, "No, ma'am," then gestured for her to head out before he did. She brushed by him, smelled him as she did, her bare pussy tingling again as she pulled open the door. She mumbled another, "Sorry," to the woman waiting, cringed at the loud female gasp that came from behind her as Casper exited on her heels.

She didn't look back, imagining the picture he made, big and bad and not giving a shit that he was coming out of a place he had no business being. Instead, she hurried to the bar, sensing without seeing that she did so alone. That Casper moved on, leaving the saloon. Leaving her to deal with whatever fallout resulted from their entirely inappropriate—oh my God, she was so, *so* stupid—encounter. Typical of him to walk away.

When she stopped to pick up her food order, Arwen was waiting, arms crossed on the bar top, a dark brow pointedly arched. "Here's the thing, sweetie. I'm all for you and Casper hooking up, but I'd rather it not be in my restroom. We try hard to keep things here family-friendly, you know."

"I know. I'm sorry. It should never have happened, and it won't happen again." Faith reached for the brown paper bag with the Hellcat Saloon clawing-cat logo the other woman pushed toward her, avoiding Arwen's gaze as she did.

But Arwen held tight, not letting go until Faith glanced up. “Are you sure? Because the look on Casper’s face said otherwise.”

“That look was about something else.”

Arwen’s expression said she wasn’t buying it. “Fine, next time the two of you need time alone for . . . something else, you can use my office. Just lock the door. And clean up when you’re done.”

“There isn’t going to be a next time. But please, please don’t tell Dax it happened this one.” It was a plea of too little too late, because who knew how many others had seen Casper follow her? “I don’t want Boone to find out.”

“Best way to make sure he doesn’t is to get a room in San Antonio. You’ve lived here all your life, Faith. You know what Crow Hill’s like.”

“I do. It’s just—” She stopped herself because she and Casper had made a deal not to tell anyone.

“It’s just what?”

A deal he’d just publicly rendered void. She took a deep breath, shaking her head, her eyes brimming with tears. “He’s so, *so* damaged. So broken. I didn’t know. I honestly didn’t know.”

Arwen’s gaze softened. “This is probably not the right time for me to say I told you so, is it?”

But she had, and Faith hadn’t listened, and now she was in over her head—and possibly in with her heart.

TWELVE

WHAT IN THE hell was wrong with him?

He'd been handed what he needed on a silver platter. No strings save for an insignificant one. No digging into his background—though she didn't need to dig as he'd opened his big mouth and told her—or into his finances to prove his ability to repay what was going to be a hefty sum.

And because his pride and his ego were all wrapped up with his dick, he'd said no.

So what if it was Faith making the offer?

It was an offer. It was easy money. It was the cash he needed.

A way out of the hellhole he'd walked away from years ago that was now sitting square in his lap.

All of his personal capital—and what a crock of a concept, as if he'd ever owned anything more than his truck and his rodeo gear and clothes to see him from one Laundromat to the next—was tied up in the ranch.

The well scheduled to be drilled in the Braff pasture by Trinity Springs Oil was months away from producing, and years away from throwing significant change the ranch's way. Besides, Faith had made it clear.

The bank wasn't going to offer him a loan based on mineral rights, especially when he was one-third of a partnership owing the price of a few good souls. Jesus.

He'd come back to Crow Hill for the good part of his past, the only part he missed, the one part worth anything. He'd come back to Crow Hill to ranch and raise hell. He and his boys had been doing a lot of the former, very little of the latter.

But he couldn't give his all to the ranch or to his boys if he was having to piecemeal the house back together, and pay for it one horse at a time. And he'd never get this thing with Clay fixed right if every time he turned around he was sucked into some new emergency repair.

He couldn't raze it. He couldn't sell it.

Taking Faith's money solved everything. It really was as simple as that.

He stopped the truck in the middle of the county highway halfway between town and the ranch. Saying no was a fool thing to do. A blanket yes would be just as dumb. He'd take the money, but they'd make it legal, just like she'd said.

They'd draw up an agreement. He'd pay her back with interest. And he'd let her have her stupid party. He could live with all of that. But he wasn't going to let her call the shots on what he did with the house. Or how he spent her cash.

That much, she had to know. Then there was the issue of Clay. An agreement would no doubt have Faith spending time at the house. Meaning the boy couldn't be there. The dog either. Tonight, once he and Faith settled things, he'd move them both to the ranch.

He made a bat turn in the middle of the road and headed back to town, hunting down the apartment complex where she lived. It was small, no more than a dozen units, which should make it easy to figure out which door was hers. He circled the parking lot, found her car, and backed his truck into an empty slot at the far end of the row.

The first gated patio he came to was fussy with potted plants, sun catchers, and a couple of those Indian things webbed with feathers hanging from the edge of the terracotta roof. The table on the second held an overflowing ashtray next to a pile of Hot Wheels. *Nice*.

The third apartment appeared to be the most likely of the four on this side, since the last one had two racing bikes lashed to the wrought-iron posts, and so he backed up. The unlocked gate swung open, and he knocked before he could talk himself out if it.

Then he parked his hands at his hips and waited, figuring he'd interrupted her supper if she'd had any appetite left after all that had gone down between them.

She had a napkin in her hand when she opened the door. Her eyes widened, then narrowed curiously, and she cocked her head to the side to look over his shoulder.

He cut her off before she could say anything. "In the bathroom. At the saloon. You said *first of all* when I asked you what catch came with your money."

"Hello to you, too."

"Sorry. Hi. What's the rest? After the party catch, what else?"

She leaned a shoulder against the doorjamb, crossed her arms, ignored the fact that he had to bat away the bugs circling her porch light, and that he was sweating like a pig in the leftover heat of the day. "I'm not giving you the money if I don't get a say in what you do with it."

Goddammit. He cupped a hand over his chin, rubbed it as he thought, as he jumped from the frying pan into the fire, because what else was he going to do? "If you want a say, then instead of paying you interest, I give you fifty percent equity. My house. Your money. An equal partnership."

"Why would you do that?" she asked, her brow knitting into a frown.

"Because I don't want to get left high and dry if you decide to pull the plug. If you're in this for half the house's value, you'll be less inclined to screw me over."

She considered that a long moment, then said, "You know if you want to buy me out later, you're going to end up paying me more than what I put in, even with interest added."

Didn't matter. He'd have as much trouble paying her ten bucks as a million. "I know. But at least the house will get done, and done right."

She took her time thinking while he swatted at moths and mosquitoes, finally stepping out of the doorway and nodding him inside. He brushed by her, taking off his hat and scrubbing a hand over his buzzed hair. God*damn*, he needed a beer.

He was insane. That's all there was to it. He should've turned and walked off the minute she'd demanded a say in more than how they fucked, but here he was and here she was and all he could say was, "Nice place."

"It's comfortable. I've got plenty of room. Very nice neighbors."

He lifted his nose. "Smells like you've also got Arwen Poole's ribs."

"I do. Would you like some?"

"I'm fine."

"Casper, it's a half-rack with a loaded baked potato, a side of green beans, and a big square of chocolate cake for dessert. There's more than enough for two."

He'd seen her eat. He wouldn't take that bet. "Okay then. Thanks."

The look she gave him wasn't quite a smile, but it was close enough that when she motioned him forward, he went with her to the kitchen instead of retreating out the front door. He stopped at the end of the table where her food was laid out next to a hardcover book.

"What're you reading?" he asked as she gathered the foam takeout containers, carried them to the microwave, and popped them in while she pulled down dishes for him.

"Something I bought at Kendall's the other day," she said moments later, dividing the now warm food between them, then adding a bit more to the plate she'd got out for him.

He tossed his hat to the seat of an empty chair, settled his hands at his waist. "About earlier."

"I'd rather not talk about earlier."

"I was only going to say—"

"Don't say anything—"

"—I'm sorry."

Her hands stilled, then she picked up the plates and returned to the table where he waited. "What are you sorry for?"

"For forcing you—"

"You didn't force me." She held up a finger, as if making sure that was clear. "You would've left the saloon in handcuffs if that had happened."

And he'd have deserved nothing less. "You told me to leave you alone. I didn't leave you alone."

"That's not the part I want you to be sorry for," she said as she sat, closing the book and pushing it aside.

He took the chair across from hers. "I'm going to need some help here then."

"Fine," she said, scooting closer. "I want you to be sorry for not listening to me the first night we were together. When I told you I wasn't going to do anything to risk Boone finding out about us."

Ah. That. "No one saw us."

"Someone saw me coming out of the ladies' room and you following."

"So I went into the ladies' room by mistake. Shit happens," he said, tearing a bone from the rack.

Before he could get it to his mouth, she reached for his wrist, holding it as well as his attention. "What if the woman worked at the high school? What if she mentioned to one of my parents that she saw me and you come out of the restroom together? What if one of my parents then asked Boone what he knew? See what I'm saying?" she asked, letting him go. "We're not being careful. We have to be careful."

"Fair enough," he said, sinking his teeth into the meat and wondering if she'd meant to use the future tense. "Now tell me about the money."

"There's nothing to tell," she said, her gaze falling to her plate, to her fork and green beans. "It's my money. That's all you need to know."

Hmm. He was pretty sure there was something here she was holding back. "Doesn't seem right for partners to keep secrets."

"And yet, it happens," she said, blowing him off. "I'm sure you've kept a few from Dax and Boone."

He had. He was keeping one now. Keeping one from Faith,

too. A secret named Clay. But he wasn't letting up about the money. If she had it and Boone didn't . . . "You a closet gambler or something?"

"Good lord, no," she said, frowning. "I'm not a gambler. The money's free and clear. No bookie's going to come demanding a cut."

"And you didn't embezzle from the bank."

She hesitated for an extra long moment, then reached for his plate and took it away. "You need me to show you the way out?"

"I'm not done," he said, grabbing for his ribs.

She held them out of reach and said, "You are done."

He shook his head, making a *gimme* motion. "Not with the food."

"Then no more questions about the money," she said, letting him have the plate but only after he grunted his agreement, earning himself a roll of her eyes.

"There's just one more thing," she said, wiping her hands on a paper towel. "I need to ask you what you know about the house."

He thought back to their sharing chicken fried steak at the Rainsong Cafe. "Didn't we already have this conversation?"

But she ignored his question to ask one of her own. "You don't have any idea how your father came to own it?"

"Not a clue." He licked barbecue sauce from the fingers of his right hand, looked up to catch her watching the motions of his mouth. A fire lit in his gut, and he let it grow, the flames flicking their way lower. Then he realized something was going on here, something she'd been obsessed with now for days. "What do you know that I don't?"

"The day you came to the bank? I started thinking about the house. What you might get for it if you sold it. If it would be worth fixing up first. That sort of thing." She gathered up her hair, held it to her head, cocked back in her chair. "So I looked at the tax and property records."

He stared at the strands that fell from her fingers, wanting to bury his nose beneath her ear, against her neck, at her throat. "That's one thing I do know," he finally said. "Suzanne kept the taxes current."

"Yeah, you're good there. You're also the owner of a piece of Texas history."

"What?" he asked, still caught up in breathing her in and not sure what she'd said.

"That house was built by Zebulon Crow."

"What?" he asked again, but this time he'd heard her.

She let her hair fall, leaned toward him. "Any idea how your father ended up owning a house that belonged to the founding family of Crow Hill?"

"No fucking clue."

"Do you have a number for your mother?"

Yeah. Like he'd have Suzanne on speed dial. "Why? You think I'm going to call her and ask?"

"Aren't you curious?"

He was, but . . . "Not that curious."

"C'mon, Casper. This is a huge deal. It could make all the difference in the world to how we tackle the renovations."

Uh-uh. He wasn't getting tied up in returning the house to its roots. He wanted it done. "Faith. All I want is for the house not to fall to the ground from rot, or catch on fire from bad wiring before I decide what to do with it. After that, I really do not care."

She reached for his plate, which was empty this time, then scraped his rib bones into hers and stacked them. "If we can find a number, do you mind if I call her?"

Pit bull. Steak bone. The woman was a force. "Could be something on the papers she sent."

"Can I look at them? Since obviously you can't be bothered. And since we're partners," she added before he had a chance to bring up how nosy she was.

"We're not partners yet. Not without a signed agreement." He offered his hand across the table. "Or at least a handshake."

"This better get me your mother's phone number," she said, determination firm in her expression as she placed her palm against his.

They shook, but she didn't pull away, and he made no move to let her go. She had a tiny speck of ground pepper from the ribs just to the right of her mouth, and it hit him that she'd hate it if she knew. She wanted everything to be just so.

So what was she doing with him?

He let her go, brushed his finger to his face, saying, "You've got—"

She jerked her hand from his, wiped at both sides of her face. "You could've said something earlier."

"That would've been out of character."

"Being nice is out of character?" she asked as she got to her feet.

Getting to his, he shrugged. "So I've been told."

"Then you're listening to the wrong people."

"Who should I be listening to?"

"Me, for one."

"What would you tell me?"

"That you've got more nice in you than you think," she said, but that was all before she took him by the hand and pulled him to the front door, stopping first by the sofa for his hat. "It's late."

"It's not that late," he said, though he did reach for the knob.

"It's late enough that I need to start getting ready for tomorrow." When he made no move to turn it, she added, "And go to bed."

"I can stay," he heard himself saying. Heard himself sounding too much like a man begging for pussy. He hated hearing men beg for pussy. "But I can go."

He still didn't open the door. Still didn't turn the knob. He looked down at her from beneath the brim of his hat, not sure what he was doing. She stood with her arms crossed over her sleeveless white blouse that was properly buttoned and didn't give him a single hint about her bra. Her black skirt was slim, hitting her knees, and her legs and feet beneath were bare.

Nothing about her screamed sexy, and yet all he could think about was sex. His mouth on her tits. Her mouth on his cock. His cock sliding into her from behind. For years he'd made himself think of her only as Boone Mitchell's sister, off-limits and the source of half the grief he'd given the other man. But since having her, he hadn't once razzed her brother about the Dalton Gang's no-sisters rule.

He couldn't make her the butt of his jokes anymore, even if Boone was his real target. And when she reached up to tuck back a lock of hair that had fallen forward, he let go of the door and reached for her instead, hooking an arm around her neck and pulling her close.

Her hands came up between them, settling on his chest, ready to push him away, and yet she didn't. She stared at her fingers, flexed them against him, flexed them a second time before gathering the fabric of his T-shirt into her fists, and shaking her head as she dropped her forehead to her hands.

"Why didn't you just open the door and go?"

His heart kicked hard in his chest. "Because I wanted to stay."

"For the sex? Or for me?"

This was going to be a tough one to answer. "Faith—"

"Never mind. I know what you're going to say."

"No. You don't. Because I don't know what I'm going to say."

"You're going to say for the sex."

"If I did, it would be true." He could smell her hair, the cinnamon and sugar scent of it. "But it wouldn't be everything."

"Now you're just trying to butter me up."

"Goddamn right."

She swallowed then, lifted her gaze. "I told myself after the restaurant I was done being stupid with you."

He lowered his head, brushed his lips against the corner of hers. "I thought we did stupid pretty well together."

Shivering, she kissed him back, then said, "I can't be stupid. I don't care how good you are."

His cock jumped at that. "Am I good?"

"As good as the hundreds of women you've had before me have told you, no doubt."

"I hope you're asking how many there've been and not how you compare."

"I wasn't asking either one, but now I'm asking both."

"And you'll be waiting till kingdom come for an answer."

She groaned. "Why do you do this to me?"

"I'm not doing much of anything yet."

"But I'm going to let you."

Hallelujah. "That's good to hear."

"For you maybe."

Or not. "If you don't want me here—"

"I do want you here. I just . . ."

That sounded like an invitation to him. He moved his arm from her neck to her waist and scooped her close, bringing her body to his, her breasts to his chest, her hips to his fly, her cheek to his when he lowered his head and inhaled. She smelled like barbecue and beer. She smelled like Faith and good sex, and his cock went tire-iron hard, but he didn't press.

He'd do that soon, press and urge and let her know exactly

all the ways he wanted her. But after his not being nice in the saloon's restroom, and being too caught up in lust in the ranch house kitchen, and being too aware of all the noises they'd made in his bed, he owed her another side of himself. And he owed himself a long, *long* night.

She parted her lips, and he slid his tongue between to find hers, toying with her softly, and swallowing a groan when she drew her thumbs to his nipples, circling them, squeezing them, digging into the flesh around them the way she'd learned quickly he liked.

He wanted to touch her, to unbutton her blouse and heft her tits in his hands, to lean down and suck the pebbled centers, to hold them with his teeth, and tongue the tips. He wanted to bruise the soft skin over her collarbone, scrape her with the stubble of his now two-day beard. He wanted to treat her in the ways that made him most happy and do things to her that got him off.

But this was about her, and she had doubts; hell, *he* had doubts. Scaring her off wouldn't do either of them any good, and he wasn't ready to put an end to whatever this was that had sprung up between them when he'd only been looking to get laid. Except that wasn't true. He'd been looking at her since she was fourteen years old and he was a randy sixteen with no concept of boundaries.

But he hadn't been looking *for* her. For anyone, really, but he would've never looked for Faith to come to his bed. To give herself to him. To want him.

Who the hell had ever wanted him?

And so he let her set the pace, let her take control. It really wasn't that hard. Especially when she reached behind him to lock the door, flicked off the lights in the living room, and laced their fingers together to lead him to bed.

THIRTEEN

HER BEDROOM MADE him think of a southern plantation, her bed a queen-sized four-poster of draped and gauzy whites. A ceiling fan whirred overhead, stirring waves in the fabric wrapped loosely around the frame's corners. The floor was hardwood and glossy, the braided rag rugs tossed around the room the only bits of color.

It made him feel really shitty about bedding her on dirty sheets. "This is not the room I would ever have imagined you naked in."

She stood facing him at the side of the bed, her quick fingers tugging his T-shirt from his jeans. "Have you imagined me naked?"

"Since you were fourteen years old," he said, growing impatient and stripping off his shirt when she stopped to stare up at him.

"Perv. You thought about me that way back then?"

Should he be honest? "I thought about every girl with great tits that way back then."

"I had great tits?"

"Then and now," he said, forcing himself to go slow as he started at her throat to unbutton her blouse. "I have a thing for tits."

"I hadn't noticed," she said, the words droll, the corner of her mouth trying to turn up.

"Probably hard to since I've got a thing for pussy, too." He pushed her blouse from her shoulders, slipped his hands to her back to release the catch of her bra. He waited just a second, taking a breath, anticipating, before letting it go. The cups weren't fancy—just a bit of ribbon, a bit of lace—but the flesh they bound in place . . . "Damn."

"Thank you," she said, trailing a finger from his breastbone to his belt buckle.

"No. Thank you." He bent, took a nipple into his mouth, swirled his tongue around the tight pebble before moving to its twin. She tasted like cinnamon and sugar, like cream, like Faith. Like a big, fat gift he didn't deserve, and that had him wrapping an arm around her and bringing her close. He didn't want her coming to the same realization and changing her mind.

Especially after what had gone down between them a short time ago. He'd been angry. He'd wanted to strike out, to make her hurt. But the way he'd gone about it hadn't been smart. Neither had it been effective. He'd stopped being angry as soon as he'd stepped through the ladies' room door and seen her reflected expression.

None of what he'd been feeling mattered. He'd had to have her. She was mad and flushed and gorgeous, and where another man might've shown better judgment, his cock had been too greedy to care. It was close to being as unthinking now, the smell of Faith's skin making him fence-post hard.

One nipple caught with the edges of his teeth, he pinched the other, twisting it, pushing her to stop him because he didn't think she was ready for all the things he wanted to do. But she didn't stop him. She covered his hand with hers and pressed into him, holding him there, her breaths shallow, her heart beating with an insistent rush.

He replaced his teeth with his lips and sucked her, laughing against her flesh when she groaned, her other hand coming up to cup the back of his head. He wanted her out of her clothes. He wanted out of his. He wanted to slam his cock into her cunt until neither one of them had the strength left to think. All of that after having her earlier. After losing himself in her just days before.

It didn't make any sense, this need he had to make his mark, to brand her as his, to own her. It didn't make any sense, but he was hosed up in the truth of it, that she was getting to him, worming her way inside of him, prying out secrets he preferred to keep hidden . . . and those things just wouldn't do. But this would do, this filling her with his cock and drowning in her body.

He let her go, reached for the zipper and button at her waistband, undoing both. She shimmied out of her skirt, and he dropped to one knee, burying his face between her legs and breathing her in along with the lingering scent of his cum. She smelled like the sea, rich and liquid, and he slid his tongue along the seam of her lips, tasting her salt, her sugar, tasting himself. Then he slipped into her folds, found her hole, and speared her.

The sounds she made were breathy and anxious, little whimpers and deeper, urgent pants. He loved that she was noisy. Loved that tight-as-a-one-lane-road Faith Mitchell was a girl who knew how to let go. Loved that he was the one making her sweat. Making her slick. Making her reach for the post of her bed to keep from falling.

He licked her, and pushed into her, and pulled out, and sucked on her clit, tugging hard, then using just the tip of his tongue to flick and to tease. Her knees buckled, and he caught her, braced her, crooked a finger deep inside of her and played her, rubbing her pillow-like G-spot while his tongue stroked her clit, circling, coiling.

She writhed against him, shuddered, and cried out his name. He stayed with her, gave her what she needed, and finished her, lapping her juices as they dripped, easing his finger from her pussy, his tongue sliding from the top of her mound up her belly to her navel, to her breastbone, and as he rose to stand, to the hollow of her throat, then her mouth.

He kissed her, sharing her flavor and scent, his tongue, his joy at making her come, his own desire. And then he let her go, tugged off his boots, and stripped out of his shorts and his jeans. Scooping Faith into his arms, he crawled onto the bed, rolling them to the middle of the mattress and covering her, pinning her, his thighs in line with hers and pressing down.

"You taste good. You smell good. You feel so damn good."

"There's a whole lot more good in me, but you're going to have to let me move to prove it to you."

"You have nothing to prove to me, woman," he said, threading his fingers into her hair, holding her head still, moving his mouth to her jaw, her throat, returning to her ear, healing the tiny bruises he left with soothing touches of his tongue. "I *am* sorry, you know, about earlier. In the saloon—" was all he got out before her fingers came up and stopped him.

"Shh," she said, rubbing a thumb over his top lip, moving it to the lower and tugging down. "Let's not talk about that. Let's forget about that. Let's pretend it never happened."

He would never forget, and he would never pretend. If she didn't want to talk about it, fine, but something told him her denial was less about what he'd done to her than the fact that she'd let him. Let him, instead of walking out and leaving him alone in the restroom before things got out of hand.

But he let it go because he didn't have it in him to keep up with a conversation anyway. His cock was full and tight, and he raised his hips just enough to prod his way between her legs. She wiggled and closed around him, tugging on him with the muscles of her thighs.

He sucked in a hissing breath, kissed her fingers, then dropped his forehead to her pillow, turned his face toward hers and growled into her ear. "I'm going to fuck you," he said, and her nipples pebbled, her thighs trembled, her fingers dug grooves in his shoulders. "I'm going to fuck you hard."

"Yes," she said. "Please," she begged. "That's what I want," she told him, pulling her legs from beneath his, drawing her knees along his sides, opening for him, shifting her hips to better align their bodies. Making it easy for him. Making him want her even more than he already did. "I want you."

God, what it did to him, hearing that from her, being wanted by her. He took his time pushing into her, drawing out the slow, steady thrust as long as he could, wanting it to last forever, the sensation of filling her, of possessing her, of being lost in her.

Once he hit bottom, he stopped, and she let out a contented sigh. It blew along his cheek, his ear, soft and warm and comforting, when he wasn't here for comfort or contentment. Being with her, being inside her . . .

It was eating him up, getting in his way. But here he was because nothing in his life had ever given him this same sense of being himself. And even when she called him on it, she didn't try to change who he was. How could he not enjoy her?

She pumped him with her pussy's muscles and he grinned, loving her impatience. He lifted his hips, pulling back until only the head of his cock remained wrapped inside her, and then he withdrew that last little bit, leaving her with only his tip.

Beneath him, she squirmed and bucked up, reaching for him, her hands clawing their way down his back, her heels pushing against his ass, eager, insistent. Greedy. He laughed, the sound wicked and dark in her sweet southern bedroom. The contrast of good and evil, pure and base, had his hard cock growing harder, his balls drawing taut.

He wanted what she wanted and so he gave it to her in long, rhythmic thrusts, putting himself into her, giving himself up to her, taking away every bit of her that made him feel good. She was wet, scented like sun and surf and sweetness, and he buried his face in her neck and let his cock have its way, stroking, fucking, sliding deep.

Her pussy lapped him up, sucked him in, milked him and gripped him and held him when he hung at her entrance, waiting until he couldn't wait anymore then thrusting until his muscles quivered and his cum gathered to blow.

At that he started all over again, delaying his orgasm while she climbed toward hers, the soles of her feet rubbing up and down his calves as she, too, slowed.

He growled into her ear, "What're you doing?"

She laughed, a sound just as wicked as his, but even more so for its softness, its innocence. Evil, evil wench. "Same thing you are. Having fun."

Yeah. At his expense, because he wasn't going to be able to hold on much longer. "We can do this again, you know."

"I plan to," she said, and pushed her lower body up against his, pulling him back down by his cock. "Several times."

"That so," he said, rolling just enough to the side to slip one hand between them, finding her clit and working it. She used the same space he'd created to join him, showing him what she liked before ringing her fingers around the base of his cock.

"I want you to do me from behind," she said, and he thought of her ass in the air, his cock slickly coated and sliding deep, his balls slamming against her, and groaned.

"I want to do you from behind," he said, and the images of her mouth and hands coming at him that way turned his groan into something feral.

He was done. So fucking done. He reared back and thrust forward with all he had in him, driving into her as his balls gripped hard and his cum readied. And then she bit his neck, licked the spot with the flat of her tongue, blew over the damage, and said, "Ride me hard."

Pumping. Driving. Banging. He did it all, his cock hitting bottom, her pussy swollen with her arousal. It felt like she was giving him head. He thought of her tongue flicking against him, her fingers squeezing him, her lips sucking at the gathering of nerves, and he came, spilling into her with furious bursts that seemed never to end.

The sensation was crazy wild and ripped from his core, and it was all he could do to stay conscious. He felt her contractions as she followed him, as she shuddered beneath him, as she turned her head to the side and cried out with her mouth at his biceps and bit him.

Once she'd calmed, he pulled away and settled in behind her, his arm across her midsection, and his legs tangled with hers. He held her to him as her heartbeat slowed and her breathing calmed, and he tried not to think what he would do if he woke in the morning to find her gone.

FOURTEEN

"GRAB YOUR THINGS," Casper said, walking into the kitchen the next evening to find Clay ready to open a can of microwavable soup.

"Oh. It's you. Late again," the boy said, popping the pull top as if Casper hadn't spoken at all.

Yes, he was a shit for not getting back here yesterday. He'd spent longer than he'd thought working on the holding pen, then on his way back here he got distracted by Faith and her offer to pay for his house. He'd ended the day wrapped up in her body and lost the rest of his mind, only to wake long past sunrise, cursing, his truck screaming as he floored it all the way to the ranch.

He was a shit, but that didn't keep him from being shittier to cover it up. "You keep telling me you're okay on your own. I didn't think you'd mind."

"I don't mind."

"Good. Now grab your things. I'm taking you and Kevin to the ranch."

Clay's eyes went wide, though Casper couldn't tell if with fear or excitement. "Now?"

"Yep." He reached over, gave a reassuring slap to Clay's shoulder, only just stopping himself from ruffling the boy's hair. He set the top back on the soup and put the can in the fridge. "Right in time for dinner. Lucky for you, it's Boone's night to cook, not mine."

"Who's Boone?" Clay called back as he loped up the stairs to the room he'd claimed as his own. Kevin followed him up. Kevin followed him down.

Casper waited for the both of them before answering, realizing he hadn't said much of anything to the boy about who he was now, what he did. The broken-down ranch where he did it. The boys he did it with who had saved his young life. "Boone Mitchell. One of my partners in the Dalton Ranch. We have a third, Dax Campbell, but he's pretty much moved out of the ranch house."

Clay slung his backpack over his shoulder. "So there's room for me?"

"There'd be room for you even if Dax was still there. It's not the size of this one, but it's a pretty big house." And in a little bit better shape, though not by much.

"Where's he live?"

"Over on Willowbrook Avenue with his lady, Arwen." Casper headed for the back door. "She owns the Hellcat Saloon."

"The, uh, Hellcat Saloon?"

"Yeah." The look on the boy's face spelled out the word *guilt*. Casper thought back to the takeout containers he'd found here when he'd found Clay. "I'm guessing you've eaten from there."

"A couple of times," the boy said, nodding, walking out onto the porch. "Good food."

"I'll take you there sometime," Casper said, digging his keys from his pocket. Sometime when the boy showing his face in public wouldn't bring down the law. "You can order from the menu. Then you can leave a really big tip for Arwen to make up for whatever you stole from her."

"I didn't take anything from the kitchen. I swear." Guilt in all caps. "But I did take a couple bottles of Coke from the back porch. And water."

"Like I said. A *really* big tip."

"Am I supposed to tell her what it's for?" Clay asked, falling into step, Kevin beside him, as Casper made for the street.

"You don't have to. Just make sure it gets into her hands and one of the kittens doesn't pick it up."

"Kittens?"

"It's what she calls the girls who work there." He opened the tailgate, motioned for Kevin to jump into the bed. Clay tossed his backpack in, too. "They wait tables and do bar top dances."

"I've seen that. In movies." Clay climbed into the cab, waiting until Casper had done the same before adding, "Someone pours booze on the bar and lights it and the girls dance in the fire."

"Arwen's place is more G-rated." Or it was until he'd followed Faith into the ladies' room and turned it triple-X. Yeah, he was some kind of cock-driven class act, putting Faith in that position when she had so much to lose.

Enough. He'd beaten himself up about it until he couldn't see straight. And she'd told him last night to forget about it. That wouldn't happen, but he would put it away. "Just so you know, I'm going to talk to a lawyer."

"About me?"

Casper nodded, pulling off Mulberry Street onto Main. "I'm taking a big risk here by not turning you in. You know that, right?"

"Yeah," was all the boy said.

"Okay. Just so we're clear."

"What'll the lawyer do?"

"I won't know until I talk to him, though I'm pretty sure he'll need to let New Mexico know you're safe."

"But not where I am? Because you know they'll send someone to get me."

"I don't know," Casper said, draping his wrist over the steering wheel. "If someone comes to get you, I'll fight to get you into a better situation, but I don't have any rights here. I don't have any leverage to make that happen. The law's not going to be on my side. The law may not give a shit."

Arms crossed, Clay slumped in his seat and turned to stare out the passenger window. "I screwed up."

"Yeah, you did," Casper said, realizing it took a lot for the boy to admit his mistake. Realizing he admired him all the more because of it.

They fell silent for the rest of the drive, heading out of town on the county highway, then down the long private road into the ranch. He watched as Clay shifted in his seat, sitting straighter, sitting forward. He tried to contain his excitement, fighting a grin, flipping back his hair to prove he was still cool, still unmovable. Not a little kid thrilled by the idea of being a cowboy.

Unwanted emotion rose in Casper's throat, jammed there like a feisty calf caught in a chute. This was stupid. Sure the kid was happy. He wasn't piled in a too-small room with others he didn't even know. And he wasn't living in a shithole, digging food from Dumpsters, scraping dried soap from the bottom of detergent boxes to wash his clothes.

But it seemed like more than that. Like hope. Like for all he'd screwed up, it wasn't the end of the world. And for all the heartache he'd known, there was something out there to reach for, a promise that things would get better. They were the same thoughts that had run through Casper's mind the first time he'd visited the ranch.

Dax had been driving, Casper beside him, Boone hunched between the two captain's chairs from the extended cab's second row of seats. All of them had better things to do, but Boone's parents were friends with Tess and Dave and told the elderly couple they'd send the threesome to lend a hand.

What they'd told the threesome was entirely different. The boys would work for the Daltons, give the pair their best, and not backtalk. They would not lie, cheat, or steal. They would not raise so much as an ounce of hell. They would not take one step out of line.

If Dax or Casper expected to ever be allowed into the Mitchell home again, or if Boone expected to ever be allowed out, they would do right by the Daltons for as long as the Mitchells saw fit.

It hadn't taken but a week for Casper and the boys to decide ranching wasn't a bad gig. It fit their rowdy ways yet reined them in by giving them structure. They'd worked their asses off, learning what it meant to be a steward of the land, burning a pasture to encourage new growth, watching a newborn calf slide into the world and wobble to its feet. Repairing pens, culling cedars, shoveling horseshit out of stalls and cleaning tack.

"You're going to have to earn your keep," Casper broke the silence to say.

"That's fine."

"Mostly at the house. There's just the two of us living there now, like I said, but the schedule we've been keeping all summer, we haven't had much time to clean since moving in. Dax's sister, Darcy, did some. But the house could use a good scrubbing."

Clay snorted. "You want me to do housework."

"Yep. That won't be all, but it'll fall on you."

"Whatever," the boy said, then after a pause asked, "Can I cook?"

"Sure."

"Cool. What about the house and the construction?"

Now that Faith and her mystery money had entered the picture, Casper figured even he would be in the way. "We'll need to go through the contents the next few days before the crews start, but that should be it."

"Will I get to ride a horse?"

That brought a smile to Casper's face. He looked over. "Do you know how?"

Clay shook his head.

"We can probably fit that in. Boone can show you how to care for the tack. Saddles and such. And you can probably take over seeing the dogs are fed and watered."

"You just have two? Three, with Kevin?"

"Once in a while a stray will show up, but Bing and Bob are the main thing."

"What about cats?"

"The Daltons, the couple who used to own the place, they had a tom who kept varmints out of the feed in the barn. Not sure what happened to him. If any come around, you can see to them, too."

Clay sat straighter then. "Is that it?"

The house was two stories, painted white but faded, the shutters on the windows once a dark pine green. The structure squatted on the left of the main ranch yard. The barn, big and brown and sprawling, as well as the corral and the new holding pen was to the right, along with the chutes used for sorting and working the cattle.

Nodding, Casper tried to see the place through young eyes, hopeful eyes. Eyes that had taken in too much garbage and hurt. That had found escape in words printed on the page. That had watched out for predators, for guns, badges, and spinning cherry-tops, for places to hole up safely to sleep.

The boy had said he'd seen worse than what he'd found in the house on Mulberry Street. And suddenly feeling like he might be sick, Casper knew that he had. That he'd shared the chilling fear Casper had known, the crawling hunger, the pain of heat and cold.

As the fence line fell away and the yard opened up in front of them, as Bing and Bob scampered to meet his truck and Boone climbed down from the cab of the flatbed, as Dax walked out of the barn leading Flash, the fringe of his chaps swinging, it took all the strength Casper had not to weep.

FIFTEEN

"Tell me again why we're doing this legal crap in Luling instead of using Darcy or Greg."

Though Faith had wanted to drive, Casper had insisted, which meant his eyes were on the road and he wasn't able to see the exasperated expression she was finding herself forced to perfect just for him.

Pain-in-the-ass cowboy. "For the eight millionth time, it's about privacy."

"Yeah, yeah, but lawyers can't talk about confidential client stuff, so what's the deal?"

They'd been over and over this the last week since she'd set up today's appointment. He was being purposefully obtuse, and that meant he wanted something. His habit was to goad her when he did. "The deal is, I don't want Darcy or Greg even knowing about this partnership. I don't want anyone in Crow Hill knowing. Not now. Not yet."

"Might as well add *not ever*," Casper said, and since he had, she didn't have to. When she remained silent, he let it drop with a heavy, frustrated sigh, asking instead, "So who's the shark in Luling?"

She closed her eyes, dropped her head against the truck's padded seat back, deciding she was insane. The sex was one thing, but no anniversary party could possibly be worth having to put up with this man. "A friend from UT."

"Someone who won't blab?"

Good lord. "She won't blab."

"Someone who doesn't know me so won't question the state of your mental health?"

"That was a consideration."

"Someone who knows about your money?"

It took a lot of willpower not to reach over and slug him. "I'm not talking about this with you."

"So you've said."

"And yet you keep pushing."

He paused for a moment, either letting what she'd said settle, or thinking up more ways to aggravate her. He came up with a good one. "I was thinking of putting a full disclosure clause into our agreement. If I have to tell you everything I spend your money on, you have to tell me where you got it."

"Then you can just turn this truck around," she said, her hands balled into fists in her lap. "Because you'll be signing that contract on your own."

"Prickly little thing, aren't you?"

About this, yes. She was. "Besides, I'll know what you're spending my money on since I'll be signing the checks. If we were going to make such a deal, I'd rather know about where you lived before moving into that house in Crow Hill."

He shrugged, a motion that said nothing, revealed nothing, much like the blank look he kept on his face any time she pressed about his past, which kinda made them even. She imagined his eyes might show something more, but they were hidden behind a pair of aviator shades that surprised her with how much attitude they added to his face.

"Best I can recall, we lived in Houston until I was about seven," he said, glancing into his rear-view mirror then back at the long, flat highway. "I went to kindergarten and first grade there. Second, too, I'm pretty sure. Third grade is when I remember new teachers and a different building, really small, and not knowing anybody."

"Still in Texas?"

"Yeah, we moved a lot after that, but we never left the state." He punched the accelerator, zoomed around a truck pulling a livestock trailer. Faith waved away the smell of cow shit, and Casper snorted. "I need to get you on a horse. Let you get a whiff of what I deal with every day."

She'd been to the ranch often enough to have an idea. "Thanks, but no."

He laughed, a deep burst of unexpected emotion that had her curling her toes. She couldn't remember ever hearing him let go with that sort of honesty. Not outside of sex, anyway, but even then he held a lot of himself in check, as if afraid she might look at him too closely. As if afraid anyone would.

He sounded happy. Relaxed. She hadn't realized until this moment that most of the time he was stretched to the end of a tether, the tension ready to snap, or to whip him back and wind him up. He'd been like that years ago, too, bouncing, on edge, only letting his hair down when he had a longneck in his hand. And that couldn't be good, needing that sort of crutch to get by before even reaching adulthood.

"What?" he finally asked. "No compassion for the working conditions faced by a struggling cowboy?"

She scoffed at that. "We all have our burdens. Mine are pantyhose."

"I hate your pantyhose."

"So you've said," she replied, and swallowed the itch of his words.

He reached over, placed his hand on her thigh, slid it higher. "You probably wouldn't be so uptight if you ditched them. Wore stockings and garters instead."

"You think I'm uptight?" she asked, ignoring the second part of his supposition. Trying, too, to ignore his touch and having a hell of a hard time.

"It's probably not you as much as the job," he said, but he left his hand where it was.

She picked it up and moved it for him. "Is this because I wouldn't release the ranch's money for your house?"

"It would've been easier than going through all this legal shit."

"No, it would've been an unacceptable risk." Right. Did she really expect him to understand why that was a bad thing? "But then I don't think you'd know a risk if it reached up and took a bite out of your ass."

"I don't know what the hell you're talking about."

"Then maybe you're the one who needs to get a whiff of the messes you get yourself into on a regular basis. And I'm not just talking about the livestock."

"Do I smell like cow shit?" he asked, lifting an arm to sniff his pit.

Could one be convicted for throttling a man so purposefully obtuse? "Not today."

"But sometimes?"

Wait. He was serious? "It's not a big deal, Casper. Boone

smells the same way. I imagine Dax does, too, though I don't get that close to him."

"Well, hell."

That had her smiling, his concern that he carried his livelihood with him in such a distasteful way. "Hey, it was your choice to take up ranching. You should've known the hazards of the job."

"Like pantyhose and banking."

"Yeah," she said. "Like pantyhose and banking."

He was quiet for a minute, pensive even, checking the traffic. "I don't know that I necessarily ever wanted to ranch. I mean, I didn't have a lot of choice in high school. At least not if I wanted to keep hanging with the boys. But Dax and Boone were the ones who kept it up after we all left Crow Hill. I rodeoed."

Because something in his nature, or in what passed for his nurture, drove him to be reckless, to take those risks he denied. To be arrogant and mean and dangerous . . . And yet being here with him now, it was hard to see any of those things.

Sure, someone passing on his left and glancing over might drop back for fear of being mowed down, the picture of which brought a private smile to her face. She supposed he might intimidate people who didn't know him. Maybe even some who did.

The way his T-shirt fit his arms and chest left no doubt as to his strength, and with the brim of his battered hat pulled bad-guy low, his eyes hidden behind the dark aviators, and the stubble on his face speaking to his don't-give-a-damn . . . She could see it.

But the rest, the things she knew, the way that stubble felt against her inner thighs, her labia, the things she saw in his eyes when he looked up at her from between her legs . . .

"Why rodeo?" she asked, her voice catching on the arousal that was bringing her nipples to peaks. "Did you go to the big one in Houston while living there?"

"Hell no. That cost money. We didn't have any more then than we did after moving here." He thought a minute, huffed, then added, "Guess Suzanne hadn't yet discovered she'd been sitting on the rent all that time. Or maybe it took Leroy leaving for her to realize she didn't have any marketable skills."

Leroy. That was the first time she'd heard him speak his father's name. "She worked as a waitress, right? Before she . . . Before the other?"

"Before she starting whoring?"

She gave a quick nod. It was hard to hear him talk about this part of his past. How difficult it must've been for him to have lived it.

She wondered how old he'd been when he'd discovered what she was doing. If he'd been twelve when they moved to Crow Hill, and his father had left soon after . . . At least he hadn't been too young to know the meaning of the gossip and the disapproving looks. And at least he'd had the boys at his back by then.

"Waitresses don't even get minimum wage. At least that's how it was then. Tips make 'em or break 'em. And being broke was pretty much how we stayed. Seems to be the one lesson she taught me well," he said, the accompanying snort derisive. "Why make your own money when there'll always be someone offering a handout?"

She closed her eyes, opened them again after she'd subdued the scream clawing at her chest. "Do you think that's what this is? That I'm offering you a handout? Because that's not—"

"Relax, Faith. If I thought this was a handout, I wouldn't be giving up half a day to drive us to Luling," he said, which didn't do much to salve her. "Don't people do these things by fax or email or something?"

"Some things, yes. This particular thing, no. Sorry. It shouldn't take long to go through the paperwork, and since you have no concept of the speed limit, we should be back for you to get dirty and smelly in no time."

"Gee. Thanks."

She laughed. "You make it so easy, you know."

"What? To make me self-conscious?"

"Seriously? You're not, are you?"

"I will be now."

"Well, don't be. It's in your clothes. It's not in your skin. Your skin smells like . . ." God, could she even put it into words? The way he smelled and how it made her think of only good things? "Like fresh air. And sunshine. And . . . the earth, I guess."

"Huh. I was hoping it made you think of sex."

Her nipples pebbled again, but her banking armor of blouse and blazer hid her reaction. "If we're having sex, then I suppose it does."

"What about now?"

"I told you. You smell fine."

"Why don't you lean over here and make sure?"

"Casper—"

"Right here," he said, tapping the side of his neck.

"I can't reach you," she said, her stomach tumbling, her heart flipping, her throat tightening around the rest of her words.

He reached a hand to her hip and freed her seat belt. "Now you can."

"And if you drive off the road and I go through the windshield?"

"Oh, Faith of little faith."

She rolled her eyes at that, but couldn't help the grin forming at the corners of her mouth. Shifting in her seat, she leaned toward him, her nose just above the collar of his yoked western shirt.

"You smell fine," she said, sliding back to where she'd been sitting.

"What about right here?" he asked, and she looked over to see him popping open the top two mother-of-pearl buttons.

She stopped in the process of buckling her seat belt, thinking it was her fault the man got away with half of what he did. But that didn't stop her from bending toward his chest, her nose in the hollow of his throat.

She breathed deeply, closed her eyes, and filled herself with him again. Horses and hay and clean sweat and Ivory soap and sex. That, most of all, because smelling him took her there, to her bed, his bed, the ranch kitchen, the restroom in the Hellcat Saloon.

Then she sat back, saying nothing until he asked, "Well?"

"Yeah. You smell like sex."

It was the wrong thing to say, of course, because he jammed his foot on the accelerator, sending the truck screaming down the road. She was left speechless and breathless and waiting, her pulse in her throat nearly strangling her.

Left, too, with nothing else to say, and the realization that she didn't have it in her to stop him. Not in this, not in anything he did. He would have his way. Because that's what reckless people did. Lived in the moment, lived for the thrill. Never thinking consequences would catch up with them.

He didn't bother with a blinker, or with slowing for the rest area's posted speed limit, tearing into the empty parking lot and reaching for her as he braked. Shifting into park with his left hand as he gathered her hair at her nape in his right. Pulling her to him without so much as a by-your-leave.

He kissed her then, met her halfway between the seats, and slammed his mouth against hers. He pushed hard with his lips, slanting first one way then the other, finally using his tongue to deepen the contact, groaning when she cupped his face in her palms.

He was warm, the stubble of his beard against her wrists like a match to a striking strip, setting her on fire. Her breasts, her belly, the small of her back, her feet and her knees and her shoulders. She felt him everywhere. Wanted him everywhere.

It was a needy kiss, desperate with ignited lust, wild with unexpected longing. And all she'd done was tell him he smelled like sex. Not the act, or the scents that rose from slick bodies and sheets, but her fantasy. She'd never felt the things he made her feel.

He slid his tongue the length of hers, toyed with hers, played and mated and wound up with hers. His hunger burned her. He was hot to the touch, his face near to blistering. She blindly sought out the controls on the dash and turned the a/c to high.

Casper laughed, the sound low and throaty, a vibration in her mouth. She thought he'd pull away then, but he toned the kiss down, mumbling against her as he caught at her lips and nipped her, held her with both his mouth and his hand. She held him, too, his face, his thigh, her hand squeezing, massaging, his muscles jumping into her touch.

It was when he reached for her, urged her into his crotch, wrapped her fingers around the bulge of his cock straining there, that she knew they had to stop. This couldn't happen, she told herself, measuring him, his girth, his urgency. Not here, not now, she added, still holding him, squeezing him. Squeezing her pussy, too, moisture seeping to dampen her panties.

All of this was wrong, what they were doing, what she was feeling. He tempted her in ways she didn't know how to resist, and she was suddenly swept to another place and time when a desire less consuming than this one had gone so wrong, ended so badly. Hurt her. Hurt others.

Had she learned nothing at all?

"We need to get back on the road," she said as she pulled from him slowly.

"Or we could get a room," he said, leaning toward her and rubbing his nose against the skin beneath her ear. "You smell like sugar. Or cinnamon. Something sweet."

She brought up both of her hands and pushed against his chest, reluctant to do so because he felt so good and warm and strong and resilient. "We have to go. We have an appointment."

He sighed, his breath warm as it feathered into her hair, but he moved back into his seat, his chest rising and falling as if he'd wrestled a runaway steer to the ground. "I'm not sure I can do this."

"Do what?" she asked because the same words had been hanging on the tip of her tongue. "Be my partner?"

He stared out the windshield, his hands on the wheel, his pulse at his temple throbbing. "What if we decide to end things?"

"The sex?"

He nodded.

"Then we finish the house. I throw my parents their party. You and I go our separate ways except when it comes to the ranch finances." When he remained silent, she grew nervous, her palms clammy as she crossed her arms. "Unless you don't think we can do that."

"What I don't think is that I can hold onto that house knowing I didn't pay for it."

"Why?" She didn't understand. She was trying, but he made things incredibly difficult. She thought they'd settled this last week.

"It's a debt I don't want to owe."

Because he was trying to right past wrongs? Or because it was a debt to her? "Casper, you're making this more complicated than it is."

"No, Faith. I'm being realistic. We sign this agreement, we're bound together to the tune of a half million dollars at least." He looked over, the aviators hiding his eyes, but not the tic in his jaw, or the grim curl pulling at the sides of his mouth. "That's a forever kind of bond."

And Casper Jayne didn't do forever. "We haven't signed anything yet. Arwen's offered the Hellcat Saloon for the party—"

He interrupted her with a snort. "Your folks? In the Hellcat Saloon?"

"Whatever. I can use the money you don't want to owe me to rent the Crow Hill Country Club," she said, hating the bitchy tone to her voice. Hating more that frustration had her adding, "And you can let the house on Mulberry Street fall down around your ears. Should make it easier for you to move on, bail on Boone and Dax, return to your vagabond ways."

He said nothing, continued to stare her down, the angry flare of his nostrils making her want to rip his sunglasses away. But she didn't. She turned in her seat to look out the passenger window and waited for him to decide, half expecting him to slam his hand against the steering wheel until it broke or he bled.

But he didn't. He put the truck into gear, saying, "Let's go," as he pointed them down the road toward Luling.

She closed her eyes, let her head fall against the glass, and wondered if his instincts had been right, and everything about this partnership would turn out to be wrong. Wondered, too, why he was the one thinking straight, and she was the one who wasn't.

SIXTEEN

EVERY WEEKEND, LIKE most working people, Faith spent a good part of her time off cleaning. It wasn't how she wanted to spend those precious free hours, but there was never enough time during the week to get it all done.

She would much rather have gone out to the Dalton Ranch, saddled Sunshine, if Boone wasn't out wrangling, or Flash, if Dax was busy elsewhere, and ridden until she was exhausted, her thighs aching, her backside sore, her head full of fresh air and sunshine, career stress pounded out of her by the horse's hooves as they galloped across the land.

Taking Casper's horse, Remedy, was out of the question. Like his owner's, Remedy's personality ran to reckless, making the two of them a perfect match. And making the horse best avoided, since she doubted she'd be able to control him any better than the cowboy who saddled him daily.

She supposed it was time to buy a horse of her own. Boone had been after her to for a while, driving home the point that Sunshine, Remedy, and Flash were ranch employees and not hers to play with whenever she got the whim.

She'd driven home her foot on the toe of his boot at that, letting him know she did not show up to play on a whim. She didn't think she'd ever had a whim in her life—unless offering Casper the money she hadn't touched since it hit her bank balance counted.

But from Monday through Friday, she did little more than load her breakfast dishes into the dishwasher. She did the same with any dishes she used at supper if she cooked instead of eating at the Blackbird Diner or the Hellcat Saloon.

She wiped down her bathroom after showering each morning, and tossed her comforter over her sheets and called it making her bed. But that was the extent of her day-to-day housekeeping. Vacuuming, mopping, laundry, and anything heavy duty had to wait for the weekend.

Still, if she'd had a choice between a Saturday and Sunday cleaning her nine-hundred-square-foot apartment top to bottom, or excavating her way through the disgusting two hundred fifty square feet that made up just Casper's kitchen, she would've opted today for the first.

Her entire place had never been as dirty as this one room. The years and the elements had a lot to do with the filth, but a whole lot of it—most of it, she was pretty sure—was what his mother couldn't be bothered with and had left behind. And that had Faith thinking.

Had Casper grown up in these conditions? Had he been fed out of cans and boxes? Had Suzanne Jayne heated his food—the detrital evidence circumstantial but convincing—with a cigarette dangling from the corner of her mouth, a bottle of Jack in her free hand? Or had he been on his own after his father left, fending for himself the best he could?

How much of this had Boone known? Had he been here, seen this unholy mess? Or had things not been so bad before Casper left Crow Hill, giving Boone no need to intervene? Considering how often her brother had brought Casper home to dinner, she doubted such was the case.

And that had anger boiling through her, bubbling up the edges of her rational side until it spilled over to make her crazy, and she kicked out at the dishes and garbage stinking up this pigsty.

She couldn't help but be more than a little morose as she pictured the teenager Casper had been, the cocky heartthrob, wild and reckless and hot, living here. She hated thinking *this* place, historical significance or not, was what he'd called home, where he'd come after school, where he'd done his homework, where he'd eaten and watched TV. If he'd had a TV. Where he'd slept. It made his love of the Daltons and his dedication to the ranch, then and now, that much more poignant.

The ranch was where he'd learned another way of life, where he'd been fed Tess Dalton's pies and casseroles, where he'd been shown Dave Dalton's stern discipline, where he'd seen two people who cared more for each other than themselves, where he'd been shown the workings of a family forged not by blood but by loving bonds.

"You don't have to do this, you know."

She was sitting on the edge of the sink, too focused on pouring soap crystals into a pail of filling water to look up, though she'd heard his steps when he'd entered the room, and her pulse had leaped in her chest. "The cleaning crew will be here Monday to do the heavy lifting. Someone still has to go through the rooms and make sure there's nothing here of value."

"Trust me," he said, scraping the sole of one boot against a wad of something nasty stuck to the floor. "There's nothing here of value."

"You'll have to excuse me if I don't take your word for it," she said, shutting off the faucet. "You haven't been here in ages. Who knows what you've forgotten?"

"I haven't forgotten anything."

Something told her that no matter the good it would do him to purge this piece of his past from his mind, he never would. She got to her feet, tossed her sponge in the bucket to soak. "Fine, but I'm going to look around anyway. And I'm going to start in here, and I need more light than the fixture is putting out. This window will come clean, or it will come out."

"Do what you gotta do," he said, and she finally glanced over to see his eyes dark, his expression harsh and feral. "But I'll take care of looking around."

Now he was making her curious. What didn't he want her to see? "It's too much for one person, Casper."

He met her gaze, his finally softening as if he'd pushed aside the worst of what he'd been thinking. "You're going to be asking me about everything anyway, so I might as well do it myself."

"Sounds like you don't want me here," she said, tugging on protective gloves and turning to tackle the chore.

"No, I'm just a realist."

Standing with a foot in each side of the dual kitchen sink, she huffed and puffed as she scrubbed at the window above it, soapy water from her sponge dripping down her arms. "I don't want to be accused of not holding up my fifty percent of the workload."

"Jesus, Faith. The fifty-fifty deal does not include you cleaning what got left here when Suzanne lit the hell outta town."

"Funny you should mention your mother," she said, a bump overhead bringing a frown and an upward glance.

When she looked back, Casper was staring. "Nothing about my mother is funny."

From the little bit Faith knew about Suzanne Jayne, she'd have to agree. "How long ago did she leave Crow Hill?"

"Why don't you find that out when you call?" he asked, his brow rising with the question.

He didn't need to know that she'd already left two messages since he'd brought the paperwork with his mother's phone number by the bank a week ago. "I'm asking you."

He sighed and gave up. "Why do you want to know?"

Better. "Being in here has me thinking about you living here with her."

"And you wonder why I don't want you in here," he muttered after biting off a string of bad words.

But Faith pressed on. "I've also been thinking about you hanging out at the ranch with Dax and Boone."

He pulled a big plastic trashcan closer to where she stood, opened a cabinet door to the left of the sink. "We didn't exactly hang out. Dave would've strung us up by our bootheels if he'd caught us doing anything but working our asses off."

"Did you have chores around here?"

"Did I ever spend time here, you mean?"

Hmm. "I remember riding with Boone to drop you off sometimes."

"Was that you?" he asked, chuckling. "That little girl giving me the puppy-dog eyes."

"I did not give you puppy-dog eyes," she said, glaring at him as she looked down.

His mouth was crooked, a half-grin making it so. "You did. And I was pretty sure you were looking to give me a whole lot more."

"I was not," she said as more banging drew her gaze upward. "And what the hell is going on upstairs? You've got a bad tree limb or rats or something."

"Pretty sure I've got both."

"Well, as soon as I'm done here I'm going to go see what it is," she said, rinsing her sponge in the bucket and ringing it out.

Beside her, Casper shook his head, then reached to grab the sponge from her hands. "No, you're going to go home and enjoy what's left of the weekend. I'll deal with—"

And then a teenage boy stepped from the service staircase into the kitchen.

Well, that explained the tree limb and rats. But it didn't explain why Casper was muttering under his breath. She waited for him to finish, then asked, "Who's that?"

Casper turned. "Oh, hey. Clay, this is Faith. Faith, Clay. He's been helping me out around here."

Clay raised a hand, a shank of blond hair falling into his face. He shook it back, all cool and full of himself. "Hey. Sorry. Kevin needed to go out."

"Kevin?" Good lord. "There are more than one of you?"

"Kevin's my dog," the boy said as the shaggy white beast lumbered by and out the back door he nudged open with his nose.

Blinking away her confusion, she looked from the door back to the boy, then to Casper, then to the boy again. "He knows his way around."

"He's pretty smart. Anyway, nice to meet you." Another raised hand. "I'll go keep an eye on him."

She waited until the screen door had banged closed, then took back the sponge and asked, "What was that?"

Casper shrugged. "Clay taking Kevin out for a piss."

"Let's try this again. Who's Clay and why didn't I know about him?"

"Because I forgot to tell you?"

"Casper—"

"Fine." He breathed in, scrubbed both hands down his face. "I took him on before you and I made our arrangement."

Took him on? "Ah, I thought maybe you'd forgotten about that. That we have one. And that every part of this renovation is included."

"You're really taking this fifty-fifty thing too far."

"If I recall correctly, it was your idea." One she'd jumped to accept for some ridiculous reason. "And now I'm wondering what else you've forgotten to tell me."

All Casper did was shake his head. "Clay's not part of the deal."

"Casper—"

"He's just a boy who needed a way to earn some money, okay," he said, tossing mug after tumbler after highball glass into the trashcan to break.

"My money?" she asked, hearing a witch in her voice.

Casper heard it, too, and frowned. "No. I'm using the money Royce Summerlin's paying me."

"Wait a minute." Obviously she needed to stop and eat the lunch she'd skipped because every word out of his mouth had her dizzy and reeling. "You're working for Royce Summerlin?"

"Now *that* I know I told you about."

She remembered that morning in the bank . . . "You didn't tell me you'd gone ahead with it."

"I thought our arrangement only covered the house." He

shoveled a stack of plates on top of the rest of the broken glass. "Not what I do for money in my spare time."

She stood, went back to scrubbing at her frustrations and the glass. "Must be nice, having spare time. I know Boone wishes he did."

"Boone could give up sleep the same way I'm doing."

"He'll have to if you break your neck and he has to take on your share of the work at the ranch."

"I'm not going to break my neck. Two-thousand-pound bulls, remember? My neck's still in one piece."

"Ribs, then. Your arms. A leg."

"Faith, I'll be fine."

She reminded herself he was a grown man, which didn't help because grown men should know better. And grown men shouldn't be so good at changing the subject. "That doesn't answer my question about Clay."

He dragged the trashcan to the back door. "I don't want to talk about Clay."

"Is he from Crow Hill? What's his last name?"

"Whitman."

Huh. "I don't know anyone named Whitman."

"Do you know everyone in Crow Hill?" he asked after he'd maneuvered the full can onto the porch and returned with another that was empty.

"Believe it or not, yes. Or if I don't know them, I've heard of them. I grew up here. I work at the only bank. My parents are both employed by the school district. It's hard not to be familiar with most everyone around."

"He's not from here."

"From where then?"

"I met him in Albuquerque. I knew his mother."

She slowed her scrubbing, the bubbles of soap bursting, the light from outside trying so hard to get in. "You slept with his mother, you mean." When he didn't deny her charge, she found the courage to ask the obvious. "Is he yours?"

"Mine? Hell, no. He's too old to be mine."

"That's bullshit." Scrubbing again. Scrubbing, scrubbing, scrubbing. "You could totally have a kid his age."

"Okay. But he's not mine. I was in Albuquerque six years ago. And he's fourteen."

"So what's he doing here now?"

"Helping me out with the house."

"What about his parents?"

It took him too long to answer, and then he only came back with a question. "What about them?"

"Good lord." And then it hit her. "Is he a runaway?"

He stood at the back door, hands on his hips, staring out, she assumed, at the boy and his dog. "Just drop it, okay? I'm handling it."

He was harboring a runaway and called that handling? Was he out of his mind? "Do you know how much trouble you could be in? How much trouble *he* could be in?"

"I'm handling it, so butt out."

"We're business partners. I can't butt out of what involves me."

"This does not involve you," he yelled before holding up a hand and reversing the step he'd taken toward her. "I'm sorry. Let me do that again. This," he said, his voice level and calm, "does not involve you."

"Casper—"

He was nearly on top of her when he hissed out, "His mother's dead. Dead, okay? He came here because he doesn't have anyone else."

She swallowed, dropped her gaze from his to the bucket of black water. "That doesn't make sense."

"Since when does life make sense?"

"What about foster care?"

He huffed. "Yeah, that always turns out well."

"I'm not that naive. I know it doesn't. But it's how the system's set up."

"The system could use some improving."

"Agreed, but it doesn't fall on you to do that."

"I'm not trying to improve it. I'm trying to give Clay a chance."

"To do what?" she asked, finally looking up. "Learn there aren't consequences? That he can cut and run and not have to answer for it? Is he staying at the ranch?"

"Most of the time, yeah," he admitted.

Crap. "Don't tell me Boone's okay with this."

"Boone knows what's up. Dax, too. And I'm going to talk to a lawyer. Get things sorted out legally."

She supposed that should make her feel better, but she wasn't there yet. She peeled off her gloves, rubbed at her forehead. "I cannot believe this. Every time I think I have a handle on you, you pull another rabbit out of your hat and I realize I don't know you at all."

"Are you trying to know me?" he asked, coming closer, his eyes dark again, his expression feral. "Do you want to know me? You need to really be sure, because I can tell you some stories—"

The screen door opening cut him off and surely saved her. She looked past Casper as Kevin and Clay came back in. He gave her another iffy wave on his way to the staircase. "Clay," she called out before thinking about what she was doing, just knowing she had to step in.

"Yes, ma'am?"

"Are you working on something upstairs, or does Casper have you up there hiding from me?"

The flush on his face was the only answer she needed. She looked over at the man responsible for the gray hair she'd found this morning. "We could use another pair of hands in here."

"Yes, ma'am," was all he said.

SEVENTEEN

The Hellcat Saloon was dark and cold, and just what the doctor ordered. Since the trip from the bank didn't give her car's a/c enough time to cool the interior, Faith had made the drive over with her windows down. If she was going to breathe in hot air, it might as well be fresh.

She really should do something about a new car. And one day, she really should go ahead and think about buying a house. Or building a house. She'd lived in the same apartment since returning to Crow Hill after graduating from UT. She'd been driving her car just as long.

It was stupid to have so much money and do absolutely nothing with it. But spending it meant explaining it and admitting to having it and that led back to the reasons why. She didn't ever want to talk about the why. She tried not to even *think* about the why.

Her family knew, and had kept the secret for her sake, but

also because of what her actions had cost them. The gossip. The legal kerfuffle. Thankfully, not their jobs. And now she was having to hide it from Casper when he might actually be the one person sympathetic to the crap she'd gotten herself into. He was the one who kept telling her she was too tight.

Well, look what happened when she let down her guard. Was it any wonder? And now this thing with Clay. What in the world had Casper been thinking, hiding the boy now for over two weeks? God, her life. Every day seemed to come loaded lately with *one more goddamn thing.*

"Quite a stir being caused over on Mulberry Street," Arwen said as Faith climbed onto a stool at the bar.

Still caught up in her musings, she frowned and asked, "What's that?"

"Mulberry Street. Seems to be all anyone is talking about." Arwen swiped a towel across the bar top, picked up a stray stir stick and peanut shell. "I'll bet Casper hates the attention with the fire of a thousand Texas suns."

"Can I get a frozen margarita?" Faith wasn't taking the bait. She'd promised Casper she wouldn't blab any more than she already had.

"Sure, sweetie." Arwen disappeared beneath the bar and came up dusting her hands. "Strawberry? Pineapple?"

"Mango would be great, if it's still on the menu."

"Yep. I'll have Adelita mix one up," the other woman said, waiting another beat before adding, "just as soon as you tell me about everything going on at the house."

Faith sighed. She supposed discussing the renovations in general terms wouldn't count as blabbing, unless she revealed things only someone close to the project would have knowledge of. "How about I tell you what little I know as soon as I've got a margarita in front of me? Large, please."

"And a plate of nachos. I'm not letting you drive home on nothing but one of Adelita's large drinks."

"Fine," Faith said, knowing the bartender's generous hand with tequila and that Arwen was right. She also knew nachos would accompany her liquid dinner a lot better than fries.

"Good girl." Arwen slapped the bar top, then walked away to place the order.

While waiting, Faith leaned her elbows on the bar and massaged her temples, trying not to think about anything. Not work or Casper. Not the house or Casper. Not her money or Casper. Not how sore her inner thighs were or Casper.

But the applied pressure didn't help because it made her remember his hands and his fingers and the way he used his thumbs, the circles he rubbed at the base of her skull, on the soles of her feet and her shoulders, how he did the same between her legs with the head of his cock, spreading her moisture, teasing her clit—

"Here ya go."

Faith reached for the glass with both hands and swallowed a quarter of the contents, stopping only to avoid the pain of an oncoming brain freeze.

Arwen moved the glass, slid the plate of nachos in front of her. "Did you come here just to drink?"

"No. I had a reason. Give me a minute and I'll find it."

"You do look exhausted."

"I'm not sure exhausted covers how tired I am. I've got to get more sleep."

"Going to bed alone's the best cure for that."

"Yeah, well, it's not like I plan these all night things," she blabbed, reaching for a tortilla chip loaded with refried beans, pico de gallo, chile con queso, and thick jalapeño slices.

"I think that's a Dalton Gang thing. Going all night." Arwen twisted her hair against the back of her head and secured it with a pencil. "Dax was the same way. I'd wake up to find him inside me and that was it."

Good lord. "As happy as I am for you? There really is a thing as too much sharing."

Arwen laughed. "Sorry. Just figured we could bond over the whole gang member old lady thing."

At that, Faith nearly choked. Then she finally relaxed and laughed. "Is that what we are? Old ladies of gang members?"

"Or something. Though I'm still waiting for my official grim reaper riding gear."

"I'm not sure they make that stuff for horses."

"Thank God, though my ass would look great in chaps. Now tell me about the house."

"Sure," she said, trying to decide how much an old lady of a gang member, as opposed to a fifty-fifty partner, would know. "It's coming together. Diego Cruz, he works part time at the ranch?" she asked, just to be sure Arwen knew. "His parents own a janitorial service, so Casper cut a deal with them to do the major clean-up inside, getting rid of what furniture's still there, window coverings, all the crap in the yard, things like that."

"Is there a lot?"

"Some. None of it worth anything, he says. I know Casper junked a ton of small stuff. Broken dishes. An old toaster oven. What used to be a TV cabinet. Suzanne's things."

"You were there?"

"For some of it. On the weekend."

"Hmm."

"What does that mean, hmm?"

"Nothing. Go on," she said, filching one of Faith's nachos.

"John Massey was good friends with Dave Dalton, so Massey Construction worked out a payment plan Casper could live with. They'll be starting the construction next Monday." Meaning Faith had one more weekend to spend making sure the inside of the house was cleared. "And, yes, I contributed my financial skills to the project to make sure no one was getting screwed."

"Good to have friends in high places."

"You know Crow Hill as well as I do. You can connect everyone in town through six degrees of separation, if not less."

"Still. I'm surprised he's moving forward so quickly. I thought he'd need more time to get the cash together."

"He's working part time for Royce Summerlin," Faith said, reaching for her drink and downing another quarter.

"That's right. Dax mentioned he was breaking horses for extra income, but I didn't put two and two together. Guess I thought the money would be going into the ranch." Arwen replaced Faith's damp napkin before she returned the glass to the bar. "Royce must pay a lot better wages than I do."

"I honestly have no clue what Casper's making from Royce." And that was the truth. "All I did was look over the Massey paperwork." Another truth. "And since that money's not part of the ranch partnership, he's not obligated to run it through me or the bank." A final truth, though there were so many bits and pieces she was leaving out that the whole thing felt like a lie.

"Makes sense," Arwen said as Faith used one chip to scrape beans onto another. "But you didn't come here to tell me about the house. Or Casper's finances. And you said you're not here to get drunk, but that there was something . . ."

Lord, she mused, holding up a finger while she chewed. The party. Of course. "I came here to offer you a compromise."

Arwen frowned. "I didn't know we had anything to compromise on."

"It's about the anniversary party. I've found another venue," she said, rushing on to keep Arwen from asking for details. "But

Boone and I decided we want to serve barbecue, and before I ask Smokin' Joe's about catering, I'm here to ask you."

"Smokin' Joe's won the July Fourth cook-off."

"Smokin' Joe's isn't owned and operated by one of my very best friends."

"Well, that's certainly true."

"So you can work me up a quote?"

"Sure thing. I need all the information you can give me. Date, time. How many people are you expecting? What crazy items does Boone want on the menu?"

"I see my brother's reputation is alive and well," Faith said with a laugh, waiting for Arwen to find a pen and order pad to scratch out some preliminary notes. "But we're not doing anything crazy. Except the beer, I guess. You know how my dad is about his funky little brewhouse labels."

"I think we've got plenty to make the coach happy. We've just taken on three new microbreweries, though the good stuff does not come cheap."

And Boone would know if she went over their budget. He knew beer as thoroughly as their father did. "I don't care. Boone can get as bent out of shape as he wants to. This will be my treat. He and Daddy love comparing notes on new finds. It'll be fun."

They spent the next thirty minutes discussing menu items, the meats—brisket, chicken, ribs—the sides—potato salad, cole slaw, ranch beans, Texas toast—the relishes—red onions, sliced dill pickles, cheese-stuffed and grilled jalapeños—and the desserts—chocolate pecan sheet cake, banana pudding, peach cobbler.

"And I'd love to have fried okra for Boone, but not sure that's feasible. It's never as crispy reheated as when first out of the oil."

"I'll see what I can do." Arwen smiled as she scribbled the last note. "I love how happy you are to have him home."

"You think I'm happy, you should see my folks. It's like Momma can't wait for Sunday morning services to be over so she can hurry home and get lunch ready. I don't remember her ever hurrying when it was just the three of us."

"He comes to church?"

"He's been a time or two, but usually he spends Sunday morning working, then the rest of the day at the house."

"I never did understand his leaving," Arwen said, tapping the eraser end of the pencil on the bar. "Except for the fact that there's not a lot of reason to stay here—unless one has a family business to keep running."

"And so many of the kids we went to school with do."

"I know. Josh has taken over the feed store. And since Dax decided to cowboy and Darcy left the family firm, Greg, the bastard son"—Arwen paused—"is now in charge of Campbell and Associates."

"How's Dax dealing with the half-brother thing?"

"It's life. He'll get over it." Arwen grabbed another nacho, then asked, "Boone never had any interest in coaching football? I can see him going all Friday Night Lights."

"Not in coaching. Not in business." She tried to picture her brother behind a desk or on the sidelines, and failed. "Boone loves ranching, and the Mitchells are not a ranching family. He could've stayed on with the Daltons, but it wasn't the same once Dax left. Then Casper followed, and that was it. He was the only one who knew anything about how Dave wanted things done."

"And he was only eighteen."

Not even that. "He didn't turn eighteen until late that summer. Dax and Casper were already gone, and he was seventeen, trying to run the show. The hands Dave was able to find weren't taking orders from a kid, and it got to be too much."

"He never wanted to go to school?"

Faith shook her head. "He was lost without his boys. Hard to believe, with the three of them coming from as different backgrounds as any three people could, but they were his rocks. It was like he couldn't function in Crow Hill without them here. So he left." She readied another loaded nacho for her mouth. "I just don't want anything to happen to make him feel that way again."

"What way? Unable to function? Why would he?"

"Maybe not unable to function, but unable to make things work."

"Like with the ranch."

"Yeah. Especially now that Casper's so busy with the house."

"And with Summerlin's horses."

Faith nodded, thinking that he was also busy being a surrogate father to Clay. And bedding her. "It's not fair to Boone to have to pick up the slack."

"It's not fair to Dax, either."

"Oh, no. Of course, not," she said, but Arwen's comment had her frowning. "Has Dax complained about the extra work?"

"I'm pretty sure Dax doesn't feel he has the right. He bailed on a lot of hours the first few weeks we were together. He said he was using his own time, but I don't think he had any more then than Casper does now. So yeah. I'm thinking it's Boone's turn to do some slacking."

"I don't think Boone knows how to slack."

"Hmm. Does he ever see anyone? Date?"

"Date? Not that I know of. Does he see anyone? I couldn't say."

"I'm guessing he does something about sex."

"He's a man so I'm guessing he does, but he's my brother first, and I really don't want to go there."

Arwen laughed. "You know who'd be perfect for him. Everly."

“Really?” Faith asked as she drained her glass. “I thought you were going to say Kendall.”

“Hmm.”

Faith waggled a finger. “Uh-uh. No matchmaking.”

But Arwen ignored her. “Will they all be at the party?”

“Boone will be, but the guest list is mostly my folks’ friends.”

“If I’m going to do the catering, I will need help . . .”

“You have Luck and the others,” Faith said, though she loved the idea of Kendall and Everly being there with her. And matchmaking or not, she didn’t think either of them had met Boone . . .

“I do,” Arwen said, taking away Faith’s empty glass. “But I’m all about two birds and one stone. Or in this case, two girls flying free and one very hard man.”

EIGHTEEN

"I GOT AN UNEXPECTED phone call today," Casper said, watching for a hint of guilt, or at least curiosity, in Faith's expression.

She was too busy looking at the pages of the Cruz Cleaning invoice spread across the bleached-within-an-inch-of-its-life kitchen island to look up. "Oh, yeah?"

"Yeah." He'd been on his way to Mulberry Street to pick up the bill left there by Alberto Cruz when he'd seen her car at the Hellcat Saloon. Since she was the one wielding the Ebenezer Scrooge pen, he'd called, inviting her to make the trip with him.

She was obviously still under the influence of what she'd described as a fish bowl of a margarita. Either that, or she couldn't be bothered to pay attention to him when there were dollar signs swimming in front of her eyes.

He tried again. "They left a voice mail."

"Who?"

Jesus. "Someone at the Texas Historical Commission."

"Interesting," she said, running a finger along a line item and screwing her mouth to the side.

He didn't know if she was talking about what he'd said or what she was looking at. "What's most interesting is that they had my phone number."

"Okay."

"I'm figuring you gave it to them."

That finally brought her head up. Her brow knitted into a frown as she considered him. "What?"

Jesus H. "Have you heard anything I've said?"

"You got a call from the Texas Historical Commission. And you think I gave them your phone number."

"Did you?"

"I did not."

"Well, hell."

"What did they want?" she asked, folding up the bill from the cleaning service, returning it to its envelope, then stuffing it into her purse.

"To talk to me about the house. To come see it. To find out what I know about its history so they can start digging for whatever documents will prove what I say." Not that he'd said anything. And he sure had nothing to prove.

"What did you tell them?" she asked, pushing her hair from her face and staring up at him as if she'd never seen him before.

Jesus H. Christ. "Are you sure you only had one margarita?"

"Yes, I'm sure. What did you tell them?"

He pushed away from the island, crossed to the sink to stare out the window at the yard. It was nothing but dirt, but it had been cleared of all debris and detritus. He didn't think he'd ever seen it look so empty. "I haven't called them back."

"But you will, yes?"

He turned around, hooked his palms over the lip of the sink at his sides, and leaned into it. "I'm not having one of those ugly brown historical markers posted out front."

"Why not?" she asked, crossing her arms. "It's an amazing honor. You own a piece of Texas history."

Lot of good it was doing him. "I don't want a bunch of yahoos stopping by to gawk."

"It's not like they'll be coming inside."

"You say that now, but just wait."

"You know," she said, finally grinning. "You could be singlehandedly responsible for a huge bump in Crow Hill's economy. Visitors filling up on gas at Bandy's. Stopping for snacks at Nathan's. Dropping by the Blackbird for lunch. Touring the Lange's winery."

Ah, but that's where she was wrong. "Not singlehandedly. This wouldn't be happening without you."

She shrugged it off. "Something no one will ever need to know."

"I know. And it bugs the crap outta me."

"Why?" she asked, frowning.

"I've seen the bills. I know what you're putting into this place."

"So?"

"The money. Where'd you get it?" he asked, because that was what was bugging him most of all.

She crossed to the old six-burner stove Massey Construction would be hauling off next week and picked up one of the broken grates. "That's my business."

"We're in this business together. Fifty-fifty, remember?"

"The business of putting your house back together," she said, dropping the grate back in place. It clanked, and the clank echoed, and then she said, "Not the business of my bank account."

Casper was quiet for a long moment, wanting to let it go but unable to. The woman was an enigma, straight-laced yet bound in secrets, and he couldn't figure her out. "I don't think you earn enough to have put aside that much in savings. And you don't seem like the type to have taken a risk on the market, even when the market wasn't shit."

She said nothing, just made her slow way around the kitchen, which was now empty of trash.

"And if it was an inheritance, I'd think Boone would've come into some money, too, and I know that didn't happen unless he's holding out on me and Dax."

She shot him a glance. "Boone would never do that."

"Exactly. Which is why I'm pretty sure you didn't inherit your fortune."

"It wasn't an inheritance. And it's not a fortune."

Then they had different ideas of what made one. "You're writing four- and five-figure checks like picking up a penny from the pavement."

"Then it's a wee little bitty one," she said, holding a thumb and index finger a half-inch apart.

"If that's the case, it shouldn't be such a big deal to tell me about it," he said, and then he waited, because he was all out of arguments and wasting his time.

She circled the kitchen island, braced her forearms against it on the opposite side, and looked across the room at him. "What are you doing about Clay?"

And here we go with the change of subject. "What about Clay?"

"Have you let the authorities in New Mexico know he's here and safe?"

"Not yet," he said, holding her gaze.

A dark brow went up. "Why not?"

"I still need to talk to Greg."

"Greg Barrett?"

He nodded. "I want to know what options are out there."

"Options for what? And why not Darcy?"

"Options for Clay. And because I don't want her involved. She's Dax's sister." He huffed and crossed his arms. "I know how sisters worry about the trouble their brothers get into."

She stuck out her tongue at that. "Are you thinking of having Clay stay here? Permanently?"

"I don't know. Would it be so bad if he did?"

"Would he live with you? In the house?"

"I live at the ranch. And there's plenty of room for him there. Plenty of chores, too."

"Hold on." She lifted a finger. "I'll get back to Clay in a minute."

"You don't have to," he said, but it was a pipe dream like most of his others.

"After all the work and money we're putting into this place, you're not going to live here?"

"Why would I?"

"Because . . . Look at it, Casper. Why wouldn't you want to live here?"

He didn't need to look at it. He knew every square inch by heart. "It's a near thirty-minute drive to the ranch. I work at the ranch. Living there means I roll out of bed and into the barn or onto a horse. It's easy. The house there is comfortable. This place . . ." He knocked his knuckles against the countertop beside him that was chipped and cracked and ready to be replaced. "This place is going to be too much. I'd have to worry about what I might carry in on the soles of my boots."

"You leave your boots on the back porch of the ranch house now. I've seen them out there. I've *smelled* them out there."

His boots were only part of it. "If I live here, I have to pay more for gas for my truck. And there's no way I can afford to cool this place. Even if I broke horses for the rest of my life."

"You don't have to break them now. I'm paying for the house."

"I'm paying to feed and clothe a fourteen-year-old boy."

"That's temporary."

"Maybe. Maybe not," he said, defensiveness seeping into his words.

She straightened and crossed her arms, mirroring him. The kitchen island was a sea between them. "I didn't think you were serious."

"I don't know that I am. Not yet. But I do know I'm not going to just throw him back to the wolves if there's something better for him out there."

"You think that something better is you?" she asked, her voice soft, but still doubting, as if she didn't believe he could be a parent. Didn't believe in him.

He took a deep breath, scrubbed at his face. "I said I don't know. I haven't had a lot of time to let it settle. Or to see how he fits in."

"If you're thinking about custody, it can't be about him fitting in. It has to be about him. Period. He's not a toy. Or a dog. You can't change your mind and ask for a refund."

"You don't think I know that?" he yelled, his voice echoing, coming back, repeating in his ears. "And I would never change my mind about a dog."

"Good. Because even if he'll be a legal adult in four years, if you take him on now, if you give him what no one else will, the ties you make will last a lifetime."

He didn't need to hear this. He couldn't think for the hard knot in his throat choking him. He didn't know shit about being a father figure, but he did know he couldn't turn his back on this boy.

"Are we done here?"

"With some things, yeah."

God fucking damn. He pointed a finger at her. "You keep hassling me about Clay, I'll keep digging for the truth about your money."

"I wouldn't expect anything less."

This woman. She, not a heart attack, not any bucking bronc or bull, was going to send him to an early grave.

"Are you going to drive me back for my car?" she asked, reaching for her purse.

"I could. Or we could stay here," he said, done arguing, done thinking, done digging into her truth and his soul.

"Here?"

He came to her, hooked an arm around her neck, and brought her close. "A lot more private than the ranch."

"A lot less comfortable, too."

"Maybe. But I've never done it in my own house," he said, dropping his gaze to the front of her blouse and the army of buttons keeping her safe. "Wouldn't take us but a couple of weeks to christen all the rooms."

"A couple of weeks?" She blew out a skeptical breath. "You can go that many times a night?"

"I say you try me."

"That may work in your fantasy, but not in my reality. I wouldn't be able to walk. I might not even be able to sit."

He moved his fingers to the first of the buttons. "That leaves flat on your back, my favorite position. Except for being flat on mine."

"I thought your favorite position was any way you could get it."

"And here I didn't think you knew me at all."

"I know you better than you realize."

"That so," he said, freeing more of her buttons and slipping a hand into the cup of her bra.

"I know what you're doing."

"I should hope so."

"You're trying to distract me."

"Am I?"

Her eyes drifted shut. Her head lolled to the side. "You don't want me pointing out all the ways I know you."

"That's because the only one I care about is you knowing what to do with my cock," he said, bending to pull her nipple into his mouth, sucking on her, licking his way around her pebbled areola.

She groaned, leaned into him. "Can I tell you something?"

"Anything, sweetheart."

"I get wet when you do that. And when I'm wet I can't wait for you to fuck me."

He laughed and licked harder. He couldn't remember ever hearing Faith Mitchell utter the word fuck. "I've gotta get me one of those margaritas."

"I'm a total lightweight," she said, pushing off his hat and scraping her nails through his buzzed hair. "I couldn't make heads or tails of Cruz's invoice."

"Sounds like a really good time to take advantage of you," he said, his cock twitching, thickening, growing long in his shorts.

"I agree," she said. "But not in the kitchen. We did the kitchen at the ranch house. And the bathroom at the saloon. And the parking lot at the cafe. And both our bedrooms."

"Your choice, sweetheart," he said, though the last thing he wanted to do was move. He was happy where he was, her tit in his mouth, her hands letting him know she liked having him there.

Or she seemed to be liking it until she pushed him away. "The ballroom. The middle of the ballroom. Right beneath the spot where the chandelier will hang."

First he was hearing about a chandelier, but he didn't argue. He didn't even stop to snatch his hat from the kitchen floor, but let her pull him down the house's long center hallway and into the first-floor's grand room. This room held no memories. This room had remained empty and unused the years he'd lived here. This room wouldn't strangle the air from his lungs the moment he shoved himself into her.

He might talk big about doing her in every space, but the truth was a different animal. There were some corners, some closets, some hidden crannies where he wouldn't be able to get it up, not with a thousand whores' mouths trying.

But Faith didn't have to know any of that. And thinking about those places now was about the dumbest thing he could do—especially with the woman in front of him wet and waiting.

While Faith stared up at the high ceiling and held her arms out to her sides, he jerked his T-shirt over his head and tossed it to the floor. His boots followed, then his jeans. He yanked his belt from the loops to get the buckle out of the way, laying the denim on the floor, the cotton shirt on top, doing what he could to create padding between bones and hard wood.

Coming up behind her in his socks and his shorts, he slid her jacket from her shoulders, added it to the makeshift bed. Next came her blouse, and while he got rid of her skirt, she did the same with her pantyhose. When he started to strip away her underthings, she stopped him.

"No," she said. "Not yet."

And then she backed away, her eyes wide and teasing, her mouth silently laughing. She spun, dropped to her hands and knees on his pallet, gave a toss of her hair and a look over her shoulder.

God*damn* the woman was hot. Her ass all up in the air like an offering. Her tits dangling as she moved from her hands to her elbows, wiggling her backside and inviting him in, the fabric of her panties hiding little and showing off the rest.

He was out of his shorts and on his knees, his cock sprung before he'd even taken a breath. He tugged her panties down her thighs, released the clasp of her bra to free her tits. He braced one hand on the small of her back, gripped his shaft with the other, and guided himself into her cunt, nearly losing his mind as he did.

She was right about being wet, and it was a damn good thing. She was so hot and so tight he had to work his way in, spreading her juices with the head of his cock before driving himself to the hilt. Once there, he stopped, his hands at her hips, his hips flush to hers, and let his head fall back on his shoulders.

He stayed there, throbbing, pulsing, his balls drawing hard into his body, his ass clenching as he held on to his load. This was crazy insane, the way she stripped away his control. The way she crooked a finger or wiggled her ass and he dropped what he was doing to pant after her. *And* he didn't even care, didn't try to stop himself. He just followed his dick, mindless.

She did this to him. Faith. No woman before had looked into him and demanded so much from him and seen past his walls. She wormed and dug, and he gave it up. Around her, his resistance was gone. One of these days he'd looked into why, but for now all that mattered was fucking her, losing himself in her, giving her what her ass was begging for.

He ground against her, scooting the pallet of clothing a

couple of inches before anchoring it with his knees. Faith gasped, pushed herself flush to his groin. He clenched his thighs, his buttocks, his fingers on her hips, and began to thrust, slamming against her again and again, the flesh-on-flesh slaps like gunshots in the big empty room.

Each time he hit bottom, she grunted. Each time he pulled back, she moaned. She moved her forehead to one wrist, and he felt her other hand at her pussy, playing with her clit, playing with him. He pumped, squeezed his eyes closed, pumped, opened them, pumped, knew there was no way he was going to last, and let go.

She came up on her hands when he stiffened behind her, grinding her hips in a wicked figure eight and tugging him in all the right ways. He shuddered, grunted, then felt her contractions begin to flutter before she tossed back her head and cried out.

They collapsed together, Faith on the pallet, he on the floor that had been recently cleaned, yet still smelled of mildew and rot. He nudged her to move off his clothes. "C'mon, sleeping beauty. You're going to turn into a pumpkin."

Smiling, she rolled toward him, wrapped her arms around him, stared into his eyes. "You're mixing up your fairy tales, cowboy."

"That's because I don't know a damn thing about making dreams come true," he said more bitterly than he'd intended, and then he kicked himself when she let him go and the light went out in her eyes.

NINETEEN

FAITH WAS LOATH to get up the next morning, rolling against Casper to absorb his warmth, to smell the musk of him, to feel the dip in the bed from his weight, his skin that in certain places was just as soft as hers, but in others was dusted with coarse hair and baked by the sun.

It was nice having him here. Comfortable. Comforting. And that was strange since she'd never felt uncomfortable here at all.

She'd been sleeping in this room since returning to Crow Hill after college. She'd changed out her mattress once, her furniture a couple of times, and her decor a half dozen until settling on the current look that made her think of sweet magnolias and a summer breeze.

It didn't exactly fit with the hacienda-themed complex, but with the cane ceiling fan stirring the air and the gauze panels hanging from her canopy, she could shed the stress of her banking career and relax.

Before Casper, she'd never brought a man to her bed. The very few . . . dalliances she'd engaged in had occurred elsewhere. A posh hotel room in San Antonio. Her lover's home. A blanket under the stars when she'd dated a rancher from Gonzales for several months. Her most sexually adventurous years had been in college. Since then, she'd spent most of her nights alone.

She didn't mind, really. She wasn't sure if she hadn't yet met the right man, or if she wasn't intended to be part of a couple. She was opinionated and insistent and sometimes rude, and she sure wouldn't want those qualities in a partner—a thought that had her chuckling into her pillow because of the rude, insistent, opinionated man beside her.

"Why are you laughing at seven o'clock in the morning?" he grumbled.

This from the man who worked cattle at dawn? "Why are you still sleeping at seven o'clock in the . . . Shit! It's seven o'clock?" A look at the bedside alarm confirmed it. The alarm she'd forgot to set because she'd been too busy trying to convince Casper dreams were overrated. She groaned. "I am so, so, *so* unbelievably late. And you are, too."

She tossed back the covers and flew through her morning routine, allowing herself no time to think what it meant that she'd slept so soundly because Casper had been sleeping beside her. Yes, Adelita's large margarita had helped, but she remembered him being there, remembered pushing her foot toward him and settling her sole at his knee.

Remembered thinking it strange that neither one of them dreamed.

By the time she'd showered and dressed and was hopping into the kitchen on one foot, pulling her shoe onto the other, Casper was pouring her a travel mug of coffee. His face was scruffy, his

T-shirt hanging at his hips instead of tucked into his jeans, one leg of those bunched up at the top of his boot.

He held her gaze as he handed it to her, sipping his own, saying nothing though speaking volumes. His eyes took her in—her still-damp hair flipping on the ends, her lips bare of gloss, her suit jacket folded over one arm—finally shaking his head as he glanced at her legs and her pantyhose. That had her smiling as she took a swallow of coffee. She hated them as much as he did.

They walked to the parking lot together, Casper following her to her car. She couldn't help but wonder how many of the complex residents knew the strange truck parked beside her was his, or how many would've assumed the overnight guest to be hers. Not that there would be any doubt now, the two of them together, in public, when she'd sworn to be circumspect.

Just her luck by the time she saw Boone later, he'd have heard where Casper spent the night. Last time he'd parked at a distance. This time they were side by side. It was too much to hope she could escape discovery a second time, especially with him standing there, so obviously with her.

Great, she mused, sliding into her seat and wondering why in the world she couldn't stick to her guns. This wasn't a whole lot different from the near-public display at the Hellcat Saloon. She'd promised Arwen then the same thing she'd promised herself. She would not let things with Casper get out of hand.

And yet here they were, both drinking coffee, neither of them quite put together, Casper barely dressed. Yeah. She was the queen of self-control, rolling her eyes as she turned the key in the ignition . . . and nothing. Nothing. The car was completely dead.

It hadn't wanted to start when she'd left Arwen's after Casper had taken her back there from Mulberry Street, and it had been iffy after work yesterday, but she'd thought the drive home would charge it. Visiting Bandy's Garage on her lunch hour had been the plan, but now . . . Crap.

"Can you give me a jump?"

One hand on her doorframe, the other on the top of the car, Casper leaned in. "You got cables?"

"Good lord. Don't you?"

"In the flatbed. Not with me." He straightened, held open her door. "C'mon. I'll drop you off."

"I need my car after work to go talk to Boone."

"Then give me your keys," he said, holding out his hand. "I'll stop at Bandy's and have Skeet bring you out a new battery. He can drop the car at the bank when he's done."

Hoping it *was* just her battery, she gathered her things, locked up the car, and worked the key from the ring while climbing into Casper's truck. When she handed it to him, he kept hold of her hand, and even when they reached the bank parking lot less than ten minutes later, he didn't let her go.

She tugged until he finally did, then reached for her jacket in the seat beside her, her purse on the floor, tucking her travel mug in an inside pocket. "Hold on," he said, and the tone of his voice stopped her.

She thought of her boss impatiently waiting for her to arrive, thought of today's scheduled conference with Greg Barrett and Philip Hart, thought about waking this morning, spineless and at peace. "Casper. I'm late," she said, but she didn't open the door.

"Then you'd better hurry up and pay me."

"Pay you?"

"Cab fare. You didn't think I was doing this for free, did you?"

"Actually, I did." She took in his look, the heat, the expectation, the little bit of resignation that he was asking for the moon.

The moon that never came through for the Jaynes. A piece of her heart began to tear, and she stopped it by saying, "I guess you want to be paid with something besides cash."

He cocked back, his thighs spread and the corner of his mouth smug and hopeful. "Well, sweet thing, since getting you to fork over cash takes an act of God, or a ball-strangling legal agreement—"

She cut him off before they got into another money scuffle. "What do you want?"

"How 'bout a little kiss?" He pointed to the center of his lips. "Right here. All soft and warm the way you're so good at."

"A little one," she said, giving him a measurement with her forefinger and thumb and ignoring the ragged pull in her chest. "*Pequeño*. That's it."

"C'mere then," he said, and reached for her, his voice a low, raspy brush that brought gooseflesh to her skin. "You know I like it when you talk dirty."

"That wasn't dirty. That was Spanish." But she scooted across the seat and leaned to brush her lips over his.

When she moved away, he held her shoulder and kept her there, extending the kiss, the press of his lips harder, then deepening the kiss, parting her lips with his tongue. She groaned and gave in, kissing him back the way she wanted even though she'd agreed to a much safer contact. She didn't want to walk into her office wet from wanting him.

It was too late, of course. Already her body was making room for his, opening, heating, growing loose and hungry. She leaned into him, wrapping an arm around his neck as he lifted her close, as he urged her into his lap, her back to his door as he leaned over her, bearing her down, sliding his hand beneath her skirt to her crotch.

He growled when he met her pantyhose, dug his fingers into

the fabric of the cloth panel, and tore, working his way through the opening he'd made to the one he wanted, the one hidden behind her panties, the one slick with her moisture and anxious. She shuddered, a breath of air touching her, teasing her. Telling her he was close.

And then he was there, pushing his way through her folds and into her, two fingers, then a third, and groaning into her mouth. She curled her hands around his shoulders, digging for purchase and straining, clenching, contracting her muscles and wishing for his cock because of the way he fit her, the way he knew her.

His tongue played with hers, sliding along hers, flicking and fucking until her skin felt too tight to hold the push and the pull of her need. She wanted to care that they were parked in front of the bank, that the tinted windows of his truck wouldn't hide her from anyone walking by. Co-workers. Customers. The man who signed her paycheck. The man who signed his.

But she was caught in Casper's snare and helpless. He did this to her, made her forget how important her reputation was, how hard she'd worked to restore it. That she'd sworn to never again be put in a position to worry that her behavior would be her downfall, or the ruination of someone she couldn't imagine not being a part of her life.

And look at the position she was in now—her legs spread, her pantyhose torn and worthless, her skirt rucked up over her hips, Casper fingering her in the parking lot of the bank. What was she thinking? Or why wasn't she thinking? Wouldn't that be the question needing an answer most?

But instead of pushing off his lap and shoving him away, she forced her conscience and common sense out of the truck's cab, allowing only her lust to remain. She writhed against Casper's hand, pushed her mound into his palm, grinding her clit and feeling the rise of his cock beneath her.

And then his hand was gone, and he was forcing her to sit up, reaching for his belt buckle and button fly. He lifted his hips and shucked his jeans down his thighs, his cock thrusting against his belly, his legs thick and muscled. She closed her eyes to let the tingles and electric buzz build to sweep through her body.

She wanted to straddle him, to feel him inside of her, pulsing, bold and hard and insistent. Instead she leaned forward and took him in her mouth, tasting him, the salt and the smooth cap of his head. Veins stood rigid along his shaft, and she followed them with her tongue.

He bucked up into her mouth, groaning, his hand holding the back of her head, his fingers threaded through her hair like fence posts through grass. "Goddamn, woman. All I asked for was a little bitty kiss."

She fought a smile and pursed her lips to suck him hard, pulling her mouth the length of his cock until she held nothing but the head. She swirled her tongue around him, using the end against the slit, then the underside seam, then the flat of the surface that was so tight she thought it might burst.

He was hot, so hot, and so ready, moisture weeping from his tip, slick and sticky. She swept it away, spread it with her tongue, wetting him with his pre-cum and her saliva, her pussy throbbing as she remembered the feel of him inside of her, how tightly he fit, how he stretched her to near bursting, too.

She was done. She needed him. She let him go, sitting up, hiking her skirt to her waist and tearing the hole in her pantyhose to make the room she needed. Then she straddled him, her knees on his seat at his hips, and reached between their bodies, taking his cock in her hand, sliding the ripe head through her folds to smear the moisture gathered there.

And though she was ready and wanted this more than anything, she stopped because of what she saw in Casper's gaze—an asking that had nothing to do with the size of the kiss she'd promised. He was staring, studying, looking for something she didn't know she had to give him. Something bigger than sex. They'd agreed this was all they wanted—bodies and heat and satisfaction.

Her pulse drumming in her neck, she squeezed his cock and said, "Don't look at me like that."

He shook his head, and where she was expecting a grin, she got something else entirely. A something that seemed a hopeful kind of sad, breaking her heart when emotions weren't supposed to be here. This was a reckless kind of sex, physical and dangerous, but it was not what he was asking.

She was still holding on to him, and he reached for a lock of her hair, rubbing it, tucking it behind her ear. "I'm not sure how I'm looking at you, so I'm not sure I can stop."

"You know, and you can. You very well can," she said, and guided him to her opening.

He shrugged, swallowed, but still didn't grin. "Seems a lot easier for you to say than me to do."

"You're going to ruin everything."

That got to him. She saw it in the tightening of his mouth, in the deepening of the grooves at the corner of his eyes. "That's nothing new, Faith. I've always ruined everything for everyone."

And then she pushed him inside and slid to sit on him, burying him deep until any movement she made he made, too, because he was part of her. She placed her hands on the seat back on either side of his head, riding him slowly, her hips moving up then down then pausing.

"What?" he asked, his hands at her waist to guide her, to urge her to go on.

"Please don't ruin this," she said, her voice gruff, her throat aching, her chest too tight to breathe.

"If you have to tell me that, I'm pretty sure it's already too—"

She stopped the rest of his words with her mouth, pressing them back with her lips, pushing them into his throat with her tongue. She didn't want to hear what he had to say, not about things being ruined or things he wanted from her. He was inside of her, filling her, owning her and giving himself up to her. He was hers, and it frightened her to think she held so much of his trust.

Her hips moved, her thighs, her stomach, as she worked his cock. His hands stayed put at her waist, guiding her where he wanted her to go. To the left, then up, to the right, stop, forward, and down. Over and over she did what he wanted, did what she wanted, pleasing them both.

And all the while she kissed him, deep kisses with her tongue and what she thought might be her heart. Tender brushes of her lips to the edge of his rushed out on a breathless moan, his sound, her sound, the sound of a connection she wasn't ready for.

The truck rumbled beneath them, the vibrations tickling through his cock to her core. She shuddered as his tip prodded her deeply, intimately, reaching her where she thought she was safe. She wanted him in her body, but letting him in to touch more than the physical parts of her was too much of a risk—for now. Most likely forever.

She shook her head, pushing the thoughts away. She couldn't think about forever. She didn't even want to think about now or where she was or the risk she was taking. Not when there was so much to feel. Holding on to the muscles bunched between his shoulders and neck, she let her head fall back and rode him, the steering wheel scraping her back, his cock scraping her clit.

He leaned forward, wrapped his lips around her nipple, and sucked it into his mouth, holding her there with his teeth while his tongue scraped the taut surface. He bit harder, moved to the top of her breast, and sucked on her skin, bruising her, marking her. Branding her before letting her go.

Her thighs burned with her efforts, and she needed so badly to come, to finish this, to feel Casper unload inside of her, to see his abs clench, the veins in his neck pop in relief as he strained.

She loved watching him come, loved the sounds he made, loved seeing the slide of his cock as he pushed into her and pulled out. She looked down now, reaching into her pussy and opening her lips, catching the ridge of his cock's head between her spread fingers.

Close. She was so, *so* close, and as near as his face was to hers, he had to know it, from the way she couldn't find her breath, from the way her heart hammered. He sat back and stared into her eyes, daring her to look away. She did because she had to, taking him in . . . his throat, his hair-dusted pectorals, the bisected plane of his belly where his abs contracted as he fucked her, the coarse thatch of hair cushioning his cock and his balls.

He was beautiful. So beautiful it hurt. Emotion rose to strangle her, her throat full and aching with it, her chest tight. She returned her gaze to his, licking her lips to tell him of her hunger. She wanted him to know what it did to her to look at him, but she couldn't find the words. And then she came, the heat and the tingles and tickles and the surge of sensation he aroused in her was too big to contain.

He followed, pouring into her, the tendons in his neck bold against the canvas of his flushed skin. He held her hips tight to his, shuddering as he finished silently, his eyes screwed shut, his mouth drawn tight against the noises inside.

She brought up a hand to his cheek, rubbed her thumb there, coaxing a smile before he turned to kiss her palm. Then she leaned against him, her head to his shoulder, letting him take her weight and all her worry that being with him had already cost her dearly.

TWENTY

"BOONE?" FAITH CALLED from the entrance to the barn since doing the same from the back porch of the ranch house had been met with silence. She didn't know where Dax was. She didn't know where Casper was. She assumed Clay was somewhere with him.

"Back here," came a response from the tack room.

She walked down the center of the enormous structure, glad she'd shrugged out of her suit jacket, wishing she'd thought to get rid of her pantyhose and pumps. She was pretty sure she had a pair of flip-flops in the backseat. And thanks to Casper, she had a new battery. She also had her fingers crossed she wasn't about to walk into a confrontation with her brother over his partner spending the night in her bed.

"What're you doing here?" he asked, glancing over as she stopped in the doorway.

He had what looked like an awl in one hand, doing some

cowboy thing to a saddle. Or, she guessed, looking closer, a stirrup. "Since you won't ever pick up your phone, I came to see you."

"I don't carry my phone," he said, flipping his dark hair that had grown way too long out of his face to see her. "Hard to pick it up."

"How am I supposed to get your okay on things for the party if I can't talk to you?" she asked, walking into the small room that smelled of sweat and leather and oil and hay, and catching sight of the phone on the wall. Lord. "What's that phone and do you use it?"

"It's the house line. We'll pick it up if we're in here. And you don't need my okay on everything you do."

Words he'd live to regret, no doubt, should he find out what she'd been doing. And with whom. But none of that was on the agenda for today. "I talked with Arwen about catering the party. Her prices are good. Better than Smokin' Joe's."

"Do her prices hinge on using the saloon?" he asked without looking up from his task.

"Nope. She'll bring the food to us."

"Okay."

"Does that mean you're good with me finalizing things with her?"

He shrugged. "You know what we can afford. And by we," he added, turning, "I mean we. Not you. We."

"I know," she said, feeling the urge to cross her fingers.

He went back to the stirrup then. "Guess I could pick up a couple of Casper's hours at Summerlin's so I can throw more cash at this thing."

"This *thing*," she said, reaching for what she thought was a currycomb, "is going to be a gorgeous party. Trust me. And you don't need to put yourself on the backs of any wild horses to make it happen. Everything'll be covered."

"By the both of us," he said again. "Equally."

"Equally." Which was true enough as long as they didn't count what she was paying to have Casper's house raised from the dead. And what she was paying for the beer. She ran the metal teeth of the round comb over her palm. "Are things okay with you and Casper?"

He withdrew the tool, smoothed the edges of the hole he'd made, gave her a side-eyed glance. "Is there a reason they shouldn't be?"

"I was just wondering." She forced a careless shrug. "He said something about always ruining everything for everyone. I was just wondering what he meant."

Boone straightened, popped his neck, waited another heartbeat before asking, "When were you talking to Casper?"

Oops. "He came by the bank a few weeks ago."

"Why?"

"About his house."

At that, Boone grunted. "I don't know why he's so het up on putting that place back together. It's going to take him forever and cost him a fortune he doesn't have."

Hmm. "Is he still putting in his share of the work around here?"

"He is, then he puts in more hours at Summerlin's. Enough hours that he's made what he needed to get a construction crew over to Mulberry Street, I guess. I don't know how he's fitting in time at the house, unless he's doing it in his sleep."

She'd decided not to mention anything about having paid for the construction crew. Or that she'd decided without consulting him to have the anniversary party at Casper's house. She could mention those things a few days before. Maybe. Depending on the temperature of things by then.

"I guess he's doing what he feels he has to, but it does seem like a lot. The house. The horses. All his responsibilities here."

Boone's hands stilled again. "Why the interest in Casper, Faith?"

"He's a friend," she said. When he gave her a look that said he wasn't buying, she added, "He's always been a friend. You know that. How often did he eat dinner at our house in high school?"

"A lot, but that was then. This is now."

"And now means what? I can't be friends with him? Because you said so?"

"You know how he is," he said with a grunt, getting back to work.

"He's your partner. I don't like hearing him say he ruins things because of that. That's the only reason I asked," she lied.

"As far as I know, we're fine. Other than the obvious debt we'll never pay off in this lifetime. But you wouldn't be here about that since you know more about it than anyone."

"If nothing's going on here, could he be talking about something personal? Something from his past. I mean, his mother dumped that house in his lap. I'm guessing that's been weighing on him."

"So you thought you'd ask me."

"You know him better than I do," she said, wondering if that was the truth.

"Yeah, but as often as he came to dinner, I'm sure you know enough."

"Is that what his mother told him? That he ruined things?"

"I'm not talkin' to you about Casper."

"But you know, don't you? You know about what went on in that house."

He grunted again. "Some. Maybe."

She rolled her eyes, considered stabbing him with the comb. "Is there some Dalton Gang code keeping you from telling me? Like the no-sisters rule y'all have?"

"What do you know about that?"

"You don't think Darcy and I talk?"

"She shouldn't know about that either."

"Well, it's moot now as far as she's concerned. She's happy with Josh. And Dax is happy with Arwen."

"That still leaves Casper, and he better not be breaking the rule."

And if he was breaking it, it had to be with her. "I'm an adult, Boone. He can't break it without me letting him."

"Then you damn well better not be letting him."

She squeezed her hand around the comb. "What if I did? What harm could there be—"

"Are you fucking kidding me?" he asked, spinning on her.

"No. I'm not. He's your friend. He's your partner. You obviously trust him—"

"I don't trust him with you."

"Then you might as well say you don't trust me."

"It's not the same, and you know it."

"I can handle Casper."

"Are you handling him? Is that why he's spending most of his nights away?"

She held her brother's gaze, admitting nothing, refusing to allow him a say in her personal life. "He came to me at the bank. I did some research on the house. We've talked about it. If he's spending his nights there, I don't know anything about it."

That much was the truth. The lie was that she did know where he'd been sleeping, and she waited for Boone to make the jump to the obvious. But he didn't.

"I'm not trying to be an ass, Faith. I just don't want you to get hurt," he said, leaving off the *again* that echoed between them as loudly as if he'd spoken the word.

"I know that. I don't want me to get hurt either. But I'm not nineteen anymore. You've got to let me be me. Even if you don't like the choices I make."

Another grunt, but nothing more.

"Trust me, please? When I say I'm over being stupid?" Or at least over expecting happy endings. And the dream coming true at the fairy tale's end. "And know I'll always need you there when I mess up. Because it will happen."

"You stay away from him and you'll be less likely to."

"Boone!"

"Okay, okay. I trust you."

"Thank you."

"But I don't trust him."

Gah. "You're not making this easy."

"Well, I'm not going to look the other way while you—"

"While I what? Bite off more than I can chew? Get in over my head? Make a fool of myself with another inappropriate man? Because that's what this is about, isn't it? You're afraid I'm going to repeat the biggest mistake of my life. Well, I'm not. I'm older and I'm wiser and that lesson was one I'll never forget."

He jammed the awl into the surface of the workbench, his hand a fist around the handle. "I wasn't there for you. I should've been there for you."

"Oh, Boone," she said, her throat tight as she walked close and laid her head on his shoulder. "You being there wouldn't have changed anything. It was something I was going to have to figure out for myself. If you or anyone else had saved me"—she made air quotes around the words—"I would have been more likely to dig myself in deeper, or move on to someone else just as bad for me as Jeremy. I needed to suffer through all of it, on my own, to figure out how not to make the same mistake again."

"I don't like seeing you suffer," he said, resting his head against hers before reaching for the awl and pulling it free.

"Then it's a good thing I'm not, isn't it?" Once that had settled, she thought it best to change the subject. She returned the comb to its hook. "What do you think of Clay?"

"I think Casper's insane for taking on a kid with the trouble attached to this one. Wait. How do you know about Clay?"

Good grief. This juggling of what she was supposed to know with what she actually did was killing her. "I met him at the house on Mulberry Street."

"What were you doing there?"

"Casper's using me as his financial advisor."

"You could've just said that in the first place."

Because it was okay for her to have a business relationship with him? "So you like Clay?"

"Good thing is you didn't have to hire a maid. The house hasn't been so clean since Tess was the one taking care of things."

"He cooks, too, I hear."

"You hear *that* from Casper?"

"I did, yes. We do talk about more than money, Boone. Which is why I was asking if things were okay."

"Things are fine. I've got two partners who come and go like there's not a shit ton of work here needing done. One of these days . . ."

She didn't like the way he'd let the sentence trail. It could mean so many things. "One of these days things are going to turn around for y'all."

"Assuming we can hang on till that happens."

"You know you can come to me for money. I have more than enough for you, too."

"I know you do. Just like you know the three of us have to make a go of this on our own."

To prove themselves worthy of the gift given them by Tess and Dave Dalton. "I know. But if things get to the point where you may lose the ranch without my help . . ."

He nodded. "Then we'll have a partnership meeting and take a vote."

"Do y'all really do that?"

"Hell no. Usually we work this shit out in the pens while sliding around on calf nuts."

"Gross."

"Hey. You asked."

"Guess I'll get back to town. Now that I have your okay to let Arwen cater. And your okay to live my own life," she said, lifting up on her tiptoes to brush a kiss against his cheek, and backing out the door before what she'd said registered.

"Hey," he called after her. "I never said that."

But she was already halfway out of the barn, and her laugh echoed to the rafters.

TWENTY-ONE

EMPTY TRASH BAG, dustpan, and broom in one hand, Faith wiped the sweat from her forehead in the crook of her elbow, then pushed open the door to the small third-floor room. Somehow, even with all her umpteen billion trips up and down the stairs, she'd managed to miss this one. Picking up the bucket of cleaning supplies, she walked inside with a sigh.

Saturday had rolled around again, and again she was spending her time off laboring physically when there were a million other things she'd rather be doing—sleeping being at the top of the list. Even taking care of the loads of chores she had waiting at home would be better than this. But here she was, checking off and clearing another room in Casper's monstrosity.

Thank God this was the last time she'd have to be shocked by what she found in this house. The construction crew took over on Monday, and Monday couldn't get here soon enough. Honestly, discovering where Casper had spent his time the years he'd lived in Crow Hill was making this adventure more depressing than fun.

Earlier in the week, the cleaning crew she'd hired had done the heavy lifting inside and out, leaving the more obvious personal items for Casper to store or dispose of. He'd turned over a lot of that chore to Clay, which the boy had managed without the grumbling Faith thought was the norm for teens.

Faith had been the one grumbling, but mostly to herself, and all about Suzanne and Leroy Jayne thinking *this* was any place, any way to raise a child.

Granted, Casper had left Crow Hill over fifteen years ago, and would never have seen the disrepair his mother had allowed the house to fall into. The trash was hers. The ridiculously thick layers of dirt were hers.

The rest Faith blamed on time, vermin, and the sun, wind, and rain making their way through broken windows and damaged shingles, eroding the plaster and hardwood and having no more respect for man's handiwork than they did God's.

Still, it broke her heart to see things she could tell Casper would rather she not, especially when he left her wondering why. When Clay had asked what Casper wanted done with a box of old VHS westerns and a suitcase of mismatched shoes and paycheck stubs from Bokeem's, he'd waved the boy toward the Dumpsters outside.

But when she'd asked about a small wooden jewelry box with nothing but small gold cuff links and a matching tie tack inside, he'd taken it from her hand and left the room.

She didn't have it in her to separate what this house was revealing about who he'd once been and the man he was now in her bed. It was stupid because he didn't live here anymore, and he'd lived the biggest part of his life elsewhere.

But her own teenage years had defined so much of who she'd

become; she couldn't help but think living here had done the same to him. Had sent him looking for who he was on the backs of bulls, in the beds of buckle bunnies, down the long roads he'd traveled alone, quiet roads leading to the next bull, the next bunny, the next bed.

She feared he wasn't done looking. That she'd stepped into the middle of his search.

She needed to get out of his way. She didn't want to stifle him, or make things worse. She didn't know why, but she thought she might be making things worse. As if each step he made forward was followed by two back to where he'd been before she'd pried past his secrets into the part of him he held close.

It was getting to be too much, the possibility that she would damage him further, that his opening up to her was going to backfire. An explosion like that would blow this construction project off track when the wheels were finally in motion. She needed the house done, but not because of the party.

Guaranteeing Casper a place of his own, a place to call home and a reason to stay in Crow Hill, meant she wouldn't have to worry about him bailing on his part of the ranch if things between the two of them went south. Because if he did that, it left Dax and Boone to juggle what the three of them could barely keep in the air.

Those working conditions might just be enough to convince Boone the grass did indeed look greener on the ranch where he'd worked in New Mexico. And if Boone left, their parents' grief would kill her. They'd been in her corner through everything, but that didn't absolve her of causing them so much pain. She couldn't let that happen again.

Massey Construction would be arriving the day after tomorrow. Trucks and trucks of them, she imagined, considering the bonus tacked onto the end of the contract her attorney in Luling had whipped up. She needed to finish these last few rooms and let them have it. And yet here she stood, staring out the window while Clay tossed sticks from the yard for Kevin to fetch, thinking about Casper as a father. About herself as a mother . . .

Enough. She turned from the window, setting down the bucket to look around the room. The crew had cleaned away what trash had been in here, and hauled away what furniture had remained after Suzanne bailed. Judging by the marks left on the floor, there hadn't been much. The four grooves dug in a rectangle near the door would've been a dresser, the long gouges scraped in the room's far corner made by the legs of a bed.

Frowning, she walked closer. A panel had been cut into the wall at what would've been the head of the narrow twin frame, just about pillow high. Facing the wall, she dropped to sit cross-legged in the corner and used the dustpan's handle to pry away the part of the wall that had been damaged a long time ago.

The plaster fell inward rather than out, crumbling almost to dust and revealing a small sheaf of papers tucked between the wall studs. She pulled them out, opened the stack, and spread it out on her knee. She thought at first she'd stumbled onto old homework assignments, or school projects Casper had for some reason hidden away.

But then she looked closer, read the words, saw the images scratched deep with the point of a pencil. Sketches of a woman's face, of a man's, both more caricatures than portraits, both exaggerated and grotesque. Both surrounded by blood spatters, by hatchets and knives and screwdrivers dripping red.

Her heart began to thunder. Her nape grew clammy, her chest suffocatingly heavy. She looked at the next sheet, scanned the tightly printed letters, so controlled, so perfectly sized, seeing over and over again words that stabbed and gutted her, that tore into her with claws and needles until her skin and the flesh beneath burned.

Hate. Death. Screams.

Bitch. Cunt.

Torture. Maim. Dismember.

Kill. Ruin.

Casper had written these words. Had lived and breathed and suffered these words. Had committed them to paper because they were in his head. Breeding. Growing tendrils that dug deeper the longer he'd stayed.

God in heaven, what had gone on in this house?

"What're you doing in here?"

Faith jumped, her hand flying to her throat, then to her eyes to dry them. "Casper. You scared me."

"What're you doing in here?" he asked again from behind her, his tone level, but the words clipped, less question than accusation.

She quickly stuffed the papers she'd found beneath her crossed legs, spun just enough to see him, and glared at him as if the answer was obvious. "Same thing we've been doing in every room since we took on this project."

"Looks to me like you're sitting on your ass doing nothing," he said, twisting his mouth to the side.

"And what if I am? Do I not deserve the occasional break?"

"C'mon." He gestured, the motion lighthearted, his expression anything but. "This room's not important. It can wait."

"Wait for what? When I have more free time, because that's never going to happen. We're out of here tomorrow and Massey's crew takes over."

"Then spend what you do have somewhere that matters."

"Casper, every room in the house is going to have to be

cleared sooner or later. And all of it before the construction guys get started. I can go through this one and mark it off my list just as easily as I can any other."

"Leave it," he said, more insistent this time. "Clay can do it when he's done cleaning up the shit hole he's made of the parlor."

Clay who was romping in the backyard with his dog instead of working. "Clay's got a list of chores longer than he is tall. You can't expect him—"

"Jesus H. Christ, Faith. For once, just do what I say."

She stopped, blinked, looked around. What was this room to him? It was tiny, a speck on the whole of the monstrous house. And the house was revealing itself to be exactly that. Monstrous.

"Now," he snapped. "Get your ass out here before I pull the door shut and leave you inside."

But she didn't take kindly to threats. "I'll just pull it open when I'm done here."

"You can try, but it won't do you any good."

"Why?"

"Because there's no knob on this side," he barked at her before pushing up his hat and rubbing at his eyes. "Are you coming, or not?"

His words sucked what air was left from the room. "How did you know there was no knob on this side?"

"How do you think I knew?"

"This was your room," she said, looking around rather than waiting for him to confirm it. That he'd slept in here, spent time in here, holed up in here to escape the even worse things he would've had to deal with if he'd gone downstairs.

"And now that you've seen it, you can go."

"Fine," she said, folding the papers against the dustpan as she got to her feet. And she might have done just that, respected his wishes to keep the horror of his past private, but then she saw the balls of newspaper stuffed in the holes in the wall behind the door, the holes in the ceiling, one or two in the floor in the same corner.

He followed her gaze, shook his head as if surrendering the last shred of his privacy. "Those were to keep out the spiders."

"Spiders?"

"They had a thing for this room. Came in off the tree, I guess. Down from the attic. I used to wake up with three or four on my pillow."

Tears welled in her eyes, and the papers she'd tried so hard to hide fluttered to the floor. She watched him watch them, saw the flush of red in his cheeks—shame, embarrassment, resentment—as he realized what she'd found. What she hadn't wanted him to know she'd learned.

He cocked a shoulder against the doorjamb, his lip curled upward. "Happy now?"

No, she wasn't happy now. Why would he think this discovery would make her anything but impossibly sad? "I'm sorry. I saw the wall. Where it had been sliced. I was curious . . ."

She didn't know what else to say. She didn't know how to face him, dropping her gaze to the papers spread out on the floor like a map of his life.

"Are you sorry for being nosy?" he asked as he bent to gather them. "Or sorry you had to find out who I really am?"

"This isn't who you are," she said, her voice breaking.

He laughed as he crossed the room to his hiding place. He stuck a hand deeper into the hole, came out with a box of matches. He struck one, appearing as surprised as she was when it lit. "Good to see some things around here still work."

And then he waved the flame beneath the corner of the pages, holding the burning sheaf until the fast-growing blaze reached his fingers. Then he dropped the ball of fire and walked from the room, leaving her to stomp out what remained of the glowing sparks.

As if he really didn't care if the whole house went up in an inferno around them.

TWENTY-TWO

When Casper pulled up in front of the house a week into the renovation, Faith was already parked there, sitting in her car and talking on her cell. He saw this as he walked to her door, and got a single raised finger telling him to give her a minute alone. He supposed it was better than a middle finger telling him to fuck off.

It was Labor Day and the bank was closed, so it made sense she had the day free. Massey's construction crew didn't and was laboring away, hammers pounding, saws buzzing, old wood and plaster rending, shingles raining down. At this rate they'd easily earn their early completion bonus, making Faith and her party happy.

He hadn't seen her since a week ago Saturday when she'd discovered the papers he should've burned a long time ago. Obviously, she'd snuffed the fire he'd walked out on before any damage was done. He and Clay had worked the next day alone, and he'd had to force himself to climb the service stairs to that room.

The ashes were still there, the floor around them black. He'd left the mess where it had fallen. It had been too late to clean it up then. It had always been too late to sweep away anything that had happened there.

He'd missed her in ways that surprised him. Hard to admit, especially when it wasn't the lack of sex burning a hole in his gut. He'd missed *her.* Her mouth. Her attitude. The way she had of making him take a step back before saying something he'd regret. The way she had of making him face the words that came tumbling out of his mouth anyway.

There'd been a whole lot of tumbling going on, and he actually hated himself less than he thought he would for putting his shit out there. God*damn* but he'd been putting his shit out there. He figured the papers she'd found were the last straw. He'd scared her off. He knew it. She would've been in touch otherwise. He wasn't sure he had an excuse for not calling her.

When he'd hit town earlier, he'd dropped off Clay while he'd run to Lasko's to pick up a load of feed. In all the sorting and packing done the last four weeks, no one had thought to get rid of the food supplies Casper had bought for the boy, and Clay had stored in one of the cabinets built along the parlor's long front wall.

Casper stood there now, wondering if Faith would come looking for him, or if she'd drive away once she finished her phone call now that he'd arrived. As far as he knew, she hadn't come here to find him, but then he'd given up his cell to cut down on his costs and was relying on the Daltons' old answering machine for his messages. Sometimes he even managed to check for them.

He'd most likely get a phone for Clay once the boy started

school, and since the semester was already two weeks in, he knew he couldn't put off making an appointment with Greg any longer. The only reason he'd waited this long was that it was going to kill him to give Clay the bad news he sensed would be swinging their way.

The boy was happy. And he had to admit to feeling the same way because of it. But he couldn't see either of the two states involved or any court at any level taking emotion into account before the gavel fell and the bars rattled shut.

"I was talking to your mother."

"What?" He hadn't heard her come up behind him. He thought he'd been watching for her to leave her car, but seems he'd been somewhere else and missed her. He was doing a lot of that.

Missing her.

She looked good. She'd skipped the business suit and heels, skipped the ratty T-shirts, sneakers, and knee shorts she'd worn while cleaning. Today she had on boots and jeans and an airy sort of top that had him thinking about her four-poster bed. It laced up with a ribbon tied between her breasts, like a corset, but a loose one, hanging just short of her belt and showing a strip of skin.

He liked that strip of skin, her smooth flesh beneath the white fabric. It had him swallowing, thinking about how soft she was, how sweet she tasted. How much he'd missed her.

"I was talking—"

"I heard you the first time," he snapped.

She tossed her arms out wide in a gesture of aggravation. "Then why did you ask me what I said?"

"Because I couldn't believe I heard it."

"Do you want to know what I found out?"

"No," he said, walking away, stopping, coming back, his hands at his hips. "But you're going to tell me anyway, so . . ."

"Your father—"

"—if he was my father—"

"—won the house in a poker game."

"What?"

"Your father . . . won the house . . . in a poker game." She spoke each word slowly as if he was some kind of idiot.

She knew him well. "Who from?"

"The last name on the deed before Leroy Jayne was Maximus Crow."

"If I had a chair, I'd sit down," he said. "Because that is just a shit awful name."

The look she gave him was pure exasperated Faith. "Now I have to wonder about the relationship between the Jaynes and the Crows."

"You'd already discovered a Crow built the place."

"Yes, but I assumed the family had given it up a long time ago," she said, crossing to the parlor cabinets. "Especially since it had fallen into such disrepair before y'all moved here."

"Hey, you talked to Suzanne. She knows more than I do."

"I wish she knew where your father was so I could talk to him."

He didn't have anything to say to that. He hadn't seen or heard from Leroy Jayne in over twenty years. The man could be dead. The man should be dead. And Faith had better not get a burr up her butt to go finding out if he was. He didn't want her around that man. He didn't want to have to kill him but he would to keep her safe.

"Casper? Is this stuff Clay's?"

He glanced down to where she was nudging the toe of her boot through the boy's things. "Yeah. I brought him by to grab the stuff he forgot. Guess that's his being a kid."

She reached for a book, looked at the title. "That little thief."

"Hey now," he said, reaching for her arm. "This house is one big echo chamber. Keep it down or he'll hear you."

"I don't care if he hears me." She jerked from his grasp and waved the book at him. "Kendall special ordered this title. She told me that it had gone missing off her shelves."

He rubbed at his forehead. "Then he'll pay her for it."

"What else has he stolen?" She dropped the book onto the pile of Clay's things. "Because I can't imagine that's it."

Of course, she couldn't, though it would be nice if she'd think about why. "He took food out of the Hellcat Saloon's Dumpsters. You know, to have something to eat. And a couple of sodas from cases on the back porch. I already told him he'll need to settle up with Arwen."

"Good," she said, still fuming. "You don't know much about this kid, do you? Beyond seeing him a few times six years ago."

And here we go. "I know he came looking for me. That's enough."

"You could be getting into something you're not equipped to handle. Christ, for all you know, he could have a juvie record."

"He doesn't have a juvie record. Except for the running away from the foster home part." Though even as he said it he found himself admitting he didn't know anything of the kind.

"Are you sure, or is that what you're hoping?" she asked, her voice tempered low, though her tone was fierce and demanding and mad. "Have you talked to an attorney? Has your attorney talked to the New Mexico authorities? Have you done *anything* about making sure none of this blows up in your face? Or in his?"

Or in Boone's, she might as well have added. "What I know is that he's done what he's had to do to get by. Just like I did."

"That's not an answer. That's an excuse." She closed her eyes, took a deep breath, opened them, and looked into his. "You need to take care of this. Now."

What he needed was time and space before he forgot all the reasons he'd been missing her. "I've got to go out to Summerlin's for a bit before I head back to the ranch. Can you feed Clay and get him home?"

She closed her eyes again, shook her head, then grabbed the book from the floor before answering. "Yes, I can feed him and get him home, but don't think I don't see right through your ploy."

His heart wasn't in teasing her but he tried. "Ploy? Me?"

"You think if I spend time with him I'll be more forgiving."

No, mostly he'd been thinking he needed to get the fuck outta here. "It's worked so far, you spending time with me."

"Has it?" she asked, her head cocked. Then she brushed by him before he could answer, stomping out of the house, calling for Clay on her way, and leaving Casper to box up the things he'd dropped the boy by to do.

And then it hit him. Oh, the woman was sneaky. She'd left before he could on purpose. It was her way of making sure he had to clean up some of the mess his harboring a runaway had brought down. A small mess, sure, but one he had a hand in.

One of many he needed to face.

TWENTY-THREE

"I HOPE THIS WILL be okay," Faith said as she and Clay climbed from her car. They slammed their doors and stepped one after the other from the parking lot into the Blackbird Diner. "I wasn't sure what you might like."

"I like food," he said, lifting his hand to return Teri Gregor's wave.

Faith thought of Boone as a teenager, shoveling up multiple helpings from the family-style bowls set on the table at supper. Then she realized Clay seemed totally at home, instead of self-conscious like she'd expect from a runaway. Weird.

"You know Teri?" she asked as they slid into their booth.

"Casper's brought me food from here a few times. The burgers are totally dope. Last time I ate four chili dogs." He reached up, shoved back the long shock of hair falling over half his face. "Think maybe I'll have something different, though."

"Anything you want," she said, reaching for a laminated menu and handing one to him.

"You might want to take that back after you see how much I can eat."

"Four chili dogs gives me an idea," she said, and found herself smiling.

"Plus onion rings and a shake on top of that."

"I work at the bank. If I need a loan, I've got connections."

He grinned, a goofy kid grin, not the grin of a boy who'd crossed two states to find a cowboy who'd once bedded his since deceased mother. Christ, but had Casper managed to complicate his life, and now by extension hers.

She hadn't been thinking. She should've gone straight to the ranch and rustled up something from what groceries the boys had instead of dining in public with a teenager the regulars would realize wasn't local.

But since they were already here . . . "I saw your stuff in the house. I guess you like to read."

He nodded. "My mom used to take me to the library a lot. And you can always find something in the trash behind bookstores."

"Did you learn that from your mother?"

"They throw away stuff that's worn out," he said without answering her question.

She reached into her purse for the Nesbø title and set it on the table between them. "I don't think they throw away stuff that's brand new."

He straightened, sat back in the booth, and distanced himself from her and his crime. "You better check with Casper before you call the cops."

"I don't answer to Casper." And at least Clay hadn't denied culpability. "Do you have any money?"

He nodded. "Casper gave me some. So I wouldn't be totally broke. And for doing chores."

"Good." She dropped her gaze back to her menu. "We'll stop by Kendall's on our way to the ranch. You can pay her for the book."

"Who's Kendall?"

"A friend of mine. She owns the bookstore." Without looking up, she pushed the paperback closer to him.

After a moment, he took it, then their waitress arrived for their order, her interruption perfectly timed. That done, Faith changed the subject. "How're you liking the ranch?"

"It's good. I haven't got to go riding yet. Everyone's busy, and I've got a lot of stuff to do at the house." He stopped then, as if waiting for her to accuse him of other crimes.

The fact that he was mulling over this one was enough. "I know they appreciate your help. Even if you're stuck cleaning up after them."

He shrugged off her empathy. "Casper says he'll take me out when they move the pairs from the Braff pasture."

"I'll bet Kevin's enjoying himself." And how many times had she thought about this boy making his trek in the company of a dog?

"Yeah, he's all about Bing and Bob. They're like the Three Musketeers, or whatever."

Like Boone and Casper and Dax. Which took her back to thinking about the future, for those three boys and for this one.

"Are you going to be okay? If things don't work out with Casper?" She had to ask. Because he had to know his time here would most likely soon end.

"You mean if I can't stay?"

Being the bearer of bad news was never fun, but she needed to know Casper wasn't getting Clay's hopes up unfairly. "I know Casper wants you to. It's meant a lot to him, having you here."

"Think so?"

"I do. He doesn't have anyone either. Not really. Just Dax and Boone. They were pretty much his family the years he lived here before."

"I remember hearing him talk about them. Back when I was a kid."

Good lord, he was still a kid, didn't he know that? She swallowed, waited until her heart had stopped breaking, then asked, "Was that part of why you came to him?"

"I don't know," he said, tapping the end of his knife on the table. "Maybe. He was always funny."

"Funny?" *Or drunk?*

"He made my mom laugh. She didn't do much of that. I kinda got the feeling I was an accident, you know." More tapping, then a frown and another admission. "That she hadn't really wanted me around in the first place."

She wondered if he'd told any of this to Casper. "Did you know your father?"

He shook his head, going quiet while their waitress set their plates in front of them. Once they were alone, he went on. "No. She usually had a guy around, but never for long."

Just while the rodeo was in town. "I'm sorry."

"It was okay. I hung out with kids from school, ate at their houses. Spent the night sometimes so I didn't have to worry about getting to school."

The same way Casper had hung out with the boys, had come home with Boone for dinner, had slept on the futon in the Mitchells' den. She reached for the ketchup, squirted a pool onto her plate, watched it spread and thought of the words Casper had written, the images he'd drawn.

"Why would you have to worry about getting to school?" she asked, snapping the top of the bottle though there was little left to keep inside.

Clay reached for it, looking from her face to her plate. "We didn't live in the district exactly. So there wasn't a bus. And it was too far to walk. Mom would take me when she was awake in time. But I missed a lot."

"Are you behind because of that?" And here he was missing more.

He gave an embarrassed nod. "This last year really sucked. I had to change schools because of where the foster home was. I didn't know anyone there. And my classes were split between seventh and eighth grade."

When, at fourteen, he should probably be in ninth. "I'm sure once you're settled in a permanent home, you won't have any trouble catching up."

"Yeah. Like that'll ever happen," he said, adding mustard to his ketchup and stirring them to orange with the first of his four corn dogs.

She hated hearing him so defeated, but he was probably right. Teenagers were rarely adopted, and he only had four more years before he'd be kicked out of the system. Four years was a very long time when there were only seven he'd be spending as a teen.

"Do you mind if I ask you something personal?" As if the things she'd been asking him hadn't been.

"I guess not," he said with a shrug, his eyes averted, his mouth full.

Using a fork, she dredged two thick-cut fries through her ketchup. "What happened to your mother?"

He chewed, swallowed, reached for his glass of grape soda and sucked half of it up through his straw. "I don't really know.

I came home from school one day and the next morning social workers came to the trailer to get me. The cops had found her during the night."

Christ. "Was it a car accident?"

"I'm pretty sure it was an overdose," he said, toying with his straw, his gaze distant.

She should've kept her mouth shut. She shouldn't have made him go back there. But then, she'd been doing a lot of that recently, hadn't she? Returning people to their pasts when she couldn't even get over hers. "I'm sorry. I didn't know she'd used drugs."

"Most people didn't. I don't even know if Casper did."

Or maybe he did. Maybe he'd turned to more than alcohol in the years he'd been away searching for who he was, trying to find his life.

"He really is a cool guy, you know."

"I guess he is." Though his being cool didn't keep him from being trouble, she mused, her stomach wrapped around the knot of that truth.

"You two hooked up?" Clay asked, waving his corn dog at her before taking a bite.

Hooked up. That brought her a smile. "We're friends. We go to dinner sometimes. I'm helping him with the house."

"Guess that makes you a pretty good friend."

"I've known him a long time." She wasn't sure what Casper had told the boy—if anything—about his years in the house on Mulberry Street, and she didn't want to prick a hole in the balloon of Clay's admiration. "He used to come home with Boone, eat dinner with us. Spend the night sometimes. But I think mostly he was on his own."

"It's not that hard to get used to," Clay said, his expression older and wiser than fourteen. "Casper knowing what I'd been through, being left alone a lot and all . . . Coming here just made sense."

Except the way Casper told the story, he barely remembered Clay. But he'd obviously—and unknowingly—left his mark on an eight-year-old boy who'd been desperate for attention.

"Casper's a good man," she said, and meant it. Not very many men would take on a boy they'd only known a few weeks and whose name they couldn't recall without prompting.

Clay dropped his last corn dog to his plate, pushing it away after only one bite. "I guess I wasn't as hungry as I thought."

"You did pretty good." Better than her. She'd lost her appetite around the same time Clay told her he'd been an accident.

"We should probably go." He scooted toward the edge of his seat. "So I can pay the lady for the book."

And with those few words her whole world flipped. She was going to do anything she could to help Casper with this boy. "Sounds like a plan."

TWENTY-FOUR

"ANY PROBLEMS SO far having Clay around?" Casper asked, jumping onto the flatbed of the ranch pickup and opening the toolbox. He tossed out a handsaw and pair of pruners.

"Nope." Boone took the saw, turned to look at the patch of cedar seedlings that had taken hold of a big section of pasture and had to come down. "Seems like a nice kid. Polite. Respectful. Haven't talked to him much."

"He's not in the way?" Casper hopped down, stretched to grab the pruners, testing the edges of the blades with his thumb. "Doing what he's supposed to do?"

Boone nodded, reaching for the gloves tucked into his belt. "So far. And, nope, not in the way."

The last thing Casper wanted to do was put more of a burden on his partners. Clay was old enough to fend for himself, but he'd never ranched, didn't know the schedule or the expectations. He was still a bit like a kid in a candy store, room to roam, acres to explore, animals and their temperaments to learn. So far, he'd fit right in, but Casper knew teen boys. He'd keep an eye on him.

"He's a hell of a cook. Gotta give him that," Boone said, planting his saw beneath the lowest branches of the closest of the scraggly trees and bending back the trunk with his other hand.

"Yep, he is." Casper pulled on his gloves to tackle a bunch of the thigh-high cedars. Damn trees dropped seeds that took root like wildfire, spreading across a pasture to choke out the grass. It was an ongoing matter of stewardship that kept the land productive for the long term.

Next go around he'd bring Clay to help, explain why the culling had to be done. Make the boy feel a part of things, give him a sense of belonging. Then pray he didn't have it all ripped away down the road.

"He was pretty quiet this morning."

"You think?" Casper asked, frowning as he moved down the line of young trees. He hadn't noticed, which pretty much made him role model of the year.

Boone took a minute to finish sawing, chucking the downed tree toward the truck as he straightened. "He's usually rambling on about something while he's frying up eggs. Barely got a word outta him this morning."

"I was half asleep and shoveling food in my face. I never did get supper last night." Because he'd stayed at Summerlin's longer than usual, making a few extra bucks that wouldn't matter in the long run. He'd never have enough.

"Might be he's worried how his being here's going to play out," Boone said, bending back the trunk of the next tree.

Hmm. What was going on that Casper had missed? Clay hadn't given any indication of being worried about what might happen to him. If anything, he'd seemed relieved to be settling in. Unless something had come up with Faith last night . . .

Goddammit. The woman had butted in where she didn't belong. He'd bet the ranch on it. "I'm gonna lay this one at your sister's door."

Boone stood and turned to face Casper. The look on his face was the one he got every time Faith's name came up in conversation. "What the hell does Faith have to do with it?"

Most likely everything. "I had to make a trip out to Summerlin's last night. I had Faith bring Clay home and feed him."

"And you think she said something to upset him?"

Said something. Asked something. The woman was like a burrowing chigger when she wanted answers. "I dunno. Maybe. He was fine when I left them. Makes sense it was Faith."

Boone blew him off with a flip of the bird and got back to work. "Makes sense you're looking to shuck the blame."

"Me? What did I do?"

"Between here and the house, you're working him pretty hard." Boone's words jerked as he sawed. "Could be he's just tired. Or he's getting sick."

"You make it sound like I'm running a sweatshop."

"You sure as hell aren't the one doing the sweating."

Grumbling under his breath, Casper lopped off one treetop after another until he'd cleared the small patch he'd been working. He tossed the pruners to the ground at the back of the truck, started gathering the foliage that, left to dry rot, would make great tender in the case of a lightning strike. Not that there was much else in the pasture to burn, but the preventative measure made a perfect case for being safe rather than sorry.

He moved to the next bunch of trees, mulling over what Boone had said. He wasn't dumping too much on Clay. Hell, at fourteen, he and his boys had been putting in fourteen-hour Saturdays on this very ranch, and that on top of school and football and hours of homework and practice each week. Running a vacuum and doing the dishes and keeping up with the laundry didn't compare.

The cooking was Clay's idea, and after just a couple of weeks Casper and Boone were placing orders, seeing what the boy could produce, challenging his skills. Clay had come through every time, and seemed to get a kick out of surprising them. Sure as hell beat a regular diet of Boone's hamburger steaks, and his own weak attempts at hash.

That was one big difference between him and Clay. He'd never had the initiative to make the best out of his situation. All he'd wanted to do was escape it, going back to the house on Mulberry Street only when he didn't have anywhere else to go. Dax's house hadn't been on the rotation, but the two of them had spent plenty of nights at Boone's, gobbling down Mrs. Mitchell's pot roast and gravy and the always warm from the oven chocolate chip cookies and apple pie.

Hell, some nights after football practice, he had come out here, checked in with Tess and Dave to see what might need doing. Tess would feed him fried Spam and potatoes with milk, and Dave would walk with him out to the barn, finding something to keep him busy so he didn't have to go home. The Daltons, like the Mitchells, knew the truth of his life in Crow Hill.

And as much as the assignment to help them out had been handed down from Boone's parents to their son, Casper suspected now the Mitchells had been just as intent on giving him a taste of structure, responsibility, normalcy—all the things they provided their children, and Suzanne wouldn't have known had they jumped up and bit her bony whore's ass.

He hefted the pruners toward the next cluster of seedlings. It hit the ground and raised a cloudburst of seedpods and dirt. Behind him, Boone's saw rasped steadily. The sweet pitchy scene of cedar tickled Casper's nose. He scrunched up his face, sneezed, sneezed again. If Clay was feeling bad, it could be allergies, cedar, or other pollen blowing in.

Guess he was going to have to make a plan for doctor bills and meds, though he was getting ahead of himself on that. Still, if he was going to take on this boy, doing it right wasn't going to be cheap. And, he mused, sneezing again, he couldn't do it any other way.

"You gonna stand there all day spewing germs?"

"I was just wondering if some of this might be why Clay's feeling bad," he said, then added before he thought better of it, "and why Faith has money you don't." He glanced toward Boone just in time to duck the saw flying at his head. "Jesus Christ, Boone."

"What're you talking about?" the other man demanded, advancing. He snagged his saw from the ground before Casper thought to grab it, brandishing it as he said, "Faith has a good-paying job. I have you for a partner. Seems pretty obvious to me."

"Not that money." Casper crossed to pick up his pruners. "The other money. The big money."

Boone tugged down his hat until his eyes were slits of big bad brother lost in the shadow of the brim. "You know about her money?"

"I know she has it. I want to know where she got it."

"How do you know she has it?" Boone asked a long moment later, his voice low and measured.

Casper thought fast. "Something she said one day. At the bank, I guess. When I wanted cash to put into the house."

"Bullshit. Faith doesn't talk about her money," Boone said, raising his fist and aiming the sharp teeth of the saw at Casper. "And you don't be talking about it either. Not to anyone. Including Dax."

Fucking hell. What had Faith gotten herself into? "Do you see Dax? I'm just talking to you."

"Well, don't. It's Faith's deal. If she mentioned it," Boone said, taking hold of another tree and bending it to his will, "and I'm more inclined to believe you happened to be in her office and eavesdropped, then ask her. Just don't expect an answer."

Like sister, like brother on that score. "You have a falling out with a favorite uncle or something? He cut you out of the will?"

Up came the saw again. "What the fuck did I just say to you? I'm not telling you anything about the money. It's none of my business. And it's sure as hell none of yours."

"Fine. Jesus." Casper took an exaggerated step in retreat, earning a roll of Boone's eyes as he got back to the tiny cedars.

It was pretty apparent that Faith's money was a sore spot, making it doubtful she would've said anything to her family about spending it on him. Hard to think Boone would be happy to learn that was the case, meaning Casper needed to be more careful about opening his big mouth.

He'd suss out the truth soon enough. He'd just have to find another way to get beyond that particular wall Faith had erected. Shouldn't be hard. He was learning his way around her defenses. A few more nights together, he'd get there.

And it wasn't like doing so would be a chore. In fact, he could see himself taking his time, making sure she enjoyed his run at the truth as much as he would.

By the time he'd settled all that in his mind and looked up, he was a good half-mile from the truck. Crap. He was going to have to make the same trip back, gathering up the tree trash as he went. No way in hell was Boone in the mood to give him a hand, much less a ride.

And then he dropped the bundle he was carrying, listening as the other man gunned the engine and drove the flatbed away, leaving him with a hell of a mess to clean up on his own, and then a hell of a long walk home.

TWENTY-FIVE

"WHAT THE HELL did you say to Clay?"

"When?" Faith asked in response, rather than wasting her time on any sort of cordial greeting. Manners were lost on the man.

Seeing him at her door when she'd looked through the peephole had surprised her. She'd already decided it would fall to her to break the silence between them, but she was not going to do it over the phone. And yet going to see him yesterday had only made things worse, or it had once she'd discovered his runaway was also a shoplifter, and that Casper, though not in denial over the crime, had tried to justify it as a matter of survival.

Right. A nearly ten-dollar paperback. The difference between life and death.

Yesterday was the first time in over a week they'd been face-to-face. She'd told him what she'd learned about the house coming into his father's possession. He'd told her he knew Clay was a thief. That was it. They hadn't talked about what she'd found in his bedroom on Mulberry Street. They hadn't talked about much of anything since he'd discovered her there.

Nothing about the words and the sketches and the fire he'd set to get rid of them. And now here he was, as if that afternoon had only happened in her mind. As if their relationship hadn't screeched to a halt when he'd walked out and left her to deal with his efforts to annihilate his past.

She thought now about inviting him in, but since he couldn't be civil, she stopped thinking about it. Let him fight the moths and mosquitoes circling her porch light. Served him right, coming to her front door and jumping down her throat.

"The other night." He pulled off his hat, waved it into the insect cloud, smacked his hand to his neck when he was dive-bombed in retaliation. "When I had to leave to go to Summerlin's and asked you to feed Clay and get him home."

She hedged. "I don't know. We talked about the menu at the Blackbird Diner."

"Wait." Casper shook his head as if dislodging something peskier than a bug. "You took him to the diner? In public?"

"You told me to feed him," she said. If he'd been nicer she might've apologized, shared her concerns that she'd made a mistake.

"Jesus, Faith. I didn't tell you to take him out and expose him to the Crow Hill gossip mill."

"Sorry." She crossed her arms, bare in her summer work wardrobe of a sleeveless white blouse. "I'm not used to subterfuge. Besides. He knew Teri. You've obviously taken him by there."

"Only to pick up food. Not to put him on display." He batted at another swarm. "Would it be too much trouble to let me in? Before I get eaten alive?"

She opened the door wider, shut it behind him, tried not to breathe deeply until he was downwind. Her body's response to him did not belong in this conversation. "I didn't put him on display. I fed him like you asked. And then I took him by Kendall's to pay for the book he stole."

"Jesus Christ." He tossed his hat to her coffee table, collapsed onto her sofa, scrubbed his hands down his face. "Jesus H. Christ."

His weariness got to her. He was fighting so much. The ranch and his lack of money. The house and his attached past. The boy and the approach of Clay's legal battles. And then it hit her. Clay hadn't told him that she'd taken him by Kendall's bookstore.

That while he'd gone inside, she'd waited at the front window, watching him shuffle to the counter to pay, his head down. That she'd mouthed a silent thank you to her friend for letting the boy off once he'd apologized and made restitution.

She returned to the kitchen and her abandoned pizza, got both of them a beer and handed his to him without a single glance at his jeans or his thighs. "He told me you wouldn't like it if I called the cops."

"I wouldn't have."

But he said nothing about it being the right thing to do. "You were just going to let him get away with it?"

"No, but I would've handled it."

She didn't say anything to that. She just waited for him to realize he hadn't handled anything yet. "So . . ."

He drank from his longneck, his gaze holding hers. "Thank you. I'm not so good with handling things."

"You're going to have to get good with it if you're planning on keeping him around."

He leaned his head to the side, cracked his neck, did the same on the other. "Yeah. I know. I'll figure it out."

"Do it now, Casper. School's already started. He's already a grade behind."

"Shit. I figured he was, but . . . He tell you that?"

She nodded.

"What else did he tell you?" he asked, his words a plea, not an accusation. He cared. He wanted to know. Seemed almost desperate to know.

She hitched up onto a barstool. "That his mother used drugs. A lot. That she most likely died of an overdose, but he doesn't know for sure. Social services came to his trailer one morning and took him away. That was it. He didn't get much in the way of answers."

"Jesus." He looked down at the longneck he'd propped on his belt buckle. "He told me she was a good mom."

"I guess the one doesn't preclude the other."

"It does in my book," he said, and drank.

"Did your mother use drugs?"

"My mother was a booze hound, which isn't much different."

"He said his mother brought home a lot of cowboys." When he didn't respond, she asked, "Do you think she took money from men? For sex?"

"She didn't take it from me," he said, and drank again.

"His mother reminds you of your mother, doesn't she?"

"Hardly."

"She came to you for sex. And left her six-year-old son alone at home."

"She came to me for sex. But she brought me home with her," he said, still drinking.

"With her six-year-old son nearby."

"At least she was there."

Until she wasn't. "Talk to him."

"What?"

"Talk to him. Don't give him chores and tell him how to do them. Talk to him. Help him. Fix this for him." The boy had unloaded, not the least bit reluctant to stop the flow of words, as if he'd needed someone to talk to, someone to ask him about his life. Someone to care what he'd been through. Someone to want to make a difference.

And he was looking to Casper to be that man.

"I don't want to talk about this, okay? I'm doing what I can. That's what matters. Clay's in trouble and he doesn't have anyone he trusts to turn to."

Just like Casper had never had anyone.

But to help him, to help them both, she needed to know Casper's side, to hear him admit it. "Why is it so important to you to be there for this boy?"

"You're asking me that? Seriously?" He gestured expansively, his expression incredulous, the bottle in his hand. "After what you saw in that house?"

But she continued to push. "You just told me his mother wasn't like your mother."

"They were both whores, okay? My mother just made a living at it, while Angie . . . Angie was just lonely."

"Were you?"

"A whore?"

She was not going to tease him about this. "Were you lonely?"

"Sometimes. Not with women like Angie around. But sometimes."

She didn't believe him. "Clay said he didn't know who his father was."

He shook his head, sat forward, draped his wrists over his knees. "You two covered just about everything, didn't you?"

"I didn't torture anything out of him, Casper. He talked. I

listened." She thought back to Clay deciding it was time to pay the piper. "He's got it in him to be okay. Whatever happens."

"I'm not going to let *whatever*"—another gesture, his arm flinging to the side—"happen. God*dammit*, Faith. I may not have grown up surrounded by family, but I know letting things *happen* is not how it's done."

"I just meant—"

"You just meant that I need to prepare for the worst. Prepare him for the worst."

She waited, let that settle, then asked again, "Why is being there for him so important?"

"Because no one was there for me!" He surged to his feet, kicking at her coffee table when his boot snagged it, disappearing into the kitchen with the longneck he'd polished off. She expected to hear him jerk open the fridge for another, but it was silence that reached her instead.

She gave him a couple of minutes, then she followed, her bare feet soundless as they sunk into her plush carpeting. The kitchen was dark, the light from the eating nook catching him in profile where he stood with his hands on the sink. It lit his cheek and his neck and his elbow and forearm beneath his dark T-shirt's sleeve.

He looked exhausted, beaten, weary in ways no amount of sleep or bill-paying money or ground-soaking rain would soothe. It cut her to the quick, that sense of defeat, as if he couldn't face one more brick wall, one more dead end.

She came up behind him, got a raised hand and a sharp, "Don't," before she got close enough to touch him. "Just . . . don't."

Fine. She made a fist, bit her tongue, turned, and left the room. He could do his man-against-the-world thing and let himself out. She was going to bed.

And she did. At least she flounced into the middle of it, fully dressed, lying back and staring at the ceiling fan, fighting with herself to stay there, not to hop up and run back and tell him all the ways she could make things better for him. That doing so would make things better for her.

Her arms stretched out across the mattress, she dug her fingers into her comforter. She had to stop trying to fix him. He'd shown her the worst of his cracks, trusting her not to twist his vulnerability, or use it against him . . . yet she couldn't bring herself to share hers.

God, she was such a hypocrite. She was the one who was really broken, who could not get beyond the mistakes she'd made in the past, who was still fighting against her adventurous nature jailed inside pantyhose and black pumps.

Wiping at the corners of her eyes, she took a deep breath, hearing Casper coming to her before she blew it out. He stopped in her doorway, leaned a shoulder against the jamb, crossed his arms and ankles, as if he had to get everything settled just right before he could speak.

She took that time to sit up, tucking her legs to the side since her skirt was too tight for anything else. And then she waited because that's how this worked. Casper weighed the truth of what he carried, coming to her only when he'd stored the part of the burden he couldn't share safely out of sight.

"I didn't mean it. Telling you not to touch me."

He'd bit off the word *don't*. He'd said it twice. Sounded to her like he'd meant it, but she kept that to herself and continued to wait. She couldn't rush him. She'd pushed him enough for one night, even if keeping her mouth shut was killing her.

After a moment, he dropped his shields and walked into her room. He settled onto the bed beside her, reached up and brushed her hair from her face, looking at her, but not into her eyes. At her ear, her neck, her shoulder. "Why in the hell do you put up with me?"

"A question I am constantly asking myself," she said, leaning into his touch.

"After everything you've seen—"

"Shh." She brought her fingers to his lips. "Where you came from, what you've been through, that's all in the past."

"Except for who it turned me into. That's all in the present."

"I'm in the present, too. You seem to keep forgetting that."

"I've been an ass, shutting you out this last week. It's just been so much, all of it. Working at Summerlin's, the house, Clay . . ."

"And the ranch."

"I don't even count the ranch anymore. It's like the monster that will not die. Sometimes I think it would be easier if it would."

But it wouldn't. And they both knew that. "The zombie ranch, eating your brain."

"If I had a brain, I would never have let this thing with Clay get to this point. I would've *handled it* as soon as I realized who he was and where he'd come from. I need to get it done."

She took a deep breath, a hopeful breath, the flutter of wings in her chest hopeful, too. "Then we'll go. Talk to whoever we need to talk to."

"I'll go. This isn't your fight."

"No, but you don't have to fight on your own."

TWENTY-SIX

"I WANTED TO APOLOGIZE again about Clay. About the other night. I shouldn't have taken him to the diner. Or talked to him without first talking to you."

Hunkered down at the rear of Remedy's stall, hunting for his missing catch rope, Casper couldn't help but grin as he listened to Faith ramble on. He had a really hard time believing she'd come all the way out here for that. More like she'd come out here because they hadn't seen each other for three days now and she couldn't wait any longer.

He'd been planning to head to her place tonight after he finished up at Summerlin's because he couldn't wait any longer either. Besides, they'd settled things about Clay on Tuesday before getting naked and losing hours of sleep. "You could've called."

"I did call," she said, pulling open the stall door and stepping inside. She had on blue heels to go with her blue skirt, and her blouse had little things fluttering over her shoulders he guessed were supposed to be sleeves. "First your cell, which I learned has been disconnected. Then the house phone where I left a message. I even called Boone, though since he doesn't keep his phone with him, I don't know why. I guess I could've tried Dax, but I already felt like a nag."

He got to his feet, the catch rope in his hand. "You're not a nag, and you don't need to apologize. You did what you thought was right, talking to him. You did what I should've done and didn't. If anything, I'm the one who owes you."

"Depends on what it is you think you owe. But speaking of owing," she said before he could detail the things he had on his mind. She held out a business-sized envelope. "The reason I'm here. I've got a bill from John Massey covering the first stage of the demolition and build-out."

"Figured you would've written a check and shown me the damage afterward," he said, looking from the rope he held to the way her blouse pulled tight over her tits.

"You don't have much faith in me as a business partner, do you? Besides, their terms are thirty days net, and I can earn enough interest in that time to put a big dent in the whole of the construction cost. I just wanted to make sure you saw it—"

Again. He didn't believe that for a minute.

"—and to find out if you've made an appointment with Greg."

Now that he believed. "Not yet. I'll be getting a check tonight from Summerlin, so I'll call him Monday first thing."

"Use the phone in the tack room and call him now."

"I'm pretty sure you just said something about not being a nag."

"You didn't need to wait to get a check. I would've loaned, not given, *loaned* you the money."

"About your money . . ."

She shook her head and finger. "The first rule of my money is that we don't talk about my money."

He'd let her think that for now as he reached for the envelope, but took hold of her hand instead, sliding the loop of the rope over her wrist. "I could torture it out of you."

"No, you couldn't. No matter your opinion of my mouth—"

"Your mouth's one of my favorite things in the world—"

"I can keep a secret. And what are you doing?"

"Tying you up," he said, lashing her wrist against the stall's door and backing her into the corner. "Give me your other hand."

"After what you just did to this one," she said, tugging at her bond, "I think the answer is no."

He reached for her hand anyway, held her gaze as he used a length of broken rein to secure her to the stall's top slat. Then he stepped back, his hands at his hips as he took her in, bound in place, annoyed, wearing too many clothes.

"Fun time's over, cowboy. Let me go. I need to get home and get dinner and get out of these clothes—"

"I can help with that," he said, and walked toward her, his grin pulling at his mouth in direct proportion to the widening of her eyes.

"You are not—"

"Oh, but I am," he said, pressing his body flush to hers and reaching behind her to unzip her skirt.

He tugged it down just enough to free her blouse from her waist, then unbuttoned it before unhooking her bra. With her arms bound to the side, he had to make do with pushing the garments out of the way as he leaned down to tongue a nipple and suck her into his mouth.

"Casper!"

He lifted his head and offered her a "Yes, ma'am" before moving to the other nipple, tonguing, sucking, his hands at her skirt pulling it down.

"Casper!"

Her groan was a mix of arousal and desperation, and her head turned over her shoulder toward the barn door. He reached for his pocketknife and switched open the blade, pulling the elastic of her pantyhose from her body and slicing through the fabric.

"You're costing me a fortune in pantyhose," she hissed. "And panties," she added as he cut those away, too, breathing her in, drawing the back of his hand over her bared lips.

When she groaned that time, he knelt in front of her, slid both thumbs into her folds to spread her open, exposing her clit that was full and begging to be sucked. The fact that she couldn't move had his cock aching for the same, but first things first.

He had uptight Faith Mitchell bare-assed and tied to a stall in the barn. Could life possibly get any better?

He leaned forward, smelling her, his cock jumping. She was salty and ripe and warm. He licked from her tight little hole to her clit, getting her juice all over his chin as he dragged his tongue through her sex. She tasted like the best sort of cream, rich and thick and fresh, and his stomach rumbled. He caught her clit and pulled it between his lips, and she gasped. So he did it again, sucking harder this time, and she hissed some words he'd never have thought to hear come out of her mouth.

"Casper, let me go. What if Boone comes in? What about Dax and Clay?"

"Let me worry about Dax and Boone and Clay." The other three were in the Braff pasture to mammy off some pairs and wouldn't be back until sunset. He'd let Clay ride out on Remedy, staying behind to deal with hunting down some of Dave Dalton's old gear. He was damn glad he had. "And let me make up to you what I owe."

He took her silence as surrender and put his mouth on her cunt, pulling at her lips with his, tonguing her clit, and circling it, teasing, lapping, making her wiggle and moan. He liked making her moan. Liked making her want him, making her come.

Liked that bound against her wishes, she still shuddered when he pushed his tongue into her, fucking her, pulling out slowly and paying attention to the warm, wet flesh he'd exposed. His thumbs held her open, and his tongue did the rest. He pushed hard when she ground against him and used just the tip to tease her when she clenched and backed away.

But he'd learned what she liked, what it took to send her over, and he put his mind to a task he loved. To one he was cocky enough to know he did well. He could read her, and he loved following her lead, loved that she could tell him to go slow, to push harder, to use his teeth, to stop being so goddamn gentle.

He thought he loved that most of all, and it had his cock thickening. Then he groaned into her, and she shuddered and came in his mouth, fluttering, shivering, and tightening before letting go. Once she was done, he kissed her there, and on her belly, and on her thigh where he bit her and left a mark.

Then he got to his feet, and on his way up her body he stopped to do the same to her tit. There was something about the reminder of where he'd been, what she'd allowed him to do—

"Untie me," she said. He murmured, "Yes, ma'am," against her throat, reaching for both wrists at the same time, sliding his tongue into her mouth as he freed her, rubbing his thumbs over her wrists before bringing her hands to his crotch, cupping her fingers over his cock and surging into her palm.

She broke away from his mouth to breathe, her gaze catching

his, saying something it was too dark in the barn to see. But he stayed there, wondering, and he was still staring into her eyes, falling into her eyes, when the barn phone rang.

He rested his forehead against hers and whispered, "Don't move."

He wasn't done with her, but when the phone rang again, he stepped out of the stall and hoofed it across the way to grab it. "Royce, hey," he said, watching as Faith shook the straw from her skirt and stepped into it, moving when he'd told her not to, making him want to bend her over his knee and correct that.

"I've got a new Arabian arriving this weekend. Think you could spare a few extra hours next week?"

He was staring at Faith, her hair disheveled, her hands at her hips as she looked around for the envelope with Massey's bill. She'd yet to fasten her bra or her blouse, and her breasts swung free, bouncing just enough as she turned this way and that. He thought of the taste of her tits, the tight nipples like tiny little grapes rolling against his tongue.

"Jayne. You there?"

"Sorry, Royce," Casper said, closing his eyes and leaning against the workbench. "I'm in the barn. Hard to hear. What did you say?"

"I could use all the hours you can spare next week. I've got a sweet little filly coming in on Sunday. I figure to let her settle in for a bit, then have you come out Monday. Was hoping you could spare at least half the day."

"I can probably swing it. I'll need to check with the boys, but we're not exactly a high-priority operation, so I doubt it'll be an issue." And then feeling Faith's hands at his belt buckle and fly, his eyes opened and he stumbled over whatever he'd been going to say next.

She opened his jeans, lifted his cock and his balls free, then shoved his shorts to his hips, stroking a finger the length of his jutting shaft, over the full head and along the underside. Then she continued using her knuckle against his sac to separate his balls.

He squeezed his eyes closed, tried to pay attention to what Summerlin was saying as she knelt in front of him, teasing him, touching him. But the next thing he knew he heard scissors, and then he felt scissors, and his eyes popped open at that.

She had him by the short and curlies, literally, her two fingers holding his hair straight while she cut her way through the thatch, trimming around his cock until he was bared to the root, a long, thick stalk she then took into her mouth.

The fingers of her one hand ringed the base of his shaft, the fingers of her other cupped his nuts, rolling them, pushing up between them before slipping deeper between his legs and finding the bud of his ass.

"Jesus," he muttered.

"What was that?" Royce said in his ear.

"Nothing. Just sounds like a hell of a horse."

That seemed to satisfy the older man, because he kept on yammering, something about lineage and coat coloration and stuff Casper couldn't really make out because Faith's finger was sliding deep into the unknown.

He had the presence of mind to cover the mouthpiece before he groaned, biting off a low, "Goddammit, Faith," as her tongue poked at the slit in the head of his cock. He was tied up by a call instead of by ropes and reins, but he was no less helpless and bound, and *he didn't give a fuck about the fucking horse.*

"I'll check in with you on Monday, Royce. You have a good weekend." Then he tossed the receiver toward the base before sliding his fingers into Faith's hair, holding her while she sucked the chrome off his trailer hitch, watching her cheeks and her lips working, the heel of her hand pushing hard against his belly above the base of his cock, and that was it.

"Hold on," he told her, moving one hand to the back of her head, the other to the horn of the saddle on the nearby rack. She held the head of his cock in the cup of her tongue, giving him a target to aim for. He couldn't aim. He could barely stand, fisting his fingers in her hair as he shot his load down the back of her throat.

Once he'd finished and found his footing and his mind, he helped her to her feet. She dusted off her knees and the back of her skirt, a Cheshire cat grin on her mouth. He nodded toward the tiny john in the corner. "Scissors? And you call me dangerous?"

Her laughter reached him above the sound of running water, then she returned and stepped close, trapping his hands between them before he got his business put away.

She raked her nails through his extra-short hairs. "Come over tonight when you're through here. We'll shower, and I'll finish that up with a razor."

Then she was gone. And not for a minute did he believe she'd come here to talk about Clay or the construction. But he really didn't think she'd come here to blow him in the barn, either, and that left him to wonder if she'd got what she'd come for at all.

TWENTY-SEVEN

"IF THAT'S HOW you handled the bulls you rode, it's a wonder you didn't get hung up to more than you did, because that, my man, was an epic fail."

Casper lay on his back, his knees raised, hands at his side in the dirt, his eyes screwed shut. Who the hell knew where his hat was. Or the air he should be breathing. Or his spleen. Somewhere in the corral, the Arabian who'd just made him her bitch stomped and snorted.

If he thought he could come back at Dax without throwing up, he would, but something told him he'd just mightily cracked a rib. Or else he'd landed on a chunk of earth hard-packed and sharp enough to leave a deep bruise. Why he'd thought it a good idea to bring the boys along to see him put Summerlin's new Arabian through her paces . . .

Squinting with the one eye he was able to pry open, he held up a finger and croaked out, "One sec."

A second pair of jeans appeared in his line of blurred vision. Then a third. Boone, he figured, and Summerlin, or one of his hands.

"Just lay still now," Royce said, putting a name to the set of bowed legs at his feet. "Doc Pope's on his way."

He wasn't going to move. He couldn't move. He would die if he tried.

And Faith was going to kill him.

He'd told her he wouldn't get hurt, that he wouldn't do anything to put him out of commission so that more of the ranch chores landed on Boone. He'd told her all of those things, and yet here he was, hoping not to puncture a lung with the jagged end of a rib, and mourning the moratorium on getting her naked in his immediate future.

He groaned. Just the thought of his cock getting hard had his balls crawling up into his body.

God*damn,* he hurt.

Beside him, Boone hunkered down, his body blocking the blinding light of the cruel, cruel sun. "Think maybe it's time to give up this shit?"

He tried to grunt but he still couldn't breathe for the elephant suffocating him, and all he got out was a squeaky, "Need money."

Dax squatted on his other side. "Fuck the money and fuck that house. We need you alive, and in one piece, my friend."

"Need hat," he said, and moments later Boone had the brim shadowing his eyes. Now if someone could do something about the dirt making mud in his nostrils and the fingernails-on-chalkboard grit in his teeth. And the railroad spike in the back of his head. And the ever-lovin' fire in his chest. God*damn,* he hurt. "Thanks."

"Stop trying to talk and listen. The house has been there for a hundred years. It's not going anywhere. The ranch is the problem."

"Boone's right," Dax said since it was obviously his turn to pile on. "The ranch was already eating us up, and now you've added the house and the horses and Clay."

"I asked." He curled his fingers, drew up a palmful of earth. "You okayed."

"That was then. This is now." Boone used a bandanna to wipe the corral floor out of Casper's eyes. "Something's gotta give."

"Clay helps," he croaked out, wanting to tell them both to fuck off but in no shape to do so. Plus, they were right, and they didn't even know about Faith. He'd taken on too much, giving up sleep to make time for it all, and paying the price.

The Arabian had let him know what was coming, and he'd been too exhausted to decipher the signs until he was already airborne. He deserved having his partners kick his ass. As long as they steered clear of his ribs. God*damn*, he hurt.

"And what happens when all this shit with Clay comes to a head and blows?" Boone asked. "Because you have no guarantee that won't happen once the law and the courts get involved."

"They won't," he said, then thirty seconds later, the pain in his back like stabbing glass shards, added, "not yet."

"Only because you've got him squirreled away like an illegal working for slave wages."

"Gets allowance," was all Casper could say, and those words were full of air and burned like a motherfucker.

"Doc's here," Summerlin said as the sound of truck wheels eating up gravel reached Casper's ears. And then things got worse with Dr. Pope touching him, poking and prodding and rolling him to one side then the other, poking more, prodding more, using his stethoscope before sitting back on his heels.

He looked from Dax to Boone. "There's a stretcher in the

back of my Suburban. I need you two to help me get him loaded up."

"I'm on it," Dax said while Casper tried to find his voice to object. Besides, what was he going to do? Spend the rest of the day flat on his back?

"Drugs," he finally said, and Mercer Pope laughed, a gravelly evil sound that Casper did not like.

"Soon, my reckless friend. First, x-rays."

"WHERE IS HE?" Faith asked, yanking off her sunglasses as she entered the ranch house kitchen. She blinked, blinked again, looked around astounded, then met Clay's gaze. "Is this you?"

"Is what me?" he asked, standing at the stove, stirring the aromatic contents bubbling in a big stockpot.

Chili powder, garlic, cumin, onions, peppers. Vegetable scraps and spice bottles sat on a cutting board along with the butcher paper from the meat. Her stomach growled. "I've never seen this kitchen this clean. I didn't even know the floor tiles were veined. I just thought they were dirty."

"Yeah, that took a while," he said, dipping into the pot with a second spoon and blowing across a bite of what was either chili or stew. He tasted it, tossed the used spoon into the sink, added salt, and kept stirring. "I had to use a toothbrush on a lot of it. And it's pretty worn from all the foot traffic. But it looks okay."

Who *was* this kid? "And that smell? You're cooking?"

"Chili. Nothing fancy. Casper likes it." He shrugged off his efforts as if fourteen-year-olds cooking chili from scratch was the norm. "Anyhow, he's upstairs."

"I'm surprised he made it up there," she said, heading toward the staircase.

"The boys tried to get him to camp out on the couch, but he was saying something about clean sheets. I didn't hear all of it."

The boys. Hearing Clay use the words to refer to Boone and Dax made her smile almost more than seeing him so happily settled. Casper rambling on about clean sheets made her smile for much more personal reasons. "Sounds like the fall didn't soften up his hard head."

"You want some chili when I bring it up?"

"Sure," she called back. "That would be great."

"Okay. I'll bring some crackers, too. And some cheese."

Shaking her head, she climbed the stairs, remembering when she'd offered to hire the boys a maid. Clay had solved that problem nicely, and even *he* looked better for it, less gaunt, less hollow, as if he had a purpose instead of having nothing. As if Casper had been the very savior he'd crossed two states to find.

God, she hoped this didn't go south the way she feared it might. It had only been a few weeks, and yet both Casper and Clay had grown more comfortable together than some fathers and sons she'd seen. Clay had obviously been looking for the structure and safe haven, the sense of belonging and family Casper had provided.

But it seemed that Casper had been needing someone, too. Someone he could care for. Someone he could be responsible for. Someone who wasn't her. It shouldn't bother her that she couldn't give him whatever it was lacking in his life, and it didn't. Except it did. And for a smart girl, she was being really stupid.

This wasn't about her. It was about the life Casper had known at Clay's age. Making that connection wasn't difficult. The difficult part was accepting that he might never need her for more than what they already shared—the companionship, the sex. Since she wasn't looking for a relationship, she should be okay with that.

But she wasn't. The fact that she'd bolted out of work an hour early at hearing news of the accident was proof. She'd been as anxious to see him and worried about his injuries as if it had been her brother or one of her parents she'd heard two of the tellers gossiping about. Of course, it would've been nice if Boone had called to let her know what had happened . . .

She stopped just outside Casper's doorway, her hand on the frame, her head on her hand, her head filled with a roulette wheel of emotions—dizzying, stunning, dangerous—rolling over her. He lay on his back, a forearm tossed over his eyes, his chest bare, the covers riding low on his hips. White tape wrapped his midsection. A strip of his boxer briefs showed white above his yellow sheet, and one foot poked out from the bottom.

She stared for longer than she should have, taking him in, all of him—the rumpled bed, the jumble of dead cell phone and keys and change on the top of his dresser, his belt on the floor, curled like a snake around the saucer of his belt buckle. His clothes in a dirty pile smelling of horse and sweat.

"I'm awake," he said, reaching one hand toward her, his eyes closed, his voice low and raspy.

"I wasn't sure. You look so . . . peaceful."

"You're not looking close enough, sweetheart," he said, crooking his finger.

She stopped at the edge of the bed and whispered, "I'm not here to have sex."

He laughed, groaned, his hand going to his bandages. "Shit. Don't make me laugh."

"Guess that means you weren't inviting me close to get naked."

"I don't even want to think about you naked." He groaned again. "Shit. There it goes." Another groan, and his hand slipped under the sheet to his groin. "Taking care of this is going to kill me."

"Why don't you not think about me naked and there won't be anything to take care of?" she asked, then crossed from the bed to the window, pulling back the curtain.

She looked down on the ranch yard, where Kevin lay between Bing and Bob, his chin on his paws, all three staring into the pasture beyond the corral as if waiting for something to happen. Seconds later it did, as Dax and Boone topped a distant rise on horseback.

At that, the trio slipped like greased pigs through the corral slats, Kevin lumbering to keep up with the border collies as they sprinted to greet the boys. Amazing, she mused, letting the curtain fall. Even Clay's dog had settled in, belonging.

Behind her, Casper grunted. "You could take care of it for me. It'll still kill me, but at least I'll die a happy man."

She turned to meet his gaze, but found his eyes closed instead. "Clay's coming up in a few with something to eat. Chili with cheese and crackers."

"Thanks, though that bucket of water's not quite cold enough. Got another?"

"The kitchen looks amazing," she offered, happy to keep both their minds off what lay—or stood—beneath his sheets. "I'd threatened Boone with hiring a maid, but I see you took care of that nicely."

"No," he said, turning his head on his pillow to look at her. "I found a runaway squatting in my house and hid him from the authorities and put him to work like a slave. There's the cold water I needed. Problem solved. At least one of my many."

The man was going to break her heart, if he didn't first break his neck. "You don't have to do this, you know. Work for Royce. End up injured even worse."

"What?" he groaned. "I'm supposed to admit where I got the funds for the house? Not that anyone's going to believe what I'm making is enough for the renovations."

Faith remembered Arwen commenting on what Royce was paying. "So you're risking your life to provide a cover story?"

"I wouldn't go so far as to say I'm risking my life."

"You got thrown from a horse who then nearly trampled you."

"How do you know what happened anyway?"

"I have eyes and ears everywhere helping me protect my investment."

"You mean you have Boone," he said, grimacing as he shifted to sit.

"Here," she said, seeing no need to correct him. She offered her arm for him to use as a lever, then tucked his pillows behind him. "Your sheets do smell good."

"You roll around in them with me for a while, they'll smell even better."

He never quit, did he? "This after saying me giving you a hand would kill you?"

"Yeah. Probably not a good idea." He pulled his summer-weight blanket higher on his hips. "And you can thank Clay for the sheets. He's been keeping all the laundry done around here."

"Good for him."

Casper nodded. "And the boy can cook. I think I've gained ten pounds."

"The chili smelled amazing."

"He's a regular Rick Bayless."

That made her smile. "You know who Rick Bayless is?"

He snorted. "Only because Clay told me when I walked in on him watching *One Plate at a Time*."

"Watch out, he'll be digging a pit in the ranch yard to cook a pig."

"I'm a cattleman. He'd better be cooking a cow."

She smiled at that. "How long are you going to be laid up with the ribs?"

"I'll be back in the saddle tomorrow."

Typical. "I have a hard time believing those are Dr. Pope's orders."

"Fuck Dr. Pope. I mean, don't fuck Dr. Pope. Fuck me if you're going to fuck anyone."

"Casper!" She covered his mouth with her hand and whispered, "Clay'll be here any minute." He rolled his eyes, but nodded, so she let him go and moved to sit on the foot of the bed.

"Dr. Pope wants me in bed longer than I can afford to be here."

She cocked her head. "How much do you think you can get done in your condition? Wouldn't it be better to take the days than to make things worse?"

"The ribs are broken, Faith. They can't get more broken."

"No, but they can *not* heal."

"You worry too much."

"You don't worry at all."

"Now that's not true. I worry it's going to be too long before I can get back to doing you." He stopped, cleared his throat, and added, "To doing your list. The things from the house. I know you've still got several for me to look at."

Good lord. The man didn't need to worry about jerking off killing him because she was going to do that. Just as soon as Clay, who was hovering uncertainly in the doorway, left the room.

"Here's the chili," he said, lifting the tray he held, his gaze shifting between the two of them.

"Dang, that smells good. I could eat this stuff every day." Casper nodded for the boy to come into the room, then nodded toward his nightstand. "Just put it there."

Clay did, backed away, dusting his hands together. "I'll make another pot, but I used the last of the cumin in this one. And I brought up the rest of the crackers, and some cheese. We're almost out of that, too. I put both on the grocery list."

While Casper grimaced, wiggling against the headboard, Faith said, "Why don't Clay and I go to Nathan's and pick up y'all's groceries? One less thing for you to worry about doing."

"You don't need to do that," he said, frowning.

Frowning because he didn't want her spending more of her money on him. "I know I don't *need* to. I want to. The boys just rode in, so you won't be alone."

"You want to go now? Who's going to feed me?"

She rolled her eyes. "You can feed yourself while I feed myself. Then after Clay and the boys eat, I can clean up while he gets his list together." She turned to Clay, who stood half in and half out of the room. "Sound good?" He nodded. "Then it's settled," she said, turning back to Casper as the boy loped down the stairs.

"Don't get used to this," he said, spooning up a bite after she'd handed him his bowl.

"Get used to what? Clay's cooking?"

"Getting your way."

"Is that what I'm doing?"

"Too often it seems. Not sure why I'm so off my game these days." He crushed a handful of crackers on top of his chili, added almost as much shredded cheese. "I blame you. I haven't been myself since—" And then he stopped, as if hit by a realization that didn't make him particularly happy.

"You were saying?" she pressed, because she was tickled.

"I let you take scissors to me. I don't let women take scissors to me."

"Don't forget the razor," she reminded him, too late to bite back the words.

His eyes heated, his pulse in his throat pounded, his cock rose to tent the sheet between them. The room grew still, and they both left their spoons in their bowls, and neither one dared breathe and break the beautiful tension binding them.

When the kitchen door slammed beneath them and Dax hollered for Clay, she found enough of her voice to whisper, "Casper—"

He cut her off with a shake of his head. "I changed my mind. I want you to take Clay to the store. Now would be a very good time."

TWENTY-EIGHT

"GODDAMMIT." CASPER FLUNG his newly reconnected phone across the ballroom floor, where it shattered against the stone hearth, wincing at the pull in his ribs and the explosion of electronics and glass. He still wanted to throttle Faith for the reconnection, her and her goddamn money, except who the hell knew how long he would've had to wait for this particular bad news otherwise?

She'd been halfway out the door, on her way to the kitchen to meet John Massey, but stopped and spun toward him. "What happened? What's wrong?"

"That was Becky Dixon at the sheriff's office." He took a breath, jammed his hands to his hips, ignored the kick drum throb in his midsection. "Clay's been arrested."

"What?"

"Shoplifting. And driving without a license. Seems he took the ranch pickup to town and stole a jar of cumin from Nathan's."

The boom, boom, boom was impossible to ignore. He screwed up his eyes and groaned. "What the hell is cumin, anyway?"

"It's a spice. Or an herb. For the chili."

"Jesus." He looked at her, her frown, the lines of worry at the corners of her eyes, her suit and shoes and pantyhose. This woman. She was becoming his rock. "You took him shopping just a couple of days ago. He didn't get it then?"

"I guess he forgot to put it on his list. Or forgot to check his list. I don't know. I'm sorry. What can I do? What do you need me to do?"

It was noon and they were at the house on Mulberry Street. He'd called her from the ranch house this morning after getting a message from Massey about a problem with the kitchen tile. She'd said she'd handle it, and they'd hung up, and those words had stuck with Casper all morning.

This was his house to handle. He didn't care that she held an equal share of the equity.

So he'd come to town to run the boatload of errands he and the boys had let slide, stopping at the bank to tell her he'd deal with the tile and Massey. That was when she'd handed him the phone she'd taken off his dresser, and told him it was her lunch hour and she was coming, too.

His rock, but still bossy. "He must've taken off right after I did. Why didn't he just ask me to pick it up? He knew I'd be in town."

"He forgot or he wanted to surprise you."

"I could do without this kind of surprise."

She stepped into him then, her arms coming around him gently, the weight of her head against his chest like a blanket covering his heart. She wrapped him up and warmed him with her hands at his back and her legs braided with his, their feet slow dancing without moving a step.

He closed his eyes and just held her, melting into the fit of her, the rightness of it, the comfort he found in her, the perfect sense of being. He kissed the top of her head, lingered there, breathed her in, and waited as long as he could to exhale.

"I've got to go."

She pulled back, looked up at him, her eyes damp with his pain. "To the jail? Or to a lawyer?"

Like he could afford a lawyer. "The jail, I guess. Then a lawyer."

"You want me to call Darcy?"

"No. Not Darcy." Dax would whip the skin from his hide.

"Well, her father's not practicing anymore."

"Her brother is."

That brought him an arched brow. "You're going to Greg?"

Casper thought back to the morning he'd talked to the other man in the Blackbird Diner. Thought back to the secrets Greg had kept. "Yeah."

"Whatever for?"

"He's a lawyer."

"That's not what I meant."

"Because I don't know him and he doesn't know me and I am not in the mood to deal with any Campbell drama."

"Darcy does not do drama."

"I wasn't talking about Darcy." When she mouthed a silent, "Oh," he said, "I'm going to the jail. Then I'm going to see Greg. Can you take care of the tile and granite crap with John?"

"Of course," she said. "Anything," she added, her voice so soft and caring he wanted to face-punch himself for barking at her.

"Faith—"

"Casper, go. Call me if you need me."

Was she kidding? He cupped the back of her head and

brought her to him, whispering into her hair, "I'll always need you."

Those words came back as he gunned it through the short drive from Mulberry Street to Main. She hadn't responded except to smile, and to draw her palm along his cheek, her fingers to his lips before she brought them to her own.

He meant them, those words, but it wasn't the need of a burden. He didn't need her to do for him, or fix things for him, to make things right when he didn't have means. He needed *her*, and the way things didn't feel as daunting when she was there.

Walking into the sheriff's substation ten minutes later brought back memories of sleeping off more than a few drunks in one or the other of the two puke-colored cells. He raised a hand in greeting to Becky Dixon who pointed him toward Ned Orleans's desk while she dispatched another officer to an accident scene.

"Sheriff," Casper said, pushing through the waist-high gate from the open reception area into the sleepy hub. He nodded at the sheriff, tamped down the wave of dread rising to choke him. "Can I have a word with Clay?"

"You can," the other man said, his chair squeaking as he leaned forward. "After you and I have a conversation."

"About?"

Ned gestured toward the chair at the side of his desk, waited until Casper gingerly sat. "Who this kid is, where he came from."

"What has he told you?"

"Not much except to call you."

So the sheriff didn't know about New Mexico, or Clay being a runaway, or Casper harboring him with full knowledge. He supposed that was a relief, though his gut wasn't feeling it. 'Course that could've been his ribs. "Thanks for doing that. Now what do I need to do to get him out of here?"

"Not so fast. That conversation, remember?"

"Fine. Let's talk."

"I'm assuming you won't be pressing charges for him stealing your truck—"

"Borrowed. He didn't steal anything from me."

"There's still the issue of him having no license or ID and being underage, which I'm assuming based on what I can see. And he did steal the spice bottle from Nathan's. I'm also going to guess he's Kendall Sheppard's and Arwen Poole's thief. Meaning I need to have a word with his parents or his guardians or whoever he belongs to."

"He belongs to me. With me. He's the son of a friend of mine. From out of town," he said, figuring truth and evasion would work in his favor better than lies.

"Then I need to talk to this . . . friend. His mother, I imagine? Can I get a name and a number? Or an address?"

Jesus H. This *Law & Order* shit was what happened when a cop had too much time on his hands and too few tickets to write. "She's . . . unavailable. That's why he's staying with me for now."

Ned leaned back in his chair, his hands laced behind his head. "What about the rest of his family? Someone who can vouch for him."

Because Casper vouching for him wasn't good enough? Bracing his arms on his knees, he worried his hat in his hands. "There is no other family, Sheriff. That's why he's staying with me. I can vouch for him."

Ned bobbed his head. "There's still the matter of his shoplifting. And whether or not Nathan's is going to press charges—"

"Over a five-dollar jar of some spice?"

"It could've been a penny candy. Or a ten-dollar paperback. Or two dollars' worth of soda. Stealing is stealing, my friend."

They were not friends. "I'll settle things with Nathan's. And with Kendall and Arwen." Kendall had been taken care of, thanks to Faith, but he'd still go by and make sure she knew Clay would be buying the rest of his books brand new. "And if you're going to fine him or press charges for his driving without a license, I'll see that he gets to court or whatever. Now, can I talk to him?"

The sheriff took his sweet time making up his mind, getting to his feet, leading Casper to the rear of the small building. He stopped at the doorway separating the cells from the office, pushing it open after he'd unlocked it and gesturing for Casper to walk through.

He did, the heavy door clanging shut and locking behind him. He blew out a suffocating breath and looked into the cell on his right. Clay sat on the built-in bench, his legs out in front of him crossed at the ankle, his head against the cinder-block wall, his eyes closed.

"Catching up on your sleep?"

"Nothing else to do."

So smart-ass was how it was going to be. "What were you thinking? I gave you money."

"I spent it. You said you liked the chili. That you could eat it every day."

"I didn't want you to steal the ingredients."

"It's just a jar of cumin. Not a big deal."

"It's not just a jar of cumin. It's also a book. And bottles of Coke. And who the hell knows what kind of trail you left between here and Albuquerque."

"Like I said. It's not a big deal."

Fuck this disrespectful . . . "It goddamn well is a big deal. I don't know what Angie taught you—"

Clay burst up off the bench and rushed the bars, grabbing hold and shaking, though the only thing he shook was himself. His eyes were wide and red and wet, and as angry as they were scared. "My mother didn't teach me shit, okay? She was too busy shooting herself full of heroin and fucking every cowboy who came to town."

Casper stood back, rubbed a hand down his jaw to his throat, thinking for not the first time that he was in over his head, but for the first time understanding exactly what that meant. How in the hell was he going to help this boy when he was at the root of Clay's problems?

He held his gaze, fighting the urge to walk away . . . which wasn't about running, but about getting help, doing right by this boy, making up for the life he'd lived before coming to Crow Hill. Maybe making up for some of his own.

Then Clay collapsed, the fury driving him draining away. "Are you going to get me out of here?"

"Soon as I leave, I'm headed to see a lawyer. He'll find out what's going to happen, though I can't imagine much of anything."

"And you'll take care of Kevin?"

"Jesus H. Christ, Clay. It's not like you're headed for the big house. You can take care of him when you get home."

It took several long seconds, but a slow smile spread over Clay's face at that.

"This isn't funny."

"I'm not laughing. I just like the way you said home."

TWENTY-NINE

THERE WAS SOMETHING about the smell of leather in a law firm that set Casper's nerves on edge. His saddle was one thing. The binding wrapping transcripts and precedents and what the hell into tomes was another. Not that he'd ever been in any real trouble during his life, or had any real reason to fear the legal system, but there was always the chance of his past catching up with him.

He didn't like thinking about his past. He didn't want to open himself up, even for a confidential flaying. He didn't talk to anyone about the things he'd seen and done, why he'd made the decisions he'd made. Except to Faith. Faith made it easy. Greg being a virtual stranger, and Clay being the one in the most trouble, didn't.

Even as a teen when he'd run with Dax, Casper had never stepped foot in the Campbell law firm. The building sat on Yegua Creek Road just off Main, as far away as possible from the Municipal Plaza that housed the sheriff's substation, while remaining inside Crow Hill's city limits. Its lot was landscaped in low-growing scrub and cactus, the firm, like the succulents, thriving.

He imagined the place was a lot quieter now than when both Dax's sister and father had practiced law here, too. Now it was just Greg. The bastard son. The brother Dax had never known he'd had. The son Dax was supposed to have been.

What Casper had said to the sheriff was true enough. He'd taken on a kid who had no one else, his mother a friend and unavailable. He'd left out all the rest—the mother being dead, the kid being a runaway, Casper knowing all this and not turning him in. But none of that had been relevant, so he didn't see any reason to share it with Ned.

Sharing it with Greg was bad enough.

His legs crossed, a legal pad on his lap, Greg sat in the big leather chair next to Casper instead of in the one behind his desk. His black shoes and black pants and white shirt had Casper thinking of Faith. Two of a kind. Professionals. Neither one of them smelling like a horse.

Greg clicked the end of his pen. "You want custody of this boy who's been staying in your house. The one who was arrested and is now in jail. Whose mother died a year ago, and who two months ago ran away from his foster home in another state. Is that what you're saying?"

Put that way, it made him sound insane. "It doesn't have to be permanent."

"Custody is permanent, Casper."

"What about him being an emancipated minor?"

"Is he old enough to support himself? Old enough to get a driver's license if he needs to drive to a job?"

Crap. "Okay, then, I could foster him or something."

"So, you want to apply to be a foster parent."

"I don't know. I guess."

"And he'd live with you at the ranch? Or in the house on Mulberry Street?"

Jesus. Did everyone know about Mulberry Street? "The ranch," he said, leaving out the part about how long Clay had bunked at the house. What potential parent would leave a kid in that place? Sure, it hadn't been long. Casper had lived there longer. But it was enough, and it gnawed at him. "I moved him there from the house as soon as I got the okay from the boys."

"Then they know about this, too."

"But none of this is on them. Just me."

"Has he been working for you?"

"Around the house. Some other chores. He cooks."

"Do you pay him?"

"Just room and board. A few bucks for allowance. It's not like I'm made of money here."

Greg didn't comment, just pressed on. "And you could get him to school?"

"Sure. I guess. If he has to go."

"Unless you're going to home school him, then yes. He has to go."

Jesus H. Why the hell was he turning this into a federal case? Clay needed help. He wanted to help him. "I just want the boy out of jail, okay?"

"I understand that—"

"He doesn't need to be in jail. Nobody does at that age."

"Casper, I'm on your side here."

"Then tell me what I have to do to make that happen."

Greg looked down, clicked his pen again, then lifted his gaze and made sure Casper held it. "He's a minor and a runaway. I'm not sure any of us can make that happen."

"I thought that's what lawyers did."

"Work miracles? Sometimes we do. But that's when the law goes our way. I'm not sure in this case it will."

"Jesus H. Christ." Casper brought a hand to his side, his taped ribs aching.

"What does the sheriff know? About Clay's people in Albuquerque?"

"I don't think he knows anything. Clay ditched his ID before leaving, so Ned's only got my word that I know who he is. I told him there wasn't anyone else to vouch for him."

"Knowing Ned Orleans, he's started digging by now, looking for runaways, missing kids." Greg shifted in his chair, recrossing his legs. "It'll take him a while to get answers, work his way out of Texas."

"Then we've got time. Just do what you have to. I want Clay out of there before Ned figures out what's up. That happens, he'll be shipped back and lost in the system and it'll be too late."

"I can probably get him out, but if Clay knows what's coming, that we'll be contacting New Mexico about custody, he could very well run away from you."

Casper shook his head. "I won't let that happen."

"He's run away before."

"But not from me. Even when I threatened to turn him in," he said before he realized what he was admitting. "This is attorney-client privilege, right? I can't get busted for harboring a runaway?"

"As long as Clay keeps his mouth shut, I don't see any reason Ned needs to know about the conversations the two of you had."

"So you'll help me?"

Greg got to his feet. "Let me get over to the sheriff's office. I'll see where things stand and we'll go from there."

"Thank you," Casper said, slower to stand.

"It's what I do, Casper. The only thanks I need is a check that won't bounce."

"Huh. My reputation precedes me?"

"Something like that," Greg said, though only his mouth smiled.

"But you're not asking for a retainer up front?"

"This boy's in trouble now. And you're my brother's partner. I doubt you're going to skip town."

"He'd probably take your head off if he heard you call him that. Dax."

"Yeah, well, blood will be blood. He'll get over it."

"HAVE EITHER OF you guys seen Clay?" Casper asked later that evening, walking into the barn where Dax and Boone were brushing down their respective rides. "Or Kevin, for that matter?"

"Not since you brought him home earlier," Boone said.

"Huh. I checked his room. Some of his stuff's there, but I can't find his backpack."

"Sounds like an invasion of privacy to me," Dax said, jerking his chin toward Boone. "You know, like the way Coach used to go through that one's things."

"I wasn't going through his things," Casper said, thinking this couldn't be happening, that he couldn't be so dumb. "And I'm not his old man."

"You're the closest thing he's got," Dax reminded him, heaving that load of responsibility toward him like a hay bale. Or a bag of feed.

"You didn't find a note or anything?" Boone asked. "He could've gone out with the dogs roaming, exploring. Getting his head together or something. Might've needed the time alone after this morning."

"Shit." Casper kicked at the corner of the closest stall, the impact like a shotgun blast against his side. "Greg said this might happen."

"Whoa," Dax said, rearing away from the horse toward him. "Tell me I didn't just hear the bastard's name come out of your mouth."

"You told me to use him, you dick," Casper said, knocking Dax's hat from his head, biting off a curse at shotgun blast two.

Dax snagged up his hat, dusted it against his thigh. "Why did he think Clay might split?"

"Because of his getting arrested on top of this runaway custody foster care bullshit," Casper said, leaning a shoulder into the stall. "He thought Clay might realize this newest music on top of the other would have things swinging in the favor of the law."

"I can't imagine Nathan's will press charges," Boone said, returning from the tack room fridge with two apples, handing one to Dax, slicing the other for Sunshine.

"They're not." He and Clay had stopped and paid Lizzy Nathan for the cumin before ever leaving town, and she'd graciously accepted Clay's apology, as had Kendall Sheppard when he'd made a second stop there.

Arwen had fed them both lunch, telling Clay to ask for food if he was hungry. That most folks would see his need. Dax had found himself a good woman in that one, which took Casper's thoughts to Faith, before moving back to Clay. "But he was still driving without a license. Sheriff Orleans is being an ass and making him go to court for that."

"He'll get a fine, or a warning, but being a kid and a scared one, I could see him not thinking straight." Boone rubbed a hand down Sunshine's nose and over his muzzle. "Could've sent him running. He gets taken from you, who knows where he'll end up."

Casper pushed up on his hat, rubbed at his eyes, then his jaw. "I didn't think he'd do it. I should've listened to Greg."

"Been spending a lot of time with the bastard?"

Casper gave Dax a look. "He's not that bad of a guy."

"I don't think I heard you right. Because if I did—"

Boone stepped between them, a big hand on both of their chests. "Enough. You two fighting over Greg isn't going to help Clay. Are we going to look for him? Go to the sheriff? Gather up a search party? What?"

Pacing now, Casper shook his head. "I dunno. The sheriff finds him, he'll lock him up."

"Maybe he needs to be locked up," Boone said. When Casper started toward him, he added, "For his own good. Keep him safe. Out of trouble. It never hurt any of us, and we all spent more than a few nights behind bars when I, for one, would much rather have spent them at home and been served pancakes the next morning for breakfast."

"Yeah, well, you had a mother who made you pancakes. I was lucky if the milk for the cereal wasn't sour. Or if I didn't pour out a bowl of bugs with the Frosted Flakes."

"And what Clay has is you," Boone said. "Not quite pancakes, but definitely not a bowl of bugs."

He supposed. "Getting locked up again means I won't be getting him out. It's going to make the custody thing a lot harder."

Both men looked at him, Dax the one who finally asked, "You're filing then? For custody?"

Casper nodded, waited, got the lecture he'd been expecting from Boone.

"It's gotta be about more than keeping him out of a bad situation. About keeping him from going through the shit you did. And it sure as hell can't be about guilt. You may have bedded his old lady, but you did not have a hand in how he turned out, or any of what brought him here."

Casper couldn't think of better reasons, but he knew what Boone was saying. "It's the right thing to do. He came to me. And I want him to know he always can."

"Alrighty then," Dax said. "We going out on horseback? Taking the trucks? Hijacking the sheriff's chopper?"

Casper took another swing at Dax's hat, the other man scrambling for it as Casper headed out of the barn. "Y'all take the roads to Luling and Fever Tree. I'll check between here and Crow Hill, then the other side of town. It's only been six hours. He's on foot and he's got a dog. He can't have gotten far."

THIRTY

"ANY LUCK?" FAITH asked as she pulled open her front door, tightening the belt of a short silky robe before pushing a mess of hair from her face.

He'd woke her. He hated that, but he'd had to see her. Being alone was driving him crazy, and no one else would get how worried he was. The boys, they tried, but they weren't Faith. Faith knew what Clay had come to mean to him. Faith knew what he was going through.

He shook his head, took his first full breath in hours. "Nothing. We'll start looking again in the morning. Dax threatened to take my keys and hobble both me and Remedy if I didn't get some sleep. I told him I'd be back by midnight."

She shut the door behind him, stepped into his arms, and hooked hers around his neck, holding him, being there for him. "How far could he get in twelve hours? And how are your ribs?"

He ached from head to toe, mostly in his midsection, but he was pretty sure that was his heart. "Ribs are okay. Sore. And he's obviously gotten further than anyone's searched. Unless he's holed up somewhere waiting for the commotion to die down." He thought back to Clay telling him he'd done just that on his trek to Crow Hill. "Or he could've hoofed it off road or something."

"What about a search from the air?" She stepped back to look up at him. "Dan Katz has a private plane, and Mike Banyon a crop duster."

"I wouldn't even know where to start looking." He tossed his hat to her couch, took her hand, and tugged her down the hall to her bedroom. "And I'm pretty sure that kind of attention would send him into hiding. He's a smart kid. He'd know what was going on." He sat in her desk chair to pull off his boots, watching as she shed her robe and climbed into bed.

She tossed back the covers, giving him room, inviting him in, waiting. "I'm so sorry. I wish there was something I could do."

She was doing it, and she didn't even know. He tore off his T-shirt, shucked out of his shorts and jeans and socks, crawled in naked beside her, going instantly hard. He needed her, to be inside her, to lose himself in her. "It's my fault. I should've kept an eye on him instead of siccin' him on the upstairs bathroom so I could get back to work."

"This is not your fault." She lifted her hips to pull off her panties, sat up just long enough to strip her short nightie away.

"Sure it is." He rolled over her, used his knee to nudge hers open. The heat between her legs warmed him, and he thickened even more. "I make bad decisions and ruin things."

"That's not the first time you've said that." She wiggled, drew one leg up his thigh to his hip. "About ruining things."

That's because around her he had a big mouth. "You get it

drilled into you enough, it becomes an easy excuse to reach for when things go wrong."

"Who drilled it into you?"

"Who do you think?" he asked, slipping a hand between their bodies to toy with her, ready her, arouse her.

She closed her eyes, shuddered, dug her fingers into the balls of his shoulders. "You know it wasn't true, don't you? That she was just saying that to strike out?"

"I know she never wanted any kids. So she blamed me for everything in her life that went wrong."

"Listen to me," she said as he lifted his hips, as he found her entrance, as he slid into her in one long stroke that bound them to the core. She shuddered again as he settled, then squeezed him and pulled him in deeper, keeping him close, keeping him safe. "That woman may have given birth to you, but that woman was not a parent. You were around mine enough to know that."

He'd been around hers a lot, as often as he could. "I got a kick outta coming home with Boone. I didn't show it, and I owe your folks a lifetime of apologies for being an ungrateful ass, but I loved being there. Especially at supper. Sitting down to eat a real meal at a real table was as foreign to me as eating barefoot on a bamboo mat with chopsticks."

She pushed up and ground against him, her voice shaky when she said, "You remember breakfast? Toast flying, juice spilling, permission slips for school ending up stained with syrup or milk. We were a mess trying to get all four of us out the door. Five, when you where there."

"I loved those mornings. And it had nothing to do with the food." He brushed her hair from her forehead, moved higher into her body, slowly withdrawing and watching the play of desire in her eyes as he did. "I'd like them to know they had a lot to do with me holding on."

She rubbed a thumb over his cheekbone. "They know that."

"They say something?"

"No, but they wouldn't need to. That's just who they are. How they are. Ours was the house where everyone wanted to hang out. They know kids. It's why they do what they do."

"You were lucky. You are lucky."

She nodded in answer, her eyes damp. He lowered his head and kissed her temple, the moisture there salty on his tongue. Then he surged forward when she walked her fingers from the base of his skull down his spine. "But I've never felt as lucky as I do now."

Not as lucky as him. No one in the world was as lucky as him. He wanted to take his time loving her, enjoying her fingers and hands and mouth, her soles as she rubbed them from the backs of his knees to his feet, her cunt holding his cock, forgetting everything else because she was the only thing he needed to know.

But he was hungry and in pain and in need. He began to rock, and she pushed up, biting his earlobe before whispering, "Fuck me."

He rocked harder, his throat tight with the impact of her words, her wanting him, her knowing he wanted her. He rocked harder, rubbed against her, skin to skin, the contact raw and primal. He rocked harder, harder still, burying his face in the crook of her neck, his head on her pillow, falling apart as she scraped her nails over his scalp and came beneath him.

He burned and he ached but he finished her, then finished himself, collapsing, spent, the spilling of his seed exhausting him, leaving him only enough energy for something he needed to say. He pulled free of her body, rolled her away, and spooned in behind her, his arm beneath her breasts tethering her.

She cuddled against him, relaxed, and was on the verge of nodding off when he said, "I'm not coming to the party."

It took her a minute to respond, pulling herself out of sleep's clutches to turn to him. "Because of Clay?"

"No. Because I can't," he said, shaking his head. He'd been thinking about this a while. Thinking how it would feel to walk through those doors, have everyone look at him, everyone knowing what the house had been like when he'd lived there. Knowing about Suzanne.

"Why ever not?" she asked, reaching a hand to cup his face. "It's your house. It's a showpiece. You should be the one showing it off."

No. That wasn't his house. He didn't know that house. His house was gone, and that's what he was left to deal with. "Later, baby. Time to sleep."

The next thing he knew, someone was pounding on Faith's door, and at the same time he realized the shower was running. It was up to him to see what was going on or let it go. He preferred the latter, but the pounding wouldn't stop, so he grabbed his jeans, walking barefoot through the living room, glancing through the peephole as he pulled on his pants.

"Shit," he muttered, staring down at his bare chest, buttoning his fly before opening the door to Boone. When the other man did nothing but stare, he finally said, "Faith's in the shower."

"I came looking for you."

"Here?"

"You weren't at the ranch. You weren't on Mulberry Street. Seemed the next best place to try."

"You could've called Faith."

"I didn't want to talk to Faith. I needed to see this for myself."

"And now you've seen it." Casper had nothing else to say.

Boone ground his jaw, rubbed at his chin he hadn't shaved. "Barrett's been looking for you. Called me. Called the house. Get your damn phone fixed." And that was that. He turned and walked away.

Casper closed the door, headed back to the bedroom for his boots and the rest of his clothes, trying not to think how bad this was on top of everything else.

"Who was that?" Faith asked, toweling her hair as she walked out of the bathroom.

He'd hoped to be gone before she was through. "You don't want to know."

"Boone?" she asked as he tugged on his shirt.

He nodded in answer, but couldn't bring himself to look at her. "Greg Barrett's trying to reach me. I gotta go."

WHEN CASPER RODE into the Braff pasture later that morning to resume searching for Clay, Boone was already there, leaning into his forearms stacked on Sunshine's saddle horn, his gaze trained on Dax as the other man rode through the grazing pairs.

"I should beat the shit out of you."

Unlike the rest of the beatings Casper had taken in his life, this one he deserved. "I'll get the ax if it'll make you feel better."

"It damn well might take that." The other man was hot, his anger like a brand in coals, burning away hair before searing flesh forever. "It's not even about the rule. It's about trust. You broke it. That can't be fixed."

This was what Faith had warned him about. That she'd end things between them if his actions drove her brother away. He couldn't imagine that happening, that Boone would leave over what really wasn't any of his business. But he wasn't going to risk it.

"I love her," Casper heard himself saying, the words ones he hadn't even said to Faith.

"You love your cock, you mean," Boone said, still steaming.

"No." He pulled himself straight, pushed back the brim of his hat, letting the truth of his feelings settle. "I love Faith. And I love her enough that I'll leave her alone if that's what you want. You staying here matters more to her than I ever will."

Confusion swiped across Boone's face. "Why wouldn't I stay here?"

"I dunno, but she's been afraid from the beginning if you found out about us you'd leave again."

"I'm not going anywhere. But beating the shit out of you—"

"—or taking an ax to my head—"

"—is something else entirely."

"You mean more to her than anything," Casper said after a minute, wanting to fix this.

"Not more than you, it seems."

"That's . . . different."

"I fucking hope so."

"You know what I'm saying." He was growing exasperated. He didn't know how to talk about personal shit. Cows, horses, dead grass, the feed bill at Lasko's. That he could manage. But not what he felt for Faith. "I'll walk away. If this is going to cause trouble between the two of you, I'll walk away."

They both fell silent after that, the sounds of snuffling horses and cattle brushing through what remained of the grass the only noises for miles. The sun beat down, baking Casper's back through his shirt, frying the strip of skin above his collar, browning his forearms.

These days, he looked more like he belonged to Diego Cruz's

family than to the white man who'd brought him at twelve to Crow Hill. Or to the woman who'd spread her legs to support herself, throwing an occasional box of cereal and a Benjamin his way.

"Go buy yourself a pair of shoes," she'd tell him.

"Go get a fucking haircut," she'd say.

"Go find something to eat," she'd bark, smoke from a cigarette spiraling upward to magically diffuse the hard look in her eyes.

He'd wondered more than once if she'd even been the one to pop him out, or if the two of them had picked him up at some carnival, needing the extra mouth to qualify for government handouts, not to mention a house slave to fetch their beers.

This was how he'd grown up, and this was the past he was offering Faith as part of who he was. Yeah, that's exactly what someone who loved her would do, saddle her with a mountain of trashy baggage she'd have to pick up and carry when he dropped it.

"What did Barrett want?" Boone finally asked, bringing him back to the present.

"He's been in touch with New Mexico."

"I came all the way to town for that?"

"He just wanted me to know. Guess it'll be on the bill I'm gonna have to beg Faith to let me pay."

Boone shifted in his saddle, reining Sunshine around and moving into Casper's field of vision. "I'm not going anywhere. And I don't want you walking away. She's been happier these last few weeks than I've seen her in a very long time."

That surprised him, coming from her brother, but it was good to hear in light of the hefty weight of change bearing down. Something told him he'd just taken a big step he'd never get back.

"It's just . . . Stuff happened when she was younger," Boone was saying. "Stuff that makes it hard for me not to want to beat the shit out of you because I know you and I don't want her hurt."

He nodded, stayed silent.

"She paid for your house, didn't she?"

This time he couldn't bring himself to do more than meet Boone's gaze that was once again angry and ax-wielding mean.

"Fucking shit."

"It's for the party."

"It's not for the party. It's for you."

"She said—"

"I don't give a goddamn crap what she said. Me and her . . . We were sharing the cost. Every bit of it. A split we could both afford. Or that I could afford since she can afford to buy the country club outright if she wants." He wiped his wrist across his forehead, then tugged down his hat until his eyes were lost in the brim's shadow. "She hasn't once touched that money since it dropped into her account. Except maybe to move it into others. And yet for you—"

"It wasn't for me."

"Say that again and I rip your tongue out of your mouth." The look the other man gave him guaranteed it would happen. "Did she tell you where she got it?"

This was harder for Casper to swallow. "Not exactly."

"Don't think you know what happened. And don't you dare fucking judge her for getting herself mixed up with that sonuvabitch." Boone flung a string of fucks and shits and damns into the air. "I didn't say that. And it better not get back to her that I did."

"I'm not about to say anything to her. And I'm not judging

her. Jesus. Why would I judge her? What right do I have to judge what anyone does?"

"What did I miss?" Dax asked, riding up beside them.

"Nothing," Casper grumbled.

"Uh-uh. Something is going on." He licked his finger, held up his arm. "Winds are definitely blowing mean."

Boone grunted. "Asshole broke the rule."

"What ru— Shit. No-sisters?" Dax looked from Boone to Casper and back. "What're you gonna do about it?"

Boone looked into the distance. "He says he loves her."

"Which part of him loves her?"

That earned Dax a whip across the back from Casper's quirt.

"*Yeowch*. Shit. I get it. You love her. Question is, what're *you* gonna do about it?"

That he did not know. He knew what he'd like to do, the kind of life he'd like to live with Faith in it. Hell, thanks to her, he already had the house with the white picket fence. But he couldn't see the two of them having kids, bringing them up together, making a family.

What the hell did he know about making a family? He couldn't even hold on to one fourteen-year-old boy.

"What I'm gonna do is look for Clay." He glanced from one of the men who'd been more brother than friend to the other who might end up being both, a thought that added to the teeth in his gut eating him up like sausage. "You two coming? Or you gonna sit on your asses and wait for the grass to grow?"

THIRTY-ONE

NEARLY TWENTY-FOUR HOURS after discovering Clay gone, Casper headed back to town to see Faith. He owed her an apology for bolting this morning. It had been hard to look at her, sweet from the shower, when all he could see was her brother's face, her brother's anger and censure, and know she was saddling up to ride him down with the same.

The thought that he'd fucked things up beyond all repair had sent him to Barrett's office in a blur. Then sent him to the ranch at a speed limit he'd never seen posted on any sign in the forty-eight contiguous states. He and Boone airing things, if not settling things, had let him put that worry to rest for the moment and allowed him to focus on Clay.

But the search for Clay had been a bust, and the worry was waking up. He hadn't talked to Faith all day, but his phone was out again, and he'd put in so many miles on horseback he'd promised Remedy he could have tomorrow off. A good thing for the both of them since he had an appointment with Dr. Pope. The other man would most likely give him a good reaming for getting back in the saddle so soon. But, hell, he'd had bulls do more damage.

He wasn't going to let Summerlin's Arabian—

He cut off the thought, squinting down the road, looking at the familiar figure jogging toward him. His heart dropped from his chest to his stomach, then it jumped into his throat before it settled back where it belonged. He braked to a stop, let the dust settle, and rolled down his window just as Clay reached him.

"Where the *hell* have you been—" But it was all he got out. Clay's face was a mess. His clothes were a mess, smeared with dirt and what could be blood and smelling like animal shit. And he was without Kevin. He was without Kevin. Shit. Casper shifted into park, shoved open his door, climbed down with his gut churning. "Clay?"

"I need help," the boy said, his throat working.

"What's wrong?"

"If you're going to turn me in, I'll split," he said, tears rolling down his cheeks, those same tears dousing the front of Casper's shirt as the boy buried his face against him.

Casper's arms came around him without any thought at all. "Clay, what's wrong?"

"It's Kevin," he said, backing up and doubling over, his hands on his knees as he fought to catch his breath. "He got in the way of a bull. It tossed him."

"Jesus, Clay. What were you doing in a pasture? And whose pasture? Where?"

"I figured going cross-country would take you longer to find us. And I don't know whose." He stopped, his whole body shaking with his effort to breathe. "We took off after we got back to the ranch. Then laid low for a while."

Well, that was for sure. Okay, think. *Think.* "What did the bull look like?"

Clay straightened, waved a hand. "He was big, monster muscles, kinda white."

That sounded like Philip Hart's Charolais. One of the bulls Casper had wrecked on had been a big, mean Charolais. "Where's Kevin now?"

"I had to wait till it was safe to get to him. I moved him into a ditch. I couldn't carry him any further." His voice broke, broke again, and the rest of the words flowed out with his sobs. "I think I was hurting him."

"C'mon," Casper said, his own voice tight, his throat choking up even tighter, his arm fastened around the boy's shoulder as he walked him to the far side of the truck. "Get in. Tell me where he is. I'll radio up to Mal's, let him know we're coming."

"What's Mal's?"

"Mal runs an animal shelter. Doc Neal, the vet, he's up there every day. No place Kevin could get better care."

"He'd stay there? I want to be with him. He'll be scared if I'm not there."

"Considering you're in a bit of trouble, that's probably not going to happen." When Clay didn't say anything to that, Casper put the truck in gear and went on. "What were you thinking, running like that? Not even leaving a note?"

"I didn't want to get you busted," he said, his head in his hands, shaking. "When no one knew I was here things were okay. But with the cop and the lawyer and everyone poking around . . . I didn't want a bunch of crap to fall on you for not turning me in when you found me."

Casper didn't even know what to say. This boy had lit off with his dog, heading over terrain fit for jackrabbits and rattlesnakes, barely fit for the cattle who grazed it, to keep Casper out of the law's crosshairs? How in the *hell* would he be able to send the boy back into the system now?

Clay gave a desperate sort of laugh. "We made it across two states just fine, and I can't even get outta Crow Hill without something happening to Kevin. God, I can't believe I was so stupid. I'm going to end up in jail because I was so stupid."

"You're not stupid. And no one's pressing charges. You know that." He didn't say anything about jail because that was beyond him to know.

"For the things I took, yeah. But I didn't have a license."

"True, and that'll bring you some consequences."

"And I'm a runaway. And a ward of the state."

At least the boy knew the lay of the land. "That part, too."

Clay kept his gaze averted, his head on the passenger window as the road whizzed beneath them. "He's going to send me back, isn't he? The sheriff?"

"No. Not yet, anyway." Casper thought about Kevin alone and frightened and bleeding, and gunned the accelerator. "He doesn't know where to send you, though I'll bet he's been searching through bulletins all day."

"So I get to stay on the ranch?"

"For now, yes."

"I wish I could stay forever."

He didn't want to get the boy's hopes up, but seeing him like this . . . "I'm doing my best to keep you here as long as I can. I'm not going to let you go back to the situation you came from. Not without a fight."

"You'd do that for me?"

Casper nodded, silent.

"I don't even think my mother would've done that for me."

"As much as I liked your mother, I'm beginning to think she wasn't much of one." Though he couldn't imagine her not fighting for her boy. Then again, had he even known the real her? "Neither was mine, which kinda makes me an expert on recognizing the type."

"Sucks, doesn't it?"

"It does, but I had friends whose folks knew what I was going through and showed me how to keep my head up." Those dinners and breakfasts at the Mitchells rose like a port in a storm. "I want to do that for you. Even if things don't go our way in the end, I don't want you getting into worse shit and blaming your mom. You're old enough to know what's right and what's wrong."

"I didn't mean to blame her, that day in the jail. I knew she did drugs, and there were a *lot* of guys. But she was always happy, like a kid. I kinda figured I was an accident, but at least she didn't toss me in the trash or something. I guess she did her best." He sniffed, wiped his eyes on his hoodie's grubby sleeve, turned to look at the window. "I miss her."

Casper reached a hand along the back of the seat and squeezed the boy's shoulder. Saying anything wouldn't have helped. This was Clay needing to work things out for himself, something Casper understood well. Except Casper making sense of his own shitty past had only begun recently, and his working things out fell to Faith. Without her . . .

Without her he'd be nothing, nowhere. He would've bucked under the weight of the house, the added burden of Clay, the suffocating obligation of the ranch drowning him. He needed her to know that. He needed to tell her what it had meant to him for her to find those papers, to be there while he'd burned them, even if he'd walked out of the room, and walked out on her for fear of breaking down . . .

Twenty minutes later, they found Kevin where Clay had left him, still conscious, his white fur matted brick red in a big circle on one side. He lifted his head when he saw them, but dropped it just as quickly, though he did give a few solid wags of his tail.

Casper swallowed hard, taking in the situation. Moving the dog was going to hurt him, and he didn't want either himself or Clay to get bit. A muzzle would be good, but might scare the dog more. Knowing where Philip Hart pastured his bull, it was hard to believe how far Clay had managed to carry the mutt. Kevin was not a light dog.

For sure they needed a stretcher of some kind. He did a mental inventory of the supplies in his truck, then whipped off his T-shirt, laid it out the length of Kevin's spine. "We'll move him onto the shirt then use it to carry him to the truck. Go on and let the tailgate down."

While Clay took care of that part, Casper did his best to set the dog at ease, stroking his silky ears, rubbing a knuckle between his eyes, scratching the top of his head. "Hang in there, boy," he whispered, leaning close so Kevin could look into his eyes.

"Okay," Clay said, breathless. "Now what?"

Casper stood, squatted over the dog. "I'll lift his hips. You slide the shirt under him. Smooth it out the best you can. Then we'll do the same on this end. But you stay on that side of his teeth."

"He won't bite me. He's never bitten me."

First time for everything, kid. "He knows you're there. His tail's telling you. Now, one, two, three . . ."

"CLAY'S BACK," CASPER said the second Faith picked up the phone.

"Casper?"

"Yeah. Sorry. I'm using the phone up at New Dawn."

"The animal shelter? No wonder I didn't recognize the number. What're you doing there?"

"Kevin's hurt. We brought him here." He looked out the window of Mal Breckenridge's small office to where the shelter's owner and Doc Neal were moving Kevin on a canvas litter from the back of his truck. "That's why Clay came back. Kevin had a run-in with Philip Hart's big Charolais bull."

"What? Wait a minute. Back up. I'm totally lost here."

Casper boosted a hip onto the corner of the cluttered desk, dragging the phone with him. He didn't blame her for not being able to keep up with his adrenaline-fueled ramblings. His head was a mess. He took a deep breath and started again. "Hi. How are you?"

"I'm fine. Better than fine hearing Clay's all right. He is all right, isn't he?"

"Tired and scared and out of his mind worried about his dog."

"Just like you've been out of yours worried about him."

"Yeah. This parenting thing's not for sissies," he said, rubbing the tightness from his neck. "Even if it's a temporary thing."

"It's good to hear you sounding so relieved," she said, and he heard the smile in her voice.

He closed his eyes, pictured her mouth, thought about holding her close. Breathing in her sweet scent. "It was so weird. I was on my way to see you and looked up and there he was."

"But he's okay?"

"Yeah."

"And Kevin will be okay?"

"Should be, Doc says."

"So why were you coming to see me?"

Because I love you and need you and it's been too long since I held you. He closed his eyes again, swallowed, looked back at

Mal and the doc carrying the injured dog, at the boy who was almost as tall as the men hovering.

"Casper?"

He shook off his daze. "I'm here."

"Can I do anything? Can I help?"

God, this woman . . . "You've already helped by not hanging up on me."

"Why would I hang up on you?"

"I didn't think you'd want to talk to me," he said, leaving the desk and bracing a hand on the wall next to the window. "Not after the way things went yesterday morning."

"When you bolted before I had a chance to say I told you so?"

Yeah. That. But he remained silent, frowning as he watched the group outside enter the shelter's veterinary building. He needed to finish up here and join them. Who knew what the price was going to be to save Kevin's life?

"I wasn't going to say it," Faith was telling him. "If you'd given me a chance to get over the shock, I had something else to say."

He rubbed at his eyes that were full of grit and exhaustion. "You want to say it now?"

"I talked to Boone the other day."

That had him frowning. "Before he came to your place?"

"It was probably why he knew to look for you there."

Wait. What? "You told him? About us?"

She took a deep breath, sighed it out. "I told him he had to let me live my own life. And make my own choices."

Well, this was news. And progress. "Even if that means putting an end to the no-sisters rule?"

She laughed, the sound soft and sweet in his ear. "Not specifically, but yes. We talked about you. And he's smart enough to put two and two together."

That would explain why her brother hadn't looked too surprised when Casper had opened her door. Pissed, but not surprised. But Casper couldn't have this conversation now, not here, not with his focus split between Clay and Kevin and Faith.

And he felt like a shit when he finally said, "Can we finish this later? I really need to go."

"Okay," she said, the word falling into the big, fat cavernous space his response had created between them, its echo a damning taunt.

"I'm not blowing you off, Faith." He turned back to the desk, tugged down his hat brim, thinking it might've been smarter not to call until things here were settled. "I promise. I just need to see what's going on with Mal and the doc, then get Clay fed and cleaned up."

"Sure," she said after a moment that dragged on longer than he liked. "Later is fine. But it'll be a few days. I've got party plans coming out my ears, and I'll be lucky to have time this week to sleep."

Was he ever going to catch a break? "As long as that doesn't mean that *you're* blowing *me* off."

"It doesn't. I promise. I'll talk to you soon." She hung up before he could say anything else.

He returned the receiver to the cradle, scrubbing both hands down his very weary face and trying to shake off the feeling he'd just stepped into something he was going to spend a lot of time scraping off his boots.

THIRTY-TWO

OVERWHELMED WITH SO much emotion she didn't know which way to turn, Faith stood in the hallway bisecting Casper's house and pressed her hands to her chest.

As the party crowd mingled, flowing around her like clear water over rocks, a stream of laughs and smiles and happy chatter, she fought the sharp hitch there, trapped by the buoyant joy bubbling in her throat and the sadness pulling her under to drown.

She glanced into the parlor on her left, then into the dining room on her right, knowing behind her, the large open living area and the library and den were just as gorgeously festooned. Greenery with sprigs of baby's breath hung over the window casings, cascaded from the arched doorways between the rooms.

The woodwork had been painted a glossy white, the walls a softer eggshell. Tiny white Christmas lights peeked through the leaves, dangling and shimmering in rows from the ceilings. The buffed hardwood floors picked up the soft glow, reflecting it as if from still pools.

The rooms were empty of furniture save for what the Hellcat Saloon had provided, serving tables and smaller folding ones, all covered in white linen cloths. Kendall and Everly had made a trip to a San Antonio party supply warehouse, returning with dozens of hurricane lanterns to use as centerpieces, setting them in bowls of aromatic cedar and mesquite.

Smells of fresh paint and new construction wafted in the air with simmering barbecue sauce and smoky grilled meat and blackened chilies and rich chocolate. And in the largest space on the house's first story, what a century ago would've been a ballroom, the sounds of a fiddle and a banjo and a stand-up bass tickled her from her ribs to her toes.

She was glad Casper had decided not to come. When he'd told her nearly two weeks ago that he wasn't, she'd been hurt. At least at first. Then Clay had returned with an injured Kevin, and these last few days of party preparations had consumed her. But during that time she'd also come to realize why it was easier for him to stay away.

She wouldn't want to face a multitude of people, many of whom she'd wronged, most of whom knew about her dirty little secrets and were standing in the house where she'd hid them. She'd intended to tell him that she understood, but that conversation, like others they needed to have, had been shunted to the back burner by life.

They'd touched base briefly a couple of times, one or the other of them too busy for more, talking in circles around what really mattered—Boone's early morning visit and where they went from here. But the delay had turned out to be a good thing, because while looking back on their relationship in the meantime, she'd been struck by the most sobering, god-awful truth.

It wasn't Casper's rash behavior that was going to ruin her, but her own.

He led her into temptation, yes, but she had never, not once, put up a fight. She'd gone willingly, every time, because it was what she wanted. She was the one with no self-control, the one whose actions hurt others. The one who couldn't get over the damage in her past.

The selfish one.

Look at everything Casper had done since first asking her for a sign—taking on Clay, changing the boy's life and his own, dealing with the pieces of his past she'd tossed like confetti in his face. All she'd done was renovate his house, thrown an unbelievable party, lose herself in the best sex of her life.

And every time he'd asked, every time he'd pushed and pressed and needled, she'd walked away from sharing the truth about her money. She hadn't been brave, like he had. She hadn't pulled out her mistakes, shown him who she really was, who he was involved with.

She was afraid if she did, he wouldn't want her anymore. That if he learned about her past, he would find her too reckless and move on.

The sound of her name being called from the kitchen brought her back to the present. She nudged a finger beneath her eyes, and was just stepping that way when an arm snaked around her waist and a voice at her ear asked, "May I have this dance?"

Her throat closed, and she turned, nearly speechless, her hands going to the dark blue tie Casper wore with a white western dress shirt and jeans. "I didn't think you were coming."

"You're here," he said, his smile soft, his gaze tender, his face clean-shaven, his hair newly shorn. "Hard not to want to be here when this is where you are. I've missed you."

"I've missed you, too," she told him, then scurried to keep up as he swept her into the crush of bodies twirling across the ballroom. She pressed close to him, her long, flowing skirt tangling with his knees, her thighs brushing his thighs, her breasts crushed against him. It was all she could do not to pull his head down for a kiss. "How's Kevin?"

He nodded. "He's had a rough go of it. Doc Neal says he's got more recovery ahead, but barring complications, he'll pull through."

"He's still at Mal's shelter?"

Another nod. "Doc's up there daily. Keeps him from having to come to the ranch, or for one of us to haul Kevin to town."

"I can't believe he faced down Philip Hart's bull and won," she said, catching a wink from Arwen Poole as they swung by. Then a frown from Marilee Banyon who worked at the high school with both of her folks.

"I know," Casper was saying. "He's a tough mutt."

She shook off the sense of reproach to ask, "And Clay?"

"Feeling guilty as hell."

"As he well should."

"He begged me to let him bunk at the shelter," he said, pulling her out of the way before they bumped into Josh and Darcy Lasko. "But he gave in when the doc convinced him Kevin would rest better without raising up to check on him every few minutes."

"They are a pair," she said as Casper spun her into the path of Sheila Edghill who leaned to whisper in Donna Wayne's ear, both women staring, disapproving. They pointed as they moved to where her mother stood talking to Nora Stokes.

Good lord. She was dancing with the owner of the house who had allowed her to use the place for the party. What could they possibly think was wrong with that? "Where's Clay now?"

Casper canted his head toward the rear of the house. "Knowing that kid, in the kitchen."

"You brought him?"

"He helped out. Figured he deserved to see all of this." He tightened his hold on her right hand, brought it with his to his chest. "Greg heard from New Mexico today."

She pulled back to look at him. "Already?"

"I know. It's barely been two weeks. Things look good. A couple more hurdles, but since Clay has no other family, I should be able to adopt him."

And at that, she stopped him in the corner of the room, her heart pounding. "Adopt him? You're not just going to foster?"

He reached up to tuck a stray curl behind her ear, a move she was sure everyone in attendance had to have seen. "I want him to know he'll always have someone who wants *him* and not just the money the state pitches in for his care. He deserves that. All kids deserve that."

This man. He'd come so far. "Do you know how amazing you are?"

"If I am, it's because of you."

"I have nothing to do with it," she said, barely able to swallow. He deserved better than her; couldn't he see that?

"Oh, baby," he said, his eyes brimming with emotion, more blue tonight than gray. "You have everything to do with it, don't you know?"

"Casper—"

"C'mon," he said, still holding her hand as he pulled her through a door that led to a narrow staircase rising to what would've been the quarters used in the past by the help. The quarters where his bedroom had been. "I need to show you something."

She was the hostess. She couldn't abandon her post for long. But neither could she resist him. When had she ever been able to resist him? He tugged her behind him until she was breathless—from the climb and anticipation—but they finally reached the third floor.

Casper opened the first door he came to and pulled her inside. He seemed to do it without thinking, without realizing where they were, without remembering the last time they'd been here, the fire he'd walked out on when he'd walked out on her.

The room was empty and dark save for the light from the moon, the window glass sparkling, shadows of the tree limbs painted like murals across the bare walls. He closed the door behind them, and with his hands on her shoulders, backed her into the nearest wall, bringing his mouth down on hers.

He was hungry and desperate, and his hands were in her hair, pulling the pins from the strands she'd so carefully curled. They dropped to the floor, tiny tinkles of sound in a room that was silent save for their shared breathing and the music from the ballroom seeping upward like smoke.

She reached for his wrists to hold on, thinking to push him away, but God. How could she? Within seconds she was lost, his tongue and his lips and his teeth like wicked laughter beckoning her into his gingerbread house where everywhere she turned was temptation.

She held on to him, pressed into him, took his tongue and his desperation and every breath he breathed. His chest rose like a wall in front of her, and his belt buckle wasn't the only hard thing branding her through the fabric of her skirt.

"This is the dance I came for," he said minutes later, the words rasping against her cheek, his breath hot, his pulse racing to catch up with hers.

She wanted to be here with him. She wanted so much to have him love her. But her recklessness had hurt so many people. *Her* recklessness, not his, and it was wedging itself between them now. She couldn't stop it. She didn't know how.

"Casper—"

"You can't. I know." He said it while bunching her tea-length skirt in his hands and tugging the fabric up the backs of her thighs. "Baby. No pantyhose. I think I've died and gone to heaven."

"You're messing up my clothes. And my makeup." *You're messing up my heart and my soul, and my resolve not to hurt you.*

"I'll be careful." He was at her panties now, the little fluff of lace she'd worn just for him, one hand breeching the barrier while his other worked open the fly of his sharply pressed jeans.

"You're never careful," she said, widening her stance to make room for his fingers, angling her hips so he could push one inside.

He laughed, a coarse, gritty sound like sandpaper scraping her face, or a cat's tongue lapping between her legs. Cock in his hand, his hips tilting, his full bulbous tip spreading her moisture, he pulled his finger from her pussy and slid deep.

She gasped, impaled, her eyes rolling, lids fluttering closed. He made her spineless, and she loved that he did, loved that he stripped her to her most vulnerable self. She loved him.

Oh, God. She loved him. *She loved him!*

She kissed him then, her fingers digging into his biceps as she held on for fear of falling. He gripped her backside, just above her thighs, lifting her, spreading her. Opening her for his insistent thrusts. Filling her. Claiming her. Branding her.

Her skirt rode forgotten at her waist, and the delicate strands of gold around her neck tangled together as he pushed them aside with his chin and his nose, biting her skin and bruising her, his hips slamming forward and bouncing her off the wall.

She took all of him, his length and his width and his purpose. She took his power, his strength, his need that bordered on brutal, knowing she would pay later with bruises and tears.

She didn't care because this thing between them was more than his cock in her pussy, his mouth damaging her skin. His fingers gouging her, his heart pounding as if it were nailing her body in place.

Whatever he might want from her, it never occurred to her to withhold anything. She could never turn him down. She could never tell him no. She wanted him too much not to follow.

And yet hadn't this sort of selfishness nearly been her undoing?

What in the world was wrong with her?

"Faith? Baby? Are you okay?"

"No," she said, realizing she was the one who had stopped. She wasn't moving, frozen against the wall for fear of ruining everything. "I'm not okay. I'm not okay at all."

He stopped inside of her, still hard, still thick, molded perfectly to fit her. Made for her. Her man. Hers alone. Hers. Only hers.

"Am I hurting you?" he lifted his head to ask. "Do I need to move?"

"Yes and yes," she said, though she did so without explanation.

"Okay. Give me a sec," he said, shifting to pull free.

"No. Don't."

He was still half inside her. "I don't want to hurt you."

But what about her hurting him? Yet the tears burning her cheeks as they spilled weren't about her pain, but torn from the realization of how badly she'd behaved, coming here with him and all the while knowing how this would end. "It doesn't matter."

"Jesus, Faith. Of course it matters." His breath was heavy and damp, his heart a hammer pounding from his chest into hers. "You're all that matters. The only thing."

"Don't say that," she said, crying now, pulling at his shirt to urge him close again.

"It's the truth," he said, and buried his face in the crook of her shoulder, his own face wet, his mouth soft against her skin as he kissed her.

Her back was aching, her thighs were aching. Her heart was aching most of all. She closed her eyes and blotted out all of that to know nothing but the ache between her legs. She squeezed him, and he pushed deeper, groaning, his whole body shaking as he held them both still.

And then he gave up trying, shuddering once as if he'd been hit with more than he could handle. He drove into her, confused, uncertain. He didn't say a word but she could feel the emotions spilling with the white hot bursts of his cum. She couldn't blame him. She'd turned the night's expectations upside down, messing with his head when he was just beginning to find his path.

She was the one who had ruined everything this time, stealing away the comfort and courage he'd found with her, and doing it tonight, of all nights. The night he'd had no choice but to let everyone into this place that had been his hell for so long.

What was she thinking? What in the *hell* was wrong with her? She was such a selfish bitch.

He let her down slowly, pulling from her body without having to ask if she was done, or if she was even close. She wasn't, and she wouldn't be. Not here, and he knew it. There was no need to pretend otherwise, which made this joining bittersweet.

He adjusted himself inside his shorts, pulled up his pants, tucked in his shirt. His big brass belt buckle caught the light from the moon and winked at her. He scooped her panties from the floor, handed them to her, not letting them go until she'd raised her gaze to his, which was tortured. His throat was working, his jaw was popping, and his eyes flashed with both truth and tears.

"You are all that matters, Faith. Believe it or don't. Nothing in my life comes close."

He was halfway to the door before she found her voice to call out, "Casper, wait."

But it was too late. The room was empty, the door open, the light from the windows at either end of the hallway casting shadows on the walls, crooked, broken fingers, pointing this way and that as if the direction she chose to go wouldn't make a bit of difference.

Nothing would be the same now that she'd let the man she loved walk out of her life.

THIRTY-THREE

CASPER STOOD ON the northeast corner of the porch where he'd first seen Kevin, leaning a shoulder into the column there, his hip into the railing, his back against the rear of the house. The structure was solid, sturdy, able to support his half-drunk ass while he listened to the music spilling into the night through the open windows, the deep thrum of the stand-up bass pulsing through the soles of his boots.

The last time he'd heard music in this house . . . He thought back. It had to be the night he'd graduated, after he and the boys had tossed their caps in the high school auditorium. He'd never planned to return to Mulberry Street after the Dalton Gang's booze and pussy bender, but for some unknown reason he had. As drunk as he'd been, making it back had been a miracle. He didn't remember a thing about the trip.

He did remember walking into the kitchen, having stumbled off the sidewalk where he'd parked and around to the back of the house, to see his old lady dancing, a cigarette dangling from the corner of her mouth, her arms raised overhead. She held a bottle of Ezra Brooks between two tobacco-stained fingers, an empty glass of ice in the other.

From the boom box she kept on top of the fridge, The Who's *I'm Free* played on repeat. He figured she'd been shaking her bony ass and sucking Ezra since he'd headed to the ceremony hours before. She hadn't even noticed when he'd walked inside, or seen him watching her toss back her head, smoke curling through her stringy bangs to leave a tar and nicotine circle on the ceiling.

Instead of heading upstairs to sleep, he'd hit his room and shoved what he could in his backpack, sleeping off that particular drunk in the cab of his truck in a pasture fifteen miles out of town. It was only the first of many nights spent that way. But it was the last night he'd let himself wonder if he might be leaving anything behind.

Even learning of Tess and Dave Dalton's deaths hadn't changed that. There was nothing for him in Crow Hill without his boys. He'd only come back to Texas because Dax and Boone were doing the same, and it had been too long since they'd raised some hell.

He lifted the longneck, frowning at the label after he swallowed. Jesus. This was the shit Boone drank, flavored with more than the malted barley and hops in the forties his old man had downed like water. Suzanne had preferred the men, turning to Jack and Jim and Jose to do her right. Fit right in with her career.

And goddamn if he hadn't followed in their booze-soaked and twisted-sex footsteps, hopping from one buckle bunny's bed to the next and staying drunk while he did it. The fact that money hadn't exchanged hands, and he hadn't beat the everlovin' shit outta the women he'd fucked, was the only thing that kept him from sinking to his parents' level of depravity.

He'd thought himself happy when rodeoing. His dick hadn't complained, but he knew now that his head had never been in it. Hell, his head had belonged to the booze—meaning in the end, he really wasn't any different, or any better, than either his old lady or the man she claimed had spawned him.

But then they'd taught him well, hadn't they? *Every man for himself. Me first. Look out for number one.* None of that Dalton Gang musketeer bullshit.

He'd thought he could do this. Turn this house into what it should've been all along and forget the house it had been. The house he'd known. The house he'd lived in for the six most fucked up years he could remember.

He'd thought he could do this because he had Faith. But he didn't have Faith. And thinking he did had been a bigger mistake than coming back to Crow Hill in the first place.

He wanted to believe he'd done the right thing, returning for the inheritance, taking on the partnership with his boys. And he knew he had when it came to Clay. That was going to keep him here. He was going to do for that boy everything right no one had ever done for him. It had taken Faith for him to see that he had it in him. To be an example, if not a father.

He'd stick close to home. And he'd have to do something with this house. He couldn't be coming to town and running into her. And Boone would have to damn sure keep her from coming out to the ranch. He lifted the beer again, laughed under his breath. As if she'd want to see him. She'd made her feelings about them being together more than clear.

Once again, he'd managed to ruin everything. Only this

time, he wasn't exactly sure why. He thought Faith had been onboard with their relationship. Yeah, she had her fusses, but most women did. And he wasn't exactly a prince, making her worry, making her fret. Not that he gave a damn about anything he made her feel . . . except he did. Because he loved her.

He'd never been one to stand around and brood about feelings, yet look at him, here on the back porch, his body still wanting hers, his heart heavy in his chest, his eyes aching. He didn't know what he'd done, why she didn't believe him when he'd said she was all that mattered.

The truth of that struck him harder than any arena floor he'd hit with his face. He loved her. And he'd fucked things up, and he didn't know how to fix them.

God*damn,* how was he going to fix them?

"Can you believe this house?"

The question came from one of Arwen's girls as two of them exited the kitchen and made for the stack of ice chests loaded with beer.

"It's some serious shit," said the other.

"Man, what I wouldn't give to live in a place like this."

"With a man like Casper Jayne?"

"For a place like this, I'd dance with the devil."

"Like Faith Mitchell was doing earlier?"

"I know. Did you see them?"

"The whole room saw them."

"You think there's something between them?"

"Oh, hell no. Faith's too straight-laced. Casper needs wild."

"And I guess you think you're the one to take him on."

"Honey, for this house, I'd take on Satan."

"I thought maybe that's what Faith was doing."

Thing was, he didn't believe them for a minute. Faith wasn't with him for the house. He'd bet the house itself on that. She'd talked only about what he planned to do with it. She hadn't once put herself in that picture, even though their agreement made her half-owner.

But they were right about the rest. She didn't have any reason to be with him. And he needed to get over thinking she did, that he had something to give her when both of them knew better.

His loving her didn't change any of that.

He pushed out of the darkness, stepped into the circle of light cast by Faith's hanging lanterns. "Want to hand me another of those before you take 'em in? One that doesn't taste like shit?"

"Oh. Casper. I didn't . . . We didn't know you were there."

He wasn't sure which girl had said it. He knew they worked at the Hellcat Saloon, but that was about it. "Yeah. That wasn't hard to figure out."

"I'm sorry. It's just—"

"Don't worry about it," he said, taking the longneck she handed him, his fingers brushing hers, lingering, his thumb stroking hers. It was her gaze holding his that made up his mind. "You gonna be done here soon?"

She blinked, glanced to the other wide-eyed girl and back. "Uh, I can probably clock out if you've got something on your mind."

"I do," he said, twisting off the beer's top and raising the bottle to his mouth for a swallow. "My truck's parked out front."

"Okay," she said breathlessly. "I'll be there as soon as I can."

He nudged up the brim of his hat with the longneck, walked by and heard the two of them twittering behind him as he crossed the yard. Luck. That was her name. She was Royce Summerlin's girl. Meaning this probably wasn't a very good idea.

Right now, he didn't give a fuck.

THIRTY-FOUR

FAITH MADE HER way down the staircase alone, stopping in the first bathroom she saw to do something about her face and her hair. There wasn't much to be done since her purse was in the kitchen, leaving her with no lipstick and only her fingers for a comb.

It would've been nice to have access to her cover-up for the bruise at the base of her throat. The one time she went low-cut instead of sticking to a collared, buttoned blouse. Served her right, trying to attract a bad boy. Falling in love with a bad boy. Letting a bad boy break her heart. Breaking his.

She took the last few stairs slowly, not wanting to draw attention from any of Arwen's staff bustling in the kitchen. It was an amazing kitchen, gorgeous, huge, and airy. It was meant for parties like this one. Myna Goss, who cooked at the saloon, was even frying Boone's breaded okra on the new stainless-steel stove.

It was hard to believe half of this place was hers. Hard because she would never live here. She would never cook here, or sleep here, or hear the patter of her babies' feet up and down the main corridor, or stay up till the middle of the night waiting for her teenagers to sneak through the front door long past curfew.

She wouldn't be here in thirty-five years, dancing with Casper, standing at his side, watching their grown children fight over the cost of their anniversary party. She wouldn't sit on the porch swing and listen to the crickets and the cicadas and the coyotes at the end of the hot summer days.

None of that would happen because Casper wasn't hers, even if he was her other half.

For so long she'd made wrong relationship choices, and when she'd finally made the right one, she couldn't see it for the reflection of the inappropriate things she'd done in the past, all in the name of adventure and spreading her wings. They'd brought her here, but they'd gotten in her way, keeping her in a job she hated, keeping her from the man she loved.

God, why couldn't she let herself move on?

"There you are," came a voice from behind her that had her quickly nudging a knuckle beneath both eyes.

"Hey, Daddy." She hitched a breath and swallowed, hoping to clear her throat. "You're a guest of honor. You're not supposed to be skulking back here where all the work's being done."

"Is that what I'm doing?" he asked, sidling up to her and wrapping an arm around her shoulders, lifting a hand in greeting at one breezy, "Hey, Coach," then another.

"Looks like it," she said, forcing a soft laugh.

"And here I thought I was just looking for my girl." He leaned close, dropped a kiss to the top of her head as they both watched Arwen's staff, along with Kendall and Everly, scurry around the kitchen with braziers of food—empty ones coming in from the parlor, full ones going back to replace them, longnecks and soda bottles heading for wash tubs of ice. "You and your brother managed a hell of a feat here. Neither your mother or I ever suspected a thing."

"That's the point of a surprise party," she said, her laughter coming easier this time.

"The biggest surprise is everyone else keeping the secret. We've got some friends who seem to find it necessary to tell us the state of their dog's bowel movements," he said, causing Faith to cringe. "Them staying close-mouthed about this will become known as the miracle on Mulberry Street."

"Well, I'm glad they did. It wouldn't have been as much fun if you'd known."

"I'm kinda curious, though. What in the world made you two choose this house?"

Her heart flipped. "Should we have gone to the country club? Or had it at home? Boone wanted to have it at home."

"No, sweetheart. Relax. You didn't do a damn thing wrong. I just never thought to see this house in this condition. Been a lot of work done here. A big expense."

"Casper's been doing some extra work for Royce Summerlin. Breaking horses." As if those few hours a week would explain away the money poured into this house. Her father was not a stupid man.

"And a few ribs, I hear."

"You talked to him?"

"I did."

"When?"

"Earlier. Before I saw the two of you dancing. I think you two were more the belle and beau of the ball than your mother and I."

"I helped him out with his budget," she said because nothing else came to her.

"Is *that* all it was?" her father asked, a chuckle rising up his throat as he dropped another kiss to her head, leaving her to wonder if his intuition was as strong as her mother's. "I saw him leaving a few minutes ago. I was kinda surprised to see him here at all, to tell you the truth."

Had he seen him going upstairs with her? Coming down later alone? "It's his house. Why wouldn't he be here?"

Her father laughed. "No, Faith. *This* house isn't his. This one's . . ." He gave a low whistle. "This one's something else."

She didn't think it a good idea to take credit when he had no idea she was the one who'd financed the renovations. "I guess."

"Trust me. It is." He pulled her with him out of the way of the caterers, stepping four steps up the staircase and sitting on the fifth. "I imagine that's tough for him. Seeing it now. Remembering it then."

"Did you know how things were when he lived here?" she asked, smoothing out her skirt as she sat beside him.

"Some of it, sure."

"Was it as bad as rumors have it?" She didn't need to ask. She'd seen enough. Casper had told her the rest.

Her father nodded. "Worse. Your mom and I had to come here a couple of times with Boone."

"Why?"

"Usually Casper was in some kind of trouble. He needed help getting out."

Because his mother wouldn't have cared or offered. "What was his mother like?"

"Suzanne?" He shook his head. "Sad's about the best word to describe her. Sad and self-centered. And not much of a parent."

"I never saw her that I can remember," she said, getting a whiff of freshly toasted bread as she breathed deeply to settle her nerves.

"I don't think you ever would have. She spent her time at the truck stop. She wasn't one to get involved in what Casper had going on at school."

"That makes me hurt, thinking he was here all that time with no one in his corner."

"He had your brother. And Dax. And your mother and me by extension."

But he hadn't had her. She'd been too young, too naive. She'd had very little clue as to the truth of his life then. Even now, she only knew what he'd told her from his adult perspective. Not what he'd suffered in the moment.

She'd been young, but she could've been a friend. "I wish I'd known him better then."

Her father's chuckle spoke to his protective nature. "I'm damn glad you didn't. That boy raised more hell than Dax and Boone combined. No way would I have let my little girl anywhere near him."

"I don't mean I wanted to date him." Though hadn't she? Hadn't he played into her fantasies of throwing off her straight As for a walk on the wild side? "I just meant . . . The things he's told me . . . I don't think he could've had too many people in his corner."

"You're right about that."

And it made her so sad. "Can I tell you something?"

"You can tell me anything," he said, turning a concerned frown on her. "Anytime. You know that."

"I know. I just don't want you to be disappointed in me."

"I could never be disappointed in you."

"You were. In the past."

"I was, yes," he said, sighing. "But more so in myself than in you."

That didn't make any sense. "Why would you have been disappointed in yourself?"

"Because I failed you somewhere. I didn't give you something you needed."

Was he kidding? "How can you even say that? You gave me everything!"

"Keeping your brother on the straight and narrow required a lot of time and energy, and that took away from what your mother and I had for you. But you seemed so confident, so happy. It was easy to let you do your own thing and think everything was fine."

"Oh, Daddy. Don't think that way. Everything was fine." Emotion rose like fog, blurring everything around her as she remembered the past. "But I did want to be more like Boone. To have fun, and even get into trouble if it meant not keeping my nose stuck in a book all the time. He made it look so easy. Getting the same straight As without having to work for them. Even now . . ."

"What?"

"I want to be more like him. He's doing what he wants to do. He's struggling. I know that, but he loves his work, the ranch, his boys, his damn horse."

"And you don't love yours."

"I don't," she admitted, shaking her head.

"Oh, sweetheart. You're financially set. That money's been

earning interest for ten years. Why not take it and do what you want to with your life?"

"Because I don't know what that is." She was thirty-one years old, and had no idea what she wanted to be when she grew up. How pathetic was that? "And using that money for me seems so selfish. I didn't earn it. Or deserve it."

"But it's yours."

"I've tried so many times to get Boone to let me pay off the ranch's debt. But he won't."

"So you used your money on Casper instead."

"I did." She looked up to meet the loving gaze of the man who had always been in her corner, and then rushed out with, "I paid for all the renovations."

Her father nodded, smiled, reached up to push a lock of hair from her eyes. "I was pretty sure from the start that you had."

She waited for him to say something more, but when he didn't, she couldn't stop herself from asking, "Are you mad?"

"Why would I be mad? It's about time you did something good with it."

"I didn't want to tell you. Or anyone. He has no idea how I got it. I doubt he'd be happy to find out."

"But you'll tell him," he said, his tone wise and knowing.

"I can't." It would kill her for him to know how stupid she'd been.

"Give him a little credit, Faith." He got to his feet, gave her a hand, and pulled her up. "How you came about that money isn't important here. It's in the past. Done and gone. None of that can be changed. All that matters is that you spent it on Casper for the right reason. And that reason better be more than a place to have this party."

She breathed in, breathed out, let go of the words that had been strangling her. "I love him."

"I know you do."

"Oh, Daddy." She pulled in a sob, wrapped her arms around him, and hugged him close. "I didn't think love was supposed to hurt this much. I feel like I'm bleeding with it."

Beside her, her father smiled. "That's how you can trust it, sweetheart. That's how you know it's the real thing."

THIRTY-FIVE

Though Casper had arrived late to the party, he'd been able to park right in front of the house. Perk of being the owner, he guessed, though more than likely all he'd done was block a path kept free from the street to the gate. And anyway, he only owned half. Faith owned the rest. And her car wasn't anywhere to be seen.

Bracing his arms on his truck bed, his beer dangling from one hand, he stood facing his past and his brightly lit present, but not his future because he'd just fucked all of that up. Except no matter his earlier musings, he'd come too far to accept that he ruined everything he touched.

He wasn't going to buy that things between them just weren't meant to be. He might be drunk, but he knew that wasn't the case. They'd been perfect together. They *were* perfect together. So what in his old third-floor bedroom had gone so terribly wrong?

Seeing Clay headed toward him, he shoveled the question to the back of his mind. Then he circled the truck to lean against the other side, the side with the new sidewalk, with the newly sodded yard, with the white picket fence like a big toothy grin.

Clay raised a tentative hand. “Hey.”

Casper raised his beer. “Hey, yourself.”

“I can go,” the boy said, his steps faltering, jerking a thumb over his shoulder and glancing back. “If you’re busy.”

“I’m not busy.” He took a deep breath, cracked his neck side to side. “Just needed a break from the noise.”

“Band’s pretty dope. I mean, for being country and all.”

Casper smiled at that. The kid definitely had his feet planted in rock ’n’ roll. “It’s not the music as much as it’s all the talking. Sometimes, I just can’t stand talking.”

Clay was quiet for several seconds, his hands stuffed in the pockets of the dress pants he’d bought along with a white shirt and vest. He hitched his shoulders like he didn’t care either way. “Like I said. I can go.”

“Uh-uh. You come here,” Casper said, waving him over. “Talk to me all you want.”

“You sure?”

“I’m sure.” He was done being a dick. “How’s Kevin today?”

“Better,” the boy said, bobbing his head. “Think he’s missing Bing and Bob, but there’s some cool dogs up at Mal’s shelter.”

“Good,” was Casper’s only response because his mind was drifting again to Faith. “You having fun? Country music aside?”

Clay shrugged. “House is pretty awesome.”

“Turned out okay, didn’t it?”

“You going to live here now?”

Was he? “What do you think? Would you like that?”

“To live here?” he asked, his eyes going wide and staying that way, his grin nearly reaching his ears. "Are you kidding me? Wait. Does that mean—"

"I don't know yet," he said, swallowing an emotion he thought might be pride, "but Greg says things look good."

Clay gave a fist pump and a loud, "Sweet."

"I wouldn't be countin' chickens or anything," Casper said with a laugh. "I've got to make it through the approval process."

"To foster me?"

"Or adopt you. If that's what you want." When Clay looked away, his throat working, Casper went on. "Having the house helps. Means I can prove you'll have a safe place to live. Then there's the ranch, making me a legit business owner, so the system knows I'm not a deadbeat. Plus I've got a few friends in high places to vouch for me."

"Sounds cool," he said, tossing back his hair, in control again, but only just.

Kids. Women were almost easier to understand. "You'll have to go to school."

"I know."

"And you'll have a curfew."

"I figure."

"There'll be rules."

"What kind of rules?"

Rules to keep you from turning into an asshole. "Don't worry. I'll come up with some," he said, watching Clay's gaze shift across the yard. He glanced over, saw a vision in white walking toward him. A vision wearing his mark on her throat. A vision come to save him.

"I'll get outta here," Clay said, patting his stomach. "Think I'm ready for more cobbler."

"I'm not cleaning up any puke from you eating too much," Casper said, pointing at him with the hand holding the bottle.

"Yes, sir," he said, his mouth twisting upward as he jogged away in reverse. Then he called back, "If I puke, I'll clean it up," before turning as Faith walked up on Casper's other side.

He wasn't ready for her, so he asked, "Did he just call me sir?"

"I think he barely stopped himself from calling you dad."

That nearly sobered him. "I'm not his dad."

"Which is probably why he stopped himself."

"Hope I don't fuck this up," he muttered under his breath, more to himself than to her.

"You won't. The changes you've made in him are amazing."

She was really a fan of that word tonight, wasn't she? "I haven't done anything."

"Oh, but you have," she said, stepping closer, her heels clicking on the sidewalk, a *tick-tick-tick* counting down time. "He looks . . . happy. The first time I met him he looked like he'd lost all hope."

"He's a kid. What does he know?"

"You're good with him."

"He makes it easy," he said, lifting the bottle because he'd changed his mind. He didn't need her to save him.

"I'm sorry about earlier," she said anyway, trying. But he wasn't going to let her, so he stayed silent, leaving her to finally ask, "Do you want to come back in? Get something to eat?"

"Not hungry."

"We could dance, or just have a glass of champagne and listen to the band."

"I'm done dancing. I can hear the band from here. And if I'm going to drink, it'll be Jack and it sure as hell won't be inside that house," he said, his gaze searching out Clay who was talking to Philip Hart's kid of the same age.

Faith's gaze followed. "You're not your father, Casper. You're not going to get drunk and beat Clay—"

"It's not about Clay. It's not about my father. Or Suzanne or anything but . . ."

"But me?"

And here we go. "I don't know what I was thinking, letting you do this," he said, waving the beer he really didn't want anymore. Drinking wasn't going to make any of what was going on here easier, and he was too old to work the ranch with a hangover. Then there was the part about taking on the role of a father, and he better than anyone knew that was best done sober. "Should've left well enough alone, sold the place, stuck to the ranch."

"It's okay, you know, for good things to happen to you. You deserve them." She raised a hand, rubbed it down his arm.

He spun on her, dislodging it. "Why, Faith? Why do I deserve anything good?"

She backed away, frowning. "Are you out here having a pity party? Because the sex wasn't great?"

"For you, maybe. I had a goddamn good time."

Her brows came together in a dark, somber vee. "Why are you being like this?"

"Like what? Like I've always been? A sonuvabitch?"

"That's not how you've been lately," she said, her voice going soft, that softness breaking. "That's not how I know you."

"Guess you've been living in fantasy land. Fucking the cowboy. Redeeming the cowboy. Riding the cowboy. Yeah. You do that one well."

She shook her head, crossed her arms over her middle, and held herself tight. "I don't even know what to say."

"In Spanish, they say *adios*!"

"I'm not going to say good-bye. We can still be . . ."

"Friends? *Amigos*?" He laughed, the sound ripped from his gut. "Do you really think we can be *amigos*?"

"We were friends before."

He straightened, and with his heart pounding like horse hooves at full gallop, he advanced on her, stopping with inches between them. He glared at her from beneath the brim of his hat. "I hadn't been inside your pussy before."

She swallowed, looked away, and rolled her eyes, her nose coming up a notch as she said, "Reverting to being crass won't get you—"

"I'm not reverting, Faith. Don't you get that? This is who I am. Who I've always been." He waved a hand over her head. "This is who this house taught me to be." Then he caught sight of the girl from the porch headed toward him with a wave and a big bright smile.

"Shit," he said, looking back at Faith, but not quickly enough.

She glanced over her shoulder, turned back to him, fuming. "You're right. You *are* a son of a bitch."

"Oh, I'm sorry," the girl said, slowing her pace as she approached. "Is this not a good time?"

Faith spun on her. "No, Luck. It's not a good time. And if you want to keep your job with Arwen, it'll never be a good time."

"Hey," Luck said, holding her small purse at her waist as she backed away in her heels that were almost taller than her skirt was long. "It was his idea. I thought that meant the coast was clear."

"The coast is not clear. The coast will *never* be clear," Faith said, her voice pitched low and barely audible but that much more powerful for it.

Casper watched Luck's retreat before looking back at Faith, something like hope pulling at his chest. "Did you just threaten her job?"

Faith didn't answer. "Your idea? Seriously? What the hell are you doing?"

"Getting on with the rest of my life?"

"Are you kidding me? After everything we've—"

"We've what? Done together? Been to each other? Your money and my cock make a great team, but other than that—"

It was all he got out before she knocked the beer from his hand and slapped him square in the face. He reeled, shook his head, lifted his hand to his cheek. She covered her mouth with her hands, the moisture in her eyes shimmering and threatening to spill.

He wasn't going to let her guilt get to him. They needed to have this out. Put an end to an affair that was obviously making her miserable.

He picked up the longneck, looked at what was left of the contents before looking at her. "Tell me it's not the truth."

She hitched her shoulders as if shaking off bird shit and made fists. "If I have to tell you that, then maybe it is, and if that's what you think of me, I don't know why I'm here."

He snorted. "Then go. Maybe I can still catch Luck."

"Why don't you do that? In fact, why don't I find her for you?" She advanced, stabbing a finger to the center of his chest and causing him to wince. "Your cock and her daddy's money should make a really good team."

Then she whirled away, her skirt a cloud of white against the dark of the night.

"Goddammit. *Goddammit!*" Rearing back, he slammed his fist into his truck's bed, then the door, over and over until he missed and drove his arm through passenger-side window. The glass popped and shattered. Pain bolted like lightning from his wrist to his shoulder, and he stumbled two steps before catching himself. "Aww, shit. *Shit.*"

"Casper!" Faith ran toward him. "What did you do?"

He waved her away, then cradled his hand to his chest. It was wet and sticky and a really dark color of red. “You’re going to get blood on your dress.”

“I don’t care about my dress. Let me see your hand.”

“Here,” Clay said from where he’d sprinted up from the other side, jerking open his shirt and skinning it off. He handed it to Faith. “Use this.”

“Thanks,” she said, shaking it out then reaching for Casper’s arm and wrapping him like a mummy from elbow to fingertips, grumbling words he couldn’t hear all the while.

That made him smile. Her muttering. Her attention. Clay’s concern was in there, too. He felt as if he were standing in some twisted family drama, his woman on one side, his kid on the other, his house behind him full of friends who were full of booze and good barbecue. Except none of it was real.

The only thing real was his hand swelling to the size of a bull scrotum. “I should probably go to the ER.”

“Ya think?” Faith yanked open the door with the broken window. “Get in. I’m driving.”

“It’s my truck.”

“And your hand is bleeding everywhere. Just get in,” she said, using the hem of her dress to sweep the glass from the seat to the floor. “And don’t say a goddamn word.”

THIRTY-SIX

His arm in a sling, his hand bound to his chest like a football, Casper sat on the foot of the ER table, thinking come morning, it might just be his head giving him the most hell. Damn Boone and those stupid designer beers. Damn himself and his lack of control. Damn Faith for being everything he wanted and not letting him in. Why he'd been so slow to the realization that he'd been the only one taking a knife to his past and bleeding out . . .

It was the sex. It had to be. He'd been too wrapped up in her body to see that she'd held back the rest. He knew nothing that had gone on with her between his leaving Crow Hill and now. The things she'd shared these last few weeks were things he'd been there for, the breakfasts and dinners and overnights in her family's home. Boone had been more forthcoming, hinting at a terrible happening and demanding he not judge.

After needles and x-rays and all sorts of new pain driving home the fact that he was too old to be stupid, he'd sobered enough to return to thinking about her, that room upstairs, her pushing and pulling and all those mixed signals. But thinking about her wasn't going to get them anywhere, so when he heard the strike of her heels on the tiled floor, her steps determined, he decided it was time for a come-to-Jesus meeting—whether she liked it or not.

"You're still here?" he asked as she slipped through the curtain partitioning his room from the others.

Her face was pale and drawn, with purple half-moons shadowing her eyes. They were the same color as the bruise he'd left on her throat, the one she'd tried to hide with her hair. "I wanted to make sure you were okay."

He lifted his arm. "It's just a hand."

"Three broken bones, forty-two stitches. That's *just* what it is."

Yeah. That was going to hurt. "So much for safety glass, huh."

She came to him, touched his knee, his face, then laced her hands in front of her. "Good lord, Casper. What were you thinking?"

That I couldn't let you walk out of my life. But he was stopped from saying anything by the curtain fluttering again.

"Here you go, Ms. Mitchell," said the woman wearing aqua Coleman Medical scrubs and thick white shoes. "Your copies of the paperwork."

"Thank you." Faith took the packet, holding it at her waist as the nurse turned to Casper, her cloud of red hair bobbing.

"Dr. Pope will be in with your prescriptions and follow-up orders in a few minutes," she said, checking the tape on his bandage, the buckle on his sling.

"Thanks." Casper waited on saying more until they were once again alone. He nodded toward the envelope. "What's that?"

Faith clutched it tightly, her fingers crushing the bulk of it. "Paperwork. Like she said."

"What kind of paperwork?" he asked as if he already didn't know.

"I was settling the bill."

Yeah, that's what he'd thought. "You paid my bill."

"You don't have insurance."

"And I don't have cash."

She met his gaze squarely, exhaustion grooved deep at the corners of her eyes. "I didn't want them to wrap you up and send you off to the county hospital. I wanted to make sure they took care of you here."

"They did," he said, and before she could get out another word or he lost his nerve, he added, "And now it's your turn."

"Are you kidding?" she asked, her brow a vee of knitted disbelief.

He thought back to the day in the bank when she'd accused him of being crass. "Nope," he said, letting her stew a few more seconds. Then he said, "Tell me about the money."

At that, she tightened, going stiff and stuck-up. "That's my business—"

"Fuck that, Faith. My business is your business is my business."

But she was shaking her head. "Our partnership only covers the house—"

"I'm not talking about the fucking house." Biting off a sharp, "Shit," he rubbed away the anger pounding like a horseshoe hammer in his temple. "You're going to be honest with me now. After what you did to me in that room earlier tonight, you owe me."

She spun on him, and he swore he could see the words, "I don't owe you anything," stuck on her tongue, and he knew she was right. That didn't mean he wasn't going to press. He wanted to know. He *needed* to know. Wherever the money had come from, that place had its clutches in her and she needed to pry them loose.

They couldn't go anywhere if she didn't pry them loose.

She collapsed then, leaned against the supply table beside his bed, gave a weak gesture to encompass so many things. "I shouldn't have offered you the money in the first place."

"Where'd it come from, Faith?"

She walked away, rubbing at her forehead, her heels once again clicking time. "I never wanted it. I did a stupid thing and people got hurt."

"Did you get hurt?" he asked because they were finally getting somewhere.

"Not nearly enough. Not *nearly* enough."

He'd come back to that later. "When did you do this stupid thing?"

"In college."

"And who'd you do it with?" Because he could never see Faith being stupid alone. She was too in the moment, too on the ball. Too completely aware of every single move she made.

"The son of the dean at the school of business."

Yeah, that could be stupid, but there had to be something more than a sex scandal, what with the kind of money that came her way in the end. "You did more than fuck him."

Her gaze sliced into him, her eyes narrowed, her frown wrinkled and harsh. "Yes, we had a sexual relationship. We also dated for two years."

Fine. It wasn't just sex. "This dean's son have a name?"

"What does it matter?"

It didn't, but he wanted to know. "What was his name?"

"Jeremy," was all she gave him. Then she added, "Jon."

Okay. Unexpected, but okay. "And what bad thing did you and Jeremy . . . and Jon do?"

"Jon was Jeremy's father," she said, her voice level, her gaze level, too. Both calm now. Both cool.

"The dean," he said, feeling tension like a vise in his jaw.

She nodded, her arms crossed, the envelope still in her hand. "He'd been widowed young. Raised Jeremy on his own. They were . . . well-to-do. Old money. And Jon . . . He was very attractive."

"You did the father, too," he said, and he thought his jaw might pop.

Another nod, more clicking of her heels as she paced. "I was dumb. I was nineteen."

"He was what? Forty-something?"

"Jeremy was twenty when he was killed. Jon was forty-five."

"Wait," he said, shaking off the drugs and sitting taller as if it would help catch her words. "Jeremy was killed? You're losing me here, Faith."

"Jeremy was . . . wild. Reckless. His mother died when he was a boy. Jon had been a single parent. One whose own parents had solved any problems he had with money. The best private schools. The best tutors. The best lawyers when he'd gone off the deep end of privilege. The best psychiatrists."

"This is the father you're talking about. And he told you all this."

"Yes, Jon. And he used his family money to treat Jeremy the same way. He'd turned out okay . . ."

"And he thought the kid would, too. As long as he kept on spending."

"Something like that." She stopped pacing, stood beside him

at the foot of the bed. "Jeremy had the car, the clothes, the whole look. He could get tickets to anything. Backstage passes. He flew first class. His family had, or I suppose still has, homes on both coasts. West Palm Beach. Cape Cod. Malibu. Bainbridge Island."

"You hit the jackpot."

She stiffened. "I was in love with him. Or as in love as someone can be at nineteen. I didn't need him to take me anywhere. Or to buy me anything."

But he did because that's all he'd been taught to do, Casper surmised. "So what happened?"

"Jeremy left me alone at his house one night. He had something to do," she said with a wave of her hand. "He did that a lot, left me because he had something to do. Jon came home. Found me staring out the window in the library, watching for Jeremy's car. He came up behind me. We talked. We were both worried about Jeremy, the direction he was heading. Jon put his hands on my shoulders. I leaned back against him. Then he . . ."

"He what?" Casper asked, not really wanting to know.

"He kissed my neck. He . . . touched me."

"And you let him."

She took a deep breath, was slow to blow it out, as if weighing her admission. "I was lonely. We were both lonely. And Jon . . . He wasn't a boy."

Meaning he knew how to fuck. How to show her the kind of good time his son couldn't. Or wouldn't because he was too selfish. "How long?"

"What?"

"How long were you with the old man?"

"I don't know. Several months."

"Until Jeremy-boy caught you."

"It was ugly. He was . . . ugly. Furious, and I know he was hurt, but the things he said . . ." Her shudder shook the bed, and

Casper had to force himself not to reach for her. "He'd never loved me. That was obvious. He'd been on the rebound. I caught him. I still don't know how, or why. There were dozens of girls he could've picked from."

"But he wanted you."

"And I wanted him. Don't get me wrong. I tried for a long time to make things work." She pushed off the bed, turned to face him, her focus on his bandaged hand. "The afternoon he walked in on me and Jon . . ." She shook her head, her chin trembling, tears welling. "He ran out screaming, got in his car, and took off before Jon could do more than get his pants on. Jeremy didn't even make it off the street. A big furniture delivery truck had just pulled into the intersection. Jeremy slammed into it. His car was a convertible. And he wasn't wearing his seat belt. The police said he hit the side of the truck first, then the pavement. Jon saw it all."

Jesus H. Christ. "Did you?"

"No. I'd started to run out, too, but with Jon half-dressed and sprinting after his son, I knew anyone who saw me would put two and two together."

"And that two and two could've put an end to Daddy's career."

"Honestly, I'm not sure he was as worried about his career as he was his place in the family. The prestige of the name." She looked down, picked at a rough nub of denim on his thigh. "The family had me sign an agreement. And paid me not to talk about the affair."

"Hush money?"

"That's not what they called it, but that's what it felt like. I didn't want it. I wouldn't have talked. Who would I have talked to? To what purpose?"

"So what did you sign?"

"The agreement had me giving up all rights to sue over anything arising from the affair." She closed her eyes, opened them, turned away. "I wouldn't have sued. It was humiliating. The whole process. Jon sat across the table in the lawyer's office, so put together, like he belonged in one of those old-money clubs from a British novel. He wouldn't even look me in the eye."

She took a shaky breath, blew it out, and reached for the curtain to catch herself. "I wanted out of there. To never see him again. Most of that was guilt over what we'd done, what had happened to Jeremy because of it. But a huge part of it was shame over the hurt I caused *my* family."

He watched the play of emotions ravage her face. He thought about Boone and Coach and Mrs. Mitchell having to face what their sister, their daughter had done. And yet . . . They loved her. He couldn't see them ever doing anything else, no matter what she'd been mixed up in.

"They sent me off to school, and that was what they got for it. The Mitchells' perfect daughter, sleeping with a father *and* his son, getting one killed, taking a million dollars from the other. Yeah. Something to really be proud of."

He wasn't going to beat her up over something she'd spent ten years pummeling herself for. "How did you get hooked up with Jeremy in the first place?"

"I don't know. I was bored. He was exciting."

He found himself grinding his jaw again. "Exciting."

"Yes, exciting. I was nineteen. You were gone by then. Boone was gone by then. Things weren't the same. I wasn't the same."

"No more cheerleading?"

She tossed back her head and laughed, the sound coarse and bitter. "Are you kidding? I was captain of the squad, but it was less about team spirit than it was about the leadership skills looking good on my college applications."

Huh. "Colleges like cheerleaders?"

"They like leaders period. Student council presidents. Members of the debate team."

"And you were those, too." He'd been gone by then and hadn't known.

She nodded, as if struck by an absurd truth. "I was a straight-A student with a 4.2 GPA. I was class valedictorian. I scored 1540 on my SATs. All of that got me the scholarships I needed for school, and I don't regret a minute of the work, but it didn't leave time for fun."

"And you wanted to have fun."

"It seemed like the thing to do."

"Fucking a dude and his dad seemed like the thing to do?"

"Not that. The rest. Stepping outside of my comfort zone. Living a little. Going wild," she said with an exaggerated wave of her hands. "Whatever you want to call it."

"I'd call it being reckless."

"I guess."

"Like me."

She shrugged.

"So that's why you're with me now?"

"No," she said, and he saw in her eyes that she meant it. "Not now."

"But at first."

"Maybe that was some of it."

"And the rest?"

"I think you know."

"I make you wet," he said because he was feeling mean. And hurt. And mean.

"If that's what you think . . ." She turned, picked up her purse, and stuffed the envelope with his bill inside. He leaned forward as she reached for the curtain and snagged her back.

She didn't try to pull free, but stopped.

"That's not what I think," he told her, letting her go once he was certain she wasn't going to scamper off like a calf from a chute. "I'm sorry. About all of it."

"You don't have anything to apologize for."

"I have everything to apologize for." He looked down at his hand, the bandage like a big white flag of surrender. "I know the state of the ranch finances. I should never have come to the bank and asked you for money."

She met his gaze, hers resigned, the smile pulling at the edges of her mouth a sad one. "I thought it started in the kitchen. When you caught me with the strawberries."

He groaned, his still-healing ribs aching as he did. "Yeah, but if I hadn't come to the bank, I wouldn't have spent that whole day thinking about you giving me a sign."

"Did you?"

"Oh, yeah. I thought about all the ways it might happen. But in a million years I never would've thought I'd find you bent over in front of the fridge. Your tits dangling. Your ass all up in the air. I could've popped a load just looking at you."

Of all things, her face colored. "It wasn't really a sign, you know. I was just eating out of frustration."

"Frustration?"

"Because you weren't there. You said you would be. That we'd talk more that night."

So she *had* wanted him. From the very beginning. He hadn't tempted her into something she hadn't thought about, too. "I tried, but then there was Clay . . ."

"Do you regret it? Being with me?"

His head came up sharply. "No. Never. Don't even say that. You've been the best time of my life."

"Been?" she asked, holding his gaze, hers steady while his

wobbled because he didn't know what she was asking him. What she wanted to hear him say.

"Not been," he finally said, wanting to add *are*, but that was all he had time to get out before bootheels sounded on the tiled floor seconds before Dr. Pope pulled open the curtain.

"Faith. Casper." The doc looked from one to the other before consulting his clipboard. He made no comment on what he'd heard, or even an indication that he'd heard any of the conversation Casper wanted to push him out of the room to finish. "You ready to get out of here?"

"I was ready when you whipped that last stitch," Casper said, and when he glanced over at Faith with a weak smile, she was gone, the curtain swinging in her wake.

THIRTY-SEVEN

ONCE OUTSIDE THE ER, the night air like a furnace blast after the frigid hospital temps, Faith took the first full breath she'd managed for hours. It was a shaky breath, unsatisfying, filling her lungs in short, tire-pump bursts, and it came back out just as ragged, tearing holes in the inner tube of her chest. The tears she'd been holding back burned as they filled her eyes.

She looked up, blinking rapidly, the sky a platter of indigo lit by the moon and salted with planets and stars. She wanted to blame her urge to cry on exhaustion, and emotional stress, and a successful party put to rest after weeks of fine-tuning the details. And all of those things were there, but they only added pressure to the root ball of the growing, living sadness inside of her.

That's where these particular tears sprang from. They felt like mourning, like sorrow. Like the end of something beautiful that hadn't had the time it needed to bloom. Like if she took one wrong step, she would fall and break into too many Humpty Dumpty pieces. She wasn't a fragile egg. She was strong. Look what she'd pulled off in a matter of weeks, the house, the party, the affair . . .

"Time to cowgirl up," she told herself, swiping at her cheeks and catching sight of Boone leaning against the front of Casper's truck where she'd parked it. He pushed off the grill and straightened, pulled his fists from his pockets, and held up his hands. And that's when she fell, cracked and fragile, Boone catching her before she collapsed to the ground.

She sobbed against his chest, her body wracked, her knees buckling, Boone her only strength because she had none left. She cried for Casper and his childhood and for his house and for herself. She cried for her parents and for the mistakes she'd made and for all the wrong things she'd done. She cried for Clay and for Kevin, for Jeremy and Jon.

And even when she was all cried out, she knew loving Casper was right. He was her everything, strong in ways she wasn't, selfless behind a mask of crass behavior, a lover who knew what he wanted and took it, all while seeing to her needs. He made her laugh and made her think and made her care.

He had her seeing things through his eyes, and for all he'd gone through in his life, his insight reflected great depth and clarity. He was an amazing, amazing man. How could she not love him? How could she not want to be at his side for the rest of her life?

How was she going to get him to see they were meant to be together—the no-sisters rule be damned, she thought with a sniffling laugh.

Boone brought up one hand to stroke the back of her head, and she nodded. "I think I'm okay now." But her throat was so swollen her voice came out sounding like something from a cartoon.

"Try that again," he said.

"I'm okay. I promise." She took a deep breath, shuddering with it. "God, what a night."

"Yep. Party was outstanding. You pulled off a miracle."

"It was, wasn't it?"

He ruffled her hair. "Thanks for the okra. And the beer."

"You're welcome for both."

He was quiet a moment, then said, "A heads up on the venue would've been nice."

"I know," she said, moving to his side, his shirt damp with her drooling, snotty sobs. "I'm sorry."

He pulled the fabric away from his skin. "It'll wash."

"Not the shirt, goober," she said, smacking his chest. "About the house. Not telling you."

"I knew," he said.

She frowned, treading carefully. "That I'd decided to have it there?"

"That you paid for the renovations."

"Casper told you?" she asked, looking up at him.

His dark hair was finger-combed back from his face. His dark eyes glittered, reflecting the parking lot's lights. His dark stubble shadowed his jaw. "Only after I pressed him about it."

"I guess it was kinda obvious."

"Yeah. Hard to believe he was making enough from Summerlin to turn that house around so fast."

She closed her eyes, leaned into his side. "Pretty stupid of me to think I could keep it a secret."

"We all do stupid things."

"You think spending my money on his house was stupid?"

"Depends on why you did it."

She shrugged, doubting he'd buy her brushing off the reason, thinking of the similar words her father had said. "Seemed like a good cause."

"Because it was for Casper? Or because the money was burning a hole in your bank account?"

"I never wanted the money."

"I know that."

"I felt . . . dirty, I guess, taking it. I would never have talked about what happened with Jeremy. And Jon. Not to anyone. Ever. I didn't need a payoff to hush me up."

"C'mon, Faith. You think you're the only one who's found themselves eyeball deep in shit?"

"It doesn't smell very good climbing out of it."

"Doesn't taste very good either."

Eww. "Thank you for that."

"Casper tells me the two of you are together," he said after several more seconds ticked by, the parking lot lights buzzing, pulling the moths and mosquitoes out of their way.

Together? Is that what he called it? "When did he say that?"

"I dunno. When we were out riding herd the other day."

Did he feel the same way now? Or had she ruined everything tonight in that tiny third-floor bedroom? "I tried to tell you."

"I know you did."

"I didn't want to hurt you."

"You didn't hurt me, Faith."

"I need you here, Boone. But I need him, too. I didn't know how to tell you that."

"You could've just said that you love him."

She closed her eyes, shook her head. "I haven't said it to him, yet."

"Criminy. You two need an intervention or something."

"That's not fair."

"You're not talking to each other."

"We talk. I tell him things—"

"About Jeremy."

"He knows." Finally. Though she hadn't stuck around for his reaction. What his knowing the truth of her past had changed, if anything.

"Good."

"He tells me things, too."

"Such as?"

"What it was like the years he spent in that house."

"Like I said. You need to talk. Not tell stories trying to scare each other off."

Was that what they'd been doing? Proving themselves unsuitable? Sharing the broken pieces that made up their lives? Warning each other off? Having sex before the truth of what they brought to the table became too uncomfortable?

She was too tired tonight to even think about it. "I guess I should go. I left everything to Arwen to clean up."

"Dax is there helping her."

Like the good man he was. "Can I ask a favor?"

"Sure."

"I'm without a car. It'll kill me to walk to Mulberry Street in these heels. Can I use your truck and you take Casper home in his?"

He dug in his pocket for his keys. "Take 'em off to drive. There's a hole beneath the accelerator. Get one of those caught there you'll hit ninety before you know it, and Ned won't like that."

She laughed. "Promise. And you'll get Casper home?"

"You sure you don't want to?"

"I want to. I don't think he'll let me."

"Okay then," Boone said, and nodded. "We'll stop by the folks and pick up Clay."

"Momma and Daddy have Clay?" The idea of her parents fussing over the boy made her smile.

"The way the party broke up, he kinda got lost in the shuffle."

"Tell Casper. He was worried."

"Will do. You got his keys?"

She nodded, then frowned as she dug through her purse. "I left them in the room. Crap. He doesn't need to be driving."

"I won't let him. Just leave my keys in the truck."

"Thanks, Boone," she said, reaching up to kiss his cheek, then throwing her arms around his neck. "Thank you, thank you, thank you."

"We're family, Faith. You don't have to thank me," he said, letting her go when she finally stepped away.

"That's where you're wrong. Because we're family, I have to thank you most of all."

THIRTY-EIGHT

Her footsteps on the staircase reached him before he heard her voice, and her sugar and cinnamon scent filled the room before he was ready. He knew she'd come looking for him. He hadn't planned to still be here when she did.

He'd planned, in fact, to follow Boone and Clay back to the ranch, and things had been going well until Boone's taillights had him seeing double.

He'd been woozier than he'd realized. And since he hadn't relished nosing his truck into a ditch, he'd circled the block, waving on Boone and Clay when they'd come back to check on him.

Not that he'd get far now after crunching over the broken glass out front. And since he wasn't in any shape to change a tire . . .

He braced himself as she grew near. He really wished she'd

waited. He hadn't had time to sort out the things she'd told him. He didn't care about any of them, but knew she did.

He needed to be clear-headed to say the right things. To let her know her past, like his past, had brought her here. But they'd both carried these things too long, had been weighed down by baggage they needed to cast off. It was time to let the past go.

"I thought Boone was taking you home," she said, a silhouette in the door when he turned.

"He tried. I would've punched him, but he was good enough to take care of Clay. Plus . . ." He lifted his hand that was beginning to wake up. "It would've hurt."

"How's it feeling?" she asked, coming closer.

"It's not feeling. But it will be soon."

"Do you want me to drive you back to the ranch?" She hesitated, added, "Or to my place? You can sleep there tonight if you'd like."

Sleep there. Not sleep with me. "Thanks, but I'm fine. If it gets bad before I'm ready to leave, I'll just stay here."

Time ticked away what felt like the rest of his life before she said, "I can stay with you."

"You don't have to do that," he said, needing her, wanting her. Loving her so goddamn much.

"I want to do that."

"I don't know why."

She came all the way across the room then, her feet now bare, her steps silent, stopping in front of him and looking up as she lifted one hand to his cheek. "Because I love you."

Something in his chest split like parched ground, the crack widening, deepening, aching, and making him weak. He wanted to blame it on the pain meds still in his system. He wanted to wait it out, let it heal and close, but the crack became a gully before he could move, and a great wash of sobering emotion rose to the surface.

He reached for her wrist with his good hand. He wasn't saying anything else until they got this out of the way. "You know I don't care about the money, about how you got it. I need you to know that it doesn't matter to me."

"I was afraid to tell you," she said, her voice breaking. "I was so stupid—"

"You were a girl who knew what she wanted," he said, rubbing his thumb over the palm of her hand. "You took it. A boy got hurt because he couldn't handle the truth, but he was the one who got behind the wheel. He was the one who didn't fasten his seat belt. Who didn't brake."

"It's not that simple—"

"I know it's not. Not to you. But it is to me." That's what he needed her to know. She was the only one who mattered.

"Why?"

He looked into her eyes as he kissed her hand, then said, "Because I love you, too."

"Oh, Casper," she said, but he shook his head before she said more. He wasn't finished.

"I'm all I have to offer you, Faith. Me. I don't have any sort of steady income, and I sure as hell don't have health insurance. I do have one bitchin' house, but then that's on you. I'd never have been able to do this without you." He laughed to himself. "That's the funny thing. I don't think I can do anything without you."

"Shh." She moved her fingers to his lips. "Don't say that. I've never known a man as strong as you are."

If he was strong, it was for her. Because of her. "I don't want you to regret us."

"How could I ever regret us?" she asked, her eyes shimmering in the light from the moon.

"Because I'm reckless. I don't think—"

"I'm reckless. I don't think—"

"I don't want to hurt you because of it."

"And I don't want to hurt you."

They really were two of a kind, a perfect fit. "You could never hurt me." And then he laughed. "Besides. I'm really, *really* good at hurting myself."

"Maybe having me in your corner will help you throw your punches in the right direction."

He sighed. She couldn't begin to know. "That was kinda dumb, wasn't it?"

"Epic. I'll call Bandy's tomorrow and get your window fixed."

"No. *I'll* call Bandy's when I can get the money together to have my window fixed."

"It doesn't matter who pays for it."

"Faith—"

"It doesn't matter." She took his face in her hands. "I want us to be partners. And I'm not talking about the fifty-fifty agreement we made, but true partners. Lovers. Best friends." Then she rose on her tiptoes and kissed him. "And I think you want that, too, so don't argue. Besides, if I hadn't gone after Luck, you wouldn't have had a reason to strike out."

Wrapping her close in his good arm, he leaned his other shoulder against the wall and cradled his bandaged hand close to his body, staring out the window into the shadows and the night. "Everything I knew here is gone, you know. The trees are still here, but that's it, and yet . . . I still see all of it. Every crack in the window. Every gap between the doors and the facings. Every hole in the ceiling and the wall plaster.

"But it doesn't hurt anymore because I can see Clay and Kevin playing in the yard, and I can see you standing in the kitchen sink with dirty water dripping down your arms. I can see the look on your face when I told you about the spiders. And I can see you looking at the papers I left burning here on the floor."

"Oh, Casper," she whispered, her breath a sharp sob.

"Don't, baby. I don't want you to cry. We both went through what we went through. We are who we are because of it. And now we're here, together." And then he let her go, but only long enough to reach for the jewelry box he'd brought up from his truck's glove box and set in the window.

He flipped it open with his thumb. "This belonged to Tess. The tie tack and cuff links were Dave's. They gave it to me when they knew I was leaving. Dax was already gone. I'd been itching to split for days. I meant to take it with me. I didn't mean to leave it. I'd actually forgotten about it being here."

"I could tell when Clay found it that it meant a lot to you," she said, taking it from his hand.

"It makes me think of what they had. It was never Tess this, or Dave that. It was always the two of them." He looked at her then, lifted her chin with the tips of his fingers. "That's what I want, Faith. For us."

She nodded, her throat convulsing, her eyes glassy with tears.

He pulled the false bottom from the box, picked up the ring Tess had given him without Dave knowing. The ring that had belonged to Dave's mother, and his grandmother before. The ring Dave had put on Tess's finger the day he'd proposed.

He lifted it for Faith to see, watched her eyes go wide, her chest catch. Then groaning, he lowered his aching body to one knee, his ribs complaining, his hand bitching like a mother-fucker, his heart so full of emotion he had to blink it away to see her face.

"I love you, Faith Mitchell. I love you more than my own life. I love you in ways I never knew possible. I have probably loved you longer than I've known, and I will love you forever. Will you love me, too, and be my wife?"

She buried her face in her hands and sobbed, dropping to her knees in front of him before throwing her arms around his neck and nearly knocking them both to the floor. They held each other, weaved and rocked together, probably cried a little bit together, too, but he didn't see any reason to admit to that part.

When she finally pulled back, he took her hand and slid the ring on her finger. She lifted her arm, the light from the moon glinting off the tiny diamonds.

"It's beautiful," she said reverently.

"You're beautiful," he told her, having eyes only for her.

"I guess you being reckless turned out okay after all," she said, cocking her head to one side, her smile the brightest thing in the room.

"Why do you say that?" he asked, his chest so full of what he felt for her, breathing wasn't coming easy at all.

"Think what would've happened if you hadn't broken the no-sisters rule?"

"I can tell you what wouldn't have happened." He lifted his bad hand, tucked her between his sling and his chest, wove his fingers through her silky dark hair, and lowered his head. "This."

And then he kissed her with the promise of the rest of their lives spent as one, knowing this moment in this house was what he'd look back on forever.

Keep reading for an excerpt from
Alison Kent's next Dalton Gang novel

UNFORGETTABLE

Available August 2013

"I'M NOT WEARING a costume," Boone Mitchell said, staring at his sister and the Dalton Gang member she'd tamed. Boone was the last of the hell-raising trio still standing, and he had no plans to fall—especially if falling meant wearing *O Brother, Where Art Thou?* black-and-white prison stripes the way Casper Jayne was doing now.

"It's a costume party," Faith said. "Of course you are." Her own getup consisted of boots, hat, a cropped denim vest and a matching miniskirt, both with leather tassels and brass hardware. She also had a silver star pinned to what fabric there was covering her chest. And what looked like a real gun hanging from a belt at her hip.

"I'm not wearing a costume," he repeated, glancing from one of the ridiculously garbed two to the other. *Calf nuts on a cracker.* If this is what relationships did to men . . .

"Sorry, dude," Casper said, his arms out as he tested the

length of plastic chain between the matching black shackles binding his wrists. "The woman's the boss."

"Not on my ranch," Boone grumbled, leaning against the sink in the kitchen of the house Casper and Faith shared—a kitchen that would easily hold four of the one he cooked in for no one but himself since Casper and Dax Campbell had abandoned him. The fact that they'd done so for women . . .

"It's an Old West theme, so just go as a cowboy," Faith was saying as she crossed to where he was trying to stay out of the way. She had a length of black fabric in her hands and a look in her eyes that bode no good. She reached up to tie it around his head, catching his hair in the knot and swatting away his hand when he tried to free it. "I'm not finished."

As far as he was concerned, she was. He had no idea why he'd agreed to stop by the house on his way from Lasko Ranch Supply back to the ranch when he'd known this would be the outcome. Faith had been reminding him of the charity masquerade party for weeks. She'd bought him one of the pricey tickets when she'd bought hers and Casper's, even though he'd told her she was wasting the cash.

"There," she said, stepping back with her hands at her hips to take him in. "Perfect. Or it will be as soon as you put your hat back on."

He slapped his hat against his thigh, raising a cloud of dust that had his sister waving her hands. "What? I've been working."

Faith scrunched up her nose. "Maybe you should shower first, change clothes."

'Clean clothes means a trip to the ranch. And if I go home, I'm staying.'

"You could wear something of Casper's."

"Uh-uh," Casper was quick to put in. "I don't have enough shirts that I can afford losing any to his shoulders."

"You would if you'd let me buy them," Faith said, then turned to Boone. "You'll have to go dirty then."

"Or I could just not go."

"You're going." She tapped a finger to her chin and considered him. "But you need . . . spurs or chaps or something."

"The spurs and the chaps are at home, and if I go home—"

"Yeah, yeah. You're not coming back. I guess this will have to do."

"You want me to go as a cowboy, *this* is what you get."

"Wait. I've got an idea," Casper said, turning to bound up the stairs, the plastic ball and chain fastened around his ankle thumping behind him.

Boone looked from the man he was having a hard time recognizing to his sister, who he'd never seen so happy. "Ball and chain, huh?"

"It's a good life. You should find someone to tie you up. At least once in a while."

"I've got once in a while covered. And she doesn't make me run around wearing zebra pj's."

Faith huffed. "I'm not making Casper do anything. I just told him if he wore that, then I'd wear this."

"Are Mom and Dad going to be there? Because you wearing that"—he gave her a quick once-over because she *was* his sister and he preferred not to linger—"is going to have Mom gathering napkins from the tables to make you a serape."

"Momma and Daddy are in Houston for the weekend. Texans football, I think they said." She tugged on the bottom of her vest that left her midriff bare. "Besides, if you think my outfit's going to raise eyebrows, you should see what Arwen's wearing. Dax is going to be shooting eye daggers at anyone who looks at her wrong. Assuming he lets her out of the house."

Now the Dax part of that equation would be worth seeing.

But Boone wouldn't be looking at Arwen just like he didn't look at Faith. She belonged to his partner, making her family and off-limits. "Doubt he'll have much choice, the party being at the Hellcat Saloon and Arwen being hostess."

"Well, he'll have to get over it. Having her place chosen to host the library's fund-raiser is a huge coup. Kendall was afraid the committee would vote down the suggestion and we'd end up at the country club where everything would cost twice as much."

"Kendall?"

"Kendall Sheppard. She owns the bookstore? You danced with her at the folks' anniversary party? She's on the library board."

"Right." One of the few eligible single women in Crow Hill, and a friend of his sister's. Meaning he crossed paths with her often enough to make Faith's matchmaking obvious. "I guess that means she'll be there tonight."

"She will. As will Everly Grant and Lizzie Nathan and Nina Summerlin. You'll have a great time."

Before he could tell her his idea of a great time would have all four women in his bed, not on a dance floor, Casper clattered his way back into the kitchen. "Here," he said, handing Boone a leather gun belt. And a gun. "Buckle this on, and with the Zorro mask, you're set."

Boone spun the cylinder looking for bullets, happy to find he wouldn't accidentally be shooting anyone, or his own foot. "Like two eye holes in a black scarf is going to fool anyone?"

"The point isn't to fool anyone," Faith said, tying on her own mask that was a lacy-looking metal cut-out and didn't hide much of her face at all. "The point is to have fun. To dance and drink and flirt and pretend that you're someone else for a few hours."

"I like who I am. I don't want to pretend I'm someone else."

"Then don't. Just dance and drink and flirt."

"I don't want to—"

"Just drink. Jesus, Boone. You can do that, can't you?"

"Sure he can. Especially with all that drinking going toward a good cause." Casper pulled a long strip of drink tickets out of Faith's top, tore off half of them, and gave them to Boone. "Sheriff here's made of money. She can buy more."

Boone folded the tickets and stuffed them into his pocket while Casper stuffed his between Faith's breasts. She slapped at his hand, took care of the tickets herself, then handed him a plain black mask that Boone supposed was prison issue to go with the stripes. He snapped it into place, rolling his eyes as Faith lifted his hair to hide the elastic, yelping when she pulled too hard.

Seeing the two together had Boone smiling. And after all the years he'd spent enforcing the Dalton Gang's no-sisters rule to keep them apart. Still, the time had needed to be right, and the sixteen years he, Casper, and Dax had spent away from Crow Hill before returning to take on the ranch they'd inherited had given both Faith and Casper a chance to get their act together. It had been a lot of years, but it had been worth it.

"Wow, y'all look great," came a voice from the doorway into the house's main hall.

"Hey, Clay," Boone said to the fifeen-year-old boy Casper was in the process of adopting. "You and Kevin up to holding down the fort? Because say the word and I'll grab a pizza and we can hang out and watch all the Bruce Willis movies you want."

"Kevin and I got it covered," Clay said, reaching down to pat his scruffy mutt that was the size of a few of the calves Boone had moved from the Braff pasture this morning. "And I think tonight's going to be *Star Wars*. We did most of *Die Hard* last weekend."

"See?" Faith waved Boone and Casper toward the door where Clay was standing. "Clay and Kevin have it covered. Let's go."

Boone jammed his hat on his head and followed the sheriff and her prisoner to the front of the house where his truck was parked on the street. He'd drink up the tickets Casper had given him, doing his part for literacy, and hope like hell he didn't end up the night wearing prison stripes. Or worse—dragging home his own ball and chain.

ABOUT THE AUTHOR

A native Texan, **Alison Kent** loves her cowboys and is thrilled to be writing about them for Berkley Heat. She is also the author of more than forty contemporary and action adventure romances, and *The Complete Idiot's Guide to Writing Erotic Romance*.

If there's a better career to be had, she doesn't want to know about it, as writing from her backyard is the best way she's found to convince her pack of rescue dogs they have her full attention. Alison lives near Houston with her petroleum geologist husband, where every year she fights the heat to grow tomatoes, and spends way too much time managing a feral cat colony.

You can find her online at alisonkent.com, on Twitter at twitter.com/alisonkent, and on Facebook at facebook.com/author.alisonkent.